THE
BUCKET
LIST

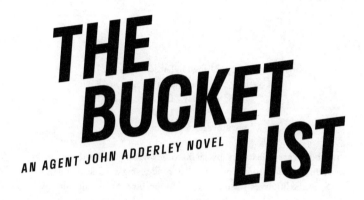

THE BUCKET LIST

AN AGENT JOHN ADDERLEY NOVEL

PETER MOHLIN &
PETER NYSTRÖM

TRANSLATED FROM THE SWEDISH BY IAN GILES

OVERLOOK PRESS, NEW YORK

This edition first published in hardcover in 2021 by
The Overlook Press, an imprint of ABRAMS
195 Broadway, 9th floor
New York, NY 10007
www.overlookpress.com

Abrams books are available at special discounts when purchased in quantity
for premiums and promotions as well as fundraising or educational use.
Special editions can also be created to specification. For details,
contact specialsales@abramsbooks.com or the address above.

Library of Congress Control Number: 2020944983

Printed and bound in the United States

1 3 5 7 9 10 8 6 4 2

ISBN: 978-1-4197-5218-6
eISBN: 978-1-64700-196-4

ABRAMS The Art of Books
195 Broadway, New York, NY 10007
abramsbooks.com

PART 1
2019 & 2009

1

BALTIMORE, 2019

He lay in bed looking up at the white ceiling. The contours of the discolored plaster-board panel were gradually becoming clearer. The stain looked like a ghost, or maybe a balloon. Something a child might have drawn.

John knew he was in the borderlands between sleep and wakefulness. He had no idea how long he had been drifting between the two worlds.

He tried turning his head to see where he was. A second later he was hit by a wave of pain. Its epicenter was at the back of his head, rippling out to the rest of his body. He closed his eyes and tried to find somewhere inside himself where he could take cover. There was no such place.

He waited until the worst of the pain dissipated and decided to take in the room using senses other than sight. It smelled of cleaning fluid—but it lacked the synthetic scent that products like that often had. No lemon or meadow flowers, just a clinical smell of cleanliness.

He discerned a beeping sound to his left. The noise was repeated at intervals of a few seconds and had to be coming from some kind of technical equipment level with his head.

Using one hand, he slowly gripped the steel frame of the bed and let his fingers slide along the structure until they encountered something that seemed to be a wire. He took hold of the cable and lifted it high enough for him to see.

At the end was a plastic cylinder with a red button. He pressed it and waited for something to happen. After just a few seconds, he heard the sound of a door opening and footsteps approaching. A woman in a white coat with her hair tied in a bun at the back of her neck leaned over the bed.

"Are you awake, John? Can you hear me?"

He nodded imperceptibly and received a smile in return.

"You're at the Johns Hopkins Hospital in Baltimore," she said. "We've performed surgery on you to treat the gunshot wounds to your chest."

As he listened to the nurse's voice, he became aware of the postsurgical pain. It was different in nature—less explosive than the neck pain, more gnawing in its character. Like a second layer of pain.

The woman continued to update him about his condition. He had lost a lot of blood and had been unconscious when he was brought into the emergency room twenty-four hours earlier. They had then operated and the doctors had managed to stop the internal bleeding. The bullets—two of them—had missed his vital organs and passed through his body.

"Water," he managed to say, taken by surprise at how feeble his voice sounded.

The nurse picked up a cup with a straw from the table and helped to put the straw to his lips. John was overenthusiastic and sucked up more water than he could swallow. He coughed and the white-clad woman had to wipe his chin with a napkin.

"It's hard to drink when you're lying completely flat. Would you like me to angle the bed?"

He nodded.

The nurse pressed a button on the wall and the head of the bed was slowly raised.

Finally, he had a view of the room. Next to the bed on his left was a stand on wheels holding intravenous drugs. John counted three transparent tubes supplying his body with a concoction of chemicals through an insertion in the crook of his arm. The beeping he'd heard was being emitted by an instrument monitoring his breathing and oxygen.

The closed curtains in front of the two windows were thin and they let in more sunlight than he would have liked. The door into the corridor also had a pane of glass in it. It was inset at the top and big enough to let him see the policeman on guard outside.

John slowly turned his head and saw the other bed. He was apparently not the only patient in here.

As he saw the face, pain exploded at the back of his head again.

There—just a few steps away—was the man who twenty-four hours earlier had put a pistol to the back of his neck.

2

KARLSTAD, 2009

Voicemail again. Heimer knew she could see he was calling even though it was almost midnight. Her phone was practically glued to her hand and was always going off at every hour of the day. When one continent closed for business, another would open—and she was always available when the troops needed their commander.

But when he—her husband—wanted to get hold of her, she chose not to pick up. Sometimes he was tempted to borrow a phone from someone on the management team and call Sissela from it. Just to see if she picked up.

Heimer looked through the huge picture window and was surprised by how dark the water outside was. Emelie would be returning to Stockholm soon and summer would be officially over. He thought about how he barely recognized his daughter when he'd picked her up at the station in June, a week before Midsummer. The transformation into a well-turned-out economics student had happened so quickly that he almost couldn't remember what she looked like now.

Sissela had naturally been overjoyed when Emelie started her course the previous autumn. All of the past was forgotten and the heiress to the family firm was at the finest of educational institutions. He'd not been quite so convinced. He made an effort to patch up their relationship during the summer; he really tried to win back Emelie's trust after what had happened. But she refused to let him in.

He called Sissela again. Why the hell wasn't she picking up? If he called three times in an hour, surely she understood it was important?

Heimer sat down at the kitchen island and reflected on what a shitty day it had been. It had started with a quarrel over breakfast. Throughout the academic year, the reports from Stockholm had been good. Emelie said that she'd passed her exams and was getting along well with the other students. Heimer had privately questioned the exam results with his wife. Their daughter had inherited his dyslexia and he knew how hard it had been for him during his architecture studies. But Sissela waved away his objections and asked why he didn't have more faith in his only child.

But yesterday the castles in the air had collapsed. A business associate of Sissela's who was close to the president of the School of Economics reported concerns about Emelie. Her attendance was poor and she'd barely been seen in the corridors lately. Naturally, Sissela called the president and didn't let up until the poor devil had come clean about her daughter. Out of a possible sixty credits she could have earned during two terms, she'd only managed twenty-four. She didn't even take her two most recent tests.

Breakfast had turned into a cross-examination in which Emelie was confronted with her lies. Heimer tried to get his wife to calm down, but it seemed as if she had already forgotten about their daughter's mental state in recent years—how close they'd come to losing her.

The morning ended with Emelie's disappearing into her room and then leaving the house with a backpack. Just after that, Sissela also departed, leaving him in the wreckage of what was meant to be a family—left alone to clean up after others, as usual.

He spent the morning in the wine cellar trying to bring some order to it. He had been lazy about maintaining inventories over the last few months and their insurance was only valid if he kept the list of bottles updated. The project of rearranging the wine cellar had worked and when he had laced up his sneakers to run the twelve kilometers prescribed by his fitness program, he felt better. But this improved state of mind didn't last long. After dinner, which he cooked and ate alone, the final illusion relating to his daughter's new life fell apart.

Heimer had gone into her room. It hadn't been his intention to pry. He just wanted to spend some time there. After she moved to Stockholm, he did that sometimes just so he could remember how it had once been the two of them against the world.

Opening the top desk drawer was something he had done on impulse. It wasn't fully closed, and he'd meant to close it. At least that was what he told himself. But instead, he opened the drawer and the stack of old schoolwork there put him on alert. It looked suspiciously planted. He picked up the papers and found a bag of white powder.

There was only a little left at the bottom and he ran his middle finger through it to collect some. He pressed his finger to his upper lip and immediately recognized the chemical, bitter taste of cocaine.

Since then, he had tried calling his daughter at least eight times without getting through. Somewhere, deep down, this was what he'd sensed but hadn't wanted to see. The new Emelie was too perfect. Time after time, the therapists in rehab reminded them that the journey back from mental illness was long and often full of obstacles. But for his daughter, the stay at Björkbacken had seemed like a miracle cure. A nineteen-year-old girl, acting out and with a taste for drugs, had gone in, and a young woman who had gotten into the School of Economics and wanted to become involved with the family company had come out. And it had only taken six months.

Heimer left the kitchen island and began to wander aimlessly around the house. The soles of his leather shoes creaked on the whitewashed monochrome parquet and he felt like the only guest at the most deserted of parties—overdressed in a shirt and jacket when he might as well shuffle around in slippers and a dressing gown. There wasn't anyone here, after all.

He changed into beige chinos and the black polo he had bought in Milan. The top fitted his toned, wiry upper torso well. He could thank running for that. There weren't many men at forty-eight who were in this kind of shape. Granted, his hairline had crept up and the skin around his eyes had become creased. But he liked his face—it had aged with dignity.

Sometimes he would secretly buy the gossip magazines if he and Sissela had been to a premiere in Stockholm. Being one of the people in those photos was something he loved—and he liked to compare himself and Sissela to other couples. The Bjurwalls—Heimer had taken his famous wife's name when they married—as a duo were hard to beat when it came to radiating status and style.

Heimer returned to the kitchen. He made a sandwich, but he only managed to eat half of it. His thoughts returned to Emelie and where she might be. She had been so angry when she had left the house that morning, and he really wanted a chance to talk to her—in peace and quiet, now that the worst of the anger had dissipated.

He went back into his daughter's room and sat on the bed. It struck him how badly the new Emelie suited the old one. White blouses and cashmere sweaters were stored on hangers next to black hoodies and band t-shirts. A Burberry bag sat on the floor next to a yellow crate of vinyl records. And the clearest contrast of all was the sleek MacBook in a leather case next to a tower PC with three monitors and a headset worthy of a fighter pilot.

Above the desk was a reminder of another era: a group photo of the Striker Chicks from the first competition they had participated in, at Dreamhack in Jönköping. Emelie was on the far right, a head taller than the other girls on the team. Her blonde hair had been dyed dark at the time and was in a short pageboy haircut. Her makeup was harder-looking and there were two piercings on her upper lip that Sissela had been really upset about.

Heimer looked away from the photo. He wanted to go out running again. He just wanted to drain his body of energy and feel the taste of blood in his mouth. He wanted to forget what a spineless amoeba he had been, if only for a while.

Then he heard the door opening downstairs. There was the dull thud of a bag being dropped on the tiled floor and the rattling of the hangers swinging against each other on the coatrack. Then weary footsteps on the stairs.

"Would you pour me a glass of water, darling?"

Heimer went into the kitchen to meet Sissela. He saw her take off her high heels and sink onto the sofa in the adjacent living room. She was barely slurring her words, but it was enough for him to grasp that she was inebriated.

"Of course," he said, making an effort not to show how irritated he was that she had been unreachable all evening. Emelie needed their support, so it would be stupid to start yet another fight.

He pressed a glass against the watercooler in the door of the refrigerator. While cold sparkling water poured out, he observed his wife on the sofa. The platinum blonde hair with the stubborn lock that refused to stay in place behind her ear. The aristocratically shaped nose that he knew she was so satisfied with. And the chin that she stroked a little too often these days. The doctor made the skin too taut during the last operation. It didn't look natural for a woman over forty, she often complained. That was surely the whole point of plastic surgery, he had thought to himself, but Heimer didn't say anything. If Sissela wanted to look natural, she could've kept her old chin.

He put down the glass of water on a coaster covered in a Josef Frank print, to protect the coffee table.

"Thanks," she said, drinking half of it in one gulp. "Sorry I'm late. The meeting went on forever and I completely forgot we were having a wine tasting afterward. I managed to get a few bottles to bring back for you. The new guy on the board is co-owner of a vineyard in South Africa, and when I told him about your passion for wine he absolutely insisted you got a case."

"Do say hello and thank him from me," said Heimer, sitting down in the Lamino armchair.

He hated it when his wife did this. What made her think that the bottles from that horse trader would be worthy of a place in his cellar? Didn't she understand the care with which he curated his collection? The scant space left was promised to some Bordeaux wines he hoped to acquire at an auction at Sotheby's later in the autumn.

"Have you heard from Emelie this evening?" he asked.

"No," she said. "Isn't she at home?"

He shook his head, while his wife pulled one leg up onto the sofa and began to massage her own foot. Heimer tried to remember when she had stopped asking him to do that after her long days at work in uncomfortable shoes.

"She's not well," he said, getting up.

With a gesture, he indicated that he wanted her to do the same, and together they went into their daughter's room. He opened the drawer and pointed at the bag with the remnants of cocaine.

"Is that what I think it is?" said Sissela.

He nodded.

"I feel so betrayed," she added after a period of silence. "First all of her lies about business school and now this. She promised she would stop."

"We've been naïve—we should have known it wouldn't be this easy."

"You mean I've been naïve. You never believed that she was better."

That was exactly what he meant. But he was glad she reached the conclusion on her own.

"She's not picking up her phone," he said. "I'm going to go out and look for her."

"Is that really smart?" Sissela replied. "She'll probably come back soon, and when she does, I want us both to be at home. Emelie listens to you more than me."

Wrong, he thought. She used to listen to him more, but that was before her time at the Björkbacken treatment center.

As usual, he let Sissela decide and they drank chamomile tea because she said it calmed the nerves. When it was after one and their daughter was still not home, Sissela went to lie down in the bedroom. Heimer curled up on the sofa and pulled a blanket over himself. If Emelie tried to sneak past him, he would wake up. He promised himself that he would really try to talk to her. Somewhere inside her was the old Emelie, the one who trusted him—and this time he didn't plan to let her down.

3

BALTIMORE, 2019

The spot where the man had been lying was empty; the bed was gone. The machines that had been connected to his body had been switched off and placed on a cart by the wall.

The man's face reminded John of why he was in the hospital, but then he once again lost consciousness. When John next woke up, it was dark outside the windows. Day had turned to evening—he didn't know just when. There was no clock in the room.

The nurse came in again. She stood next to the bed and looked concerned. She said that blackouts were unusual with gunshot wounds to the torso and wanted to get a doctor. John protested. His head no longer hurt and the pain in his chest had been dealt with by the morphine. After some hesitation, the woman capitulated.

"What happened to the man who was lying next to me?" John said.

"He's gone back into surgery. It didn't go quite right the first time, so the surgeon wanted to take another look," the nurse said, before stopping herself.

Maybe she had said too much about the other patient. There was strict confidentiality in hospitals. John wondered how much the nurse really knew about the men she was caring for. The police guard outside the room was hardly likely to be commonplace at Johns Hopkins.

She wished him good night after he had promised to ring the buzzer if he felt dizzy again. John waited until the woman left the room before he shut his eyes. The fragmented memories from the Port of Baltimore had suddenly made sense when he saw the man's face. Despite his body's protests and the pain at the back of his head beginning to throb, he forced himself to go back to that container where he had been convinced his life was going to end.

Abaeze was there together with the rest of the familiar faces. And Ganiru, of course. Always Ganiru. He's the one who called the meeting. Now he led them through the labyrinth of containers to the northern end of the port. Finally, he stopped in front of one of them and removed the bar so that the heavy doors swung open.

He nodded at Abaeze, who was nearest, to indicate that he should go inside. Then John and the others followed. They positioned themselves along the walls and watched as Ganiru tried to close the doors behind them. The lock system resisted, but once he nudged it with his hip the bolts slid into the right position and what little light was still streaming in as a result of the early spring sunshine was shut out.

A second later, a weak light on the ceiling of the container was turned on. John looked up and saw a builder's lamp hanging from a hook. Ganiru took a few steps forward and reached for the light source. He unhooked it and held it in front of him at chest height. Its cold, white glow illuminated his face from below and made him look like an angry ghost.

"Sit down."

John glanced at the others. It felt strange to get down onto the dirty floor.

"Sit down," Ganiru repeated.

This time, the men obeyed, sitting and leaning back against the corrugated steel walls. John felt the cold metal chill him through his shirt.

"What's this about?" Abaeze asked.

If he had said anything like that to Ganiru, he would have received a couple of hard slaps for his trouble. But it was different for Abaeze. He'd been there longer and had a higher status within the group.

"I never thought I'd have to say this, but one of you has talked."

John was grateful that his face was in darkness and couldn't give away anything as Ganiru spoke. He'd had nightmares about the boss's huge hands around his throat so many times: the thumbs pressing in just below his Adam's apple, pressing until he couldn't breathe.

"How sure are you?" Abaeze said, this time in a lower voice.

"One hundred fucking percent. We've had problems with deliveries being stopped by the DEA. So, I told you all about a phony consignment being shipped in by air. Guess which crates the pigs opened?"

Ganiru swept the construction lamp around like a flashlight over his men. The beam moved from face-to-face, lingering for a few seconds on each one.

"If anyone knows anything, now's the time to speak up," he hissed.

When the boss's dark eyes passed over John, he tried to raise his hand to his forehead to wipe away the sweat. It wouldn't obey him. The signals from his brain weren't getting through—somewhere inside him the system had collapsed.

Ganiru again. The roar echoed inside the container.

"Fucking answer me!"

When no one said anything, he pulled his pistol from the shoulder holster under his jacket and put it on the floor in front of him. He gave the weapon a sharp kick, making it spin on its own axis. John followed the rotating barrel with his eyes. The pistol was on its final lap and the odds looked bad. Eventually, however, the barrel decided to move past him and stop at one of the other men.

Ganiru picked up the weapon, put it back in the holster, and hung the lamp on the ceiling hook. Then he pulled the loser in the sick game of roulette up from the floor and dragged him toward the doors. Using his spare hand he opened the container and pushed the man so hard he fell onto the asphalt outside.

Ganiru turned back toward the faces inside. He looked calmer now. He smiled cautiously, as if the game with the pistol hadn't been meant seriously.

"I'll shoot one of you every ten minutes until I find out who squealed," he said, going outside.

There was a booming in John's ears when the heavy doors once again closed and the light was reduced to the white glow of the construction lamp. A second later, two rapid shots were fired outside the container.

The silence that followed was dense, as if all the men inside the four steel walls were holding their breath and no one wanted to be the first to exhale. Eventually, the absence of words was so oppressive that the man closest to the door spoke.

"Take it easy—no one's been hurt," he said. "Those bullets are in the ground. I don't believe shit about that seized shipment. No one in here is stupid enough to talk, right? Ganiru's always been paranoid. He's just testing us."

John was almost willing to buy it. He sounded so reassuring, so believable. Soon it would be over, and they'd all laugh about it. The boss would buy the drinks at the miserable place by Patterson Park that his cousin ran.

John tried asking his brain to raise his right arm again. His nervous system remained on strike.

"What do you think, Abaeze? You know him," said a voice farther away in the semidarkness.

Abaeze appeared to be deep in concentration and merely shrugged his shoulders, as if he didn't care about anything other than his own thoughts.

Then the lock mechanism rattled again. A narrow crack of daylight appeared, and it grew wider when the door was opened halfway. Something was pushed into the container and then the light disappeared again. Ganiru's voice was faintly audible through the steel wall.

"Five minutes left."

John saw several of the men leap up and form a semicircle around the body on the floor. Someone shook it to get a response, at first carefully and then more roughly. Then the face fell to one side and through a pair of legs there was an eye staring at John. The other had been shot out.

The man who had just tried to calm down the others stumbled toward the far corner of the container and threw up in a series of noisy convulsions. The rank smell of bile and half-digested fajitas quickly spread through the cramped space.

Several of the men began shouting and blaming one another for this or that. John remained glued to the floor and tried to get his thoughts into some sort of order. They changed tack every five seconds and it was impossible to connect them up into anything comprehensible.

Abaeze stood in the middle of the container and tried to separate two men who had started throwing punches at each other.

"If we don't stay calm, we're all going to die," he shouted.

The men reluctantly stopped fighting. They realized the only one with a chance of stopping Ganiru was Abaeze.

"When he comes back, I'm going to tell him who squealed. I'll never forgive myself for letting someone die before I put two and two together," he said, sitting down again.

The other men also sank to the floor. Then there was an odd silence in the container. Frightened men lined along the walls avoided one another's gazes. Finally, someone dared to ask the question.

"Who is it?"

Abaeze shook his head.

"When Ganiru gets here."

John wondered how much of the chaos whirring inside his head was visible on the outside. His breathing was so quick and shallow that he was panting like a child with fever. But no one noticed. Everyone was focused on themselves, calculating. Their word against Abaeze's if they were the one named. Who would Ganiru believe?

The container doors opened again, and the boss stepped nonchalantly over the dead body on the floor. Ganiru must have noticed how all their eyes turned to Abaeze.

"Is there something you want to tell me?" he said.

Abaeze didn't hesitate. His voice was powerful and layered with contempt.

"He's the one who talked," he said, pointing.

John saw the finger was pointed at him and immediately felt the other men's gazes. Their eyes contained not only hatred, but also a measure of relief. If he lost, they would win. First prize was the honor of getting to wake up tomorrow morning.

But how could Abaeze know? If he did know. He could simply have chosen someone at random to avoid being accused himself. John had been with them for the least amount of time—that alone made him a suitable scapegoat.

"Are you sure?" Ganiru asked.

"Yes. He left his phone in the car one time when he went for a piss. There were a bunch of odd messages. I didn't get it then—but now I know what they were about," he said, directing a gobbet of spit at the traitor.

John stared at the blob of saliva a couple of inches from his feet. He felt sick, but he managed to suppress the nausea. Would Ganiru really go for this? Did he really think that infiltrators communicated with their handlers like that?

Apparently he did. He saw Ganiru aim his weapon at him.

"You've broken my heart—what little of it that's left."

John wanted to defend himself. To tell the psychopath so many shit-filled lies that he wouldn't trust anyone ever again. But his tongue was just as paralyzed as the rest of his body. He couldn't say a word.

"Let me do it," said Abaeze. "I'll sleep better tonight if I can ice the bastard myself."

Ganiru nodded appreciatively.

"He's all yours."

Abaeze pulled John up from the floor. It was a humiliating way to die. He'd been trained to act under pressure but now he was letting himself be led to slaughter like a helpless animal. Ganiru held the doors open so that Abaeze could drag him outside. At least the final breath he drew would be of fresh air.

"On your knees," Abaeze ordered him.

John was shoved over. He put out his hands so that he landed on all fours with his back facing Abaeze. He was also grateful that the rest of the men had stayed in the container. Death was a private matter and he didn't want to share his last moments with them.

He turned around and saw Ganiru hand over the pistol. He heard the metallic sound as Abaeze clicked the safety off. The barrel was pressed to the back of his head and his face forced to the ground. John followed a crack in the asphalt with his gaze until it vanished beneath another container.

This was the end, the final chapter—he was convinced of it.

The film playing in his mind paused when he heard the door handle. He opened his eyes and saw the policeman in the corridor helping the nurse push a bed through the doorway. It must be Abaeze returning from surgery. John looked for signs of movement, but the man did not seem to be awake.

The nurse parked the bed next to John's and connected the monitoring equipment to the patient. Then her pager beeped and she left John alone with the sleeping Abaeze.

John studied the heavy body that barely fit into the bed. The man had to be almost six and a half feet tall and well over two hundred pounds. The skin on his face was so black it was almost blue. His nose was wide and the furrows on his cheeks were deeper than John had previously noticed. The thick arms resting on top of the blanket were by no means toned from the gym. The strength was wrapped in a layer of fat, but was no less impressive for that. John understood why Ganiru found him so useful. People struggling to pay their debts to Ganiru often found hidden reserves when Abaeze showed up to collect.

Then there was a cough from the sagging mouth. John jumped. The cough was followed by several more and it was clear that the man was regaining consciousness.

John considered whether to ring his buzzer but stopped himself when Abaeze opened his eyes and turned his head toward him. It took a few seconds before the giant man seemed to understand who he was looking at. Then he smiled weakly and said:

"So, you're alive, huh?"

John returned the smile.

"Yeah, and we both know who I have to thank for that."

4

KARLSTAD, 2009

Heimer tasted the freshly pressed juice and noted that the oranges weren't up to par. They'd started carrying a new variety at the market and it wasn't as sweet as its predecessor. He rinsed the juicer and poured two glasses of juice, handing one to his wife, who was sitting at the kitchen island. They usually ate breakfast there, since it was the only place with light from the east. On clear days, they could see the sun rise over the treetops.

The window had been added to the plans at the last minute and Heimer was glad he had insisted. Given the location of the plot next to Lake Vänern, it was natural to try to let the water influence every room. But Värmland wasn't just lakes—it was also forests. Heimer was pleased with that phrase. He'd used it to convince the architects to change the plans yet again. In exchange, he had promised it would be the last change that had an impact on plumbing or load-bearing walls—a promise he broke just a day later, when he had woken up with a fresh vision for the master bedroom and adjoining bathroom.

He had never felt better than when they were building the house, and for once Sissela kept out of the way. He was the trained architect and she had respected that. Even if he hadn't worked for many years, the knowledge was still there.

Heimer looked at his wife as she raised the glass of juice to her lips. Her hands looked old. It was the one part of the body that no expensive miracle creams or plastic surgery could fix. If you wanted to know a woman's age, all you had to do was study her hands. It was as reliable as carbon-14 dating.

Then he thought of Emelie again.

His thoughts only managed to turn to other things for brief periods before returning to her. It felt as if someone had put his rib cage in a vise and was slowly turning the screw to increase the pressure. He longed to be outside, running on the trail. He wanted to run so fast and so far that he would taste blood. Anesthetic for the brain through an exhausting physical challenge.

"It's half past ten," said Sissela. "We have to do something."

Her voice was quiet but decisive.

"This juice," he said. "Isn't there something off about it?"

"It doesn't feel right. The cocaine in her room . . ."

"She'll probably get in touch soon," he interrupted.

"I'm worried that she's hurt herself again. Maybe she's with Magnus—they've been hanging out a lot this summer. I'm going to call Hugo."

Heimer watched his wife disappear into the library with her phone. Hugo Aglin was AckWe's finance director and one of the few colleagues of Sissela's who spoke to him even occasionally. He had built a house not far from their own and a few times had asked for advice that Heimer was happy to provide. It was rare that someone from the company thought he was capable of anything other than spending his wife's money. Most of them treated him like Sissela did—with affected enthusiasm for his eccentric interests. Offering encouraging applause for the child until the door was closed because the grown-ups needed to talk. Hugo was the only one of them he had shown around the wine cellar. The rest of the gang couldn't tell a Barolo Riserva from grape soda, which meant they had no business being down there.

It wasn't hard to understand why Sissela was happy that Emelie had started to spend more time with Hugo's son. He was—in every way—more suitable company than the girls in Striker Chicks with their arms around one another in the photo in his daughter's room. Sissela usually referred to them contemptuously as computer nerds when Emelie was out of earshot.

Heimer didn't know what to think about Magnus Aglin. His slicked-back hair undeniably helped Tynäs to live up to its epithet of being "the Hämptons."

Sissela had been annoyed when the columnist in the local paper (*Nya Wermlands-Tidningen*) had put two dots on top of the A in the name of America's colony of the wealthy, and—in her view—had ridiculed the place where they lived. Heimer however thought it made an amusing point. After all, the small headland with the waters of Lake Vänern on either side was home to none other than the newspaper's owners.

The other prominent resident of Tynäs was the dance orchestra conductor who had sold millions of records. It amused Heimer that they had bought the plot next door to his and built a house that made the musician's previously impressive home look like a basic summer cabin. He had never objected, but during the construction there had been something strained in that otherwise velvet-soft baritone when they had greeted each other in the supermarket.

The column in *NWT* had been titled "Different Worlds" and depicted not just the well-to-do corner of Hammarö outside Karlstad, but also the areas around the paper mill at Skoghall. The socioeconomic profile of that area was different and the residents had to put up with the smell of sulfur from the production of paper pulp.

It wasn't far from Tynäs to Skoghall—less than ten kilometers. But after having lived on Hammarö for many years, Heimer knew that the distance between the two was greater than that. The two places were like planets in different solar systems.

He cleaned up the breakfast things, with just enough time to finish before his wife returned from the library.

"Magnus was still asleep, but Hugo promised to speak to him as soon as he wakes up. The kids apparently had a party at the house yesterday and it's quite possible that Emelie was there. He didn't think we should worry."

Sissela sounded calmer now—more like a CEO and less like a concerned mother. Heimer decided it was the right moment to leave her on her own for a while. He needed to take that run. His body and head needed it.

Fifteen minutes later, he headed out on his usual route. He checked that the GPS and heart rate monitor on his new Garmin wristwatch were activated. Then he put the earbuds in his ears and switched on his MP3 player. He was going to run a shorter route today, which meant he ought to manage to maintain a tempo of 3.40 minutes per kilometer.

The first long stretch uphill was after just eight hundred meters and acted as a watershed. On good days, he enjoyed feeling the power of his legs as they flew over the ground, propelling him up the hill. On other days, he could feel the lactic acid by the end of the climb. Those days, he knew it was going to be a rough circuit.

He glanced at his watch, which showed him the first kilometer had been quick. His body was responding well today, despite his thoughts about Emelie. Or perhaps because of it. Worry drove him forward across the terrain. He needed to torment himself, to hover as close to his breaking point as possible. It was the only way he could silence his thoughts.

Once he conquered the hill, the wide path turned left and continued alongside the water. This was Emelie's favorite part of the route. She said it was because of the views of Lake Vänern below. He liked to tease her and say it was more to do with the fact that it was an easy stretch to run so she could catch her breath after the climb.

He loved their conversations while they were running. In the beginning, he had had to twist her arm. Every kilometer on the trail could be exchanged for twenty minutes at her computer. She had accepted the arrangement in exchange for him promising to watch her for a while every day when she was playing.

It was an eye-opener for him. He hadn't had a clue what *Counter-Strike* was before Emelie introduced him to the secrets of the game. The premise was simple. Two teams of five. One team played the terrorists, the other the counter-terrorists. Everything was played online and at a pace that had initially given him a headache, but had then fascinated him. He quickly realized that Emelie and her teammates in Striker Chicks were talented and had earned their reputation on the e-sports sites.

"What do you think Mom would do if I was as good at tennis as I am at *Counter-Strike*?" Emelie had said, the first time she managed to run two whole laps with him, earning almost five hours of game time.

The words had hit him. He knew exactly what Sissela would have done—she would've let the whole world know that her daughter was a rising star and she would have flown in a private coach from America.

From that moment, Heimer had decided to reappraise the gaming. His daughter had found something she loved to do, and his job was to support her. After showering, he told her to call her friends in Striker Chicks and invite them to the house. Then he drove them all to the computer store and instructed them to fill the car with everything they needed to get better at the game. He would pay the bill.

The look Emelie had given him when he had closed the trunk on a mountain of new computers and gaming gear! He had saved that look and treasured it as his dearest possession. But that was then. This summer, she hadn't come out on the trail with him even once.

His watch beeped again and drew his attention to his kilometer time. Three minutes and fifty-eight seconds. It wasn't good enough. The thoughts of Emelie had made him lose his rhythm. He forced himself to increase his pace.

When he returned after his run, he saw that Sissela had a visitor. Hugo Aglin was standing next to her by the kitchen island, pointing at a laptop. Perhaps it was just the light from the screen, but he thought his wife's face looked unusually pale.

"Sorry if I don't say hello properly, Hugo, but I'm dripping in sweat," Heimer said, holding his arms in the air to show his clammy hands.

"You have to see this," Sissela said, her lips so tightly pursed that her voice assumed a hissing tone.

"It's a photo on Emelie's Facebook page," Hugo explained. "Magnus showed it to me when I asked if he knew where she was."

Heimer had only a vague understanding of what Facebook was. He had heard Emelie talk about it and grasped that it was some kind of online notice board for friends. He approached the kitchen island and saw that his socks were leaving sweaty footprints on the parquet.

Hugo turned the screen toward him so that he could see the photo. It showed Emelie's forearm, with the strange tattoo that she had been so secretive about. The motif consisted of three squares, of which two had a V-shaped tick in them.

Heimer saw it by accident just after his daughter had returned from Björkbacken and he'd tried to get her to explain what it meant. She had been reluctant, but eventually she had said it was a bucket list. Three things she promised herself she would do before she died. When he had asked what these were she had merely shaken her head and said she wasn't going to tell anyone.

"Look," said Sissela, pointing at the third square, which had previously been empty. "She's cut herself here. She's carved the final tick right into her skin."

5

BALTIMORE, 2019

It struck him that he didn't know the name of the man who'd saved his life. To John, he had been Abaeze—Ganiru's right-hand man and obedient foot soldier in Baltimore's Nigerian drug cartel. But the truth was different. He realized that in the port, seconds after the pistol had been fired. He waited for the bullet to drill its way through his skull, taking his life with it on its way out the other side. Instead, the loud bang left his ears ringing. It was then, when the loud noise hadn't stopped, that he realized he was still alive.

The next moment, John had seen Ganiru lying on the asphalt clutching his kneecaps. Apparently his protector had fired not just one but two shots at their leader.

Then Abaeze had ordered him to run. The first steps had been the hardest, but the connection between his head and his feet was soon re-established and John's legs started to move more and more quickly.

That was when the first shot had rung out behind them. The men in the container must have figured out what was going on when they heard Ganiru's shouting. They started in pursuit of the traitors, with no hesitation about using their weapons. If the SWAT team hadn't arrived just a few minutes later, the two of them would be dead.

"How're things, son?" Abaeze said, shifting himself into a slightly more upright position on his pillows so that his face rose above the side rail of the bed.

He seemed to be wide-awake—not disoriented, as John had been after his surgery. Abaeze was at least fifteen years older than he was, but the fact that he had used the word "son" was overdoing it. John would be thirty-five next year and people rarely got his age wrong—they certainly didn't underestimate it.

"Yep, totally okay," he responded unconvincingly. "What about you?"

"Complete shit. It feels like someone has shot me in the stomach," he said, surprising John by laughing, then quickly relapsing into whimpering when his surgical wounds were stretched by the movement of his stomach muscles.

"Fuck me, that hurts. I need more painkillers. You don't happen to know a dealer, do you?"

He laughed again. John had never seen a person so completely transformed. The drug dealer Abaeze and the convalescent Abaeze shared the same robust body—but apart from that they had nothing in common. One had been taciturn and serious, the other a perfect facsimile of a bedridden stand-up comic.

"Who exactly are you?" John managed to say. Of course, he could guess the answer—but he still wanted to hear what his roommate had to say.

Abaeze suddenly became serious.

"Brodwick wouldn't be happy about us talking about that. He'll probably want to debrief us separately, first."

Brodwick—as in James E. Brodwick. The head of the FBI field office in Baltimore. John had guessed right. Abaeze was an undercover agent—just like he was. But why hadn't he known there was another mole in Ganiru's cartel? Brodwick probably had his reasons. Yet he still couldn't help but feel hoodwinked by his own side.

At the same time, John realized that this wasn't the time to be touchy. Without Abaeze, everything would have ended differently. He was the one who had kept a cool head and found a solution. What had John done? Fuck all. He had been frozen, unable to move.

"I thought I was dead. When you shot Ganiru, I mean. I had to check that my brains hadn't been blown out."

"Sorry about that," said Abaeze. "But I had to make it look real."

John involuntarily put his hand to the same point on the back of his head—the place where the muzzle of the pistol had been pressed against him.

"At least tell me your name, so I know who to thank."

"Trevor—and if I wasn't in so much damn pain, I'd shake your hand. You?"

"John. My name's John."

It felt odd to say his real name. For almost a year he had been someone else. The Bureau had carved out an identity for him, with the kind of violent résumé that would catch the eye of Ganiru's HR department. He'd been set up with an apartment on Belair Road and then left in peace to do his job. It had taken time, but soon enough John had won the confidence of both the underlings and Ganiru. His tasks as errand boy had become more advanced and one Sunday early last spring he had been invited to a beautiful house in the suburbs. It was then—once he had been introduced to Ganiru's wife and test-driven his Lamborghini—that he realized he was truly inside.

Brodwick had pushed all the right buttons when he recruited him from the Homicide squad in New York City. He told him about a unique opportunity to make a difference and how undercover agents were the FBI's most important weapon against organized crime. John could understand why Brodwick was making an effort.

It couldn't be easy to find candidates willing to take the risk. John accepted the offer but had been naïve about what the new life would involve. The illicit drugs trade went on around the clock. Meeting anyone on the outside was out of the question. In the circles he moved in, you kept an eye on one another.

A woman in a white coat came into the room. John didn't recognize her. She had short hair styled into a consciously boyish, tousled look. She wore no makeup, and yet her face was so perfect it could've graced the pages of any fashion magazine.

Trevor seemed much brighter all of a sudden. Despite the fact that he had just woken up after his second round of surgery, his grin stretched from ear to ear.

"Hello," the woman said. "Do you know where you are?"

"In heaven with one of God's angels," he said, and let out his biggest laugh yet.

Is this guy for real, John managed to wonder before remembering the debt of gratitude he owed him. The woman didn't seem to care. She was presumably used to patients commenting on her appearance.

"Take it easy, so you don't ruin your stitches. You've had surgery on your abdomen for your gunshot wound."

She continued telling Trevor about his medical status. His injuries sounded worse than John's. It would be some time before his neighbor could eat unaided.

Trevor listened attentively and then asked whether the nurse could speak to the doctor and get him to increase the dosage on his painkillers. Now it was her turn to laugh.

"Sorry, I didn't introduce myself properly. I'm the doctor. I'm the surgeon from the trauma team—I performed both your surgeries."

"Oh, Jesus! I'm the one who should be apologizing," Trevor said.

"There's no need," she said. "And of course you can have more morphine. I'll speak to the nurse and have her adjust the dose."

The conversation was interrupted by the door opening. The man who entered was wearing a dark suit and offering the usual lopsided smile. John was never able to decide whether it was friendly or just supercilious. The doctor turned around, clearly irritated.

"I asked you to wait outside," she said.

"You said I could see them."

She sighed.

"I said you could see them *after* I checked to see if they were up to it."

He shrugged his shoulders.

"They seem okay to me."

"And you base that observation on your many years of practicing medicine?"

John couldn't help enjoying the moment. It wasn't often someone put Brodwick in his place. The boss was noticeably perturbed but still retained the smile and went for the soft touch.

"My apologies, doctor. Of course, it's for you to make the assessment. Five minutes are all I need."

She shook her head.

"Go home and get some sleep. If there are no complications, then a conversation might be in the cards tomorrow morning. At the earliest."

Brodwick raised his hands in a disarming I-give-up gesture. In one hand he had a blue plastic folder and in the other a laptop.

"Okay, fine. But surely you can give him these for the time being," he said, nodding toward John's bed.

The doctor took the folder and put it together with the laptop on the bedside table as Brodwick vanished back into the corridor. Then she turned her attention to John.

"I read in your notes that you've been having issues with headaches and that you've lost consciousness."

"Yes, that's right," said John, putting his hand to the back of his neck again.

"Does it hurt now?"

"No, it comes and goes."

The doctor wrote something in her notebook. John didn't like the concerned expression.

"We'll have to X-ray your skull tomorrow morning. But now I want you both to try to rest."

Trevor was asleep within minutes. John reached for the folder that Brodwick had left behind. The movement hurt his chest and he hoped that the surgical drain hadn't been dislodged from its position. The ceiling lights had been dimmed, so he had to use the reading lamp to see.

The folder contained mail addressed to his real identity, John Adderley—sent to his old apartment in New York. The Bureau had made sure it was forwarded and had held on to it for him.

He glanced through mail from his dentist, the bank, and the IRS, before focusing on the two letters that stood out because they had handwritten addresses on them. He saved these for last. One of them was a thin envelope containing nothing but a photograph. The picture was of him together with his colleagues from Homicide back in New York. Several of them were wearing Santa hats. The bar's dark wooden fixtures and the Irish flag in the background indicated that the photo had been taken at their regular haunt just a block from the police precinct.

John turned the photo over and read the greeting. "Don't know if you'll get this—don't have your new address. Anyway: good luck in the private sector, you damn deserter."

That was the official version—he had moved to Baltimore to take a job with a private security company that provided personal protection for CEOs.

John smiled. He hadn't thought about life in New York City for a long time. He examined himself in the picture. The arms around his colleagues' shoulders looked so puny. Ahead of infiltrating the cartel, he had worked out like a madman to fit into his new criminal life. John now felt no shame about admiring his reflection in the mirror after his morning shower. He liked his new biceps and six-pack.

His face was also different in the picture. He'd still had his hair then—dark and curly. It came from one half of his genes. When Brodwick had suggested he shave it off, John at first hesitated. He was worried about whether Ganiru would think he looked sufficiently African, with his light brown skin. Brodwick had dismissed that as nonsense and handed him a trimmer. He hadn't looked back. The shape of his face was more defined and more masculine without hair on his head. He was never going to look like the guy in that picture from the bar again.

John put the photo back in the folder and opened the last letter. It was a brown padded envelope with foreign stamps. He reached inside for the contents and put them on his lap: a newspaper clipping, a flash drive, and a handwritten letter.

It was a greeting from a parallel universe that he knew existed, but which he had become so good at suppressing that it had almost faded away.

The letter was from his mother, whom John hadn't seen in twenty years. She had stayed in Sweden when his father brought him to New York after the separation.

Reluctantly, he picked it up and began to read.

John!

This time you have to come home.

He got no further than that before his guilty conscience got the better of him. He could hear his mother's voice through the messy handwriting and his eyes immediately filled with tears. The words went straight to his heart and made him see himself in a new light. What he saw wasn't flattering: a spineless person who had stuck his head in the sand and chosen the truth that best suited his own purposes.

John considered whether to read the rest of the letter, but decided not to. Instead, he looked at the newspaper article. It was from *Nya Wermlands-Tidningen*, from just a few weeks ago. He started with the caption beneath a photo of two serious men looking into the camera.

The Chief Commissioner of the Värmland County Police together with Bernt Primer, the recently appointed head of the force's new unsolved cases team. "Cold case initiatives like this have been tried and tested both abroad and elsewhere in Sweden with good results," says Bernt Primer, of the new project. The team will start work this autumn and their first task will be to re-examine the circumstances surrounding the disappearance of AckWe heiress Emelie Bjurwall ten years ago.

John understood their choice of this as the first case—they picked the one that would ensure the greatest media exposure. The police in Sweden seemed just as anxious about public opinion as the organizations he had worked for. The FBI and NYPD never missed a chance for good publicity and were willing to go a long way to avoid bad publicity.

He put down the article, realizing how tired he was. The doctor had ordered him to rest. At the same time, he knew that it would be hard to sleep. It would be better to try to stay awake for a little longer. He reached for the computer that Brodwick had brought. If he couldn't face reading the letter from his mother, he might as well browse the contents of the flash drive she sent.

It was an extensive investigation, which was reflected by the large number of files and documents on the tiny gadget. The media had devoured the story, which always meant the police added more resources. The company that the missing girl was to have inherited was an international Swedish success story, even ten years ago. Nowadays, there were several stores in every major American city selling AckWe jeans and casual fashion. It was presumably the same everywhere else in the world.

John began by reading about the history of the company on Wikipedia. It was surprisingly easy to understand the text in his old mother tongue. The odd word here and there gave him trouble, but he could usually work out the meaning from the context. He thanked his lucky stars that he had watched Swedish movies and kept his language skills going over the years.

The company had been founded in 1931 by the children of an emigrant who had brought denim back home to Värmland. The name AckWe was in honor of the local anthem "Ack Värmland, du sköna"—Värmland the beautiful! The heiress, Emelie Bjurwall, would have been the fourth generation to head the company. John examined an old photo of her posing with her mother, Sissela, at the opening of a store in London. She couldn't be more than ten years old, but she already had a practiced smile for the camera. The caption quoted her as saying how beautiful she thought AckWe clothes were, and that she looked forward to leading the company herself one day.

When it came to the details of what had happened to the girl, the Wikipedia article was extremely reserved. All it said was that she had disappeared in 2009 under unclear circumstances, in the Tynäs area on Hammarö just outside of Karlstad, Sweden.

John closed the article and began to search for a summary of the case—something to give him an overview. He finally found a chronological summary of the case based on the presumed victim's activities.

The final sign of life from Emelie Bjurwall had been a photo posted publicly on her Facebook page. It showed a tattoo on the girl's left forearm. The design comprised three squares with ticks; the one closest to her wrist had not been tattooed but carved into her skin using something sharp.

Based on the blood clotting, the medical report had determined that the wound was relatively shallow and that Emelie had been alive when it had been made. It had not been possible to ascertain whether she was dead or alive in the photo. Nor had it been possible to determine whether she'd taken the photo herself.

On the other hand, Facebook had released data that established the location of the phone at the moment the photo had been uploaded, with a good degree of precision. The patch shown on a map in one of the documents covered an area of just one thousand square meters. The circled area on the map was the tip of a promontory called Tynäs—just half a kilometer from the house where Emelie had been to a party the night she disappeared.

Data from her cell phone company confirmed the information from Facebook. Emelie's phone had pinged towers in the area until all contact had been lost later that night. Either the battery had run out, or someone had turned the phone off.

John followed the Karlstad police's attempts to piece together the clearest possible picture of the girl's activities over the evening. Witnesses agreed unanimously that she had left the party at around midnight, and the photo had been posted on Facebook at 1:48 A.M.

Finding out what had happened during those two critical hours was at the heart of the investigation.

6

KARLSTAD, 2009

Just twenty minutes after Sissela had called the police, the buzzer at their gate rang. When Mrs. Bjurwall called, you came. This apparently also applied to the police. Heimer was expecting uniformed officers, but the person who took the call must have assigned top priority to the case and passed it directly to Criminal Investigations Department.

He recognized the younger of the two detectives from the boating club. His name was Bernt Primer and they had done a night watch together. Heimer had shown him his Nimbus 405 Flybridge as they patrolled the jetties down by Lövnäs Church. But Primer had never mentioned that he was with the police. Or Heimer hadn't been listening. He could remember having been out fishing with him a couple of times, but he had quickly grown tired of his company, irritated by the torrent of words flowing from the man's mouth. He knew half the boating club and had something to say about every one of them.

Heimer had never set eyes on the other police detective before. He would have remembered. The man had a large birthmark running across his balding pate that extended over part of his face. It was impossible not to think of Mikhail Gorbachev—the old Soviet politician who had talked about glasnost and perestroika and had brought down the whole Eastern Bloc. Heimer was sure the man had already heard this plenty of times from people with less sense of decorum than Heimer had.

The obvious questions were soon dispensed with. When had they last seen Emelie? Yesterday morning, when she had stormed out after breakfast after an argument. Did they know where she was going or whom she was meeting? They didn't, but Hugo Aglin—who had stayed with them to wait for the police—filled in the holes. His son had explained that Emelie had been one of the guests at his party. When Hugo had returned home late that evening, the house was full of young people. This had been a surprise, since his son had said he was going to sleep over at a friend's.

Exactly when Emelie had left the party was unclear. Hugo hadn't seen her there, but on the other hand he had gone down to the spare room in the basement to sleep. Hopefully, his son and the other teenagers would know more. The police would need to speak with them.

There was no doubt about it that Gorbachev was the higher ranking of the two detectives. Heimer noticed that he sat forward on the edge of the armchair, as if he wanted to get closer to Sissela and himself on the sofa. The glass coffee table between them was slightly too wide. If you leaned back, you ended up too far away from each other for it to feel comfortable when speaking at a normal volume. It was one of the few purchases for the house that he actually regretted.

They got to the Facebook picture. Hugo was sitting on a pouffe by the short end of the table and had just shown the police officers the photograph of Emelie's forearm.

"What does the tattoo mean?" said Gorbachev.

Sissela looked at Heimer.

"You know more about that than I do," she said.

"Emelie says it's a bucket list."

The policeman raised his eyebrows.

"A bucket list? What's that?"

"A list of things you want to do during your lifetime," Heimer explained.

"I see. And what things does Emelie want to do?"

"Only she knows that."

"You discussed it?"

"Yes, but she refused to explain it. At least to me."

"And what about you?" said Gorbachev to Sissela, brushing a few imaginary crumbs from his trousers.

Heimer noted that he had a self-conscious manner with his wife. She brought that out in men—especially those who weren't accustomed to her world.

"No, and I know there's no point in asking," she said.

"Do you know when she got the tattoo?" Primer interjected.

"It must have been after she came home from Björkbacken," Heimer said. "At any rate, that was when I first saw it."

"Björkbacken? In Charlottenberg?" Gorbachev said in surprise.

Heimer knew he was on thin ice. Sissela kept the stay at the residential treatment center for young women a secret. Officially, Emelie had been interning abroad at one of AckWe's many offices.

"Our daughter was going through a difficult time and needed the kind of support and treatment that they offer there," Sissela said in a neutral voice.

If she was annoyed that he had disclosed family secrets, she didn't show it. Heimer glanced at Hugo to see how he had reacted, but the director of finance seemed unaffected. Either he was just as good as his boss was at maintaining his mask or she had already told him about the treatment center. Personally, he had no intention of keeping secrets that would come out anyway.

"That carving on her arm—could she have done that herself?" said Primer.

Sissela replied quickly and Heimer saw that she intended to handle the narrative about Emelie.

"I can understand what you're thinking, Detective Sergeant. And we don't want to hide the fact that Emelie hasn't always been so kind to herself. So yes, she may have cut herself."

Hasn't always been so kind to herself.

Well, that was one way of putting it, Heimer thought to himself. He remembered the empty pill bottle on the toilet seat and Emelie's lifeless eyes as she lay in the bathtub after he had finally managed to pick the lock with a kitchen knife. It wasn't until they had pumped her stomach in the hospital that she finally came to.

"How has your daughter been feeling lately?" said Primer.

"Much better," Sissela answered. "She's taken control of her life and last autumn she started at the School of Economics in Stockholm."

Naturally the story begins there, Heimer thought to himself—rather than with her failed studies or the drugs he'd found. He considered whether to say something and couldn't think of any reasons to keep quiet.

"She had a bag in her desk drawer with the remains of something I'm almost certain was cocaine," he said, not addressing anyone in particular.

"Yes, that's right," Sissela hurried to add.

Now that the cat was out of the bag, she wanted to be the concerned mother.

"Heimer and I are worried that she might lapse back into depression. It's not unusual to encounter temporary obstacles during the rehabilitation process."

"The most important thing right now is that we find Emelie," Gorbachev said, inching even farther forward onto the edge of the armchair in an attempt to foster intimacy across the wide glass table. "Do we know how this picture was taken?" he added.

"It must have been with Emelie's phone," said Sissela. "We've called it lots of times without getting hold of her. Yesterday evening, it was still ringing—but now it goes straight to voicemail."

"We'll have our tech people deal with that," said Gorbachev, jotting the number down in his notebook.

He then explained what would happen next. A formal missing persons report would be filed and all police departments across the county of Värmland would be issued a photograph of Emelie. But there was no cause for alarm. She had argued with her parents and sometimes young people disappear only to return a few days later.

After all, she was twenty and didn't need to report all of her comings and goings to her parents.

Then the detective with the birthmark paused. It was clear he was choosing his words carefully.

"If anyone makes contact with you, I'd like you to call me right away," he said.

Sissela looked at him.

"Makes contact?" she repeated. "So that's what you think—that she's been kidnapped?"

"We don't think anything," he replied. "But you're a well-known family and we have to consider all the possibilities."

Heimer saw his wife nodding thoughtfully. They hadn't discussed it, but he knew she had gone over all the possible scenarios in her head. It was out of the question that she would have overlooked kidnapping.

"I'll get you a photo of Emelie," she said, vanishing into the library.

There would be plenty to choose from. Since their daughter had started at university, Heimer had noticed his wife had regained her interest in photography. The empty pages in their family photo album had been filled with images that reflected her aspirations.

In the photograph that Sissela selected a few minutes later, Emelie was wearing a white dress with a braided leather belt around her waist. Heimer saw that it had been taken on Midsummer's Eve earlier that year. His daughter was looking at him from beneath the brim of a straw hat. She was wearing her blonde hair down and it framed her freckled face.

His rib cage was back in a vise again. The air was being pressed out of him with each turn of the lever. He looked away from the photograph and let his gaze linger on the Lars Lerin painting on the wall just above Gorbachev's head.

"Are you alright, Heimer?"

He felt Sissela's cool hand on his back.

"Oh, I'm just so worried," he mumbled.

7

BALTIMORE, 2019

The cart the nurse pushed in was laden with a new batch of intravenous drugs.

"Ah, exactly what we need. More drugs!"

Trevor laughed at his own joke and then groaned at the pain in his abdomen. It didn't seem to matter how much it hurt. He was compelled to laugh. John noticed it was infectious. His neighbor's positive energy wasn't a façade—it was something that seemed to come from within. A force of nature expressed as a good mood that was impossible to resist.

John had been woken early in the morning for his X-ray. When he returned to the room again, he had fallen into a long, dreamless, morphine-fueled sleep. Now the spring sun glimpsed through the thin curtains was high in the sky, and he realized it must be almost lunchtime. Possibly even later. John remembered the conversation between the doctor and their hotheaded boss the night before. If she gave the okay, the debrief would begin this afternoon.

"Have you seen Brodwick today?" he asked, once the nurse had left the room.

"I don't think he dares come back until he has permission. It was almost worth the bullet in my stomach just to see him being put in his place by our favorite doctor."

Trevor expended great effort turning toward him. It was clear he was in greater need of painkillers than John was.

"Are you worried about the debrief?" his colleague continued.

"Not at all," John replied. "Just wanted to know if he'd already come by."

That wasn't the truth. The prospect of the initial conversation was playing on his nerves. Brodwick would tape it and pass the recording on to the prosecutor. Maybe it would even be played in court. He couldn't say anything that differed from Trevor's statement. It would kill his credibility as a witness, and the defense would exploit it. At the same time, he didn't want the whole world to find out about his breakdown inside the container at the port.

"Take it easy," said Trevor, as if he had read John's thoughts. "Brodwick'll find out what he needs to know. How resourceful we both were in a high-pressure situation. That you realized that I was an agent too, and together we improvised a plan that got us out alive."

"Together?" said John.

"Yes, together. Brodwick isn't the sharpest tool in the box. He doesn't understand fieldwork so there's no need to burden him with too many details."

"And exactly how did I realize you were undercover?"

"I whispered it into your ear while we were on the way to the container. That was when I realized what was about to go down."

John nodded slowly while silently repeating his witness statement to himself.

"Thanks," he said, really meaning it.

"You're welcome. Now I've saved your life *and* your ego."

Trevor laughed again and this time it didn't seem to hurt as much. Maybe the nurse had taken into account the patient's tendency to laugh at opportune and inopportune moments when adjusting his morphine dosage.

"On the other hand, I don't understand why you care what those macho dicks at the Bureau think," he continued. "After the trial, we still get to start our lives over somewhere far away from all of this."

Of course, Trevor was right. John should be thinking more about the future and less about his legacy at the FBI. The cartel was more than just Ganiru, and it would do everything it could to find the squealers after the trial—no matter where on the planet they were. That was why they were going to be given new identities and placed into witness protection.

"Let me give you some advice: make sure you make your demands now," said Trevor. "Once you've testified and the judge has struck his gavel you won't have any bargaining chips."

John waited for the laugh he thought was coming. But this time it didn't. It was clear that Trevor had spent a great deal of time thinking about what was to come.

"It's your family that matters," he said. "The deal you cut with the Bureau will determine what your future life is like."

John started. Did Trevor have a family? John had thought it was impossible to combine it with the role of infiltrator.

"So, it's not just you who has to disappear?" he said.

"No, my wife too. And our daughter."

"Your daughter?"

"Yep. She'll be one year old this summer."

John tried to keep up. If Trevor's daughter was that young, he must have become a father while infiltrating the drug cartel.

"She was a beautiful accident," Trevor said with a smile when he spotted John's confusion. "When my wife found out she was pregnant, I was already in deep with

Ganiru's gang. I demanded they get me out as soon as possible, but I knew it'd take time. That's why Brodwick doubled up on his agents in the cartel. As soon as you were inside, the plan to pull me out was going to be activated and then you were supposed to stay for as long as it took to uncover whoever Ganiru reports to."

John nodded. He understood why Brodwick hadn't said anything. It was about protecting him and his colleague. The less John knew about the agent he was supposed to take over for, the better it was for everyone involved.

"So were you at the birth?" he said.

Trevor's eyes suddenly filled with sadness.

"No, unfortunately. Our precious bundle of joy had the good sense to make her entry into the world the same weekend Ganiru's cousin got gunned down in Cherry Hill. Coming up with an excuse to leave town right then was impossible."

"But you've seen her?"

"Jesus—of course I have. I've been there twice," said Trevor, his face lighting up again. "She's something else. Like a curly-haired angel. She has a temper too—at least when she doesn't get her way. Gets that from her mother."

"And which characteristics have you provided?" said John.

"She eats like a horse, or so I hear. That must be from me."

Trevor gave another booming laugh and managed to knock over the water glass on the nightstand.

"What about you—is there anyone going with you?" Trevor said when he had caught his breath.

John shook his head.

"No, it's just me."

It felt lonely when he said it aloud. Especially when comparing it with Trevor's new life as the father of a young child. John had difficulty seeing himself in that role. Granted, he was younger, but it wasn't really about that. Several colleagues his own age in New York had had one or two kids. It was really the experience of growing up as the child of a dysfunctional marriage that had left its mark on him.

His parents' love story was a shining example of how "opposites attract" was a poor strategy for choosing a life partner. His father originally came from Nigeria and had moved to New York City in the mid-sixties. John had heard the story of how he had met his mother many times. Not as a romance, but as a cautionary tale of how women can turn men's heads. A blonde twenty-six-year-old woman from Sweden had walked into the bar where his dad worked in the South Bronx. She was in New York on an art scholarship and was living in the neighborhood. One thing led to another and a year later she was pregnant. He left America for her sake and they bought the house in Sweden that became John's child-hood home.

"Think with your big head, not your little one. The only good thing to come out of our marriage is you," his dad would say years later, as they sat at the kitchen table in the apartment on the Lower East Side.

By then, John was a teenager and sick of hearing stories about his mother. He had been twelve when his parents separated, and his dad took him back to New York. There, his dad had borrowed money to buy a bodega on Eldridge Street.

Which memories of his mother were his own and which had come from Dad's stories, he wasn't sure. But the fact that she hated her job and took every chance she got to paint instead was something he did remember. She would be cleaning her brushes in the kitchen when he got home from school. The embraces she pulled him into smelled of cigarettes, cheap wine, and turpentine.

"Your mother didn't understand what being a family involved. She drank and messed around with paint instead of taking care of you. And helping out with the money was something she had zero interest in."

John was surprised how much of his father's lecturing had stuck. But if you boiled down the sum total of his wisdom, there were really only two takeaways: work hard and look out for women. As a teenager, he hadn't much liked that message. Neverthe-less, he had, subconsciously, taken it on board. There had never really been a lack of women—John could thank his looks for that. But he had never had any long, more serious relationships. Work always came first.

When Dad passed away a few years ago, the pastor had asked whether John wanted to say a few words at the funeral. At first, he accepted. He stayed up all night, pen in hand. In the end, he just got angry with him. His dad had gone on and on about what a hopeless person his ex-wife was. But on the rare occasions when John had asked about his mother or their years in Sweden, the answer had always been the same—that it wasn't something he needed to think about. All he needed to know was that the two of them were better off without her.

When he had gone to bed, the script for the funeral address consisted of just one single world. Bastard. Crossed out twice—once his conscience caught up with him for writing it. The next morning, he called the pastor and requested an extra hymn instead.

John was so absorbed in his thoughts that he didn't notice the doctor standing in the room. She must have crept in while his dreamy, morphine-addled brain had been time-traveling.

Trevor once again apologized for mistaking her for the nurse. The doctor turned to John, who immediately felt the back of his head beginning to throb again. He remembered the claustrophobic sensation from that morning when he had lain with his head inside a metal tube listening to the sound of the MRI.

"The X-rays look good," she said, while John tried to read her facial expression. It was difficult. She looked serious, although the news she was delivering sounded positive.

"There's no trace of any suffusion or bleeding from the trauma to your head. We can't find any physical issues that would explain your pain," she continued.

John had been expecting a "but," which didn't come. Instead, it was silently present in the word "physical." She couldn't find any physical problems. All that left were psychological ones.

He was obviously aware that the point at the back of his head that hurt was where Trevor had pressed the pistol for those long seconds when he had thought his life was over. But at the same time, he simply couldn't accept the doctor's easy diagnosis. *Psychosomatic*—that was the word her profession adopted when their knowledge could take them no further.

"So, you mean it's all in my head?" he said.

She must have detected the hint of hostility in his voice, because she took a half step back from the bed. It was done unconsciously, but it was obvious enough for an undercover agent trained in body language to notice.

"I didn't say that. All I was saying was that we didn't see anything on the MRI that deviates from the norm."

"And what are your conclusions based on that?"

"That we have to keep looking for the cause of the pain. There are some neuro-logical tests we can run, but we can't rule out emotional trauma."

"Then I suggest you run those tests," he said, the words sounding harsher than he intended.

The doctor responded by jotting a few lines in the notebook that she always seemed to carry around. Then she smiled and said that the nurse would be in shortly to re-dress his wounds. The fact that John had taken out his frustration and power-lessness on her didn't seem to have dampened her mood.

When she left, Trevor turned toward him.

"It's probably best if we start behaving ourselves," he said. "Otherwise she might cut down our morphine."

"Don't bite the hand that drugs you," John replied, pleased to have found a rejoin-der he thought Trevor would appreciate. And he was right—Trevor laughed so loudly the guard outside peered in to check that everything was alright.

———

After his wounds had been re-dressed and the bags of fluids changed, Trevor said he was going to rest. John supposed he ought to do the same, but he wasn't tired after his long slumber in the morning.

He opened the laptop again and pulled up the Swedish investigation file, scrolling through the witness statements from the house where Emelie Bjurwall had been to a party the same night she had disappeared. The most interesting account was from a kid named Magnus Aglin. He was twenty years old and the host of the party, which had taken place at his father's house.

Magnus seemed to have known Emelie for a long time. Her childhood home was just a kilometer from the Aglins' house.

John pulled up the six-page transcript of the interview. It had taken place at the police station in Karlstad the day after the disappearance, and had been led by Detective Inspector Anton Lundberg.

INSPECTOR LUNDBERG: How did Emelie seem?

INTERVIEWEE AGLIN: What do you mean?

LUNDBERG: Well, was she her usual self?

AGLIN: Yes, I guess so. She was happy. In a party mood.

LUNDBERG: Drunk?

AGLIN: I imagine so.

LUNDBERG: How drunk was she?

AGLIN: As drunk as everyone else.

LUNDBERG: I understand. Was she drunk when she arrived?

AGLIN: Like, yeah.

LUNDBERG: "Like"? How am I meant to interpret that, Magnus?

AGLIN: Well, she was drunk when she got there. She'd had a few drinks.

LUNDBERG: Do you know where Emelie had been before she came to your party? Did she say anything about that?

AGLIN: I don't know. She had probably warmed up somewhere else.

LUNDBERG: Was it just alcohol at the party?

AGLIN: What do you mean?

John understood where Lundberg had been going with this. Emelie's parents had found a bag with traces of cocaine in it in a drawer in her bedroom. It was perfectly plausible that she had taken it before arriving at the party. But Magnus hadn't noticed that Emelie had been under the influence of anything other than alcohol. He also denied that there had been drugs at the party. John wished the detective had pushed the boy harder on that point. After all, these were spoiled upper-class kids and if Sweden was anything like the States, cocaine was the most popular drug in those circles.

The tattoo on the girl's forearm was another thing that Lundberg had taken an interest in.

LUNDBERG: As you know, a photo of Emelie's tattoo was posted on Facebook the night she disappeared.

AGLIN: Yes.

LUNDBERG: I'm curious—do you know why she has that specific tattoo?

AGLIN: It's a bucket list of things she wants to do before she dies.

LUNDBERG: Did she tell you that?

AGLIN: Yeah.

LUNDBERG: Okay. And whenever she does any of these things on the list, she has a tick tattooed into the box? Have I understood correctly?

AGLIN: Yes, I think so.

LUNDBERG: Do you know what's on Emelie's list?

AGLIN: No. She wouldn't say. She doesn't like talking about it, period. The thing about it being a bucket list, I had to drag that out of her.

LUNDBERG: In the photo uploaded to Facebook, the final tick has been carved using something sharp. Do you know if she did it herself that evening?

AGLIN: Not that I saw.

LUNDBERG: Did anything happen at the party that might have caused her to carve that tick?

AGLIN: How should I know? Like I told you, she didn't want to talk about the tattoo.

John opened the browser and searched for "bucket list + tattoo." The search brought up countless images and links to tattoo parlors around the world. But he couldn't find a single picture that showed three checkboxes in a row. Emelie Bjurwall's tattoo seemed to be unique and decidedly personal.

LUNDBERG: Think hard, Magnus—did Emelie say or do anything that evening that made you react? Something that stood out? Anything?

AGLIN: No. Like what? I wasn't with her that much. I talked to them in the beginning but then I was mostly out by the hot tub and . . .

LUNDBERG: Them? Which them?

AGLIN: Emelie and that other girl.

LUNDBERG: The other girl—who was that?

AGLIN: I don't know. A friend, I guess. They came together.

LUNDBERG: Okay. So, when Emelie arrived at the party, she came with this female friend?

AGLIN: Yes.

LUNDBERG: What do you know about her?

AGLIN: Like, nothing. I've never seen her before.

LUNDBERG: Isn't she from round here?

AGLIN: No, I don't think so. I would have recognized her if she was.

LUNDBERG: So, you spoke to her?

AGLIN: Just a few words.

LUNDBERG: What did she say?

AGLIN: How am I supposed to remember that? Nothing in particular. Just the sort of stuff you say at parties.

LUNDBERG: Like what?

AGLIN: Haven't you ever been to a party? I guess I asked if she was having a good time or something.

John could feel the interrogator's frustration. Something told him that a brisk smack on the side of the head might have done Magnus Aglin some good. But Lundberg had displayed—at least according to the transcript—an impressive degree of patience and hadn't allowed himself to be provoked.

LUNDBERG: Do you remember the friend's name?

AGLIN: Emelie called her Maja, I think.

LUNDBERG: But you're not absolutely sure?

AGLIN: Yes, she said Maja.

LUNDBERG: Last name?

AGLIN: No idea.

LUNDBERG: What did this Maja look like?

AGLIN: Well, pretty good-looking, I guess. Dark hair. Slim. A bit too short for my taste.

LUNDBERG: Age?

AGLIN: Same as us, or maybe a year older.

Lundberg hadn't gotten any more than that out of him. John decided to take a break from reading the interview and rest. He wanted to find out more about Maja. She ought to be able to tell them more about Emelie—she could provide the key to the missing girl's state of mind and tell them what they'd been up to on the night in question.

He looked for an interview with her in the files, but strangely enough there was nothing. Instead, he skimmed the transcriptions from the police interviews with the other partygoers. They didn't know who Maja was either and weren't able to do much more than confirm Magnus Aglin's description of her. John continued reading the investigator's notes from the conversation with Emelie Bjurwall's parents. It was the same story. They didn't know anyone by the name of Maja and had never heard their daughter talk about a friend with that name.

It was all very peculiar, John thought to himself. This young woman had clearly been at Magnus Aglin's party, together with Emelie and around twenty other people. Despite this, no one had provided the investigators with enough information for them to find and question her.

John continued going through the investigation records and noticed how the police had expanded their search to a wider and wider area. Inquiries had been made at the hotels and hostels in Karlstad and its surroundings. But none of them had had a guest by the name of Maja on the dates in question.

The School of Economics in Stockholm had also been contacted, as well as the treatment center where Emelie had been a resident for a period. But these—and a large number of other initiatives—had all been fruitless. The investigators seemed to have done what they could to find the mysterious friend. Yet the fact remained—and it was undeniably a strange one—that ten years later, Maja's identity still remained unknown.

John returned to the final part of the interview with Magnus Aglin. Lundberg had concentrated on finding out more about Emelie Bjurwall's departure from the party.

> LUNDBERG: Do you know what time it was when she left the house?
> AGLIN: Yes, it was just after twelve.
> LUNDBERG: How do you know that? There are so many other things you
> don't remember.
> AGLIN: I tried to get her to stay. I checked my phone and said she couldn't
> leave at midnight.

LUNDBERG: Why did you want her to stay?

AGLIN: If you're having a party, you don't want people cutting out too early. Especially not Emelie.

LUNDBERG: "Especially not Emelie?"

AGLIN: She's a classy addition to a party. Especially since she came back from Stockholm. Before, you couldn't see what she looked like in those crappy hoodies she used to wear. Whatever—the point is, it's not good if the AckWe princess leaves. People might get the impression I throw lame parties.

LUNDBERG: Did she say why she was leaving?

AGLIN: She was meeting someone.

John looked up from the screen. The more he read, the more interested he became. Given that his mother had taken the step of sending him the investigation, he felt obliged to try to understand what had happened to that girl. He focused and continued reading.

LUNDBERG: Who was she going to meet?

AGLIN: She didn't say.

LUNDBERG: What did she say?

AGLIN: Just that she was going to meet someone and would be back later.

LUNDBERG: But she didn't come back later, did she?

AGLIN: No.

LUNDBERG: Did she leave by herself?

AGLIN: I think so.

LUNDBERG: Her friend, Maja, didn't go with her?

AGLIN: No, she stayed—I'm sure about that.

LUNDBERG: What was Emelie like when she left?

AGLIN: What do you mean?

LUNDBERG: Well, was she angry, sad, nervous, frightened, or anything like that?

AGLIN: No, nothing like that. She seemed totally cool.

LUNDBERG: And you didn't get the impression something had happened? That she'd had a fight or anything like that?

AGLIN: Not that she told me about.

LUNDBERG: Do you think she was meeting a guy?

AGLIN: Maybe.

LUNDBERG: "Maybe"? If you know something, Magnus, it's important you tell me about it.

AGLIN: But I don't know anything. Maybe she was going to meet a guy. Or a girl. Or Papa Smurf. Don't you get it? I. Don't. Know.

LUNDBERG: Okay, okay. Is there anyone who might know?

AGLIN: Yeah, that girl she came to the party with. Maja. She probably knows.

LUNDBERG: Anyone else?

AGLIN: Maybe—Emelie knew lots of people at the party. Those of us who grew up out here have been hanging out together for a long time. I guess you should do your job and talk to them. Isn't that what the police do? Question people? Are we done now?

That was it. Lundberg had released the insufferable Magnus Aglin and done exactly what the boy had suggested. It was his job, after all. He had asked the same question of everyone who had been at the party and to a number of other people in Emelie's circle. But as with the question of her friend, Maja, the result was disheartening. No one knew who Emelie had agreed to meet that night.

8

KARLSTAD, 2009

He couldn't remember when they had last eaten take-out pizza. Sissela opened the lid of hers and cut it up in the box. Heimer got plates and asked her to transfer the slices onto the china. They had to maintain some minimum standards.

They sat at the kitchen island with a view out over Lake Vänern and the fairway. A couple of sailboats running on their engines moved slowly past, heading toward the harbor in Karlstad. It was getting dark, so all Heimer could see were the lanterns and silhouettes of the boats' hulls and masts.

Sissela's gaze also lingered on the view through the window while she ground the food down with her molars. She had seemed hopeful after the meeting with the two police detectives—and calmer, too, once she had taken control and the search had been initiated. But now she was back to waiting and it was something Heimer knew she didn't like. Perhaps she had expected a quick result. The phone should have rung already, with Gorbachev reporting that Emelie had been found.

Heimer took a mouthful of wine—a Chianti Classico from 1997. It was obviously overkill for the lumps of dough on the table. He had read that production output had been lower than usual that year, since there had been frost in April that had damaged the crop. But the few grapes that had been harvested were clearly of the best quality. He could sense the characteristic sharpness in his mouth. Chianti was one of his favorite regions in the old world, and even though many claimed it was overpriced, you really did get what you paid for.

"I don't understand why she's doing this to us," Sissela said, while her gaze remained fixed on the boats outside.

Her voice sounded judgmental. Heimer knew she didn't intend to come across like that, but that was how he perceived her. Always quick to point out the weaknesses in others.

"Business school was a mistake," he said.

He shouldn't be drinking right now—he knew that.

"How can it be a mistake? Going there was one of her goals in life," she said, turning to face him.

How long had she been staring at that lake? Emelie wasn't going to come walking across the water, if that was what she thought.

"So, you think the first tick on her arm was about business school?" he said.

"What else would it be about? She got the tattoo after Björkbacken, when she decided to go to business school."

Heimer shook his head. "You're wrong about that."

"So why did she get it then?"

"I don't know. But there is one thing I know—business school wasn't what she wanted. It was what you wanted."

"I had nothing to do with it. I was just as surprised as you were when she told us she'd applied."

If he hadn't already started on his second glass of Chianti, he would have capitulated—but he couldn't stop now. The words inside wanted to get out and if he suppressed them yet again he would suffocate.

"Don't you understand that's how it works in your family? Nothing needs to be said out loud. Everyone understands what's expected of them. You're sitting here actually believing that your daughter made a whole new start in life just because she's dressing like you and going to your old college? Damn it, it wasn't a new start. She gave up. She ignored what she wanted and tried to make you happy instead."

He watched her tear a crust from her pizza and put it in her mouth. A flake of oregano got stuck to her lip and she wiped it away with a napkin.

"All changes are good changes when it comes to Emelie," she said.

"You still don't get it, do you? She didn't change. She might have looked different, but it didn't mean she felt better. The only thing that's happened is that we're out of the loop. We have no insight into her life. She didn't even dare tell us how badly school was going."

Sissela interrupted him. "You have to stop living your life through Emelie. She's an adult and she can make her own decisions. That's something you have to accept."

Heimer looked down into his glass and saw the surface of the wine rippling in time with the tremors of his hand. Anger shot through him from the deepest place within him, spreading out to the finest capillaries in his fingers.

"The same way you accepted it when she wanted to focus on gaming?"

He was on his feet before he realized it. His chair tottered on its rear legs before falling to the floor.

"That's absolutely not the same thing," she said. "You saw for yourself how she was, sitting in front of those screens for hours every day."

Their fights always followed the same pattern. When he raised his voice, Sissela would lower hers, thus gaining the upper hand. Heimer assumed that she used the same tactic at work. He decided not to walk into that trap again. This time he was going to make his point. Slowly, he righted the chair and sat down again.

"You're wrong. She was never happier than when she was gaming. If you had watched her you would have seen that."

"So, you think all that violence and shooting had nothing to do with her being unwell?"

"No, it's a sport. Like any other sport. You must be able to see your own role in this! She felt like she was letting you down, that she wasn't living up to the family's expectations, and God knows they aren't the easiest ones."

"See my own role in this? What do you mean by that? Is it my fault that Emelie . . ."

Her voice faltered and she turned her face back to the window. She had come to a halt. She always came to a halt there. She couldn't say it—couldn't express the words. Couldn't accept that their daughter had tried to take her own life.

"You've pushed her too hard, Sissela. And it's sad that you can't acknowledge that."

Heimer drained his wineglass in one go and poured a refill from the next bottle. Inebriation helped him to stay calm, but he knew it was deceptive. If his state of mind shifted—even just slightly—the wine would become fuel to the fire.

Sissela met his gaze and he saw that his words had hit the mark. Her eyebrows were drawn together and there was even a furrow on her botoxed brow. This was the closest to being off-balance he had seen her in a long time.

"I'm going to call Dad," she said.

Heimer woke several hours later because his neck hurt. It was at an angle of almost ninety degrees against the armrest of the sofa. The room was dark except for a dimmed lamp. He remembered that he had lain down to rest a little after the pizza and wine. But he must have fallen asleep, because his tongue felt fuzzy and he had a string of saliva at one corner of his mouth.

He sat up to reach for the wineglass on the coffee table. There were two mouthfuls left and he had no intention of letting a vintage this good go to waste. He swirled it in the glass, smelled the hints of earth and ripe cherries, and finished it. Then he draped the dark blue lambswool blanket over his legs. Sissela must have put it over him before she had gone to bed.

He looked at his watch, which said it was just after two. He got up and checked that the kitchen island had been wiped down and the pizza boxes put in the recycling.

Then he rinsed the wineglass, filled it with cold water, and went to the window over-looking the lake.

He drank slowly while his eyes adjusted to the darkness outside. Slowly, he began to make out the ripples on the black surface below him. He thought about Emelie's tattoo again. There was something about it that had been nagging at him, and only now did he realize what it was.

In the photo she had posted on Facebook, two of the squares had ticks tattooed in them. The design hadn't looked like that when she had visited at Christmas. Back then, only one of the boxes had been ticked—he was sure of that. Emelie had been wearing a short-sleeved red dress on Christmas Eve and he saw the tattoo when she had reached to pass a dish of food.

She must have done something big ahead of the summer break, something that meant she could get the tattoo of the second tick. He pressed the glass of cold water against his forehead to keep his thoughts clear. It was so contradictory. Emelie was clearly not well and had lied about her grades to avoid disappointing her family. At the same time, she had been ticking off another goal on her bucket list. How did that work?

His thoughts continued to spin around in his head, becoming entangled in the darkest part of himself. The picture he had just conjured up, of his daughter's tattooed forearm, felt unbearable. He thought about the final tick—carved into the skin like a wound—and shut his eyes.

Heimer imagined cutting through the black surface of the lake outside, and sinking quickly through the water, as if a force were pulling him to the bottom. It didn't feel unpleasant—more like liberation.

When he opened his eyes again, he heard himself crying. First quietly, then more loudly. Sobbing, he sank to the floor with his back to the panorama window. He smacked the back of his head so hard against the thick glass that it felt like his head might explode.

Sissela wasn't to blame for Emelie being gone. She was just doing what she was programmed to do—preparing her daughter for the role awaiting her. Just as her father had drilled her. Whether or not the family's daughters wanted to take over the company didn't matter. It was a matter of duty and responsibility toward something greater. Almost like a religion.

It had been up to him to make Emelie understand that she actually had a choice. That she was free to do whatever she wanted with her life. He had seen it as his most important duty and yet he hadn't backed her up at a critical moment.

Perhaps he was blowing what happened out of all proportion. But it was impossible to ignore the fact that there was a correlation between his betrayal and the events that had ended with his daughter's attempted suicide.

Striker Chicks had won an online tournament for players from across Scandinavia. Heimer thought back to the dinner he hosted for all five girls in Karlstad to celebrate the victory. They had scarfed burgers and talked about becoming the first girls' team in the world to make a living playing *Counter-Strike*. They asked him if he knew anything about agents' contracts. He had laughed and told them to calm down. Then one of the girls had shown him an email from an agency in London that said they represented e-sports stars.

"If things go well in Seoul, they'll probably want to sign us," she had said jauntily.

Heimer hadn't understood a thing. Seoul? What was that all about? The friend had read his puzzled face and explained.

"Didn't Emelie tell you? First prize in the tournament we just won is entry into a competition there. They pick up the tab—business-class flights, hotel, food—everything."

Heimer knew that *Counter-Strike* was something that was getting serious for the girls. They were eighteen and rising stars in a field no one in the adult world knew existed.

When his daughter had fallen asleep that evening, he had sat down with Sissela and told her what he found out at the restaurant. The response had been as expected—but even more intense. This had gone too far. The amount of time Emelie spent playing computer games was bad for her. It was time they put a stop to it, before things got completely out of hand.

Heimer had protested and said he took the opposite view. That gaming gave her a purpose. That it was something she had achieved on her own and could be proud of.

Sissela had changed tack, arguing that gaming was having a negative impact on Emelie's already-weak studies. A trip to South Korea during the school year wouldn't help her grades. When Heimer had realized that she wasn't going to change her mind, he gave up trying to persuade her. It would have been pointless and simply ended in another huge fight.

So the Striker Chicks had gone to Seoul without Emelie. The agency found a replacement and the team came in third. A few weeks later, it emerged that the girls had signed a contract with the agency behind Emelie's back and that the new girl was taking her place on a permanent basis. Emelie was no longer part of Striker Chicks and was forced to watch as her friends took a year off from high school to move into an all-expenses-paid apartment in London.

Heimer banged his head even harder against the window. Why hadn't he stood up for her when he had known how much gaming meant to her?

He thought about how quickly Emelie's world had fallen apart after that. All the time and energy she'd previously spent on *Counter-Strike* was now spent partying or sitting listlessly in her room, refusing to come out. Depression had taken a firmer hold of her by the day.

Sissela handled the issue as she usually did—by asking someone else to deal with it. A string of therapists had been brought in and Emelie had seemed to take a perverse delight in messing with them. Once, she claimed that her parents hit her if her grades weren't good enough. That they didn't care that she had dyslexia.

In the middle of this circus, Heimer saw it was more than just teenage rebellion and disappointment at what had happened with the Striker Chicks. Emelie felt trapped—chained to a future she didn't want. But he could never have imagined things were so bad that she'd attempt to take her own life and have to be admitted to a treatment center.

Sometimes, he thought the transformation that had happened after Björkbacken was a way for Emelie to punish him for betraying her. She had made it clear to him that their pact was broken and she had thrown herself into the Bjurwall side of the family. From then on, she had treated him as the sad person he was. A clown living on his wife's money and spending his days doing things he thought were important. Like finding a case of Margaux of the right vintage or cutting a few seconds off his personal best for a 10K run.

He could have dealt with the contempt from others—but not from Emelie. She was his daughter—they belonged together. The way she treated him made him furious and miserable at the same time. He pounded the back of his head against the window with such force that his vision flickered.

The sound must have woken Sissela. She was standing in front of him in her pearlescent, shimmery white nightdress, which made her look like a ghost in the low light. She didn't say anything—she just sat down on the floor. She carefully took his face in her hands. He could smell her hand cream—a faint scent of rose water.

"It's my fault," he sobbed.

She hushed him and let him sink his head into her lap. Then she stroked his hair slowly until there were no tears left to cry.

9

BALTIMORE, 2019

The doctor really knew how to rile Brodwick up. When she pushed back the time of the debrief, Brodwick lost it. He said that he represented the FBI and could basically do whatever he liked. The doctor replied that she was medically responsible for the patients and that if he didn't respect that then he wasn't welcome at the hospital. It ended with a compromise. The debrief was postponed—but just overnight, instead of for forty-eight hours as the doctor had said at first.

The nurse came into the room and said it was time to go. Trevor was up first—Brodwick wanted to start with him. She rolled him away in his bed and almost two hours passed before he returned. He looked tired, but winked at John from his pillow. Trevor had told Brodwick what he needed to know and nothing more.

Then it was John's turn. The policeman helped the nurse to maneuver the bed into the corridor. The doctor was standing in a doorway farther along it, talking to Brodwick. He assumed she was issuing final exhortations to him not to push the patient too hard. The boss smiled his lopsided smile. He was presumably providing her with the assurances she wanted to hear.

The nurse adjusted the angle of the bed so that John was sitting more upright and then pushed the bed into the meeting room. Then she turned on her heel and left the room without giving Brodwick so much as a look.

"I really hope they're treating you better than me," the boss said in the nasal voice that was his other distinctive characteristic alongside the lopsided smile. It had taken John a long time to realize that he actually talked like that and wasn't afflicted with a long-term cold.

"She likes me, that's why she's messing with you, I reckon," John replied.

"I guess it's those velvety eyes you're into. I can't really disagree with that."

Brodwick took his jacket off and pulled the chair closer to the bed. Then he fixed a microphone to the collar of John's white hospital pajama top and checked that it was connected to the smartphone on the adjacent table.

"Shall we get started?"

John nodded. He was ready.

The first part of the conversation was a report of his time as an undercover agent in the Nigerian drug cartel. He reported what he had seen, being careful not to exaggerate. Everything he said had to correlate with previous surveillance and describe things that he had personally witnessed. If a statement was about something he'd heard secondhand from someone close to Ganiru or the leader himself, he made sure to emphasize this.

When it came to the events that had taken place at the port, he stuck to the alternative version that Trevor had come up with. It felt so plausible that John almost believed it was the truth—that he had really been a take-charge FBI agent who'd kept a cool head and together with Trevor had improvised a scenario that had fooled everyone else in the container.

When Brodwick was satisfied he stopped the recording.

"Well done, John. You and Trevor did a fantastic job. But I want to warn you now that this was just a warmup. The Nigerians will have an army of lawyers and it's my and the prosecutor's job to make sure you're ready. But we have several months ahead before the trial and crunch time, so don't worry."

"Sounds good," said John, who saw that the conversation was slipping into the next phase. The one that encompassed the decision he had made late the night before and that he had to be ready to defend.

"Well then," said Brodwick. "We need to discuss the terms of your witness protection arrangements. The Bureau obviously has a process for this, but I wanted to start the conversation."

He got up and checked to make sure no one was listening outside and that the door was shut.

"Have you given any thought to where you might like to disappear to?"

John looked him in the eyes. There was no room for hesitation.

"Sweden."

Brodwick laughed. "I assume you're joking."

"I'm not joking."

"Jesus Christ, John. You've got family in Sweden. You grew up there. It's too risky."

"But any traces of my background there have already been erased, right?"

"Yes—the digital ones. John Adderley disappeared from all the official databases the same day you accepted your mission to infiltrate the cartel. We've also got confirmation from the Swedes that you've been erased from their population register. But the people who know you—they still exist. How many people in New York know you grew up in Sweden?"

John sighed inwardly. This was the weak link in the plan.

"I don't actually know. Not as many as you might think."

"One is all it takes, John. Don't be naïve. Ganiru is a heavyweight, but the cartel won't go down with him. There are even uglier customers out there, with even more resources. They'll do everything they can to find you and Trevor. It's not only about revenge—it's about making an example of you. Showing the consequences of disloyalty to the cartel."

"I understand that and I'm willing to take the risk."

"You're willing to take the risk—sure. But that doesn't matter if the Bureau isn't."

Brodwick's lopsided smile returned to his face, seeking to smooth over the show of power he had just made.

"It's for your own sake," he continued. "Come on—we both want the same thing here: to give you a good, safe life."

John shook his head.

"We don't want the same thing. I want a Swedish identity and you're saying no."

Brodwick folded his arms. The smile was gone.

"The Bureau has its rules. Witness protection isn't granted for environments where the person under protection has connections to their past life. No ifs, no buts."

John paused for a moment. He had known the conversation would end up here and he knew what the next move had to be. Yet, he still hesitated. It was a betrayal of his employer and might ruin his relationship with the Bureau forever. He forced himself to think about the first lines in the letter from his mother again—about the bigger picture. About the sort of man he wanted to be.

John!

This time you have to come home.

"A Swedish ID is my condition for testifying in the trial."

There. Now he had said it. Crossed the Rubicon. Rolled the dice.

The reaction was immediate.

"What kind of fucking drugs are they giving you in here? Have you completely lost your mind?"

Brodwick stood up, his face completely red. His pulse was throbbing so hard in the knotted artery at his throat that for a moment John thought the man leaning over him was going to have a stroke.

"Think damned hard. When you make an ultimatum like that you declare war on your own. On the FBI. You must realize you can never win?"

John fought to remain calm. The morphine coursing through his blood helped.

"I don't want to start a war with anyone. I want to testify against Ganiru and make sure he goes down for life. All I ask—after risking my life every day for almost a year—is the option to choose where I start over."

"And you can—so long as you follow the Bureau's rules for witness protection. I don't understand why you're so determined to end your days being tortured to death. Because that's what'll happen if you go to Sweden. Sooner or later, they'll find you there."

"It's my life and I make my own decisions."

John waited for yet another outburst of rage, but Brodwick decided to change tactics. He reined in his anger and switched to negotiation instead.

"We're very grateful for your contribution and I'm certain we can bend the rules a bit when it comes to your monthly allowance. You should be comfortable, John—you've earned it. Pick a country with a nice climate, white beaches, and low expenses. Then you can live like a king without having to think about anything except which drink to order and which girl you're going to go out with."

"That sounds wonderful, but it's not what I want."

Brodwick sat down again. Apparently he had the weight of the Bureau's collective troubles on his shoulders, given the protests from the chair.

"Because you want to go to Sweden," he sighed. "A country full of polar bears, socialists, and Nigerian hitmen. And where you're putting not only yourself in danger, but your family too."

"Like I said, I'm willing to take the risk."

"And if I don't agree—what then?"

"You already know that."

"Yes, but I want to hear you say it one more time, since you can't really be so dumb that you actually mean it."

"I won't testify."

Brodwick leaned forward in the chair and put his hands on his neatly pressed suit trousers.

"We've already got your intelligence reports and the recorded witness statement you just provided. Together with Trevor's testimony, that's enough to get Ganiru and the other bastards put away."

"Maybe. But don't you think the jury will wonder why I'm not there during the trial? The lawyers will cross-examine and my absence will be a good place to start if they want to poke holes in the credibility of the witness statements."

Brodwick got up and adjusted his trousers so that the fabric once again reached down to his patent leather shoes. He put on his jacket, put the phone and microphone in the inside pocket, and headed for the door.

"And what now?" John said from the bed. "What happens now?"

The boss turned around and shrugged his shoulders.

"Nothing. There's no point discussing witness protection for someone who doesn't intend to testify, is there?"

He gave his lopsided smile again, but this time his eyes were ice-cold.

"You're on your own now, John."

10

KARLSTAD, 2009

Heimer realized that whoever was pushing the buzzer down by the gate wasn't going to stop any time soon. Sissela was already at the bedroom window, wrapped in her dressing gown and peering between the curtains at the road below. In one hand she had her mug of morning coffee and in the other a vibrating phone.

"It's a reporter from *Aftonbladet*," she said. "He must know Emelie has gone missing."

"Is he calling or buzzing the intercom?"

"Both, presumably," she said, rejecting the call.

Unlike Heimer, Sissela didn't seem particularly bothered by being disturbed at home like this. Years spent in the limelight had made her immune to the pushiness of journalists. When Heimer complained about the constant press coverage of AckWe, she generally defended the reporters. "We're a public company and they're just doing their jobs," she usually said.

The scribblers on the finance desks were rarely much trouble. They had some grasp of the fact that even a CEO had a personal life and wasn't always available for comment. But the man standing at the gate was another beast altogether. When a reporter from one of the evening tabloids caught the scent of a story, he didn't let go.

"I'm going to take a shower," Sissela said, going into the bathroom. He saw the contours of her body through the frosted glass that separated it from the bedroom. He knew the ritual by heart. First, turn on the water, then hang the dressing gown on the hook by the mirror, and then step under the warm, soft jets.

Part of him wanted to get out of bed, wrench open the door, and push her against the glass wall. He wondered what would happen if he actually did it. Would she be indifferent and ask him to stop? Get angry and ask how he could think about sex when their daughter was missing? Or be turned on and ask him to continue?

She was lathering her stomach right now and her hand slid over her breasts. Heimer felt himself growing hard under the duvet and he put his hand down to push back the beginnings of his erection. There had been something there last night when she had comforted him. A closeness from another time that he missed. He had almost forgotten that they had once been in love and had barely been able to keep their hands off each other.

He had been her *Counter-Strike*, her revolt against her parents and the predetermined path laid down for her. Sissela's father had made it known that he considered Heimer to be a phase his daughter had to get through before she found a candidate with a more suitable last name for the role of husband in the AckWe family. But then she had gotten pregnant and Heimer said jokingly that they should head to Vegas to get married. They were in their early twenties and he never thought she would say yes. But she had taken him at his word and booked two tickets.

He would never forget the first dinner after the trip, when they told her parents about the baby and the wedding. Sissela had held his hand under the table and the angrier her father had become, the harder she had squeezed. Heimer was still convinced that she had kept Emelie more to annoy her father than because she had wanted to become a mother at such a young age.

"Hello? Anyone home?"

The voice from downstairs made him jump. The timing was almost uncanny. Allan Bjurwall never used the intercom or the doorbell. He behaved as if the house were his own and in a way it was—even if Heimer didn't like to admit it.

The old man must have taken the first flight from Marseille after speaking to Sissela last night. He lived in a large stone-built house outside Aix-en-Provence for part of the year and he didn't usually like to leave it. But a missing grandchild was a matter of sufficient gravity to merit a trip home.

Heimer met him halfway up the stairs from the foyer. His father-in-law spoke the way he looked. His voice growled, as if it belonged to a bear. He probably weighed one hundred and thirty kilos without being especially tall. His provençal diet had made his waist expand, but despite that his face had kept its shape. His silver hair and neat beard were reminiscent of Kenny Rogers in his later years.

Heimer tried to avoid the mandatory handshake by shoving both hands in his trouser pockets and nodding by way of greeting. But Allan followed etiquette and when he proffered one of his giant paws there was nothing to do but reach out and hope the bones inside his hand weren't crushed.

Heimer explained that Sissela was in the shower and offered Allan coffee. He didn't want any. He had already had two cups to keep himself awake during the drive from Arlanda airport and his stomach couldn't take anymore.

"I hope you haven't spoken to that man outside." Allan said, nodding toward the road.

"No, of course not."

"He'll write something anyway, which will bring more reporters round, so better be prepared."

Allan sat down at the kitchen island and asked whether they had heard anything more from the police. Heimer explained that the head of the investigation had contacted Sissela earlier that morning. He had said that the search would be focused on a small area at the tip of the Tynäs promontory. According to the cell phone company, that was where Emelie's phone had been when it lost contact with the network.

"Do you think she's tried to harm herself again?" said Allan.

Heimer didn't know how to answer, and in the silence that followed the question, conversation died out—as it had on so many other occasions. Each of them had grown tired of trying to like the other and had instead adopted the strategy of having as little to do with the other as possible.

When Sissela finally arrived in the kitchen she hugged her father and thanked him for coming. Heimer thought Allan looked awkward—unaccustomed to that kind of show of emotion from his daughter. When she had freed herself from his embrace, Heimer noticed Sissela was wearing the closest thing to normal clothes that her designer-stuffed wardrobe permitted: a pair of dark jeans and a ribbed blue cardigan over a white tank top.

"Are you going somewhere?" Heimer asked.

"I'm going to help in the search for Emelie."

Allan cleared his throat and appeared to look for the right words to change her mind.

"Let the police handle it. There'll be photographers and reporters there and you're not ready for that. Anyway, we have other matters to discuss."

"What could be more important than finding Emelie?"

There was an edge to Sissela's voice that seemed to disturb even her authoritarian father.

"There's nothing more important than that," he said. "But it's the police's job and the best thing we can do is leave them to work in peace. And as I said, we've got a few practical issues to deal with—whether you like it or not."

Allan presented his plan for managing the company in the short-term. If necessary, he would temporarily return to the post of CEO while Sissela went on leave until Emelie returned. All statements to the press would go through him, and neither she nor Heimer would need to be involved. Allan would be the family's voice to the outside world and give them the space to look after each other and Emelie when she was back home.

"She hasn't even been gone two days, Dad."

"I know, and hopefully she'll be back this afternoon. But it's just as well we plan for the possibility that it might take a little longer. It never hurts to be prepared."

Sissela thought for a while and then finally nodded in consent. Then she got up and began to go down the stairs and toward the front door. Allan ran after her.

"But I thought we agreed that . . ."

She interrupted him.

"We're in agreement that you'll handle the press. But I'm still going to look for my daughter."

She slid her feet into a pair of red Wellingtons, opened the front door, and went out onto the drive. Just a few seconds later she returned.

"What is it?" Heimer asked.

Sissela took a deep breath, composing herself.

"There are people all over the road. Reporters and TV cameras. I think they just filmed me through the gate."

Heimer realized what had happened. *Aftonbladet*'s reporter must have published an article, which meant every other news outlet in the country had been alerted. The heiress being reported missing was a good story and it wasn't that far from Karlstad to Stockholm.

"What are you going to do?" he said.

"What I've said all along. Look for Emelie."

It was impossible to stop Sissela—Heimer realized that much. Even her father knew that a campaign of persuasion wouldn't work and merely shook his head.

"Wait, I'll call the detective sergeant," said Heimer, when his wife made a move to open the door again. "He can pick us up."

A little while later, Bernt Primer was standing in the foyer. He looked concerned after having driven through the swarm of reporters at the gate, all wanting to know whether Emelie had turned up.

"They're out of their damn minds," he muttered.

Primer explained that he would take them to the tip of the Tynäs promontory, where the search had just begun. The weather forecast said it was going to start raining soon, so there was no time to lose.

Heimer helped Sissela into her raincoat and reached for two umbrellas from the hat stand. He put on the waterproof windbreaker he usually wore on wet-weather runs and a pair of large Wellingtons.

"Ready?" said Primer.

Sissela nodded and then the detective opened the door. The cameras clicked on the other side of the fence as they walked toward the car. When they slowly passed through the gate, they could hear the reporters' questions for Sissela through the window as they sat in the back seat.

"Have you heard from Emelie?"

"Any comment on reports that she's been kidnapped?"

"How concerned are you?"

When she wouldn't answer, they tried Heimer instead. A lumbering young man from one of the TV channels pushed forward to his side of the car and shouted as loudly as he could:

"How is your wife?"

Heimer had to marshal all his willpower not to wind down the window and put his fist in the man's chubby face. The question was ridiculous and insulting at the same time. Partly because it was obvious to anyone who could see Sissela's tense face that she was not at all well. And partly because he was Emelie's father and the question should have been about how he felt. He was his own person with his own feelings—not just a dad doll propped up next to his wife.

Primer kept his hand on the horn and finally managed to get through the cluster of media people. He accelerated away and drove the short distance to the cordon, where a policeman raised the blue-and-white tape so they could park on the other side.

"Follow me," said Primer, leading the way. The rain hadn't yet started falling, but judging by the dark clouds it wouldn't be long before the umbrellas were needed. They walked between sparse pine trees, heading toward the water. The detective stopped level with the foundation of the old jetty where the boat to Karlstad used to stop.

They were at the spot where the popular Tynäs Restaurant had once stood. The archipelago eatery had burnt down at the end of the seventies and all that was left were parts of the foundation. Around them, Heimer saw uniformed police officers searching the stony ground for traces of Emelie.

Right away, he felt it becoming difficult to draw enough air into his lungs. He had to try to pull himself together. If he let thoughts of his daughter overwhelm him, it would end with him breaking down in front of Sissela and the police.

Primer exchanged a few words with one of the uniformed officers, who said they had still found nothing of interest. Then the three of them continued farther along the promontory. The terrain became barer, mostly naked rock. Several ledges ran down to the water, as if someone had terraced the rocks to create the ideal sunbeds for visitors.

Heimer spotted a policeman on a flat rock ahead of them, waving his nearest colleagues toward him. They gathered around him, seeming very interested by something he was pointing at on the ground.

Primer saw that something had happened and hurried over to the spot. Heimer and Sissela followed him and got there just as one of the men peeled off from the group to approach the detective sergeant.

His face was red with exertion.

"We've found something, and we need to get Forensics here as soon as possible, before it starts raining."

11

BALTIMORE, 2019

John tried to gather his thoughts after the conversation with Brodwick. It had gone just as badly as he thought it would. He hadn't predicted that the boss would give in during their first meeting; he had expected some back-and-forth. John reckoned coolly that time was on his side. Whether he was right remained to be seen. The Bureau's decision-making was characterized as much by politics and big egos as it was by reason and a desire for a good outcome.

He hoped that Trevor's meeting with Brodwick had been less complicated. Trevor had been in an excellent mood when he had been allowed to meet his wife a few minutes ago. The nurse had washed his face and shaved off his stubble before rolling him to the private visitors' room.

A sketch pad and a selection of pencils in different thicknesses and hardnesses were lying on John's bedside table. He had ordered them via the hospital's patient services and was surprised at how quickly they came. Trevor had been curious about the contents of the package and John had told him about his passion for drawing. His mom had taught him how to draw. On good days, she'd had the patience to sit with him in front of the easel. The key thing was to keep an eye on the light—how it fell and how it cast shadows. Together, they created still lifes of footballs, hot dogs, and various other things that captivated small boys.

When as an adult he had joined Homicide in New York City, he found a way of using his drawing skills as part of his job. He secretly started to make what he called "investigation pieces." His rules for these pieces of art were simple: one sheet of paper per investigation, and only significant things could be committed to paper. It could be words, symbols, drawings . . . The freedom to visualize the case any way he wanted, and the limited space, helped him refine his thoughts.

Naturally, he had eventually been caught with a pencil in his hand late one night in the police precinct. It hadn't been long before John was nicknamed Picasso. But the digs had petered out once the other cops saw that the investigation pieces were useful. Eventually, they became a natural, accepted part of John's working methods for a case. When he left New York, the guys had framed some of them as a going-away present. They had been decent about it and picked cases that had been solved and the perpetrator convicted.

Given the extent of the Swedish investigation file he had been sent, he was grateful for the pad and pencils on the bedside table. They would be needed in order to distinguish what mattered from what didn't, as he dug deeper into the material ten years after the fact.

On the third day after Emelie Bjurwall's disappearance, the case had taken an unexpected turn. The investigators had found traces of blood on a rock by the water. The police no longer believed she had disappeared of her own volition, which had initially been their theory. It was easily adopted, given the girl's turbulent backstory and the fact that she had taken cocaine on the night in question.

Suicide also became a less plausible scenario the longer they went without finding a body. The police had dragged the water off the Tynäs promontory, without any results. The wind and current also meant that a body would have drifted back to shore.

The rock where they had made their finding was situated just five hundred meters from the house where Magnus Aglin had thrown his party. John went gone through all eighty-six pictures from the scene. A long string of rocks along the water's edge. Some were flat and smooth, others taller and more jagged. John guessed that during the summer months it was a popular place for sunbathers who wanted to avoid the bigger beaches.

The blood residue had been found just two or three meters from the water, and according to the lab report it belonged to Emelie Bjurwall. It wasn't just the blood that had interested the investigators, but also its volume. The attacker—or nature—had rinsed most of it away, but the size of the remaining stain allowed them to estimate that the girl had lost almost a liter of blood.

It was impossible for that much blood to have come solely from the wound on her forearm that was visible in the Facebook photo. Everything indicated that someone had taken Emelie Bjurwall against her will and might even have killed her.

Twenty-four hours after the blood was analyzed, the next piece of surprising news had arrived from the laboratory in Linköping. John understood from the investigative material that the Forensics team had continued to search the area with a fine-tooth comb. Pretty soon, they had found a number of smaller stains close to Emelie's blood. These had taken longer to analyze, but when the answer came, it sent the investigation in another new direction.

They had found semen on the rock.

The discovery was completely counter to the police's latest theory that someone had kidnapped Emelie to get at her family's money. Sexual violence was very rare in connection with abductions. Maybe the daughter of billionaire Sissela Bjurwall had just been in the wrong place at the wrong time and had walked into the path of a rapist.

Reading between the terse lines in the reports, John sensed the investigators' intense interest in the finding. Semen was forensic evidence that could tie a suspect to the scene of the crime. If the perpetrator had a previous conviction, he would be in the police DNA database and all they had to do was bring him in.

They ran the search but were disappointed. No hits. John wondered how many profanities had echoed around the walls of the police station in Karlstad that day. Few investigators wanted to do more work than necessary on a case. They wanted to wrap it up quickly—above all for the sake of the victim's loved ones, but also to ensure they looked efficient in the eyes of their bosses and the general public.

John read on and noted that the Swedish police followed the same procedures as the Americans. A comprehensive DNA check of all local residents and other men in Emelie's social circle was initiated immediately. He got the feeling that every single police officer in Värmland had been somehow involved in the investigation during this period. However, the witness statements, the interviews, and reports were primarily signed by the same people: a handful of detectives who had formed the core of the investigation.

He scrolled through the folders. The laptop became warm and the fan began to whirr noisily. The battery was hot against his thighs through the thin blanket and he had to put the laptop down for a while.

He sank back into the pillow and put his arm over his face to shield his eyes. There were two things that didn't fit with the theory of a sexual crime committed by an unknown assailant.

One: the mysterious meeting.

Magnus Aglin, who had thrown the party, had told the police that Emelie left the house to meet someone. The investigators had expended considerable time trying to find this someone without success. This might have been because the person was the perpetrator, or because they simply didn't want to admit to meeting Emelie at that time of day. Of course, it was possible that Magnus had been lying and that the person didn't exist. Whichever of these options was true, none of them supported the scenario of an unknown assailant.

Two: the tattoo.

Was it possible that it was pure chance Emelie had carved a tick into the final square and publicly posted the photo on Facebook just before being attacked by a rapist? It wasn't completely impossible, but it sounded like too much of a coincidence to satisfy John. There remained the possibility that it was the attacker who had carved the tick and uploaded the photo. In that case, it was no regular sex crime. There was something else to it—another motive where sex was just one component and Emelie was not a randomly selected victim.

John reached for the laptop again and pulled up the picture. He clicked on the shortcut to switch to full screen and let the pale forearm fill the monitor from edge to edge. Three squares, two tattooed ticks, and the final one carved into the skin with the contours of a fresh wound. A bucket list—if the girl's own words were to be believed. But exactly which goals in life had Emelie Bjurwall achieved at such a young age? John felt intuitively that the photo contained an enigma and that if he stared at it long enough the answer might appear.

John had fallen asleep while reading the Swedish investigation files and only woke up when Trevor returned. The wheels squeaked as the nurse rolled him back into the room. The angle of the bed meant John could see his colleague's face. It was familiar but also different. Gone was the sly mouth, always ready to laugh. The twinkle in his eye had been replaced by bleak emptiness.

It wasn't Trevor.

It was Abaeze.

The distance between his neighbor's two personas was perhaps not so great. The darkness lay within both of them.

"She's changed her mind," he said. "What happened at the port is too much for her."

His voice was dry and matter-of-fact, as if he were submitting an intelligence report to Brodwick.

"She wants a divorce. She thinks the Nigerians will find me and she doesn't want to put our kid at risk."

"But surely you'll get to see your daughter again?" said John.

"No. She wants me to relinquish custody."

12

KARLSTAD, 2009

During his forty-eight years of life, Heimer had never previously had anything to do with the police. He hadn't even been inside a police station except on the few occasions he had renewed his passport. He wondered how common that was. Most people surely encountered law enforcement every now and then. Break-ins, damage, and pub brawls were in the papers every day. But Heimer had avoided it all. It probably had something to do with the area he lived in. Crime rarely made it as far as Tynäs. At any rate, not the sort of crime that involved violence and bloodshed.

The room he and Sissela were in was on the second floor of the police station, with a view down onto Infanterigatan. Her father wanted to come with them, but they both agreed it was best if he stayed home. The metal-framed table in front of them had a greenish sheet of laminate glued onto its wooden surface. The brown plastic chairs seemed to have been designed to be easily stacked rather than to be sat on comfortably.

Detective Sergeant Bernt Primer stuck his head around the door and offered to get them coffee. They wouldn't have to wait much longer; there was just another interview they needed to wrap up first. Before Heimer had time to decline, Sissela replied that they would like two cups, with milk. Primer vanished, probably toward the coffee machine Heimer had seen in the corridor earlier. It had a sticker attached to it that said "Warning: cop coffee."

Sissela adjusted her skirt for the umpteenth time and looked worried. Gorbachev—or Anton Lundberg, the actual name of the head of the investigation, as Heimer had learned—had called that morning and asked them to come to the police station. New information had emerged. What it was, he hadn't wanted to discuss on the phone.

Heimer thought back to the last time they had met the head of the investigation, the man with the birthmark on his forehead. It had been at their home, around a week ago. He had thought Sissela would break down when the detective had spoken bluntly about their finding on the rocks—the large amount of blood from their daughter. Instead, she had fallen silent and disappeared into her own thoughts.

Then the questions had followed in rapid succession: ordered, logical, and unsentimental. Gorbachev—it was impossible to think of him as having another name—had come to grips with who he was dealing with and had stopped wrapping his answers in tissue paper. The police were working on the basis that this was not a voluntary disappearance. Semen had been found next to the blood residue, which indicated that Emelie had been the victim of a sex crime and that the perpetrator had taken her from the scene.

Primer, who had also been present during the conversation, had looked grave as he'd opened the bag and taken out a DNA testing kit. He had explained that the police were taking samples from all men in the area. Just routine.

Heimer had struggled to stay calm. What sort of routine gave the police the right to imply he'd had sex with his own daughter? Sissela had noticed which way the wind was blowing and had discreetly put her hand on his forearm, as if trying to transfer a little of her own superhuman calm to him.

Eventually, he had given in and opened his mouth for the cotton swab. He had felt Primer scrape it against the inside of his cheek to capture enough saliva. Then the detective had put the sample in a transparent container and put the lid on.

Only when the policemen had left the house had Sissela allowed herself to fall apart. Heimer had led her into the bedroom and sat next to her until she fell asleep with one hand in his and the other clasped tightly around her pillow. The fact that she had needed him had suppressed Heimer's own anxiety—for the time being at least.

The scrape of the chair leg as Sissela stood up brought him back to the dreary room in the police station, where even the plastic flower in the window looked like it needed watering.

"It's more bad news—I can feel it," she said, after doing a circuit of the table. "Otherwise, why wouldn't that Primer man look me in the eye?"

"I don't know. But if it is bad news, I don't think they'd keep us waiting."

Sissela sighed.

"How on earth can it take twenty minutes to get two cups of coffee?"

It was rare that she showed her frustration. But when she did, it was always in situations like this, when her patience was being tested.

When the detective finally returned, he was followed by the head of the investigation. The coffee seemed to have been forgotten, and he was grateful not to have to drink it given the sticker on the machine.

Gorbachev greeted them and Heimer did his best not to stare at the birthmark. The head of the investigation was more neatly dressed today than on previous occasions, in dark chinos and a contrasting jacket without any wear on the elbows—as if he had prepared for meeting Sissela Bjurwall.

"We've got a match on the semen we found by the blood residue," he said. "It matches a DNA sample we took during the investigation."

The interview, Heimer thought to himself. It must have been that person that the detectives had been talking to. The pressure on his chest returned and he felt faintly nauseated. He scanned the room for a wastepaper basket in case he needed to throw up, but he couldn't see one.

"Who is it?" said Sissela.

"A nineteen-year-old. His name is Billy Nerman. We arrested him just before I called you."

"Has he said anything about . . ." Sissela swallowed a couple of times before she continued. ". . . anything about Emelie?"

"No, he says he doesn't know what happened to her and that he's never been to that end of Tynäs."

"But how's that possible? It's his semen?"

"Yes."

"But then he must have been there, mustn't he? He must know where she is now?"

Sissela had raised her voice and then covered her face with her hands. It was all too much for her. Gorbachev leaned forward, resting his crossed arms on the laminated surface and making the table wobble slightly.

"We've only questioned him on a preliminary basis, and we'll continue shortly," he said. "But first I wanted to find out if you know anything about Billy Nerman. Is he someone Emelie spent time with?"

"I've never heard the name. Have you?" said Sissela, turning to Heimer.

"No, never."

"Do you think you could look at a photograph? It's important for us to find out whether he knew your daughter, and if so, how."

Sissela nodded slowly, and after a discreet glance from the head of the investigation, Primer opened the folder he had placed on the table. The photo showed a young man with a neutral driver's license–appropriate expression.

"He's Black," said Heimer with surprise in his voice that he was unable to conceal.

"Yes, he's Black," said Primer, as if repeating the comment made it less loaded.

Heimer examined the photo carefully. He tried to push away the nausea that kept welling up. Instead he focused on whether he had seen the young man before. He had always had a good memory for faces and if their paths had crossed he would have remembered it. He didn't meet that many Black men. But his memory bank was blank.

"He's not from Tynäs, I take it?" said Sissela.

In other circumstances, Heimer would have laughed at the question. The man in the photo would shock the living daylights out of the ladies in the Hämptons.

"He lives outside of Skoghall," Gorbachev replied.

Sissela pushed the photo back across the table—it was clear she didn't want to look at it anymore. Primer understood and put it back in the folder, which he then closed.

"I'm sorry we couldn't be of any more assistance," she said, getting up.

Heimer was grateful that his wife was so clearly showing that the meeting was over. He didn't know how much longer he could have stayed in that airless room without bringing his breakfast back up.

Primer escorted them to the stairs. Heimer saw that the entrance to the corridor on the opposite side of the building had more security. The windows were reinforced and there were several keycard readers by the door. He looked in and saw that a red light was illuminated above one of the rooms. Perhaps that was where he was—the boy whose semen had been found on the rock. Gorbachev and Primer would go back to grilling him and Heimer had no idea what he would say. That realization made him quicken his pace down the stairs. He needed fresh air.

13

BALTIMORE, 2019

John had guessed right about the FBI's decision. Far too many resources and the reputations of people with bigger salaries than Brodwick's had been invested in the operation against the Nigerian drug cartel. The absence of a star witness from the trial had to be avoided. If the price was bending the Bureau rules for witness protection, then when all was said and done it wasn't that high a price.

John could almost hear the conversation that had taken place in a windowless conference room at headquarters in Washington, where he assumed the issue had been raised. *What's the worst that might happen? The agent is killed in a country far away across the Atlantic. What the hell. It was his own choice. The most important thing is getting a conviction and showing the taxpayers they're getting their money's worth.*

Brodwick returned to the hospital the next day. He brought a long contract in which John confirmed that he had chosen his destination of his own free will and that the Bureau had discouraged him. If his boss felt defeated, there was no sign of it. In order to survive in the upper stratosphere of the FBI, you needed Teflon skin. No shit could stick. John knew that Brodwick had his sights on a corner office in Washington.

From his new position of strength, John made the final demand that would guarantee his cooperation during the trial—the crucial piece of the puzzle that he needed if he was going to help his mother. He wanted Brodwick to get him a job in county CID in Karlstad, with a position on the cold case team. The new identity would consequently need a Swedish police ID and an appropriate résumé for the job. Brodwick hadn't protested. HQ had put its foot down and it would be career suicide not to give the witness what he wanted.

When it had come to the Bureau's start-up capital for the new life, John had been more compliant. To Brodwick's surprise, John accepted the first offer without even attempting to negotiate. When they had gotten down to the practicalities around transferring John's existing assets, his boss realized why. John had large cash balances and plenty of stocks and other securities that would need to be transferred to his new identity without leaving any traces.

Brodwick looked just as surprised as John had been at the reading of the will after his dad died, when the lawyer told him he was the sole heir to more than twenty million dollars.

The bodega on the Lower East Side hadn't been worth much when the old man had taken it over at the end of the nineties. But during the financial crisis, he had managed to buy the building and expand the business until it took up the whole ground floor. He'd rented out the apartments on the three floors above.

At the same time, the neighborhood had shed its skin, making way for bearded hipsters with expensive tastes. Real estate prices had ballooned, resulting in a fortune beyond John's wildest dreams when his dad had finally sold it all.

Yet he had spent his final years in solitude in that run-down apartment a stone's throw from the store. If he had been tight with his money before, it got worse after the sale. Without the business to manage, he had slipped into depression—with the heaviest cloud the fear of losing his assets.

That day at the lawyer's office with the view of lower Manhattan, John had decided never to let himself be paralyzed by money. That very afternoon, he had bought his first tailored suit and a pair of shoes at Corthay and made an appointment to view an apartment in Hudson Square.

Brodwick hadn't asked any questions about where his money had come from—he merely noted it would be a challenge for the accountants at the Bureau to transfer such significant sums to a new identity abroad. But it would be taken care of. Just like everything else John wanted, so it seemed. He couldn't help enjoying the situation. Brodwick had been transformed into a genie in a lamp.

When night fell, John switched on the reading lamp and propped the sketch pad up on his crossed legs in bed. He liked the calm that descended on the hospital at this time of day. There were fewer people running up and down the corridors and not as many phones and alarms going off.

He looked at the sketch depicting the house where Magnus Aglin's party had taken place. On the roof, he had positioned four gothic letters that formed the name MAJA, as an aide-memoire about the mysterious friend the police had never managed to identify. At the gable end of the house was a clock, the hands of which showed twelve—the time Emelie had left the party to meet someone. Beneath the clock he had written a question mark, followed by Mr./Ms. X to remind himself that this person was unidentified. The strange tattoo on Emelie's forearm was there too: the squares with the ticks telling everyone that the most important things she wanted to do in life had already been done.

He reached for the pencil case on the nightstand and opened the lid. Using one of the softer pencils, he drew the shape of a rock and then switched to a harder pencil to mark the police's findings: a heart for the blood and a penis for the semen. But when he came to visualize the prime suspect—the young man whose DNA matched the semen—he ground to a halt. He switched pencils yet again and ran his thumb over the lead tip. Yet he still felt unable to put it to paper. He just couldn't.

John closed the sketch pad and put the pencil case back on the nightstand. Maybe it would be easier to continue with his investigation piece if he read the interview transcripts. He filled his lungs with air and closed his eyes briefly. Then he turned the laptop back on and forced himself into the account of the first conversation led by Detective Inspector Anton Lundberg and Detective Sergeant Bernt Primer.

DETECTIVE INSPECTOR LUNDBERG: Do you know a girl named Emelie Bjurwall?

INTERVIEWEE NERMAN: No.

LUNDBERG: Okay. But you know who she is?

NERMAN: Yes, I guess so. Everyone does.

LUNDBERG: Why don't you tell us what you know about her, Billy?

NERMAN: I don't know anything except that her mom is filthy rich.

LUNDBERG: Why is her mom so rich?

NERMAN: She owns those clothes stores—AckWe.

LUNDBERG: Yes, that's right. You know quite a bit, really, don't you Billy? Did you hang out with Emelie?

NERMAN: No, I said I didn't know her.

LUNDBERG: But you would like to hang out with her?

NERMAN: What the hell do you mean?

LUNDBERG: Take it easy, Billy. I don't want to upset you. I'm just trying to get to the bottom of this.

NERMAN: Get to the bottom of what?

LUNDBERG: Well, your relationship with Emelie.

NERMAN: But I don't know her! Why are you asking so many questions about her?

LUNDBERG: Where were you on Friday night a week or so ago? The four-teenth of August?

NERMAN: [inaudible]

LUNDBERG: Say that again. The recording can't pick it up if you move the chair at the same time.

NERMAN: I was at home, alone. My mom was working the night shift.

LUNDBERG: Did you go out at any point during the evening?

NERMAN: No.

LUNDBERG: And you didn't meet Emelie Bjurwall?

NERMAN: How fucking dense are you? No, I didn't meet anyone!

LUNDBERG: So you weren't on the promontory at Tynäs that Friday night?

NERMAN: What the hell are you talking about? No.

LUNDBERG: You're absolutely certain?

NERMAN: Yes, I'm certain. I've never been to Tynäs.

LUNDBERG: Not ever?

NERMAN: No, never.

LUNDBERG: Do you know what, Billy? I think you're lying.

NERMAN: What?

LUNDBERG: I think you were at Tynäs last Friday night and that you either met Emelie Bjurwall there or that you went there together.

NERMAN: I've never met her. What the hell is this about?

LUNDBERG: Do you know why you're here?

NERMAN: No, I don't know. Is it about that thing at the party? If it is, then let me tell you that that fat bitch is lying. I didn't do anything—she was up for it.

John stopped reading and clicked through the folders on the computer. What incident was Billy Nerman referring to? At first, John thought it was something that had happened at Magnus Aglin's party on the night of Emelie's disappearance. But after searching for a while, he found the answer. The incident Billy was alluding to had taken place a year or so earlier. It was documented in a closed investigation like so many others John had encountered during his law enforcement career.

The scenario: a party filled with drunk teenagers. A girl drinks too much and falls asleep on a sofa upstairs. Three boys decide to have a little fun. They pull down her top and take photos of her breasts. One kid goes further than the others. He has sex with her, but the girl wakes up and pushes him off.

Two weeks later she reports the boy—Billy Nerman—to the police for rape. He is questioned by the police and tells his version of events. The girl was drunk but hadn't fallen asleep. She was up for it and consented. The story is backed up by his friends and the investigation is closed due to lack of evidence before it even reaches the prosecutor's desk.

John analyzed what bearing the incident had on the Emelie Bjurwall case. Billy's actions were despicable, but did that make him a more plausible culprit in the Emelie case? The answer was probably. If the girl was telling the truth, it at least demonstrated that he was capable of crossing lines that most other men wouldn't. John angled the reading lamp so it didn't create a glare on the computer screen and continued reading the interrogation.

LUNDBERG: Forget about what happened at the party. This is about something more serious. We've found traces of blood on the rocks at the tip of the promontory in Tynäs. Emelie Bjurwall's blood. And right by that we found semen. We took a DNA sample from you and compared your DNA with the semen. And we got a match. So, you see, Billy—we found your semen next to Emelie's blood. And you're saying you've never been there. You must understand why I'm confused.

[SILENCE]

DETECTIVE SERGEANT PRIMER: Aren't you going to say anything, Billy?

NERMAN: [inaudible]

LUNDBERG: Could you speak up, please?

NERMAN: I didn't do anything.

LUNDBERG: I know this must be tough for you. But believe me when I say that it'll feel much better if you tell us where Emelie is now.

[SILENCE]

NERMAN: I don't fucking get what you want . . .

PRIMER: What is it you don't understand? How you came to rape her? How everything could go so wrong? Because it was a mistake, right? Or had you decided to do it a long time ago?

NERMAN: No.

PRIMER: Okay, so you made your mind up when you met up with her Friday night?

[SILENCE]

LUNDBERG: Where's Emelie now?

NERMAN: I've never met her! And I don't know where she is! Are you deaf or something?

PRIMER: I don't know what you think you'll gain from sitting here and telling us lies. We know it was you. How could your semen end up next to her blood if it wasn't you? Can you explain that?

NERMAN: No.

LUNDBERG: You can't undo it. But if you tell us where Emelie is, it'll be better. That's the chance you have now to make things right. I've met so many people like you, Billy—and they all feel better once they've come clean.

NERMAN: Fucking moron.

LUNDBERG: The interview subject is pointing his finger at the interviewer, so I think we'll take a short break. Give you a while to think about what we've talked about, Billy. The interview has been interrupted at 10:42.

So far, the policemen had followed standard procedure, John thought to himself. They had gotten Billy to deny that he'd been at the crime scene, before presenting evidence that exposed the lie. When he then stuck to his story, they put pressure on him to confess through subtle nudges, and promises that he would feel better afterward. It wasn't uncommon for suspects to deny the crime at first. On the contrary, it was a natural human instinct. Over the years as a homicide detective in New York City, John had developed a certain skepticism toward suspects who confessed to everything too quickly. They were usually scapegoats who were confessing to others' crimes.

LUNDBERG: Resuming the interview with Billy Nerman. The time is 11:15. Have you had some time to think about what we talked about earlier?

NERMAN: Yes.

LUNDBERG: Is there anything you'd like to tell us?

NERMAN: I don't know what to say. There's nothing to add. I didn't do anything.

PRIMER: Do I have this right? You claim you were at home alone the night Emelie Bjurwall disappeared. You didn't meet her?

NERMAN: No.

PRIMER: But how is it that your semen was on the rocks next to her blood? Can you explain that to me?

NERMAN: Someone must have put it there. How the hell should I know?

PRIMER: You think someone planted your semen on the rock?

NERMAN: I don't fucking know!

PRIMER: Had you had sexual intercourse with anyone who might have been able to obtain your semen?

NERMAN: What?

PRIMER: It's a simple question—did you sleep with anyone before Emelie's disappearance?

NERMAN: No, I didn't!

PRIMER: In that case I find it very hard to see how someone could have
   planted it.

[SILENCE]

LUNDBERG: Billy, all we want to know is where the girl is. If you tell us that,
   we'll take a long break. You can get something to eat and drink. It'll
   feel better if you talk to us.

[SILENCE]

PRIMER: Evidence doesn't lie. There isn't anyone on earth who believes what
   you're saying. Your only chance is to tell us exactly what happened. It'll
   help you in your trial.

NERMAN: [inaudible]

LUNDBERG: Do you understand what we're saying? This is serious. I want
   you to tell me where the girl is.

NERMAN: I'm done! I'm gonna sue you for harassment!

John read the later interviews. The investigators' frustration had grown each time, and
he could see why. The transcripts were near duplicates with just minor variations. The
threats if he stayed quiet were increased, and the rewards if he talked became more
generous. But Billy had stuck to his story and continued to proclaim his innocence.
The only thing that had happened was that he had changed his mind about not having
legal representation. From the second day onward, he had had a public defender in
his interviews. But that hadn't changed the answers to the questions.

   He clicked on a photo of Billy Nerman that had been taken just after he was
arrested. It showed a morose young man who was staring into the camera with that
ballsy I-don't-give-a-shit attitude that you only had when you were under twenty. He
searched for similarities, but soon realized they looked pretty different. Billy's skin was
much darker and his face rounder than John's own. The eyes were different too. While
John's were a greenish brown, the ones in the photo were decidedly dark brown. The
hair, on the other hand, was strikingly similar. The unruly black curls were identical
to his own before he had shaved them off.

   John tried to remember his brother and summoned up a disparate collage of
images in his head. The two of them on a playground that time Billy fell off the swing
and hit his knee so hard that they had to go to the hospital. A birthday party where
Mom had forced them to wear ugly matching shirts with lions on them. And the brown
cord sofa where they used to curl up and hide under a blanket when their parents were

fighting. John had held his hands over his little brother's ears so that he wouldn't be scared by all the shouting.

John was twelve when they had separated—Billy just eight. He didn't remember much about the end. Just that Mom had admitted to having an affair with one of Dad's friends. Billy hadn't really understood what half brother meant, but John did. They had the same mother, but different fathers. That meant they weren't whole brothers—just half.

On the final evening in the house, they had sat together under the blanket on the sofa and eaten popcorn, even though they weren't allowed to. In the morning, his brother had stood in the hallway, his face suffused with emotion, shouting that he wanted to come with them to the airport. He had clung to John's sleeve so that he was dragged toward the door, making the rug crumple up like an accordion.

"Pull yourself together, Billy!" his dad's voice had rumbled as he forced his hand away. "The plane won't wait. We have to go."

He had finished the sentence in English while glancing into the kitchen. Mom had still been sitting at the table. She had taken an ostentatious drag on her cigarette to indicate that she had no intention whatsoever of taking responsibility for the chaos she had caused.

Over the following years, there had been no phone calls or letters. Not even a postcard on birthdays. John guessed that his mother had tried to reach him in the periods when she felt better, but that his father had thrown everything away. Maybe John should have sought her and his brother out when he had got older and could make his own decisions, but he had felt a certain reluctance. Life had moved on and he hadn't wanted to ruin things by stirring up old shit. "We look forward, John. Not backward," had been one of his father's catchphrases during his kitchen-table sermons.

But then Billy had been arrested. John had recently been hired by the NYPD and at the time he was still living at home with Dad. It had been hard to find his own apartment in New York. He had seen an article about the incident purely by chance, when he had been on the *Aftonbladet* website, trying to keep his Swedish alive.

John had done a double take when he realized that the missing girl lived in Tynäs by Hammarö. During his lunch break, he had Googled the case to find out who the suspect was. He had found a thread on the Flashback forum and almost fallen off his chair when he saw the name Billy Nerman. That evening, he had told his dad, but his father didn't want to listen.

"That's not our concern," he had said, disappearing off to the bodega's cash register.

A week later, they had been forced to discuss it again. A padded envelope addressed to John had landed on the doormat. He had opened it and found a flash drive inside with the same content that he had received in the hospital just a few days ago—large chunks of the preliminary investigation against his half brother.

Just like now, his mother had enclosed a letter. She had begged and pleaded with him and his father to help Billy. She knew he was innocent, but he would still be put away if no one did anything. He came from the wrong side of the tracks and the police already seemed to have made up their minds.

John remembered that he had hidden the letter and waited until the next day before showing it to his dad. It had been a Friday and they had been celebrating the weekend with beer and peanuts in their favorite armchairs by the window. John had known his father didn't like it when he talked about their time in Sweden, but he thought this time was different: Billy was really in a tough spot.

John had suggested they book tickets to go to Sweden and do what they could to help him. When all was said and done, Billy was family and they had to help family.

The reaction had not been the one he was hoping for. His father had put down his beer so hard the foam had surged out of the neck of the bottle. Billy was no goddamn part of this family. He was the child of a whore without a drop of Dad's blood in him. Billy's mother had created that monster herself and Dad wasn't going to clean up her mess. Nor was John. He had to think about himself. About his life in New York and his career with the police department. What did he think would happen if it came out that he had a brother in Sweden who raped and murdered young women? He would be put on patrols in the worst neighborhoods until he could no longer handle the sneers and left the force. Once and for all, John had to get it into his head that Sweden was a closed book. As far as his dad was concerned, someone could drop a bomb on that godforsaken socialist hellhole.

John had never seen his father so angry. The fact that Billy was actually part of John's family—that they shared a mother—didn't ever seem to have crossed his mind. But the letter had gone unanswered, nevertheless. John had backed down and tried to forget the whole thing.

He thought about the cord sofa in the house outside Skoghall again. It had smelled of dried-up macaroni and slices of sausage from their dinners in front of the TV. Smells were strange—they could stick in the memory with a different level of intensity relative to pictures and voices. John had failed the boy who had sat next to him as they watched kids' TV. Who cared whether Billy was guilty or innocent? Who cared what his father would have said? The fact remained that his brother needed him and he wasn't there for him.

14

KARLSTAD, 2009

"How can they just let him go?"

Sissela looked at Heimer, who had just hung up after speaking to Primer.

"As long as they can't find Emelie, there's no victim," he said.

"But what about the blood? Surely that proves she's a victim of violence." Heimer could see the frustration on his wife's face, but at the same time he knew that the news was no surprise to either of them. Gorbachev and Primer had seemed resigned over the past week and had implied that the prosecutor was losing interest. Billy Nerman continued to issue denials under interrogation and his lawyer demanded that his client be either charged or released.

"According to the prosecutor, it's not enough," he said. "A lawyer would claim that Emelie had sex with him of her own accord. Or that he just masturbated there."

"Is he still claiming not to know how the semen got there?"

"Yes, apparently."

"The bastard can't even come up with a lie."

It wasn't often that Heimer heard his wife swear. The outburst was such a departure from her usually controlled way of expressing herself that she almost seemed like another person. At the same time, it made her human. Heimer realized it was in moments like this that he felt—if not love—tenderness toward his wife.

"Darling, I don't know any more than what Primer told me," he said. "Call him yourself."

Heimer held out his phone, but Sissela shook her head.

"Later—and I'll speak with the prosecutor myself."

She went to Emelie's room and he followed her. They sat down next to each other on their daughter's bed. Heimer ran his hand over the white coverlet. The linen rustled slightly.

He found himself thinking that they had once sat like this with Emelie between them, many years ago. She must have been in fourth or perhaps fifth grade. Their daughter had been chosen by the school body to lead its St. Lucia's Day procession. Everyone had wanted her at the head of the line with the crown of candles atop her blonde hair. Everyone—except Emelie. She had been panic-stricken about the long verses she was expected to read aloud in front of the pupils and parents in the auditorium.

Sissela had tried to bolster her confidence the night before the big event.

"It'll be fine. You and Dad can practice together," she'd said, rushing off to another meeting.

Heimer remembered how they had crammed those verses. He had helped her to write a cheat sheet, but it didn't seem to matter how much she practiced. There was always a word that moved or got skipped.

"You don't have to do it if you don't want to," he had said, aware of what a trial it was for someone with dyslexia to read aloud in front of an audience.

Emelie had crossed her arms and looked at him defiantly. As if what he had said was the strangest utterance she had ever heard. Of course she wanted to be the Lucia. The others had chosen her.

Finally, she had managed to get through the verses without making any big mistakes. They were as close to finishing on a high note as they would ever be. He had hugged her good night and gone to turn on the TV.

After the late news, he went to look in on her. He noticed the light creeping out through the narrow crack between the door and the threshold to her room. He had knocked on the door carefully and a moment later it went dark inside.

"Are you okay, Emelie?" he had said.

She hadn't answered, but he heard quiet sobbing on the other side of the door. He had opened it and saw her lying with the duvet over her head. Heimer sat down on the edge of the bed and stroked his daughter's back in the dark. The slender body shook with tears.

He had turned the light back on. On the floor there were a pair of scissors and some coils of blonde hair.

"What have you done?" he had said. His voice had sounded harsher than he'd intended and he'd immediately regretted it.

Emelie had cried even harder under the duvet.

"Sweetheart—it's alright," he'd said more softly, trying to pull the duvet from her face.

She resisted with all her might.

"I promise not to be angry," he said.

"Really?" she sniffed.

"Yes, really."

He had let go of the duvet so she didn't feel pressured. Slowly, she pulled it down to reveal her face to him. It hadn't been as bad as he had feared. Heimer had arrived in the nick of time, before she managed to hack away more than a few centimeters on one side.

"I don't want to be the Lucia," she had said. "I thought if I cut my hair I wouldn't have to be. Lucia has to have long hair."

He leaned forward and squeezed her wet cheeks.

"You don't have to cut your hair off for that. You just have to say no. But I don't understand. I asked you if you wanted to be Lucia earlier and you said yes."

Emelie had begun to cry again and pulled the duvet back over her face.

"Mom's taken the day off to watch me tomorrow."

"Yes, but Mom doesn't want you to do anything you don't want to do. I can tell her you've changed your mind."

"No," she had said from beneath a layer of down. "You can't say anything. She'll be mad that I cut my hair."

Heimer had felt tears welling up too. He brushed them away so that Emelie wouldn't misunderstand and think he was upset because she had let him down.

"Won't you pull the duvet down so I can see you?" he had said.

She did as he'd asked. Her eyes were red-rimmed and snot ran out of one of her nostrils down to her lip. The love he felt in that moment was unconditional.

"I have an idea," he had said, taking her face between his hands. "When Mom comes home tonight, we'll say you have a fever and can't be in the Lucia procession. Then we'll stay at home tomorrow and watch movies. How does that sound?"

If Heimer closed his eyes, he could still feel the weight of that slim body as she threw her arms around his neck as though she never wanted to let go.

"What are you thinking about?" said Sissela, bringing him back from his reverie.

Her hand sought his, but Heimer didn't want to take it.

"Emelie," he said. "I'm thinking about Emelie."

15

BALTIMORE, 2019

John looked at Trevor, asleep in the adjacent bed. Trevor had only been awake for a little while, when the doctor had done her morning rounds. He'd replied monosyllabically to questions about his health and then pulled the blanket over his head again. No coarse jokes or rumbling laughter. None of what John had come to associate with Trevor was left, and he noticed how much he missed it.

As soon as they were both well enough to leave the hospital, they would be moved to one of the Bureau's safe houses. They would spend a number of months there preparing for the trial. But once that was over they would part ways and never be allowed to make contact with each other again. Brodwick explained how it worked. If the drug cartel did manage to find one of them, it wouldn't be possible to extract from him where the other was by means of torture. It was the same model used by terrorists organized into autonomous cells.

Trevor's voice sounded wheezy when he woke up.

"Did I miss lunch?"

"Afraid so," John said. "Do you want me to call the nurse?"

"Later maybe. Guess I haven't got much appetite."

His friend hadn't strung together this many words since his wife had visited. John didn't know whether to turn the conversation to what had happened or to wait for another time. Trevor solved the problem for him.

"Minette was my rock," he said. "We've been together for almost fifteen years. Long before I got into this shit. She's always been there—you know what I mean?"

John nodded and saw Trevor reach for his wallet on the table next to him. He searched for a while and then passed a photograph to John. John accepted the photo but hesitated before looking at it. Trevor had already told him his wife's name, and now he wanted to show him a picture of her. Brodwick wouldn't like this. They were supposed to know as little as possible about each other. But refusing to look would be disrespectful to Trevor.

"She's beautiful," John said, after looking at the woman smiling into the camera. She was sitting at an outdoor café, the light strong on her face.

"A better wife than I ever dared hope for," Trevor said, putting the photo back in his wallet. "I've had her here all the time, in a secret compartment."

John knew that despite the risk of the wrong people finding the photo, while Trevor did his job he needed to have it with him, close to his body, in a concealed place.

"We're going to become very lonely people, you and I. Neither one of us knows what it's going to be like, living a life where we're always watching our backs . . . where anyone might be out to kill us," Trevor continued.

John realized once again how little he had thought about life after the trial—how absorbed he'd been by his job as an infiltrator. All the focus had been on the big task at hand—providing the Bureau with what it needed to put Ganiru away. The risks had given him all the kicks he needed: a couple of bungee jumps a day without knowing whether the cord would hold. He both loved and hated it—mainlining adrenaline as if there were no tomorrow.

"I need something to write on," said Trevor, holding out his hand.

John tore a sheet from his sketch pad and handed it over, together with a pencil from the case. Trevor wrote something and passed the paper back to him.

https://secure.connection.com
Username: unknown_325
Password: BuckWickFord

John understood immediately what it was.

"As soon as I can get to a computer on a secured network, I'll set up an account for you," he said. "If you log in, you'll find a contact in the address book. It'll be me. I know we're supposed to be in a safe house together for several months. But the Bureau might have other ideas and separate us tomorrow. Now you know how to get hold of me."

John didn't know what to say. Brodwick had been crystal clear—no form of contact was permitted. All communication left digital footprints that could be traced. But a life in the shadows, always on guard, never being able to let anyone else in—there would be times when that got very tough.

"Jesus, Trevor. I don't know," he said.

The man stared at him. It was good to see him do that.

"I just thought you might need a friend. Someone you don't have to lie to about who you really are. I reckon it'll do me some good anyway."

"It's not about . . ."

Trevor interrupted him. "I know, the rules say different. But if you do want to contact me later, at least there's the option. What you choose to do is completely up to you."

John looked at the note with the login details again. The password puzzled him. BuckWickFord. What did Trevor mean by that? Then he understood. It was an anagram. When the letters were reordered they formed the pithy phrase: Fuck Brodwick.

John laughed quietly and looked at his friend, who saw that the penny had dropped. The grin on his face made him look like a schoolboy who had just come up with the perfect prank.

Two cheese sandwiches later, Trevor was asleep again and John opened the laptop. The Swedish police investigation had completely sucked him in. He realized that he would soon be just as dependent on it as he was on the painkilling morphine.

He read about where the investigation had gone after Billy Nerman's release. The police had put surveillance on him in the hope that he would lead them to Emelie. It had been fruitless, apart from the surveillance team saving the kid from some angry Karlstad locals who'd decided to take the law into their own hands with knives and crowbars.

John didn't know whether there was a Swedish equivalent of the American expression "no body, no crime." Regardless, the principle was most definitely applicable in this instance. If Emelie wasn't found, it would be hard to charge Billy Nerman.

There were voices in the corridor and John looked up from the screen. Through the glass he saw the policeman outside get up from his chair. The man spoke to someone and then the burly silhouette was replaced by a slimmer version. Shift change, John thought to himself as he checked the time. By this point, he knew the guard rotation schedule.

When the voices died down, he put the laptop on the nightstand. The handwritten letter from his mother was still in the bottom drawer. John hadn't touched it since he had opened the envelope and seen the first few sentences, but now it was calling to him—as if his mother would no longer accept his excuses for not reading it. He reached for the letter and steeled himself for its contents.

John!

This time you have to come home.

They say in the papers that they're going to bring in your brother again. He didn't do anything to that girl. I know it. But they think they're better than us. We're just dirt on the sole of their shoe. They'll never listen to us.

Billy won't be able to handle it. Not again. Neither will I. I'm dying, John. I don't have much time left—that's what they say, the people who know these things.

Dear boy of mine, please come back to us and help your brother. You didn't come the last time I wrote. But this time you must. This won't end well—I can feel it in my bones.

I'm sending you one of those things you can stick in the computer. The lawyer who helped me last time made it for no extra charge. He probably felt sorry for me.

Hugs from your mother.

John read the letter several times. There were no tearful digressions, just bald statements about the situation as it stood. It was a direct approach that he understood.

I'm dying, John, his mother had written.

Apparently she was sick. She didn't say what was wrong, but there was no doubt that it was serious. He didn't believe in God or fate, yet he had to admit that this cry for help came at a time when he was receptive. He had been given a second chance and this time he was going to take it.

In his head, he made two rules for his time in Sweden. The first was that he would find out the truth about his brother. Not the version that a contemptuous police force had predetermined. But also not the one that a mother who loved her son wanted to see. The Truth. With a capital T. Come what may. Everyone had to take responsibility for their actions. That applied to his half brother too.

The second rule was a time limit. Brodwick had been right when he said that all it would take for the Nigerians to pick up his scent was for one person to mention his Swedish mother. He had three months. If he hadn't managed to cast any light on Billy's innocence or guilt by then, he would leave the country. Swedish passports were handy like that. It meant he could live anywhere in the European Union. He had never been to Berlin, Rome, or Paris. All three appealed to him and it might be safest to rotate. Spend a few months in each place before changing location—at least in the early years.

But his fantasies of being a flâneur in the capitals of Europe would have to wait. First he had a job to do—and he was going to do it to the best of his ability.

That much he owed to his family on the other side of the ocean.

PART 2
2019

16

Of all the seats on the plane, John had been assigned the one with a faulty screen. The flight attendant informed him that unfortunately the plane was fully booked and that he'd have to make do without in-flight entertainment.

"We'll take extra good care of you," she said, hurrying on down the aisle to escape the dissatisfied passenger.

Seven hours in an uncomfortable seat wasn't something he was looking forward to. If he had been paying, he would have opted for business class, but it was one of the Bureau's shell companies that had booked the tickets, which had meant there was no room for extravagance.

He reclined the seat the small distance that was possible and reflected on what had happened over the past few months: his time at the Bureau safe house outside Baltimore, the heavily guarded trial, and finally the successful convictions. John had made eye contact with one of Ganiru's henchmen in the courtroom when the jury foreman had said the word "guilty." The hatred in the man's eyes had blazed. He'd shaped his hand into a pistol and fired a symbolic bullet into John's head. The message was unambiguous. John was a dead man.

Later that day, he and Trevor had celebrated with a *Godfather* marathon. It had been their last night together in the secret hideout. When John had woken the next morning, his friend's room was empty.

The flight attendant was back. John asked for a water and a beer. He turned down the offer of the vintage champagne that was usually only served on the other side of the curtain, in business class. He couldn't be bought that easily. He got out the document Brodwick had given him after the trial and read it again—not that he needed to, but just to send his thoughts in a different direction.

Forward.

To what was to come.

Fredrik Adamsson, thirty-four years old, adopted child of mother Irene and father Birger. Just after he had started school, the family moved to Springfield, Massachusetts.

After two decades, his parents retired and moved back home, while their son remained across the Atlantic. Both parents had died around a year ago in a car crash.

Fredrik had spent some time in Sweden because of the funeral, and he had decided to put down roots in his old home country.

He'd never been married and had no children. Two addresses were listed in the population register: his childhood home in Årsta and an address in Stockholm's Södermalm, where he had lived since his return to Sweden. He had no criminal convictions and no disputes with the Swedish Tax Agency or any other government authority.

The food service ended and the cabin lights were dimmed. John felt his eyes growing heavier and the letters on the page began to blur. He put the document back in his bag, closed his eyes, and sank into a shallow sleep, which was all he could manage in the uncomfortable seat.

When the plane finally landed, his black suitcase was one of the first bags to appear on the luggage belt. John grabbed it, cleared customs, and headed into the Arrivals hall. He scanned the row of taxi drivers holding up signs with names on them and approached one—an anemic young man who looked like he needed a square meal and forty-eight hours of sleep before he got behind the wheel.

"Fredrik Adamsson?" said the driver.

"Yes, that's me," John replied.

The journey to Karlstad was a quiet one. The driver displayed no willingness to talk and John was grateful for that. It was mid-October, which meant the landscape outside was wet and gray. Rain had been falling constantly since they had left the taxi stand at Arlanda and the drops formed beautiful patterns on the rear windows. Many of the red barns visible alongside the E18 highway had rickety walls and sagging roofs that couldn't keep the damp out. Buildings were sparsely distributed at the dividing lines between the fields and John saw tractors and rusty cars in the farmyards outside them.

John recognized most of the place names—Västerås, Örebro, Karlskoga—but he had no memories of the family ever visiting them. They hadn't been able to afford outings.

His father had run a convenience store in Sweden too, but it hadn't been anywhere near as lucrative as the store he had later bought in New York. His income had been modest and his mother's wages at the paper mill even worse. And she had often called in sick. As a child, John and his brother had learned to keep out of the way when the worst arguments erupted. At the time, he hadn't understood why their parents always had to fight. As an adult, he thought the real mystery was why they had ever gotten together.

It was hard to imagine two more mismatched people. He, the down-to-earth, dark-skinned man with roots in the southern hemisphere. She, the dreamer, the free spirit from the north. It hadn't taken long for the passion to die down. Then a tortuous daily existence took hold, which for him involved a never-ending string of responsibilities and for her an equally long string of cheap bottles of wine from the store where all Swedes bought their alcohol. John realized he had forgotten the name of the shop. He'd find out when he arrived.

He was grateful that Fredrik Adamsson had lived in the States for so many years. It would explain his accent and any cultural missteps in the coming months.

The driver signaled right and exited the highway in the pouring rain just after the sign welcoming visitors to Karlstad. John had a reservation at a Best Western hotel called Gustaf Fröding—a name that was unfamiliar to John but that every single person in Karlstad probably recognized. Was he an old-time king with connections to Värmland? The Swedish monarchs were usually called Gustaf—that much he remembered from school. A little later, Google would help him find out the name of the liquor store and the years when Gustaf Fröding had reigned.

The driver came to a stop under the canopy on the hotel driveway and carried his heavy bags into the lobby. He was surprisingly strong for someone so delicately built. John thanked him and pushed a bill into his hand. The anemic-looking man seemed surprised, but he muttered "great" and then disappeared back out to his car.

John realized he had just made a mistake. They didn't tip in Sweden. It was strange that he'd forgotten, given that his dad used to complain about the socialist Swedes who didn't know how to reward good service.

Behind the reception desk, a blonde woman in glasses asked if he wanted to check in.

"Yes please," he said.

"And the name?"

"Fredrik Adamsson."

It still felt weird to say it, but he knew he would quickly grow used to a new name. He made the Nigerian one he'd used during the operation in Baltimore his own in a matter of just a few weeks.

"Welcome to Best Western, Fredrik," she said, handing him a keycard. "You have some guests waiting in one of our conference rooms. I'll show you through."

John waited silently while she summoned a colleague to take his things up to his room. Then he followed her toward the conference rooms, which were on the right down a corridor beside reception. There were photographs hanging on the walls that she explained were part of a series called "Värmland Up Close." The series consisted of photos of nature taken with little depth of field. Moss on a rotting tree stump. A reed sticking through the ice. An orange flower—which upon closer examination was the funnel of a chanterelle.

They were the kind of photos that ought to have made John feel nostalgic about his local roots. In reality he felt anything but at home. Granted, he was glad there was an ocean between him and the people who wanted him dead, but he was still on the run. It would take more than a close-up of a mushroom to change that.

"They're in the Dungen Room," the woman said, pointing at a door.

He thanked her and watched her disappear back toward reception. Then he took a deep breath and knocked. The door was opened immediately, as if the woman behind it had been waiting with her hand on the handle.

"Mona Ejdewik, National Crime," she said, proffering her hand.

Then she nodded at the man beside her.

"And this is Bernt Primer, Chief of Police in Värmland."

John scrutinized them. The woman was the older of the two—probably around sixty—but in conspicuously better shape than her male colleague. She was wearing jeans in a size that not many women of her age would have been able to button up. Her black top was short-sleeved and showed off a pair of toned arms.

He recognized Bernt Primer from the photo in the newspaper clipping his mother had sent along with the police investigation files. With his round face, gray-flecked stubble, and a jacket that was two sizes too big for him, he was the epitome of a small-town cop. At the same time, there was an alertness in his eyes. John had read masses of transcripts in which Primer had been lead interrogator, and the man was no fool. In a strange way, it felt like John already knew him.

John realized he was still thinking like an undercover agent. The difference this time was that no one knew about his mission. When he had demanded that Brodwick arrange the job on the cold case team, he had been worried that the Bureau would find out that his brother had been the chief suspect in the AckWe case. But apparently there were limits to what the FBI knew about its agents. Billy had never actually been charged with the crime and therefore wasn't in any database.

Mona invited him to sit down at the oversize conference table. She had a formal tone when she spoke and a natural air of authority.

"First, a few simple rules. No one in Sweden—including myself—knows your true identity. We know you've worked for the FBI, that you speak Swedish, and are in witness protection. But we don't want or need to know more than that. As of now, you are Fredrik Adamsson, a Swedish-American from Stockholm who has gotten a job here in Karlstad. Bernt will be your supervisor and you can discuss all issues relating to the job with him. Issues pertaining to your security you should discuss with me and no one else."

"Understood," he said. He appreciated her clarity. It was almost like taking orders from Brodwick.

"Well, that's my cue," Primer said jovially in a broad Värmland dialect. John had forgotten what it sounded like. It was almost like another language.

"I just want to welcome you and say that I hope you'll be happy here," his new boss continued. "We probably won't have the resources you're used to, but I know you'll be a real asset to the team."

"I'm sure you've got a highly skilled department," John said.

"We do our best in any case," Primer replied, looking almost abashed. "Do you think you can start as soon as tomorrow? I'd like to introduce you to your new colleagues at our weekly meeting."

"No problem."

"That's great. We only started this cold case team a few weeks ago, so we're just starting to get systems in place," Primer said, taking a folder out of his bag and placing it on the table. "Some homework for this evening if you're not too tired from your trip. It's a summary of the first case we've taken on—a missing girl whose body was never found."

John picked up the folder but didn't open it.

"I'll read it right away," he said, although he was already at least as familiar with the folder's contents as his new boss was.

"That's great," Primer said with a smile, patting John's upper arm rather tentatively. "Oh, and I need to give you these too. You need to be able to get around town."

He pulled some car keys from the inside pocket of his jacket and passed them to John.

"It's outside in the hotel parking lot. A 2016 SEAT. You can use it until you get your own car. If any repairs are needed, just talk to the boys in the garage down at the station."

John thanked him and took the keys. He glanced at the small metal disc attached to the keyring. The big S of the logo was completely unfamiliar.

Shortly thereafter, the meeting came to an end. John took the elevator up to his third-floor room. He stretched out on the bed and opened the laptop. It turned out that the liquor store was called Systembolaget and that Gustaf Fröding hadn't been a king at all—he had been a Värmland poet. John Googled some of his best known poems. They were beautiful—even if some of the words were old-fashioned and hard to understand.

He checked the time. Too early to go to bed. If he slept now, he'd be wide-awake in the middle of the night. Reluctantly, he got up, put the laptop on the desk, and began to hang up his shirts in the wardrobe. He was considering taking a shower to wake himself up when there was a knock on the door. He peered through the peephole.

Mona Ejdewik was standing there holding two bottles of beer.

"I thought we might have a chat without your new boss," she said after John let her into the room.

"Of course," he said, looking for a bottle opener.

Mona was less formal now that they were alone. He gestured to the armchair by the wardrobe and she sat down.

"For a moment, I thought he was going to ask you to sign a poster of yourself," she said. "But Primer has a point. County CID isn't the FBI. You'll need to fit in—keep a low profile."

John took a sip of the beer and nodded slowly. According to Fredrik Adamsson's fabricated résumé, he had worked as an investigator for the police in Springfield—a town not significantly bigger than Karlstad—before moving to Stockholm and getting his American police training accredited. Any FBI behavior would be out of character—or whatever they called that in Swedish.

"Don't worry, I like my identity and don't plan to do anything that jeopardizes it," he said.

The answer wasn't entirely truthful. His plan to learn the truth about his brother was hardly risk-free. If the police here discovered his true identity, he'd be thrown out headfirst. The fact that he'd participated in an investigation where his own brother was the prime suspect would certainly get out. Reporters would feast on the scandal. They'd publish his real name and photograph on every news website and social media platform, and all it would take for Ganiru's men to find him would be a Google search.

Mona stayed for half an hour and they managed to get through another beer each from the minibar before she left him to sleep. Her train to Stockholm was at seven the next morning.

John's tiredness gave way to mild inebriation. He went to the window and studied the contours of the dark trees and bushes outside. He thought about his brother and remembered how he and Billy used to hide in the big garden behind their childhood home when it was time to go to bed. It was a strange feeling after so many years to be in the same town again. But visiting him was out of the question. It was best for both of them if Billy didn't know he was here.

On the other hand, he would have to take the risk of tracking down his mother—if she was still alive. It had been eight months since she'd sent the letter with the investigation files, the letter that said she was dying. He wanted to tell her that he had listened this time. That he had come back for her and Billy's sake.

17

John had never felt as overdressed as he did when he opened the meeting room door at the police station in Karlstad. In order to not stick out, he had chosen his most basic suit: a navy wool suit from Paul Smith. His shirt was white, and he skipped the tie, as he'd heard that Swedes dress casually for work.

But he wasn't expecting this. The men in the room looked like they were on a Sunday outing with their families. The first to proffer his hand was introduced by Primer as Detective Inspector Ruben Jonsson. He was wearing light-colored jeans with what looked like a mustard stain on one thigh. His polo shirt was clean but so washed out that the once-blue fabric was now faded.

The second man introduced himself before Primer got there. His name was Ulf Törner, and he held the same rank as Ruben Jonsson. The shirt he was wearing with his worn-out chinos fit his shoulders badly and was missing a button on one sleeve.

John realized that his own attire would become the topic of conversation the second he left the room. But it couldn't be helped. He'd gone with a suit and to dress differently tomorrow would signal insecurity.

Primer kept the opening of the meeting brief. John introduced himself as Fredrik Adamsson, then told them about his previous job in Springfield and the move to Karlstad. He ducked awkward questions about how to get American police training accredited in Sweden and instead listened attentively as the others presented their own career trajectories with the force. In the meantime, he read his colleagues' body language. It was a technique he'd learned during his training to be an undercover agent, in order to quickly determine whether a person was positive, negative, or neutral toward him.

Ulf Törner was easy to read. He had turned his upper body toward John and his arms were resting squarely on the table. His face was open and he even smiled when Primer described John as an asset to the team.

Ruben Jonsson was harder to get a fix on. His facial expression and body language were neutral. He seemed to belong to that category of people who kept their thoughts and opinions to themselves.

Once they wrapped up the formalities, Ruben started to lay out the team's plan for solving the cold case of the missing girl.

"The challenge isn't finding the culprit, since we already know who killed her," he began. "It was a lowlife named Billy Nerman who still lives in the area. A lot of us would like to see him behind bars, but we need to find the body. We didn't have that last time."

John had to make an effort to conceal his irritation. He agreed that the forensic evidence against Billy was strong. But the whole point of a cold case review was to look at the case with fresh eyes. If their conclusions still led to the same perpetrator, it should be the result of police work and not preconceived notions. He understood why his mother was so anxious for him to return. She knew how tongues wagged at the police station and that Billy would never be given a fair chance.

"Have you planned the search for the body?" he said as neutrally as possible.

Ruben went up to the map attached with magnets to the whiteboard. John stood next to him and examined the contours of Hammarö outside Karlstad, where he had spent his first twelve years of life. His new colleague pointed at a boundary that someone had drawn in black ink in the northeast corner of the map.

"This area, by the Tynäs promontory, is where they found the blood and semen ten years ago. They searched the area with cadaver dogs in the early days after the girl's disappearance. We've started by going over it again in case something was missed last time."

"But I assume you're not using the dogs this time?" John interjected.

"Metal detectors. According to the girl's parents, she was wearing a silver heart pendant around her neck when she went missing."

It sounded like a reasonable plan, even if it had its shortcomings. There was a risk that the perpetrator had moved the body by car or managed to make it vanish into the water despite the inauspicious winds and currents.

"Have you questioned the suspect again?" John asked. It went against the grain to refer to his own brother that way, but he couldn't let his emotional ties to Billy influence him.

"Yes, just the once. He's sticking to his story. There's no point to additional questioning at this stage without new evidence to push him with."

John tried to imagine Billy as a grown man, but without success. To him, his brother was oddly frozen in time. It had been the same when he'd read the old interviews back in the hospital in Baltimore. It was the voice of an obstinate eight-year-old boy that he'd heard answering the interrogator's questions.

"What are we doing, in addition to looking for the body?" he said.

"I'm trying to identify a potential witness who'll hopefully tie the suspect to the victim on the night of the murder," said Ulf, who had been quiet until now.

He continued to describe what John already knew. The friend—Maja—had never been identified. If she could name Billy Nerman as the one Emelie Bjurwall left the party to meet, it might be enough to bring charges—even without a body.

"Are you getting anywhere with tracking her down?" said John.

Ulf didn't seem to like the question.

"I'm working on it," was his curt response.

John sat down at the table again and turned to Primer. The fact that their boss had been involved in the previous investigation was a drag on the team. While he brought his knowledge of the case, he was also the single biggest obstacle to fresh thinking. John saw that it was going to be a balancing act on a slack tightrope to stay in his good graces.

"What did you have in mind for me?" he said.

Primer passed the question on to Ruben, and John saw that he was the de facto head of the investigation. Maybe not unexpectedly. After all, it said *Head of County CID* on Primer's business card—this presumably meant there wasn't much spare time for day-to-day police work, even if the newspaper article had implied otherwise.

"There's one thread we need to follow up on," said Ruben. "Four years ago, the police in Gothenburg passed us details of a young woman who had taken her own life. She had a tattoo that was identical to Emelie Bjurwall's. The same design and the same position on the body. But since Gothenburg hadn't found any connection to the Bjurwall case, it didn't go any further."

John focused. This was news to him.

"But you think there may be a connection between the girls?" he said.

"Yes, it seems plausible," said Ruben. "The tattoo design is so unique that two girls of the same age can hardly have come up with it independent of each other. On the other hand, it doesn't mean the deaths are linked. But I still think we should look into it."

John agreed with his colleague with the inscrutable face.

This was definitely worth taking a closer look at.

After the meeting, Primer showed John to his office. He wondered if the others on the team had as much space, or whether the boss was still sucking up to him. In New York, it had only been the captain who'd been able to close a door behind him. Run of the mill detectives like John had had to make do with cramped desks in an open office.

Once his boss had hurried off to his next meeting, John logged on to the laptop that the IT department had left on the desk. Primer had said the police in Värmland were dedicating significant resources to digitizing old investigation files. Everything from 2002 onward was already scanned onto the server. He searched for the documents from the Gothenburg police about the girl who had committed suicide. Kirsten Winckler—that was her name—had come from a good family and had ended up in a downward spiral of mental illness and drugs, just like Emelie.

He read the autopsy report carefully and even looked up several Latin words to be sure he understood their meaning. Unless the pathologist had missed something, everything suggested the girl really had taken her own life with prescription sleeping pills, even though it was never possible to prove it with one hundred percent certainty. In theory, someone might have forced Kirsten Winckler to take the pills.

John looked up from the screen when he heard a discreet knock on the door. He cleared his throat and asked the visitor to come in. It was Ulf Törner, and in his hand he had a calendar.

"I was going to check whether you could do your week in the kitchen now," he said. "Sorry to spring it on you, but it would be easiest if you just took on Svantesson's weeks."

John had no idea what the man in the doorway was talking about, but that didn't stop Ulf from pushing on.

"He's on paternity leave. Svantesson, that is. And if you don't take his weeks then I'll have to redesign the whole schedule," he said, waving the calendar in the air.

"Yeah, I'm sure that'll be fine," said John, without really knowing what he had agreed to.

"Brilliant, thanks. Follow me and I'll show you," Ulf said, leading him down the corridor. They passed a coffee maker with a sticker on it that said "Warning: cop coffee" and reached a break room with some round tables. In one corner there was a kitchenette with a sink filled with dirty cups.

"It gets like this when there's not an empty dishwasher," said Ulf, who began emptying the machine.

John was still none the wiser. Were police officers really expected to clean up the police station themselves?

"You need to empty it twice a day. Once in the morning and once after lunch. Clean dishes go up here," said Ulf, putting the last few plates in the cupboard above the counter. "Best to run the cloth over the tables too—it makes it nicer for everyone."

Ulf rinsed the cloth under the tap, wrung it, and threw it toward John, who caught it reflexively. He wanted nothing more than to shove the blue cloth down the throat of his new colleague. He hadn't come to Karlstad to wipe fucking tables. But starting a fight on day one wouldn't be keeping a low profile, which was what he had promised both himself and Mona Ejdewik he would do.

"Sure," he said, dutifully wiping the nearest table. Then he tossed the cloth back to the surprised Ulf and returned to his office.

With a few rapid taps of the keyboard, he woke up the laptop and pulled up the preliminary investigation into Billy. He'd had an idea. He searched for the details of the treatment center that Emelie Bjurwall had been admitted to. Her parents had been questioned several times, so it took a while for him to find the document. Once he had the right one, it didn't take long to learn that the place was called Björkbacken and that it was in Charlottenberg, just one hundred kilometers northwest of Karlstad.

John closed the laptop to give himself peace and quiet to think. There was something about screens that stopped the brain from making free associations. He was happier with the big sketch pad he had brought with him from Baltimore. The sketch—his investigation piece for the AckWe case—had continued to evolve as he had read through the file in the hospital and at the safe house.

He put the sheet in front of him on the desk and wrote *Kirsten Winckler* in a blank area. Then he drew a copy of Emelie's tattoo. He started with the three squares, but stopped himself when he came to draw the ticks. How many of the Gothenburg girl's squares were filled in when she died?

He opened the laptop again and pulled up the photos of the left arm from the autopsy. All the squares were filled with ticks. If Kirsten's tattoo was a bucket list, it meant she had achieved her goals only to then commit suicide. It was tragic, John thought to himself, for such a young person to feel done with life. According to the date on the autopsy report, she had ended up on the table just a couple of weeks after her twenty-sixth birthday.

He finished drawing the tattoo and then wrote *Björkbacken* under both girls' names. Perhaps they had met somewhere, and if so, there was a good chance that it had been at the treatment center. Both had similar issues and came from well-to-do families who could afford to pay for private care.

Then he leaned back in the comfortable desk chair, deliberating. The car that Primer had organized for him was parked outside. He considered his two options.

One—go to Björkbacken. Really, he ought to check in with Primer first, but he was busy in meetings. Anyway, it would be best if his boss got used to his new employee making his own decisions. John never let paper pushers stand in the way of police work. That rule had applied in New York City and Baltimore, and he had no plans to change it in Karlstad.

Two—visit his mother, whose address he'd found online the night before. She had been living in a nursing home at Gunnarskärsgården for the last couple of years—not far from John's childhood home outside Skoghall.

He thought again about the letter he had read in the hospital and the desperation seeping off the page.

Billy won't be able to handle it. Not again. Neither will I. I'm dying, John. I don't have much time left—that's what they say, the people who know these things.

John made up his mind. The treatment center could wait.

He put the investigation piece in one of the desk drawers, grabbed the car keys, and hurried out to the parking lot.

18

The rain was pouring down, and John ran the short distance from the entrance of the police station to the parking lot to avoid getting soaked through. He unlocked the car and climbed into the driver's seat.

It turned out that SEAT was a Spanish make of car. The reason John hadn't heard of it was because they weren't sold in the States. And there was no doubt about why—the minimalist steel box was clearly made for miniature flamenco dancers and it was impossible for tall people like him to fit into it comfortably. He pushed the seat back as far as it would go, and his knees were still at a ninety-degree angle. It was almost impossible to reach the pedals without also getting his thighs stuck on the steering wheel. Worst of all was the manual transmission. The fact that the Europeans still messed around with that stupid stick shift every time they wanted to change gears was beyond his comprehension.

He had tried to swap the car that morning when he arrived at the police station. However, the man behind the counter in the basement had simply shaken his head. Automatic transmissions were only standard on marked patrol cars—they were less common on civilian vehicles. John had sworn silently when he realized he'd have to put up with the SEAT and then hurried away before the man could spot how annoyed he was.

He ran his hand over his wet scalp, put the key in the ignition and turned it. The low-powered engine started with a noisy rattle. John had been surprised to discover the car came with GPS. Before exiting the parking lot he entered the address of the nursing home. The traffic moved slowly until he reached the road toward Hammarö. The GPS showed that Gunnarskärsgården was on the same road that ran from his childhood home to the paper mill.

After crossing the bridge, it didn't take him long to get there. Once he had parked and gotten out of the car, he immediately recognized the smell. Sulfur smelled like shit, sulfate smelled like food—that was what they'd chanted on the school playground. How bad it smelled depended on the direction of the wind. On good days, the odor would disappear across the water, on bad ones it would drift over Skoghall and its surroundings.

John leaned against the car door and wondered how to approach the woman who lived in the low brick building in front of him. The plan was to show his police credentials to a staff member and request to speak to Mrs. Nerman. It shouldn't arouse suspicion, given that the AckWe case had been reopened and she was the mother of the prime suspect.

The risky moment was the meeting itself. If his mother recognized him and spontaneously called out his real name, or even worse addressed him as *my son*, someone might hear and then the rumors would start to spread. Skoghall was a small community and gossip would move faster than the paper machines in the mill.

He walked toward the entrance and once he was inside, he headed for the nurse in the small office on the right. He explained the purpose of his visit. An informal conversation with Mrs. Nerman, that was all. The nurse nodded understandingly. She said the person he was looking for was probably in her room—she usually spent the mornings in bed.

"If you just keeping going along the corridor, you'll find her in the first room after the bathroom."

John thanked her and left the nurse before she asked any questions. When he came to his mother's room, he checked that the name sign was right before raising his hand to knock. When he got no reply after two attempts, he carefully opened the door and entered.

His first thought was that he had the wrong room. The wrinkly face framed by lank, brown hair couldn't possibly be his mother's. She wasn't even sixty. There was a wheelchair parked by the bed. John squeezed past it, to the visitor's chair. He sat down and leaned carefully over the bed. He was so close he could hear the woman's breathing and smell her sour breath.

"Mom," he whispered softly.

The woman didn't react.

"Mom, are you awake?" he continued.

This time she turned slowly and opened one eye. He saw right away that she knew who he was.

"John! So you came."

Her voice was hoarse and when she tried to smile it looked wry, as if her muscles didn't want to obey her. When she opened the other eye, John saw that her eyebrow was sagging unnaturally so that it almost impeded her field of vision.

"Yes, I came this time," he repeated.

She reached out toward him with her left hand and John took it in his.

"I'm so happy to see you."

She was slurring her words slightly—he could hear that now. From her body movements, John realized she wanted to sit more upright. He let go of her hand and helped her adjust the angle of the bed.

"How do you feel?" he said, once she seemed to be in a more comfortable position, propped up on an extra pillow.

"Like I've got my just desserts." She laughed hoarsely. "Broken everywhere except in my head, where I'm unfortunately far too lucid. The rest of these folks have dementia and I've got to admit I'm jealous. It looks so nice to just slip away."

"What's happened to your face?"

"A stroke. Two years ago. My right side is paralyzed all the way down to my toes. I'll spend the rest of my life in this," she said, nodding at the wheelchair.

His mother looked at him, scrutinizing him from top to bottom as if trying to determine what had become of her lost son.

"Do you still draw?" she asked.

John smiled at her. That was her first question after twenty years. Not how he was. Not whether he had a family or children.

"Some. Not enough," he said. "What about you? Do you still paint?"

She raised her left hand, and only now did he spot the residue of oil paints on her fingertips.

"I've got an easel in the closet. The staff gets it out sometimes when they think I'm being too unruly."

Suddenly, she became serious and sought out his hand again.

"You have to help your brother," she said. "They don't care whether he's guilty or innocent. Someone has to go down for this and it's going to be my Billy."

The woman in the bed was dying and had no time for small talk. Not even with a grown son she hadn't seen since he was a child. John knew better than to underestimate her. His mother might look worn-out, with broken blood vessels standing out red on her nose and cheeks after many years of drinking. But the lioness who had shouted at a teacher for daring to criticize her youngest son was still there on the inside. It had always been like that. John was big and strong and could manage by himself, while little Billy always got in trouble and needed to be looked after.

"I'm going to make sure the investigation is fair," he said, noticing how reluctantly those words came out. He didn't want to tell his mother more than was absolutely necessary.

"How?"

John turned around to make sure there were no members of staff about to come into the room and then moved the chair closer to the bed.

"Listen to me, Mom. I'm one of the detectives investigating the case."

She looked at him as if he had lost his senses.

"You're lying. How can they let you investigate Billy? There must be rules against that."

"They don't know who I am," he said.

"What do you mean?"

"I know it sounds strange, but the less you know, the better. And you absolutely cannot tell a soul."

His mother fell silent while she took in what he had said. Then she squeezed his hand again. Her face, which had been full of worry, now looked relieved.

"Then you can make sure his name is cleared."

John shook his head and looked at her gravely. It was important that she understood. "That's not what I said. I promised to make sure it was a fair investigation. But if it turns out Billy's guilty . . ."

"I trust Billy. He's done a lot of stupid things in his life, but he's never lied to me. If he says that he didn't touch that girl, then he didn't."

John suppressed a smile that wasn't appropriate for this serious conversation. Billy had caused trouble and then persuaded his mother he was innocent countless times. But that had mostly involved innocent boyhood larks, not violent crime with apparently deadly consequences.

"You have to promise me you won't tell anyone I've been here. It's very important. Do you understand?"

"Not even Billy?" she said.

"Not even Billy. If he finds out I'm one of the investigators working on the case, it'll put him in a difficult situation. It's better for everyone that no one knows."

His mother nodded slowly. It seemed she understood the gravity in John's voice.

"He was taken in for questioning. I guess you knew that?" she said.

"Yes, that was just before I got here. How did he take it?"

"It was tough—they had him in there for over three hours. But he's a fighter. Do you know what he said when I told him I'd sent the investigation to you again?"

John shook his head.

"That it was a waste of postage. He didn't think you'd come this time either, but I said he should trust his big brother."

"You can't blame him for doubting," said John.

She looked at him gravely.

"It was hard for Billy in the first few years after that girl went missing. I don't know how many times I cleaned up bruises on his face after the beatings he got from people in town. You should've been around then—I won't say otherwise. But you're here now and that's what counts."

There was a brief knock at the door. The nurse John had spoken to when he arrived stuck her head in. He quickly removed his hand from his mother's grasp and leaned back in the chair.

"I was just going to ask you if you wanted to have lunch in your room today, since you've got a visitor."

"Why don't you leave the tray and we'll see if any of it's edible."

The nurse opened the door fully with her hip and stepped inside. John moved so that she could fold down a table over the bed and put the lunch tray on it.

"What's this?" his mother said, looking at the plate.

"It's sausage stroganoff with rice. And then some cheesecake with raspberry jam and cream on the side."

His mother prodded it with a spoon and snorted.

"You call that cheesecake?"

"It's good—I've tried it," the nurse said, exchanging a look of understanding with John before heading for the door.

He reciprocated her smile, realizing that Mrs. Nerman was not the staff's favorite resident at Gunnarskärsgården.

"Did you know that Billy has a daughter?" she said, once they were alone again.

"No, I had no idea."

"Her name's Nicole and she's almost eight. The best girl in the world."

"Is her mother still around?"

A dark look crossed his mother's face.

"That Baltic whore took off before the child even turned one. Billy hasn't exactly had his pick of the local girls, so he imported this one from Latvia. I warned him, but he didn't want to listen. Maybe it's for the best that things worked out the way they did. If she hadn't moved away, I would have—and then who would have taken care of Nicole? Those two couldn't tell you which end of a diaper was the front or back."

"You all lived together?" John said in surprise.

"Of course—that was before my stroke. Them downstairs, me upstairs. The whole damn family in one place."

She laughed hoarsely again, and John wondered if her lungs were giving out. The almost-empty pack of cigarettes by the bed told their own story.

"No, it wasn't easy for Billy," she said, lowering her voice. "He probably wouldn't want me to say this, but . . ."

John leaned in.

"But what?"

"He tried to off himself when things were at their worst."

"Off himself?"

"Yes, he'd gotten drunk and took a load of pills when I found him."

"When was that?"

"Seven years ago. Around the time the Baltic whore left. But it was okay—he made it, thank goodness. Couldn't even succeed at that, my Billy."

Her gaze drifted out the window and up toward the treetops outside. Her words lingered in the confined room. John didn't know what to say. It was still impossible to summon the image of his brother as a grown man. All he could see before him was a little boy who shouted and cried if he didn't get his way.

"You didn't bring any wine with you, did you?" his mother said.

The question was so unexpected that John needed a few seconds to reply.

"Are you allowed to drink in here?"

"No, but you can see how it is for me, can't you?"

John looked at her inflamed, red face again.

"Maybe another time," he heard himself say.

"Billy always brings something to drink. If it's good weather, he takes me out into the garden and we sneak a few drinks."

John could picture it. Mother and son drinking secretly in the garden, their nostrils pricked by the smell of sulfur. In a parallel universe where his father hadn't taken him to New York, he would have been there with them.

He nodded slowly while contemplating how to formulate his next question.

"In the letter you wrote in the spring, you said you were dying . . ." he began, not knowing how to continue.

"Yes. You don't think I look like I'm dying?"

"How bad is it?"

She rolled her working eye and laughed drily.

"I can still eat and shit under my own steam, so I'm doing okay. But if I hadn't laid it on a bit thick you might not have come this time either. Right?"

John looked at her in confusion. "So, you're not dying?"

"We're all going to die someday. Me too. Just not quite as soon as you might have thought."

The words tumbled out as if she were discussing the weather forecast for the next day. To her, it was no big deal that she had lied about her health to get him where she wanted him. Maybe he should have been angry, but he realized it would be foolish to raise his voice. The last thing he wanted was to draw attention to himself.

"How's your father?" she said out of nowhere.

John was ready and had decided not to soften the answer. His mother had never liked that kind of thing.

"He's dead," he said, looking at her to see how she reacted.

He tried to detect some emotion in the marred face, but if the news had shaken her there was no sign of it.

"Serves him right," she said, spooning some cheesecake and jam into her loose, lopsided mouth.

John sat in his parked car outside Gunnarskärsgården for a long time. It would take him an hour or so to get to the treatment center outside Charlottenberg, and he wanted to get there as soon as possible. In spite of this, he felt unable to turn the key in the ignition. Previously, he had only guessed how miserable his mother's and Billy's lives had been after he and his father had left. Now he knew.

You're here now and that's what counts.

That was what his mother had said. But was it that simple? Was she prepared to casually forget the betrayal ten years ago, when she and Billy had called on him for help and he failed to respond? John suspected it depended on which way the wind blew in the new investigation.

He sighed heavily, started the engine, and prepared to reverse out of the parking space. At that moment, a car swung onto the expanse of asphalt, forcing him to wait as it passed. John looked in his rearview mirror. He recognized the driver. It was Ruben Jonsson, driving a white Toyota Auris.

What were the odds of his new colleague from the Karlstad police turning up here and now? If he was seen outside the nursing home, it would lead to inconvenient questions for John to answer. And if there was one thing that his time in Baltimore had taught him, it was to lie as little as possible. Each lie took you one step closer to being uncovered.

The Toyota's driver didn't seem to be looking for somewhere to park—he drove it all the way up to the entrance. He honked twice and a woman came through the door carrying a bag. John leaned forward and saw the nurse who had served his mother her lunch jump into the passenger seat.

He slapped the dashboard hard. Of all the people on earth . . . Presumably, she had just finished her shift and was getting a lift home from her husband. He watched the Toyota drive off down the hill. The car wouldn't even have made it across the bridge off the island before the nurse had reported that someone from the police had come to visit Billy Nerman's mother. As soon as she described him, it would be clear to Ruben Jonsson that the visitor had been the new guy on the cold case team, the one who had come back from the States.

John took fresh aim at the molded plastic, but then stopped himself. Nothing would be changed by his smashing the car's interior to pieces. He'd just have to wait and see how Jonsson reacted. Unfortunately, there was no other choice.

19

According to the GPS, the treatment center was a few kilometers south of Charlottenberg, not far from the Norwegian border. John turned off the main road and made his way along a series of winding lanes to Björkbacken.

The building was surrounded by a tall stone wall and John had to announce his arrival outside a pair of black iron gates. The main building was magnificent, situated on a slope running down to the lake. It had its own sandy beach and bathing jetty. It was an old stately home that had been renovated and now functioned as a refuge for the troubled daughters of wealthy parents. The façade was painted in a shade of yellow with white detailing and wood carvings. On either side of the main building were outbuildings that were presumably used to accommodate patients. Or guests. John didn't know which word best described the relationship that the girls admitted to Björkbacken had with it.

He parked the car in the yard beside the westward facing conservatory with its transom windows, where the gentry would once have taken their evening digestif. On the way in, he nodded to two girls sitting on the stone steps playing backgammon. He was met in the entrance hall by a man of about fifty who he assumed was the manager.

"Fredrik Adamsson—I'm with the police," said John.

The man greeted him with his right hand while putting his left hand to his own throat.

"Welcome. I'm Torsten Andreasson—I run this place," said an artificial, robotic voice.

John guessed that the man had no vocal cords and was using a voice generator to speak.

"Is there somewhere we can talk in private?"

The manager nodded and asked John to come into his office.

"It's beautiful here," John said, once they had sat down on opposite sides of the desk.

"It's a family estate that's been passed down through four generations. When the farming no longer paid, I sold some of the land and started Björkbacken. It's a good environment for the girls. Gardening is just as important a part of their treatment as talk therapy."

Despite the fact that he needed help from the gadget at his throat, it didn't appear to be difficult for him to talk. He just had to take care to articulate his sentences clearly. He had fallen silent now and was waiting for John to state the reason for his visit.

"I'm working on an old case and trying to find a connection between two girls. My guess is that they were both treated here," he said.

The man put his hand to his throat again. "Why do you think that?"

"I know for certain that one of the girls was admitted here, and the other has a background that would make her a suitable candidate for Björkbacken."

Once John had given the girls' full names—Emelie Bjurwall and Kirsten Winckler—the man looked up from the keyboard.

"That's the AckWe daughter, right?"

"Yes, that's right."

"I read in the paper that you'd opened the investigation again. It must be at least seven or eight years since all that business."

"Ten, actually," said John. "We're taking a fresh look at it. I assume you keep records of who's been admitted here."

The man looked uncertain. "I don't know," he said.

"You don't know whether you keep records?"

"Yes, of course we do. But I don't know if I can disclose that information to you. We have a duty of confidentiality. The families don't really want to advertise that their daughters have been here."

This wasn't the first time someone had waved patient confidentiality in his face. "I don't have to tell you that this is in relation to a very serious crime," he said, fixing his gaze on the source of the robot voice. "A young woman was abducted and very probably raped and murdered."

"I understand that. But I still need to consult a lawyer before I can disclose personal information."

John got up and went to the bookcase at the far end of the room. It was filled with thick volumes, mostly about psychology and sociology. One of the shelves, however, was different. There was a collection of white books—albums with years printed on the spines. John guessed they were yearbooks for Björkbacken and he picked the one from 2007—the year Emelie Bjurwall had been admitted to the treatment center.

"Wait a second—you have no right to look at that," the manager said.

He presumably missed his own voice in situations like this. The artificial voicebox had its limits in relation to volume.

"Obstructing the police in doing their job is a bad idea. Might lead to all kinds of problems for you," John said, trusting that Torsten Andreasson would fill in the gaps. A place like this clearly needed good relationships with the police and other authorities.

The manager got up and stood next to him by the shelves, but made no attempt to take the book from his visitor's hands. John leafed through the pages. They were packed with pictures of young women working on flowerbeds, canoeing on the lake, and cooking together. The captions were general and omitted names. Nevertheless, John had no trouble spotting Emelie Bjurwall. She seemed to have participated in daily life at Björkbacken, appearing in several photos. In one of them, taken in a clearing in the woods, she was flanked by two other girls of the same age. The caption read: "The good old tent-pitching gang."

"Who are they?" he said, pointing at the girls.

The manager looked tired. He returned to his desk and sank back into his chair. John followed and put the photo in front of him.

"Is one of these girls Kirsten Winckler? It'll be easier for us both if you just answer the question."

The man leaned forward and then nodded slowly.

"It's her, isn't it?" said John, pointing at the girl to Emelie's right, whom he thought he recognized from the autopsy photos.

A new nod from the man.

"And the other girl? Who is she?"

The manager held his hand to his throat.

"I don't remember."

John sat in silence and scrutinized him. Small beads of sweat had appeared on his brow and he was struggling to meet John's gaze. It was obvious that Torsten Andreasson wanted to avoid this conversation for some reason.

"You remember Kirsten Winckler, but you don't remember the other girl?" said John.

"Exactly."

"Why are you lying to me?"

"I'm not lying. So many girls have come through here over the years. It's impossible to remember all their—"

He got no further than that before John pounded the desk with his fist.

"Bullshit. You damn well know who she is and if you don't tell me, you can expect to be charged with obstruction of justice the next time I pay you a visit. Do you understand?"

The manager appeared to be frozen to his desk chair, his eyes wide. Finally, he moved his neck in a barely perceptible nod and swallowed. John put his index finger on the photo and lowered his voice.

"So I'll ask again—who is she?"

"Her name is Matilda," rasped the metallic voice.

"Matilda what?"

"Jacoby. Matilda Jacoby. Those girls were always together. If you were looking for one, you would generally find all three."

"The good old gang," John said, noting that the man seemed to remember more about the girls' time at Björkbacken than he wanted to let on. "Did Emelie spend time with anyone else, anyone specific—someone she might have stayed in contact with?"

"Apart from Kirsten and Matilda?"

"Yes."

Torsten shook his head.

"I'm not coming up with anyone."

"No one named Maja?" said John, thinking of the friend from Magnus Aglin's party.

"No, not that I remember. I don't even think we had a girl by that name here then."

There was a knock at the door and a woman stuck her head in. She reminded the manager that he had a meeting with the family of one of the girls and that some visitors were waiting on the terrace. Torsten Andreasson looked at John and nervously spread his hands out as if to say that there was nothing else he could do for him.

"One last question," said John. "Do you know where I can get hold of Matilda Jacoby?"

The man put his hand to the voice generator.

"Afraid not. The girls were discharged at the same time but I don't know what happened to them afterward."

"Okay," said John, tearing the photo out of the album without permission before getting up to go to the door.

When he emerged onto the terrace, he put the photo in his jacket pocket and nodded at the couple waiting to meet the manager. He assumed it was their car—this year's Mercedes SUV—that was parked in front of his own car in the yard. The SEAT, by comparison, looked like an Optimist dinghy lagging behind a yacht. He waited for as long as possible before unlocking it, in the hope that the couple would go inside before they saw which car he was driving. But they were still standing there, visible through the side window, as he squeezed in behind the wheel.

He turned the ignition and released the hand brake. Suddenly, there was a scraping sound in the car. It took a second for John to realize that it was coming from the transmission, in a loud protest at his attempts to put the car into gear without depressing the clutch. The couple on the terrace looked around in horror and the man took a few worried steps forward. The two girls playing backgammon were still on the stone steps. They looked at each other and laughed.

"What the hell is so goddamn funny?" he heard himself say.

He tried to put the car into reverse again and heard it shift into gear. But the biting point came sooner than he expected. The car leapt backward, almost hitting the veranda.

The girls' hands flew up to their mouths and they laughed even more loudly.

John turned the car around and drove away across the gravel so fast that stones were thrown up on all sides.

On the way back to Karlstad, John wished the manager had offered him coffee—but maybe he'd been too brusque to deserve such a reception. He stopped at a hot dog stand and ordered an American-size cup of coffee. Leaning against the hood, he enjoyed the sensation of the caffeine spreading through his body.

The trip to Björkbacken had definitely been worth it. Not only had he managed to confirm that Emelie Bjurwall and Kirsten Winckler had known each other from their time at the treatment center, but he had also found out that there had been a third girl in their group. John wanted to find Matilda Jacoby as quickly as possible. She might know something that would cast new light on Emelie's disappearance. If the woman was still alive, that was. Things hadn't gone well for two members of the good old gang, and John began to worry that the third member might have met a similar fate. What on earth had he gotten mixed up in? Had Kirsten Winckler not committed suicide, in spite of all the evidence? Was this investigation about more than just Emelie Bjurwall, or was that John letting his imagination run away with him?

He opened the rear passenger door and took out his laptop. He couldn't get remote access to the police server that hosted investigation files, but he could check the population register through a regular internet connection. Back in Baltimore, he had made himself familiar with many of the open databases that were available in Sweden.

He connected the laptop to his phone and went online. After a few clicks, he was in the register and able to search for Matilda Jacoby. He was grateful that it was such an unusual name. The number of hits ought to be limited.

He waited while the cursor turned into an hourglass and the search was processed. After a few seconds, he saw the list of hits on the screen. There were three Matilda Jacobys in Sweden, of which only one had been born in the 1980s. The other two were well past retirement age.

He clicked on the appropriate name and was provided with all the addresses where the girl had been registered. The first was an apartment in Hallonbergen outside of Stockholm. Judging by the years, it was her childhood home. Matilda had then spent two brief periods in other apartments in Stockholm suburbs, before she had registered at an address in the municipality of Charlottenberg in 2008.

John checked again.

Yes, he'd read it correctly.

Matilda Jacoby was registered as a resident in Charlottenberg.

The cup of coffee had already gone cold. He swallowed the rest of it and looked up the address. It was only a couple of kilometers from the treatment center he had just left.

His interest rising, he checked whether there were any public records of home-owners in Sweden. He wasn't let down by his old homeland. In a long post on the Flashback forum someone described how best to stalk an ex-girlfriend who had dumped you. There was a link to the real estate registration database and instructions about which information was accessible and how to search for it.

John silently thanked the crackpot and clicked on the link. He entered the address and waited. This database was apparently run on antiquated software. The hourglass spun for what felt like an eternity before the computer spat out the result. When it finally appeared, it made him raise his eyebrows.

Torsten Andreasson.

The property where Matilda Jacoby was registered as a resident was owned by the manager of Björkbacken. The same man who had refused to disclose the girl's name and who had responded to a direct question by saying he didn't know where the girl had gone after her stay at the treatment center.

John threw the empty coffee cup to the ground, got into the car, and screeched back onto the road toward Charlottenberg. He wanted to drive through those black gates, push that voiceless bastard against the wall, and ask why he had lied to the police. But once he calmed down and thought it through, he decided to go to the address he'd just discovered. If Matilda Jacoby was there, he didn't want to give the manager a chance to speak to her before John did.

———

The house he was looking for was in a copse of trees near a sharp bend in the road that led to Björkbacken. John must have passed it driving to and from the treatment center earlier. He braked hard and had to reverse a bit in order to turn onto the patch of gravel in front of the house.

If Björkbacken was elegant and well tended, then this was the exact opposite. Several tiles had fallen off the roof and were lying in pieces in the long grass. Two of the windows facing the garden were covered in plywood and it was hard to see what color the wooden façade of the house had once been.

He turned off the engine and walked toward the front door. Nightfall was approaching and the dense trees around the lot prevented the fading rays of daylight from making it through. It seemed unlikely that anyone lived here. Nevertheless, John knocked a couple of times before trying the handle. The door was locked, but it was in such poor condition that he knew all it would take to open it was a strong tug. His grip firm, he pulled and almost fell over backward when the lock and its surround came right out of the doorframe into his hand.

Once he regained his balance, he looked into a hallway with a rag rug on the floor and a naked lightbulb hanging from the ceiling. Beneath the coatrack was something he thought looked like rat droppings, and hanging on a solitary hanger was a blue quilted coat.

He went inside and pulled the door shut as best he could. To the right was a doorway leading to the kitchen, which was spacious and furnished with a gateleg table with four mismatched chairs around it. A low kitchen counter ran along the wall, interrupted by a stove and a fridge. He kneeled to look behind the latter and saw that it wasn't plugged in.

Then he went into the room behind the kitchen. The former servant's room was furnished with a camp bed, a stool functioning as a bedside table, and a large wardrobe made from untreated wood.

He went back into the kitchen, but stopped when he saw a figure in the garden. There was someone standing under one of the trees, looking toward the house. Only when the man took a few steps out of the shadow of the leaves did John see his face. It was the manager from Björkbacken.

The two men sat down at the gateleg table in the kitchen. Torsten Andreasson put his hand to his throat and activated the voice generator.

"I suspected you'd be here."

"Why is that?" said John.

"I understand that you're angry. It was stupid of me to lie."

"Stupid because you were caught or stupid because you're obstructing a police investigation?"

John met the manager's gaze, fixing his eyes on the man until he looked away and stared down at the table.

"Both," the man said. "I like Matilda and I want to help her. She had nowhere to go after Björkbacken. The other girls went home. So I let her live here—the house was empty anyway."

"Why didn't you tell me that?"

"Helping patients privately is against protocol. As a therapist, you're supposed to maintain a certain distance. If it came out that I was letting a girl from Björkbacken live in a house that I owned, it would be bad for my own reputation and that of my business."

"Didn't she have parents who could help her?" John asked.

"No. Most of the girls who come to us come from families with money. They've been given everything, but somehow they still end up in treatment. But it was different with Matilda."

"Different how?"

"She couldn't really afford Björkbacken. I've got a friend who is a social worker in Stockholm. He called and asked whether I could offer the girl a place for the standard municipal rate. I sometimes do that for particularly deserving cases. I also think it's good for the princesses here to meet people their own age with different life experiences."

The manager took his hand away from his throat. He seemed to want to catch his breath. Maybe it was more effort for him to speak than John had initially thought.

"And Matilda had those—different life experiences?" he said, encouraging the man to carry on.

"Yes, you could definitely say that. Alcoholic single mother from a Stockholm suburb. Criminal record from a young age due to shoplifting, and then later theft and drug possession. In a normal treatment center, her story would be commonplace—but here it's something special and perhaps got some of the other girls to appreciate everything they've been given in life. Don't get me wrong, you can be unwell even if you're rich—and I have a lot of empathy for our patients. But there's no harm knowing that the world can look very different to others."

"How long was she here?"

Suddenly the manager looked sad.

"It only lasted a few weeks after she was discharged, then life out in the woods got too much for her. One morning when I came to visit, her bags were gone and the house was empty. I realized she'd gone back to Stockholm and was going to lapse into her old habits."

"And she never came back?" said John.

"Yes she did, after about six months. One evening, I saw a light on in one of the windows and knocked on the door. She opened up, looking in an awful state. She asked whether she could stay while she went cold turkey. I said that was fine. She wanted to start a new life and needed to get away from her friends in Stockholm."

"Did you believe her?"

"She probably meant what she said. But I've seen how drugs work. Some girls don't have what it takes to stop and Matilda probably falls in that category, unfortunately."

"So, she left again?"

"Yes, and came back again a few months later. And it's gone on like that for ten years. She has her own key and comes and goes as she pleases. She's usually here once or twice a year. She always looks after herself when she's here, and I usually fill the fridge so that she can feed herself."

"When was she last here?"

The manager thought. "Sometime last autumn. We hadn't put up the Christmas decorations at Björkbacken, but it was already dark early in the evening. October, perhaps. Possibly November."

John took a deep breath before asking the next question that had to be asked every time a middle-aged man offered help to a young woman.

"How would you describe your relationship with Matilda?"

The manager raised his hand to the voice generator, looking agitated.

"Can't you see that this is why I didn't say anything to you before? Matilda was a patient and I want to help her—nothing more."

John thought the man's desire to help Matilda seemed genuine, but he had learned not to rely on pure intuition. He was going to check out Torsten Andreasson as soon as he got back to the police station for any charges of sexual misconduct.

"Do you know where she is at the moment? I need to get in touch with her."

The manager looked out of the window.

"It probably won't be easy to do that. I don't have her phone number or email address. Her mother is dead now and Matilda won't tell me where she lives in Stockholm. Not even whether she has somewhere permanent to live—she's still registered here. I guess that's how you found the place?"

John nodded.

"What about her mail?" he said. "If she's registered here, she must get mail sometimes."

"Sure. It doesn't happen often, but there's the occasional letter in the mailbox. I keep them and give them to her every time she comes, and when she leaves the pile is always still on the kitchen table."

The manager smiled wryly at this tragicomic ritual.

"I'd like to take a look at it," John said.

"I knew you'd be interested," the manager replied, disappearing back outside to the bicycle he had arrived on. When he returned, he had a plastic shopping bag, which he handed to John.

"Here's all of it, sorted into folders for each year."

John reflected that it was a much more cooperative Torsten Andreasson that he was meeting this time. Maybe the letters were compensation for lying and withholding information.

"If she shows up, please call me right away," he said as he took the bag.

The manager promised to do so and John decided he could probably trust him. The man looked as though he wouldn't dare mess with him again.

20

The cramped steel box made its final journey back to the police station parking garage. The coffee John had taken away from the breakfast buffet at Gustaf Fröding slopped over the edge of the cup and burned his fingers as he changed lanes near the old barracks. Of course the cup holder was too small for the cup. The Spaniards hadn't even managed to succeed at something that basic.

John licked his fingers before the black liquid managed to drip onto his trousers. He had no intention of letting the car ruin his mood today as well. When he had finally parked in the subterranean garage, there happened to be no one around. He placed the key with the large S on the wooden counter—and took the elevator up to the ground floor. He jumped into his pre-booked taxi and asked the driver to take him to the car dealership he had seen advertised online last night.

The salesperson was a young fellow who still had a few years to go before he hit thirty. He lit up when he realized what John was after: a black Chrysler 300 SRT8 that was ready for delivery.

"Automatic," he added, to avoid any misunderstandings.

The salesperson showed him to a car a small distance away on the forecourt. John smiled to himself when he saw the cool grille and the raindrop-shaped xenon headlights glowering at him. This was completely unlike the joke he had left in the police station garage.

"Do you want to test-drive it?" the salesman said, dangling the keys in front of his nose.

"No, I want to buy it," John said, pulling out his credit card.

Fifteen minutes later, the papers were signed and the deal concluded. The pleasure he felt when he left the dealership and headed out onto the E18 highway permeated his entire body. The Chrysler was a dream on the road thanks to its 470 horsepower and a 6.4-liter V8 under the hood.

John thought about his father. His old man had always talked about getting a new ride, but had never done anything about it. He had kept on running around in a battered pickup truck that had aged and died in parallel with him. John remembered the day he had driven it to the scrapyard and watched as the presses dug into the steel. It was the first and last time he had cried at his dad's passing.

The American muscle car drew some attention when he pulled up outside the police station. John secretly reveled in the looks. He took the stairs to the second floor with more of a spring in his step than usual. He was about to knock on Primer's door when he saw through the pane of glass that the boss had a visitor. A woman with hair as dark and glossy as a grand piano was sitting in one of the visitors' chairs.

Primer seemed agitated. He was gesturing with his arms and leapt out of his seat several times. John could only see the visitor from behind, but she seemed to be the personification of calm.

"If you're waiting for Primer, I'd give him a while to calm down," a voice said.

John turned around and was met with Ulf Törner's smirking face.

"That's Erina Kabashi," his colleague added. "She claims we haven't followed protocol in a lineup where one of her clients was picked out."

"So, a lawyer then?" said John.

"The worst kind. She mucked up a case last spring as well. The guy got off and the judge said some nasty things about shortcomings in the investigation. I can understand why the boss is pissed. She's a real pain in the backside for us, but I can tell you this—if I was the accused, I'd be more than happy to have her defend me."

John peered into the office again and made eye contact with Primer. He didn't seem to appreciate his employees spying on him, and he pointedly turned the slats of the window blinds. The gesture was clear and John headed back to the stairs.

The account of his visit to Charlottenberg would have to wait for a better time, but now he had at least shown his face.

Ulf hurried after him.

"Hey, I was thinking about the kitchen schedule . . ."

John interrupted him.

"It'll be fine," he said, patting his colleague on the shoulder and then disappearing down the stairs.

John headed back out in the new car. He took the same route to Hammarö as he had the day before when he had visited his mother. This time he didn't drive all the way to Skoghall—he turned off sooner and in a different direction, heading toward the Tynäs promontory and the beautiful world in which Emelie Bjurwall had gone to a party one night ten years ago.

He parked the Chrysler on the verge and walked the final few hundred meters up to Hugo Aglin's house. It would be stupid to draw unnecessary attention to himself. He breathed in through his nose and searched for the hint of sulfur—but the unpleasant odor from the mill clearly didn't make it to this side of the island. All he could smell was the scent of wet pine after the recent rain. He looked up at the sky. It had been dry when he had driven home from Charlottenberg the night before, but judging by the rapid scudding of the clouds and their ever-darkening contours, a new deluge was coming.

Hugo Aglin's house was exactly as luxurious and over-the-top as he had expected. The façade was a combination of white render and larch paneling across three stories, with half of the top floor given over to a large terrace surrounded by translucent glass. John didn't know exactly what houses in the area cost, but there was no doubt that this was worth millions of kronor. Hugo Aglin had deep pockets. He had clearly been richly rewarded by the Bjurwalls over the course of his many years as director of finance at AckWe.

John tried to imagine the young people dancing and drinking up on the terrace. According to the police investigation, the son's party had been boozy. Magnus—or Mange, as he was known—had said that Emelie Bjurwall had arrived together with her friend, who was called Maja. After a while, she had left the party alone to meet someone. Anton Lundberg, who had headed up the investigation at the time, had pushed hard to find out who this someone was. Magnus stubbornly maintained that he didn't know.

John scanned the façade and spotted the steps leading from the terrace down into the garden. Perhaps that was the way Emelie had left. He imagined her opening the gate and passing the place where he was standing right now, before continuing along the path toward the water.

John followed the girl. He upped his pace so as not to lose the scent. He saw her right ahead of him—her blonde hair loose and flowing in the wind.

After a few minutes, the path petered out and there was nothing but rocks with the odd pine springing up between them. He stopped and caught his breath. It was beautiful here and it must have been the same on that August night ten years ago. He summoned the image of the shining moon reflected in the dark water and then followed Emelie down toward the lake.

It was easy to move over the rocks, as if nature herself had built a stone staircase down to the water's edge. Once by the lake, he reconciled the surrounding terrain with the photos of the scene where the residue of the girl's blood had been found. John had transferred the photos from the investigation to his phone so he could more easily identify the rocks. After a few minutes, he found the right one. He sat down and ran his hand over the rough surface. Something had happened to Emelie Bjurwall on this exact spot. Half a liter of blood had gushed out onto the rock and then she had vanished without a trace from the surface of the earth.

Well, without a trace wasn't quite right, he realized. The photo of the strange tattoo on the girl's forearm had been posted to Facebook at 1:48 A.M. Forensics were certain she had been alive when the final tick had been carved into her skin, but whether she had been alive when the photo was taken was impossible to tell. The question was whether she'd taken it herself or whether it was the perpetrator who had been aiming the cell phone camera. To find the answer, John recognized that he would have to pose a different but equally interesting question: why had the picture been taken? Did it have something to do with the crime that—all things considered—the girl had probably been the victim of? Or was the Facebook post an isolated incident that had nothing to do with her disappearance?

He looked at his phone again and checked his position against the photos from the crime scene investigation. Then he turned to look at a rock a couple of meters away. According to the forensics, who had searched this area, that was where Billy's semen had been found. Had Emelie Bjurwall really snuck off to meet him? And if so, why?

John found it difficult to make the story add up. His brother came from the wrong side of the island and wasn't much to look at, while Emelie was the heiress to the AckWe empire and was in a completely different league. Was it drug-related? Was it that simple? Billy was selling and Emelie was buying? There was a lot to suggest she had taken cocaine that night and perhaps she had wanted more. The sex might not have been the primary crime. A drug deal gone wrong ending in rape was something he'd encountered before. But that had been in the Bronx—not on Hammarö. And it didn't tally with Billy. There was nothing in the extensive investigation to suggest that his brother had been dealing drugs. People didn't snort lines on his side of the island—they stuck to the bottle.

John sighed. He could sit here for hours coming up with theories about how the girl had died and why the semen had been on that rock. But as long as Billy himself couldn't come up with a plausible explanation, there was only one conclusion to be drawn: his brother was keeping quiet because he had done something terrible.

John closed his eyes for a moment. He listened to the sound of the waves lapping against the rocks and the wind blowing through the trees above him. Then he opened his eyes again. He searched for Emelie, but couldn't see her anymore. She had shown him the way here and then vanished, just like she had in the investigation.

In order to make progress with the reconstruction, he left a conscious gap for the crime itself and concentrated on what had happened after the girl's probable death. The perpetrator must have gotten rid of the body somehow. The idea that she had been thrown into Lake Vänern seemed far-fetched now that he had visited the site. Divers had searched the lakebed and, what's more, it was on a promontory where the waves brought most things back to shore.

It was easier to envisage a grave being dug. According to the map that Ruben had shown him in the meeting, a large area had been searched thoroughly using cadaver dogs in the days immediately after the disappearance. But if Emelie Bjurwall had been carried to a car—or a boat for that matter—then it had been pointless. The number of places she might be buried was infinite.

John got up and walked aimlessly along the rocks beside the water. He was always able to think better when moving, and he concentrated on the timeline for that evening. Emelie's phone had lost contact with the network at 2:34 A.M., when the battery had died or someone had turned it off. According to the report from the cell phone company, it had still been in the area at that time. The phone had been connected to the same cell towers from just after midnight until the moment it stopped working.

If the perpetrator had dumped it in the area, Forensics would have found it on the ground or in the lake. The most credible conclusion was therefore that the phone had been moved after it went offline. Either through the perpetrator taking it with them deliberately or because it was still in Emelie Bjurwall's pocket when her body was moved.

John swore silently to himself. If the phone had been able to connect to a new tower before it vanished, he would have had a direction to search in. But he had no such luck and soon this pointless excursion would be brought to an end by pouring rain and a ruined suit.

He turned around and began to walk toward the car again. Halfway up the rocks, he felt that something was missing from one of his trouser pockets. He returned to the lakeside and saw his own phone in a crevice just a couple of meters from the water's edge. It must have slipped out of his pocket when he had stood up earlier.

He picked up the phone from the ground and examined the glass screen. It was undamaged.

"Just maybe," he whispered to himself, as a thought began to take shape.

It was a long shot, but it was definitely worth a try.

John closed the car door at the very moment the heavens opened. The heavy raindrops hitting the metal forced him to put off making the phone call he had been planning.

He turned on the windshield wipers and made a U-turn back onto the road. Despite the rubber blades doing their best to keep the windshield free from water, he couldn't drive more than fifteen miles per hour. He was forced to slow down even more when, far too late, he spotted a wine-red Volvo V70 parked on the verge around a bend. The car was blocking a large part of the narrow road, and John was only just able to pass without going on the verge himself.

After a few minutes, the deluge became more subdued. He connected his phone to the Chrysler's Bluetooth and dialed the number for the police switchboard. A woman's voice asked who he wanted to speak to and he asked to be put through to Lost Property. After ringing for a long time, a man with a broad Värmland drawl answered.

"Well, hello!"

John introduced himself as Fredrik Adamsson from the new cold cases team, hoping that the owner of the sleepy voice would wake up when he heard he had a detective on the line.

"Oh really . . . And what can I help you with?" the man answered, as languidly as ever.

John explained his errand. He wanted to know if any iPhones had been handed in to the police in Karlstad in the last ten years.

The man reacted—but not in the way John had hoped. A leisurely laugh filled the car. The man chuckled as slowly as he spoke.

"You bet your ass," he said. "Several hundred. At least. Maybe over a thousand. I've no idea. Do you know what model you're looking for?"

John tried to remember what the investigation file said about Emelie Bjurwall's mobile.

"When did it go missing?" the man said after a brief pause.

"August 2009."

"Then it was probably an iPhone 3G or possibly a 3GS."

"Okay," John said. "Is it possible to get a list of them with the places they were found?"

He waited for a protest about how long it would take and how much work they had to do. To his astonishment, the man promised to email precisely such a list later in the day. Primer hadn't been exaggerating when he had said that the police had invested heavily in digitization. Apparently it even included Lost Property.

"Thanks very much," he said appreciatively, giving the man his contact details before ending the call.

Once John was back on the road toward the mainland and approaching the bridge, he pulled over and stopped. His childhood home—where Billy still lived and where he had spent a third of his own life—was just ten minutes away. He calculated the risks. A Chrysler like John's passing the house wasn't commonplace in that neighborhood, but it wouldn't awaken any suspicions so long as he didn't stop or get out.

He drank the last of the mineral water in the bottle he'd been given at the dealership that morning and decided to give in to curiosity. He looked in the rearview mirror, made a U-turn, and headed toward Skoghall. When he reached Gunnarskärsgården, he detected a whiff of sulfur penetrating into the car through the vents. He thought about his mother in the nursing home. She was wasting away there, stuck with the shitty smell from the only place she had ever worked—a reminder of the shitty life she had lived.

He sped up and didn't slow down until he had left the dense housing and the gaps between the buildings were growing wider. He recognized the big oak tree by the footpath leading to the scout hut. There was only one turn to go and then he would be there. He remembered how he used to run with Billy along this road when they played down by the lake. They were always late for dinner. Their father would shout for a while, but then he would serve them their meal in front of the TV as usual.

After dinner, they would sneak downstairs to the basement where all the plastic tubs were: candy from Dad's shop that was past its sell-by date, but which was cheerfully eaten by the two brothers in pursuit of their next sugar high.

Him and Billy. Then and there—hearts in their mouths—it felt like they would never be parted.

Then he saw the sign: *Nerman's Autos – 24/7 towing – garage – service*. It was no surprise that his brother had opened a garage. John had made inquiries while at the safe house in Baltimore and discovered that Billy had started a company with the same address as their childhood home. The oversize plastic sign was being held aloft by three sturdy wooden stakes driven into the ground. The lettering, once red, had faded in the sun. If not for the black outlines, it would have been difficult to read the words.

He drove on another few meters so that he could see the house itself. It was at a reassuring distance from the road. Part of him wanted to ring the doorbell, but he rejected that idea immediately. He couldn't casually take risks like that. It was bad enough that he had turned up at his mother's bedside in the nursing home.

The place had presumably already been pretty run-down when the whole family had lived there, even if it never occurred to him at the time. Now he saw his childhood home for what it was—a barely inhabitable hovel. Yellow paint was flaking off the façade and in places the laths had given way completely, allowing the rain to drive in freely between the boards. Roof tiles were all over the place. In some places, they were missing altogether—and all that was visible were roof beams and roofing felt.

At some point over the years, the house had been supplemented by an additional building made from metal that stood on the other side of the yard. There were two tall garage doors with small rectangular windows at the top. This was where Nerman's Autos did business. The new building did not have graceful proportions. It looked as if someone had erected this metallic shack in haste directly opposite the dilapidated house, disregarding all aesthetic considerations.

Outside the workshop there was a tow truck with yellow lights on the roof and next to it there were two American classic cars. John was able to identify one of them without difficulty. It was a silver-gray Chevrolet Camaro built in the late sixties. The other was a rusty thing that he guessed was an older Dodge.

There was a metal pole sticking out from the façade with the American flag hanging from it. He shook his head, looking at the star-spangled banner fluttering gently in the breeze. It was hard to grasp why Billy seemed to love the country that had taken his father and brother away from him. If it had been John who had been left behind with an alcoholic mother, he would have found the nearest oil drum and burnt that fucking flag. Then he would have moved on to the house. But not Billy. He had bound himself even more closely to all that stuff. Not even when people had begun to see him as a murderer and rapist had he moved. Instead, he had let their mother carry on living on the top floor. John wondered whether the mother of Billy's daughter had known what she was getting herself into when she had moved here. The simple fact that she had lasted so long was an achievement in itself.

John braked hard.

He had been staring so intently at the workshop that he hadn't seen the girl on the bicycle who had trundled into the road in front of him. She had come from the driveway of his childhood home and was concealed by a hedge. Their eyes met and he saw how frightened she was. He had been a meter—maybe two—away from running her over.

Nicole, he thought to himself. That had to be Billy's kid—his own niece.

The girl kept looking at him. She was wearing a bright yellow jacket, and a strand of dark hair stuck out from beneath the hood. Her skin was paler than her father's, but the facial similarities were still visible. She was almost eight—so John's mother had said. The same age as Billy when the brothers had been separated.

The girl on the bicycle began to move again. Her slender legs pedaled for all they were worth, back toward the yard. The bike was turquoise and had heart-shaped reflectors on the spokes. John moved forward a few meters so that he could watch it retreat through the puddles.

Not until the headlights of another car appeared in the rearview mirror did he bring himself to put his foot back on the accelerator. He waited until the car passed by and was about to drive on when it occurred to him.

The car that had just driven past—he recognized it.

It was the same wine-red Volvo V70 he had seen parked on the verge out at Tynäs.

He leaned toward the windshield to try to see the registration number, but it was too late. All he could see were two red lights through a fountain of water that was being thrown up from the road in the wake of the car. Then it vanished around the next bend.

Suddenly, intense pain radiated from the back of his head. He recognized it from his time in the hospital bed in Baltimore. The throbbing pain that the doctor had claimed was all in his mind, but which felt no less real for that.

He drove the car far enough to be at a safe distance from his childhood home and then pulled over. His thoughts raced ahead. What did he think was happening? Had the Nigerians found him? It was highly unlikely. The entire federal witness protection team had John's back and he knew that they had made an effort to erase all trails that led to him. Both digital and analog. He had been in Karlstad for less than a week and if Ganiru were—against all expectations—to find him, it would take far longer than a week for him to do so.

John suppressed the paranoia and searched for other explanations for why the same car had been in both places. If it even was the same car . . . He couldn't be certain. How many wine-red V70s were there in this neck of the woods? He supposed it might be a mushroom picker who'd been at Tynäs picking chanterelles—taken by surprise by the heavy rain before going home.

John pressed two fingers to the point at the back of his head and felt the pain slowly dissipating before vanishing completely. Then he turned the car around and drove back toward town. When he passed his childhood home a second time, he avoided looking at the house. It belonged to the past, and if he was being honest, he didn't want to see the wretched thing.

21

After eating lunch in the car, John returned to the police station. He opened the door to his office and the first thing he saw was the mess on his desk. Twenty or so coffee cups were littered across it and there was a smell of sour milk. The message was unambiguous. His colleagues felt he wasn't doing his bit on the kitchen chores and this was how they were showing it.

John swore aloud and went straight to the shared kitchen. He rooted through the cupboards and drawers until he found a black trash bag. He swept all the mugs off his desk into the bag and dumped the bundle in the trash can in the parking garage.

Once he was back in his office, he locked the door behind him and took the investigation piece from the top drawer. He checked carefully that there were no coffee stains on the desk before he spread out the sheet. Ulf Törner and his brigade of coffee-break-cops could knock on the door all they wanted—he wouldn't open up until he'd put his thoughts down on the page in front of him.

He chose a pencil with a fine lead and added Matilda Jacoby next to the other two girls' names. Then he switched to a softer pencil and began to add leafy birch branches emerging from the name of the treatment center that he had added the previous day. When he was finished, the leaves surrounded all three girls' names. They had met at Björkbacken and the bonds among them had been strong.

He put the investigation piece to one side and thought about the manager at the treatment center. He still hadn't run any checks on him. He needed to know if there were any reports or convictions relating to Torsten Andreasson. John logged in to the system and fed Andreasson's social security number into every database he could access. The number of hits was zero. The man was as clean as the finest powdered snow.

He closed his laptop and spread out the mail he had been given in Charlottenberg. There was nothing wrong with the manager's sense of order. Every year was in a separate folder, just as he had promised.

John started on the most recent year and worked backward. He found some post from the Swedish Tax Agency and the pension authorities, but nothing that would help him to trace Matilda Jacoby. The manager had also kept junk mail that was addressed to her. In the folder for 2008, he found something interesting: a Christmas card from the company Awesome Ink in Karlstad.

John felt the familiar shiver that ran through his body when he found something that might move an investigation forward. It was clear from the design—a tattooed Christmas tree—what kind of business the sender ran. He knew that tattooists in the States kept detailed records of their customers' designs. If it was the same in Sweden, he would soon know whether Matilda Jacoby also had a bucket list on her forearm. With a little luck, Awesome Ink would have taken some contact details for her beyond her mailing address. Maybe an email or even—in the best-case scenario—a cell phone number.

He Googled the company and found their address in the town center. According to Google Maps, it would take twelve minutes to drive there.

John pulled over by the curb and looked into the premises across the street. The strident lettering of the neon sign stood out sharply against the gray afternoon. He cut the engine but left the ignition on so that the windshield wipers could continue sweeping the rain away.

Awesome Ink.

He had found the right place.

A courier sped around the corner, forcing him to wait before he crossed the street. The small windows of the tattoo parlor were at ground level and covered in faded photos of tattoo designs. Some steps led down to the entrance at the basement level. He went inside and found a dark room with Persian rugs laid out across the floor. Hanging from the low ceiling there was a patinated iron candelabra with five black candles, their flames fluttering in the draft from the open door.

"With you in a minute."

A bamboo curtain was hung up behind the reception desk and the soft voice seemed to have come from behind it.

"Okay," John replied, looking around.

Framed pictures of yet more tattoos covered the walls. The designs comprised everything from simple black-and-white drawings to large works of art with complex detailing. The perspective and shadows were perfect, and John realized he was in the presence of someone who had mastered the craft.

After a few minutes, a wiry young man with straggling long hair appeared from behind the bamboo curtain. His face was covered in tattoos and piercings that had been added to his skin in all sorts of likely and unlikely places. The piercings in his earlobes were the size of coins and through them he had pressed what looked like two spiral-shaped pieces of ivory.

John was about to offer his hand when the guy passed him and vanished out through the door.

"Jesus Christ, isn't it just tragic?"

The soft voice again.

John turned around and discovered a man of about fifty who was the exact opposite of the Christmas tree that had just left. Graying hair neatly combed, no piercings or tattoos.

"Can you guess what that lad's job is?"

"No idea," John answered, nonplussed.

"Home help for the elderly," the man said with a smile, shaking his head. "You just have to hope someone like that doesn't turn up to wipe your ass when that day comes."

John took a few steps toward the counter.

"Fredrik Adamsson, Karlstad CID. Are you the owner of the shop?" he said, in an attempt to reassert control after the confusing introduction.

"The parlor," the man corrected him. "Yes, I am."

"And how long have you run it?"

"I opened in the January after the arrival of the new millennium. What's this about? Is there a problem?"

John put his hand in the inside pocket of his jacket where the rain hadn't managed to seep in and took out the card Matilda Jacoby had received from Awesome Ink.

"I'm looking for a girl who I think might have been a customer here," he said. "Did you send this Christmas card?"

The man took the card and examined it carefully. John was still struggling to believe he was a tattooist. His white shirtsleeves made him look more like he worked in a bank.

"Yes, that's right. It's been a few years—but for a while I sent out cards with this design."

"To customers who had been tattooed here?"

The man nodded.

"This card in particular was one you sent to a Matilda Jacoby in Charlottenberg," John continued. "It's postmarked 12 December 2008."

"Gosh—that's a long time ago."

"Can I take it that she came here in 2008 and got a tattoo?"

"That sounds likely, but I can't be sure."

John searched his jacket pocket again and found the photo of the girls that he had torn out of the album at the treatment center.

"Do you remember her?" he said, pointing at Matilda.

The man stared at the picture of a pale girl with dark, short hair, repeating the name. "Matilda Jacoby . . . No, not offhand. But it was some time ago, like I said," he added.

John nodded as his thoughts whirred.

"The address must have come from your customer database. Could I take a look at it?"

The tattooist frowned thoughtfully.

"I'm afraid it's been lost. My computer crashed a couple of years ago, and I had to start all over again. But I've still got the folders."

"Folders?"

"Yes, every time I do a tattoo I take a photo and put it in a folder together with the customer's name. Do you know what kind of designs this girl was interested in?"

"Perhaps. Can I borrow a pen and some paper?"

The tattooist bent down and retrieved a sketch pad from the shelf below the counter. John took a ballpoint pen from the tin next to the vintage cash register and began to draw.

"Wait—I recognize that," said the man, before the three squares were even finished.

John looked up from the paper.

"Is there a tattoo like that in the folders?"

"I think so, unless my memory is failing me completely. Do you have any idea roughly when during the year she might have been here?"

John thought. Emelie Bjurwall's parents had said during questioning that their daughter had gotten her tattoo around the same time she had left the treatment center. It wasn't impossible that Kirsten Winckler and Matilda Jacoby had done the same thing.

"Try the beginning of 2008. January, February, maybe even March," he said.

The man disappeared behind the curtain and returned with a large folder bound in red leather. He placed it on the counter and began to leaf through it. He hummed gently while examining his past handiwork. John was burning with impatience. He had to leave the counter and walk around to calm himself.

"Might she be one of these?" he said, turning the folder around to show two Polaroids.

John hurried back to the counter. In one photo there were three young women showing their freshly tattooed forearms to the camera. He immediately recognized them as the gang from Björkbacken. The picture had been taken from too far away to make out any details of the design. That was presumably why the second Polaroid had been added. A close-up of three pale forearms. All featured three squares—and all had ticks in the first square.

"Oh my. I remember those girls," the man said. "They didn't have an appointment. They just walked in. It was pretty late. I had closed up, but I was still here painting. It's a bit weird now I come to think of it."

"Weird? How so?"

"They didn't say much. I mean—girls that age usually babble on and joke around, but they were quiet. Somehow serious."

The tattooist seemed to become lost in his thoughts.

"So, what happened?" said John.

"I remember explaining that the parlor was closed but that they could book an appointment for later that week. But they insisted and I didn't have the heart to say no."

"So, you helped them? You tattooed them that evening?"

"Yes. They wanted to have the same design and it wasn't complicated."

"Do you know why they wanted that design in particular?" said John.

"No, and I didn't ask. Designs can be very personal and it's not my place to pry."

"Did they say anything about why it was so urgent?"

"Not that I remember offhand."

John took a deep breath.

Think a bit harder then.

He held his tongue and made an effort not to show his irritation. The man was doing a good job given that the event he was trying to describe had taken place more than ten years ago.

"And all of them just wanted one of the squares filled in?"

"Yep," said the man, pointing to the folder. "Three squares and one tick."

John tried to picture the scenario: the three teenage girls leaving the treatment center in Charlottenberg and heading straight to Awesome Ink to get tattoos.

Did they want to celebrate their time at Björkbacken being at an end? Perhaps, but the serious atmosphere indicated something else. John had the feeling that the girls had done something they had been forced to do. As if the design were a necessary evil that needed to be inscribed into their skin.

In his head, he compared Emelie Bjurwall's arm in the Polaroid in the folder with the picture that had been posted on Facebook. He'd looked at it many times and had no problem remembering it. When she had gone missing, all the squares had been ticked. The last one had been carved straight into her skin, but tick number two had been tattooed on. On some occasion, Emelie must have returned to Awesome Ink or visited another tattoo parlor to complete the original design.

The same logic applied to Kirsten Winckler, who had had all three boxes filled in when she was declared dead in Gothenburg several years later.

"Did any of the girls come back to add any more ticks?" he asked.

"For a new tattoo?"

"Yes, to add new ticks?"

The man shook his head.

"No."

"You're absolutely sure?"

"Of course. I would have remembered that. It's such an unusual design and those girls stood out the first time, if you know what I mean."

John prepared to wrap up the conversation.

"You understand that I'll need to take the photos with me? They're evidence in a criminal investigation," he said, pointing at the folder on the counter.

The man unfastened the rings in the center and handed over the sheets of card stock to which the two Polaroids were attached. John took them and for the first time he looked properly at the names written under the photos.

Emelie, Kirsten, and Maja.

He read it again.

It definitely said Maja—the same name as the missing friend from Magnus Aglin's party.

"Did you write this?" he said, pointing at the slightly slanted lettering.

"Yes, that's my handwriting. I always write the date and names under the photos."

"One of the girls is called Matilda, but you've written Maja. Why?"

"I guess that's what she called herself," he said, with a shrug of his shoulders. "I ask customers what they're called and write down what they say."

John looked at the sheet again.

If you took the first two letters of the first name and last name and put them together it made sense. Matilda Jacoby became Maja.

A nickname known only to the girls.

There was nothing more to it than that, but John had still missed it.

But he didn't intend to punish himself too severely. This breakthrough in the investigation was still his. Struggling to remain impassive, John thanked the man for his assistance and began to walk to the door. He glanced through the small basement windows. It was still raining. He put the sheets with the photos inside his jacket and turned up his collar.

Just as he was about to grasp the door handle he came to a halt. His brain had spotted something that hadn't emerged into his consciousness until then.

"Was there anything else?" said the soft voice behind him.

John turned around and looked at the man without replying. Then he went back to the window and looked out through the wet pane of glass. This time he didn't care about the weather—instead he focused on the parked cars on the other side of the street.

What he saw sent pain shooting through the back of his head. He had to support himself on the wall to keep his balance. By the curb, four cars behind John's Chrysler, was the wine-red V70.

It was the third time he had spotted the car in just a few hours.

It was no coincidence.

Immediately, he pictured Ganiru's meaty face before him. The boss staring at him on the stand during the trial. The pain ran through him. It was as if someone was striking him repeatedly on the back of the head with a hammer.

"What's the matter?"

The soft voice again.

John felt his muscles cramping. Just as it had in the container at the dock, the paralysis began in his feet and legs.

What the hell is wrong with me?

He forced himself to look out of the window again and he saw that the driver's seat of the V70 was empty. Soon, the fragile wooden door leading into Awesome Ink would fly open and he would be face-to-face with the man who was going to torture and kill him.

He fumbled in his jacket for his service weapon. The paralysis worsened; soon his body would be useless.

"Can I do anything for you?"

John felt the tattooist's hand on his shoulder.

"Is there another exit?" he managed to say.

The man looked around as if it was the first time he had visited his own parlor.

"Yes, there is," he said uncomprehendingly, pointing toward the bamboo curtain. "But that'll take you into the basement store. What's . . ."

"Show me," John interrupted him, pushing the man toward the counter.

His muscles were still working well enough, but he had to summon all his mental strength to deal with the painful cramps. The man went through the curtain and John followed. They passed through a small room filled with tattoo equipment before they entered another even smaller office. The tattooist went over to a white fire door and began to fiddle with a keyring.

"Is there someone here? I don't understand . . ."

The soft voice was soft no longer—it was jittery.

Once the man finally found the right key and unlocked the door, John pushed past and stumbled into the dark basement. Then he couldn't move any farther. It was as if two steel cables had been wrapped tightly around his legs.

"Lock the door and wait in the office," he said, using the last of his strength to slam the door behind him.

The crash rumbled inside his head and the pain reached its numbing climax. His legs gave way and he sank to the grimy concrete floor.

When John opened his eyes, he didn't know where he was at first. Nor how long he had been unconscious. Without lifting his cheek from the floor, he let his gaze wander along the poorly illuminated basement passage. It was lined with several small storage units divided by chicken wire. The air was cold and damp. Three lightbulbs were hanging from the ceiling, but only one was lit. Farther away at the end of the long corridor there was a door ajar and a faint strip of daylight was forcing its way through the gap. It probably led to one of the staircases in the building.

John tried lifting an arm. It was stiff, but seemed to be obeying orders. He did the same thing with his legs and noted that his body seemed to be working again. The back of his head still hurt, but the pain was no longer as explosive. On the other hand, he felt sick.

He tried to gather some saliva and swallowed a couple of times before grabbing hold of the chicken wire and pulling himself to his feet. Apart from the sound of running water from the bare pipes on the ceiling, the basement was completely silent. He put his ear to the fire door leading into the tattoo parlor and listened. He could hear nothing from inside.

He checked the time on his phone. It said 3:27. He remembered he had parked outside of Awesome Ink a little after three, and the conversation with the owner had probably taken about fifteen minutes. In other words, he'd not been out cold for long.

John checked that his service weapon was still in its shoulder holster inside his jacket and then began to walk toward the light at the end of the corridor. The closer to the doorway he got, the quicker his thoughts flew on. He had to get out of the building—that much he knew. But then what? Where was he supposed to go?

If the Nigerians had managed to find out where he was, then it was certain they had uncovered his new identity too. They wouldn't have any trouble tracking every plane ticket he booked in the name of Fredrik Adamsson.

Fuck.

John considered whether to call Mona Ejdewik in Stockholm to demand that she organize his immediate extraction from the country. He would explain to her that his cover had been blown and that he had only hours left to live. But it would take time—and he would still need to go to ground and hide somewhere.

He had underestimated Ganiru's organization. The Nigerians had probably had him under surveillance at all times in Sweden. But how had the cartel managed to crack the FBI's witness protection program so easily? He simply couldn't understand.

John carefully nudged open the door into the staircase. The clatter of dishes and voices speaking Arabic were audible from inside one of the ground-floor apartments, but it was otherwise quiet. He pressed himself against the wall and went up a half-flight of stairs to the main street door.

The street outside wasn't very busy even though it was near to the town center. By a hot dog stand farther down the street toward the river there were customers waiting for food, sheltering underneath their umbrellas. He leaned forward and turned his head to the left. The V70 was there, but there was still no one behind the wheel.

John tried to plan his next step. Going out onto the street was a big risk. At the same time, he couldn't stay in the stairwell. If his pursuers kicked down the door of Awesome Ink, it wouldn't take them long to find his escape route through the basement. The tattooist wasn't likely to keep quiet about where his visitor had gone if someone pointed a gun in his face.

John had just decided to ring the doorbell to the apartment with the Arabic name on the mailbox when he saw something that snagged his attention. A man had left the hot dog stand and was walking toward the door. At first, John wasn't sure what he had reacted to. But there was something about the way the man was moving. The stooping posture. The distinctive, almost exaggerated gait. John recognized the movement. He squinted to make out the face beneath the hood, but it was too far away. Only when the man was level with the door did he see who it was.

Detective Inspector Ruben Jonsson.

John stepped back and let him pass by. After a few seconds he looked out again and saw Ruben get a car key out of his jacket pocket and unlock the wine-red V70. Then he opened the driver's-side door and got in.

John stared at the silhouette of his colleague through the foggy windshield, slowly realizing that it all made sense. How close he had been to overreacting and doing something really stupid by contacting Mona Ejdewik!

He pictured the nurse at the home. She had clearly told her husband about the visit to Mrs. Nerman. That was all it had taken to make him suspicious, so that he started following his new colleague. But the question was: how much did he know? Did Ruben know that Billy Nerman was John's brother? And if he did, had he told their boss?

John took a deep breath and had to make an effort to gather his thoughts. The situation wasn't good, but it was also considerably better than it had been a moment earlier, when he had been convinced that Ganiru's henchmen had caught up with him. Ruben Jonsson was a threat he ought to be able to deal with.

He opened the door, crossed the street, and approached the Volvo diagonally from behind. When he reached it, he wrenched open the passenger door and got in.

"Why are you following me?" he said, looking at his colleague, who was so taken aback that he dropped his paper plate of mashed potatoes and hot dog into his lap.

"Hell! You startled me."

"You've been stuck to me like a stamp for the last twenty-four hours. Why?"

The question lingered in the air while Ruben put the plate on the dashboard.

"I know who you are, John," he said, smacking his lips.

The instinctive reaction was to protest, but John realized the battle was already lost. Ruben knew his name. That meant he must have made the connection to Billy and his mother.

"When did you realize?" he said.

Ruben turned to him.

"You were unlucky with the nurse at Gunnarskärsgården. She's my wife."

"I know, I saw her getting into your car—the white Toyota."

"Crap—I didn't know that," said Ruben. "She told me a policeman had come to visit Billy Nerman's mother. I asked her to describe you. You're not exactly hard to spot. We don't have many people of color in the force here in Karlstad."

He rescued his plate from sliding into his lap again before going on.

"Granted, it wasn't that odd that you wanted to talk to the prime suspect's mother for some background information. But you didn't tell any of the rest of us about the visit, which I thought was odd. It didn't take a big leap to consider that there might be a connection between you—perhaps even that you were mother and son."

"When were you sure?"

"Yesterday afternoon. I got stuck when I checked the population register. According to that, your mother only had one kid. But I checked which school Billy went to and called the old principal. He told me there was a big brother."

John noted that his suspicions had been confirmed. Ruben Jonsson was a good detective who was never satisfied until he got the answer he was after. He cursed his doubly bad luck. Not only had the wife of a coworker seen him at Gunnarskärsgården—it had been the wrong colleague. If Ulf Törner had been married to the nurse, he would have grabbed another doughnut and ignored the whole thing.

"Okay, so what happens now?" John said.

Ruben looked at him stone-faced.

"That depends."

"On what?"

"On how you answer my questions."

John held out his hands in a gesture that indicated he was going to cooperate.

"Why are you lying about who you are?"

John realized there was no point in trying to fabricate something. Better to be straight with Ruben and hope to win his trust.

"What I'm going to tell you is strictly confidential," he said. "I'm part of the FBI's witness protection program. There's a threat against me which means I have to live under a false identity."

His colleague didn't look as surprised as he had expected.

"If it hadn't been for the issue with the population register, I would have said you were full of shit. But it's not easy to scrub data out of public records. You need someone big and powerful to make that kind of thing happen."

"Like the FBI," John said.

"Like the FBI," his colleague repeated. "It wouldn't be the first time the Swedish authorities had had their strings pulled by the Yanks."

John thought he discerned a slight crack in the stony mask, in the form of a bitter smile.

"Why are you involved in the investigation into your own brother?" Ruben asked. "You must realize how inappropriate that is?"

John did. The question was whether he should explain the maelstrom of contradictory emotions within him that had made him come back to Sweden.

"I want to know what happened," he said. "I deserve to know whether my brother is a murderer or not—and our mother does too."

"And you don't trust us to find that out for ourselves?"

"No, I don't," said John, surprised by the harshness in his own voice. "You didn't manage it last time, so why would you succeed now? It's very possible or even likely that my brother is the perpetrator. If he is, he should take his punishment. But you're not looking at the case in an open way. This is about sending Billy down as quickly as possible. Alternative avenues of investigation and new evidence aren't of any interest if they won't help the prosecutor build a case against him."

John had expected defensiveness, but Ruben seemed to take his criticism of the investigation very calmly.

"Let's say for the sake of argument that you have a point," he said. "We've gotten fixated on Billy Nerman and we're blind to other perspectives. What is there to suggest there's an alternative suspect?"

"Not much," John acknowledged. "But there are a few things worth considering."

He told him about the visit to Björkbacken. He described how the three girls had gotten the same tattoos after being discharged and explained that Maja was actually Matilda Jacoby and registered as a resident of Charlottenberg. He also showed Ruben the Polaroids he had managed to obtain at the tattoo parlor.

"So that means we know who the mysterious friend is?" said Ruben.

John nodded. "Yes, and if we can get hold of her she might very well be able to tell us who Emelie left the party to meet."

His colleague sat in silence for a moment.

"And if she says it was Billy?"

"Then we've got the forensic evidence to go with fresh witness statements. The charges will be much stronger," said John, aware that his loyalty was being tested.

Ruben didn't respond, but somewhere, deep down, John hoped that Ruben appreciated the clear statement of intent.

"For me, it's not about testifying in court," John added. "It's about the truth. I want to hear him say in his own words what he did to Emelie Bjurwall."

"Isn't the semen enough to convince you? It was found only a few meters from the girl's blood."

"I know," said John. "And as long as he doesn't have a good explanation for that, it's hard to believe anything except that he's guilty."

"At the same time, that's exactly why it doesn't work for me."

John looked at Ruben in surprise. This wasn't just a momentary crack in his poker face. The man was showing his entire hand.

"What do you mean?"

"I think it wouldn't have been especially difficult for your brother to come up with an alternative story for why his semen was on the rocks. He could have claimed he'd masturbated there. When I was a boy and lived at home, I took my dad's porn mags into the great outdoors for a wank more than once. That might not have been any more plausible than him actually raping Emelie Bjurwall—especially given he has a prior complaint against him for a similar crime—but it would've been enough for reasonable doubt if the case had gone to trial. The whole investigation relied on that piece of evidence alone."

John tried to keep up with his line of thought. "So, you think the fact that he can't explain the semen makes it likelier that it's not his?"

"Yes—in some weird way that's the conclusion I've come to," Ruben said, drumming his fingers on the wheel. "But it's probably crazy to think like that. Perhaps he was cold-blooded enough to assume Emelie would never be found, which meant there was no need to come up with a lie. He knew the evidence wouldn't be enough to charge him unless there was a body."

John looked out through the windshield again. Perhaps there was something in his colleague's reasoning, even if it seemed far-fetched.

"You asked what happens now," said Ruben.

John felt his palms go clammy, as Ruben continued. "I've not spoken to the boss yet. I wanted to find out what the situation was myself—see whether you were going to make contact with your brother and leak details of the investigation. But so far, all you seem to have done is drive by the house—so I'm willing to give you a chance to tell Primer yourself. He doesn't need to know about our conversation here. With a little luck, he won't throw you off the case. But it might also end in immediate dismissal and an internal investigation for gross professional misconduct."

"I realize this is going to have professional consequences," said John. "But the most important thing is that my true identity doesn't get out. You have to understand that there are people out there who want nothing more than to see me dead."

Ruben looked at him for a long time.

"You're welcome to continue being Fredrik Adamsson as far as I'm concerned," he said. "But it's up to Primer."

"I understand," John said in a subdued voice.

His colleague started the engine—a clear sign the conversation was over.

"I'll give you until the end of the week," he said. "If you haven't told Primer who you are by then, I will."

22

After talking to Ruben, John took the car and parked up in the inner harbor area behind the Löfbergs Lila tower. While his childhood might have smelled of sulfur, the scent here was rather more pleasant. The Löfberg family had been roasting coffee beans for four generations in the tall building and were just as much associated with Karlstad as the local ice hockey team. John remembered the sticker with the bad pun that had been stuck on the break room wall in his father's convenience store in Skoghall. The coffee with that *lila* bit extra.

He needed a walk. When it came to clearing his head, proximity to water was essential. In New York City, he had walked for hours along the East River, letting his thoughts wander freely. The harbor in Karlstad wasn't as big, so after a few lengths back and forth he nipped into the only pub that was open on a weekday afternoon in October. It was called Rederiet—Swedish for "shipping company"—and was based on the ground floor of one of the new buildings.

John ordered an IPA from a brewery he had never heard of and put the keys to the Chrysler on the bar. A few men of his own age seemed to have sneaked out of work to grab a beer or two before family life came calling. At the table closest to the door there was a woman sharing a plate of pasta with her young son. The child wasn't even school age yet and was driving his mother mad with his demands for more ketchup.

Only once half the beer had been drunk did John take off his coat and hang it on a hook under the bar. He thought about what had happened at the tattoo parlor—how he had been convinced that Ganiru's hitmen had found him, and the bodily collapse that had come about as a result of the paranoia. The doctor in Baltimore had been right. There was something wrong with his head. When danger approached—anything that reminded him of the experience in the container port—his brain short-circuited. She had wanted to send him to see a shrink, but that was where he had drawn the line. Nothing good would come from rooting around in the past.

He drained his beer in one final gulp and ordered the same again. The kid with the pasta began to cry because his mother had taken the ketchup bottle out of his hand. John turned in their direction to discover that the woman was already looking at him. She pursed her lips, her expression hostile. He couldn't understand it. If there was anyone who had a right to be irritated, it was him and the other patrons who were having their peace and quiet ruined by her bratty child.

Suddenly, he had a vivid image of Trevor. Whether it was the kid or what had happened in the tattoo parlor that had brought his friend to mind he didn't know. Perhaps a combination of both. John realized that he missed him: Trevor, who would never get to see his own child again. In moments like this, he wanted to talk to someone who understood him. Who knew what had happened in Baltimore. Who understood the risks he faced, now that he had to tell Primer that he was involved in the investigation of his own brother. All the things that no shrink in the world could understand.

John waved to the bartender.

"Can you keep an eye on this for me?" he said, pointing at the glass.

Then he took his car keys and hurried to the car, where he grabbed his bag with the laptop. Two minutes later, he was back in the pub. He opened the machine and turned it so that no one except him could see the screen. The login details for the secure email service that Trevor had given him in the hospital were in an encrypted file on his hard drive. On several occasions, he had been about to delete the file so that he wasn't tempted to get in touch with him. Today he was glad he'd kept it.

He opened the browser, logged in and began to write an email to his friend. However, the thoughts racing through his head wouldn't translate into text on the screen. He kept trying and there was always something wrong. His fingertips were wet from the moist glass. He had to put the chafing car key in his trouser pocket back on the bar. His bladder needed emptying.

After almost an hour, all he managed to squeeze out was half a page of maudlin sentimentality. He read this crap and then erased it all with a long press of the delete key. He watched as the cursor consumed the letters, waiting until the screen was empty. Then he wrote a much shorter message. *Arrived. What about you? J.*

He hesitated before hitting send. Trevor had said the service was encrypted, but John knew that every code could be cracked. At the same time, it would be more or less impossible for the Nigerians to find this exact email in the global flood of data washing over the planet each and every second. If they were careful about the contents of their messages, everything would be fine.

Trevor's words echoed in his ears.

We're going to become very lonely people, you and I.

Amen to that, brother, John thought to himself as he raised his glass in a toast to his distant friend.

Then he sent the email and shut the laptop. One of the guys enjoying a post-work drink stood beside him to order a new round. The man looked at him quizzically. John thought he was bothered by the laptop taking up space at the bar so he put it back in his bag on the floor. But the guy continued to scrutinize him and shook his head demonstratively before disappearing back to his table with the bottles of beer.

What the hell was that all about? Why is everyone here treating me like shit?

The phone in his inside pocket vibrated, preventing him from confronting the man and asking him whether he had a problem.

"It's Lost Property calling," said a Värmlander's leisurely voice. "I just wanted to say that I've finished your list of phones and sent it over by email."

John thanked him, and his mood instantly improved. The man on the phone belonged to that rarest breed of police officers—ones who worked more than they talked.

After ending the call, he got his laptop back out of the bag and put it on the bar again. It didn't take long to pull up Fredrik Adamsson's work email.

His hero in Lost Property was as concise in writing as he was on the phone. *As promised* was all it said in the subject line. But the attached file was far more extensive. He opened it and scrolled down. The rows flashing by contained dates, objects, details of notifiers, and find locations.

John pondered how to tackle the list. The most reasonable approach was to start from the beginning. If Emelie's phone had slipped out of her pocket when her body was being moved, it was probable that it would have been found during the initial period after her disappearance.

John went to August 2009, the first month after Emelie Bjurwall had been reported missing. Five iPhone 3G mobiles had been handed in to Lost Property. Four had been found in central Karlstad, making them less interesting. All things considered, the perpetrator was not going to have dumped Emelie in the main square in the center of town. The fifth had been found at a rest area on the road to Skutberget. John noted the time and place on a napkin. He remembered the popular swimming pool by the campsite. There had been a water slide there; he and Billy had nagged their parents to go to it. He couldn't remember what the terrain alongside the road looked like, but maybe it was wooded.

He continued on to September and October 2009. The number of iPhones found had increased as the phones became more popular. All phones found in proximity to water or adjacent to wooded areas were added to the napkin but none of them felt right. The places where they had been found weren't isolated enough nor on a natural route for a driver leaving Hammarö.

When John looked out of the window, he noticed that it was nearly dusk. The lights along the quay had come on, illuminating the handful of boats at anchor this late in the season. He requested a bowl of peanuts to ease the worst of his hunger and returned to his list. Halfway through November, he found an entry where the phone in question had been found on Hammarö. He read the details of its location with increasing interest.

Woods along the Hallerudsleden road close to the old dump. Approx. one hundred meters into the woods in the ravine toward the hollow, on the far side of the parking area just after the turn for Sätterstrand.

John checked the column for other comments. The phone had been destroyed long ago and there were no remarks regarding the owner. He pulled up a satellite image of Hammarö on his phone and used his fingers to slowly follow Hallerudsleden from above. It ran from the fancier areas on the island past Skoghall and on toward the southern tip of the island.

The disused dump was easy to find on the map, as was the parking spot. He examined the broad green areas on either side of the road and had to remind himself not to be overly excited. The idea about the phone was still just a guess. He remembered what Hallerudsleden looked like, though. It was the shortest route from his childhood home to the mill and sometimes Dad had let the brothers take turns sitting on his lap to steer when they had gone to collect Mom from work.

John could picture the dense woods and the sharp bends. Someone driving from Tynäs who wanted to bury a body would be hard-pressed to find somewhere better.

He downed the last of his beer and paid the bill. When he put his hand on his car keys, he heard the bartender's voice.

"Maybe you should take a cab? I can call one for you if you like."

John was so surprised he didn't know what to say. A cab? After two beers? Then he understood the skeptical looks from the mother with the child and the man who had stood next to him ordering beers. It was about the car keys. In this politically correct country, it was apparently not okay to have a couple of beers and then drive home.

John's entire being wanted to revolt. He wanted to order another IPA and spin the keys on his finger while drinking it so that everyone in the room could see what he was going to do. This was plain stupid. He was just as good a driver now as when he had stepped into the place. But then he remembered what had happened the last time he had let his inner American run free. He had dumped half the mugs in the police station in a trash can in the parking garage.

"I was going to leave the car and walk home," he said.

The bartender visibly relaxed.

"Well, that's fine then. Have a lovely evening and see you soon."

Two minutes later, John started the engine and felt the power of the Chrysler vibrating through the driver's seat. He reversed out of the parking lot and accelerated harder than usual. The first stop was an electronics store where he bought a metal detector, the second a hardware store where he managed to find a big spade on sale.

Then he set a course for Hammarö. When he reached the football pitches near the middle of Skoghall, he turned left and drove east until the streetlights petered out and dense darkness enveloped him and the car. Once he reached Hallerudsleden, he slowed down, searching for the turn for Sätterstrand. After just a minute or so it appeared. He dimmed his lights as a car came the other way and passed the crossroads. Then he returned to full-beam headlights and soon picked out the parking spot.

John pulled in and cut the engine. He silently repeated the description of the location to himself. *Approx. one hundred meters into the woods in the ravine toward the hollow, on the far side of the parking area.* He opened the door, got out, and stared into the seemingly impenetrable woods on the other side of the road. Flashlight in one hand, spade and metal detector balanced on his shoulder, he crossed the road and searched for a way into the trees. It transpired it was easier than he had first thought. The forested wall that had seemed so dense from a few meters away had a narrow opening through which a path led into the dark greenery.

He pushed away the wet branches with the arm holding the flashlight and continued onward. It was important that he took regular paces and didn't lose count. Once he had gotten a bit farther in, he noticed that the ground had begun to slope downward. He examined the terrain using the flashlight. Ahead of him was a ravine leading down into a hollow between two hillocks.

John began to descend. The closer he got to the lowest point, the softer it became underfoot. His leather shoes sank down to their tongues in the moss, and mud splashed a long way up his trousers. When his mental tally reached one hundred paces, he hadn't gotten more than halfway down the slope.

He looked around. It seemed logical for the cell phone to have been found on the slope. The angle a body would be carried at when going down a slope would be different, making it more likely that something would drop out of the pockets.

The question was whether Emelie had been buried here. John didn't think so. There was something impractical about digging on a slope. The level bit of ground at the bottom of the hollow seemed more likely.

He continued another twenty meters and then put the spade in the ground so that the shaft stood up straight like a bare tree. Then he readied the metal detector and hit the on button.

The machine immediately emitted a beep to confirm it was switched on and working. After a few seconds, the detector fell silent and John began to systematically search the area, which was around twenty meters wide and fifty meters long.

The sweep by the light of the flashlight tried his patience. It was like cutting a gigantic lawn using a trimmer, the difference being that the equipment was heavier and the grass softer.

Once he had covered about half of the area, the machine beeped. He repeated the sweeping motion over a spot next to a couple of low bushes. The metal detector went off again. There was clearly something in the ground here.

John tore a twig off the bush and pushed it into the moss as a marker. Then he fetched the spade and began to dig. The mud was heavy with moisture and he sweated in his jacket, even though the temperature had fallen markedly in the last hour.

It took time to check each spadeful's contents. He could also only use his right hand since he needed the left one to hold the flashlight. Crouching, he went through what must have been several sacks' worth of earth without finding so much as a coin.

But then his fingers felt an unfamiliar object. John moved the flashlight a little closer to his hand. Now he saw it—it was a jam pot.

Irritated, he stood up and aimed a kick at the damn thing. The sound of the sole of his shoe hitting the metal broke the silence in the woods and he heard the rustle in the clump of trees where the projectile landed.

He put the spade back in the ground and continued his relentless sweeping with the metal detector. A little while later, it happened again. The machine beeped twice as he ran it over a point in front of a tall pine that stood by itself on the edge of the flat bit of ground.

He began digging again. The soil was now—if at all possible—even heavier than it had been a few minutes earlier. Once he was half a meter deep, pausing before continuing deeper, he spotted something glittering in the glow of the flashlight. Something in the ground had been uncovered.

His trousers were ruined anyway, so John kneeled and leaned forward. He carefully prized the object out of the mud. It was a silver heart on a chain.

Emelie's, he thought to himself. It had to be Emelie's.

Blood rushed to his head, as if he had just run a marathon and was on the home stretch. By the light of the flashlight, he dug deeper using his free hand. There was something else there—something hard. He used his fingers and nails to peel back another thin layer of mud. The arched bones that were visible were, without doubt, those of a human rib cage.

A gust of wind blew through the woods and he heard it whistling past the treetops surrounding the hollow. The spruce and pine were the only witnesses to this exhumation. All he had to do was shovel the soil back into the hole, get in the car, and go back to his warm hotel bed. And his brother could carry on repairing American cars as if nothing had happened.

John shook his head in response to his own thoughts. That wasn't the promise he had made to his mother or himself. He had promised Billy would get a fair investigation, and withholding crucial evidence was the exact opposite of that. But the question was whether he trusted Primer and the others on the team. As soon as John told his boss about his connection to the prime suspect, Billy Nerman, he'd be kicked out and no longer have any ongoing knowledge of the case.

John had heard them at that first meeting at the police station. No one was interested in looking at the case with fresh eyes. The doubts that Ruben had expressed in the car wouldn't matter once the machinery was set in motion. The order from on high was to find new evidence to convict the man that everyone already agreed had committed the crime. And now John would be the one to deliver Emelie Bjurwall's remains to the police chief as a gift-wrapped early Christmas present.

The body, in combination with the blood and semen, was potentially enough to put Billy away. But it wasn't enough for John. He needed a confession to feel one hundred percent certain.

23

His childhood home looked almost abandoned. A fine wisp of smoke emerging from the chimney indicated that someone was inside, but the windows were otherwise dark. However, there was activity in the workshop. John could see a harsh blue light occasionally flickering inside the windows at the top of the garage doors.

He checked the time. It was just after ten. The daughter ought to be asleep by now. She could under no circumstances hear the conversation he needed to have with her father.

John had left the Chrysler on a gravel track a few hundred meters away and walked the final stretch. It felt strange to approach the house as an uninvited guest when the place had once been his home. He passed the kitchen door and looked up at the second floor. The boys' shared bedroom had been right there at the gable end. Its location right by the stairs had been perfect for nighttime outings while their parents slept. John could even remember which steps had creaked and which ones were safe.

He continued toward the workshop. The irregular flickering illuminated the cars in the yard for brief moments before they vanished back into darkness. He stopped and listened. The pattering sound of the welding torch on the other side of the wall was faintly audible through the thick metal.

There was no manual for a situation like this, he thought to himself. No handbook for the best way to turn up after twenty years' absence and accuse your brother of murder. He waited for the right moment, when the welding torch paused. Then he knocked on the door that was inserted into one of the two big garage doors.

"Nicole, if you're hungry then get yourself something from the fridge. I'm working right now."

The voice made John pause. It was an echo from his childhood. A grown man's voice, but with a melody he recognized.

He knocked again. The sound from his clenched fist on the metal echoed into the autumn night. He heard footsteps inside and a second later the door opened. John stared into a face covered in a mask with a tinted glass panel in front of the eyes.

"What the hell?!" the voice underneath it said.

Billy pushed the visor onto his head and gave his widest grin.

"Is that you really you, bro?" he said, pulling John into a bear hug. "Sorry if I'm all greasy and shit."

He let go of John and tried to brush away the stains on his blue overalls, which had no impact whatsoever on the filthy fabric.

"Let me take a look at you," he said, taking a step away to examine his brother. "A bigwig in a suit and fancy coat and everything. Well, I always knew it. That things would go well for you."

John managed to articulate a few stiff but polite words—but he found it was hard to know what to say. All the lines that appeared in his head felt dishonest. His brother was surprisingly similar in appearance to the photos taken ten years earlier in connection with the first round of questioning. His face was possibly a little rounder and the wrinkles around his eyes were more prominent, but the curls of dark hair were just as unruly.

"We should have a beer," he said. "Come with me so you can see what I've got."

Billy moved to let John into the workshop. The compressor in the old fridge was humming so loudly that it almost drowned out the tape player on the workbench, where Bruce Springsteen was singing about the darkness on the edge of town. Billy bent down and took out two bottles of beer.

"Cheers!" Billy said, taking the cap off. "Jesus, it's good to see you again."

"Cheers," John said, noticing his hand trembling. He put the bottle to his lips so that his brother wouldn't notice anything.

The workshop was lit by four fluorescent tubes that cast a harsh light on the room. A black car had been jacked up and two of its wheels had been taken off. The hood was up and fluid appeared to have run down from the engine into a small grate in the middle of the floor.

"A Buick Century Riviera from fifty-five," Billy said, when he saw John looking at the car. "My little gem."

"So, it's yours?"

"I bought it from a Yank in Minnesota who shipped it over three years ago. It was pretty run-down and I've been restoring it since then."

Billy put his hand on the front wing and let it trace the shape of the body.

"Well, to be specific, it's a Buick Century Special Riviera. This baby, along with the 98 Holiday and 88 Holiday, were the first full-size models to feature four doors."

"It looks good," John said.

"Good? I'll have you know this is a rarity. There are only two of them in Sweden."

His brother leaned against the bench and drained his beer bottle.

"I thought Mom was talking crap when she said you'd come back. But the old woman was right—here you are in person. Imported straight from the States."

He laughed so loudly it echoed between the metal walls.

"Yes, here I am," said John, clenching his fist in his pocket. Of course his mother hadn't been able to keep her trap shut. What else should he have expected of that drunk old cow who seemed to live her life through her youngest son? He hoped she'd confined herself to telling Billy and hadn't blabbed to anyone else.

"She said you were working for the police, but that it was top fucking secret."

John spotted an opportunity to steer the conversation in the right direction and he had no intention of letting it pass.

"That's right. I'm part of the team investigating Emelie Bjurwall's disappearance."

Billy's eyes immediately looked guarded and he folded his arms.

"But how is that possible? We're brothers . . ."

John realized he was going to have to say something about his new identity. He told Billy only what was absolutely necessary and emphasized several times how important it was that his brother keep the story to himself. Billy listened attentively and then pretended to zip his lips.

"You can trust me, you know that. I'm just so damn happy you're home and can help me out of this shit situation."

He opened the fridge and reached for another beer.

"When Primer brought me back in for questioning, it was like the nightmare had started over. Why the hell is he going through all this again? It's more than ten years since she went missing."

"What did you tell him?" John asked.

"What I've said all along. I never touched that girl. I was at home alone and didn't even meet her."

"And there's really no one who can confirm that?"

"No, Mom was working at the mill and didn't get home until late," Billy said, sounding annoyed. "How many times do I have to go through this?"

John raised his hands disarmingly.

"Take it easy, I just want to know what you've said. I assume Primer asked about the forensic evidence too?"

"What forensic evidence?"

"The semen on the rock."

"Yeah, of course he did. The idiot seemed obsessed with spunk."

"It's hardly that strange that he wants to talk about it, is it?"

Billy put the bottle down on the workbench so hard that the beer foamed out of the neck. Then he turned off the music.

"I thought you'd come home to help me. But it almost seems like you're here to put me away."

John took a couple of steps closer to his brother. It was time to clarify the situation.

"Listen to me carefully," he said. "You're in a damn tight spot. Worse than you think. I can hear what Primer and the guys down at the station are saying. You're going down. End of story. There's no one there interested in hearing your version again. But I am. I want to know exactly what happened."

"But what is it you want me to say?"

"The truth will do."

His brother held out his arms.

"That's all I've been doing for ten years," he shouted. "I don't know how my semen ended up at Tynäs. There's no reasonable explanation."

"Yes, there is. You could have raped and killed Emelie Bjurwall."

John struggled not to drop his gaze from his brother. He wanted to see each and every movement on Billy's face. However, contrary to what he had expected there was no outburst of rage. If Billy's eyes were filled with anything, it was sorrow.

"Is that what you think?"

"If you don't have any other explanation then that's what I have to think," John said.

"And my saying I didn't kill her doesn't matter to you?"

"I've questioned a lot of men who've sworn on their mothers' graves they didn't do this or that. Only for them to confess to everything the next day, when the evidence was too strong."

"Maybe. But were any of those men your brother?"

Billy put the welding mask back on and went over to a car whose front end was elevated on two jacks.

"I want you to leave," he said.

"Like hell I will. I'm going nowhere until we're done talking."

Billy shrugged his shoulders and pulled the visor down over his face. John took a few quick steps toward the car and kicked the left-hand jack out of the way just as his brother was about to start welding. The wing crashed to the floor.

"What the hell are you doing?"

Billy pulled off the welding mask. John was standing so close to him that he could hear his heavy breathing.

"I've found her," he said. "You buried Emelie Bjurwall next to the same road we used to drive along when Dad took Mom to work. Be a man and confess to what you've done."

Billy replied by giving John a hard push to the chest that made him stumble and lose his balance. Then he grabbed a wrench from the side. He raised it in the air and for a moment John thought the heavy metal implement was going to hit his head. Instead, Billy let it fall to the floor and proffered his wrists, indicating that he was ready to be handcuffed.

"Arrest me then! Might as well lock up the monster once and for all, right?" Billy shook his hands, as if the handcuffs had already been applied. "Nicole can live with a foster family. Anyone is better than this monstrosity, right? Isn't that what you think, bro?"

John put his beer bottle on the dirty cement floor and checked that his phone was still in his jacket pocket. As soon as he got back to the car, he was going to call Primer. It was time for the boss to be told exactly where Emelie Bjurwall's remains were.

PART 3
2019

24

Lunch was served on the large terrace overlooking the Mediterranean. The party from AckWe was in the shade in one corner, surrounded by empty tables. Heimer knew that his father-in-law always rented out the whole place when they came here for their annual conference of the board and management team.

The trip was a tradition that had been established by the second generation of AckWe's owners. It was a mixture of work and relaxation, to which employees' spouses were invited.

Sissela had said that the younger members of the management team found the event a little strange. Their wives and husbands had their own careers and didn't have the time or inclination to be bussed around the sights of southern Europe. Nevertheless, she defended the trips. They were part of what made AckWe unique—a publicly traded, international fashion group with the soul of a small family business.

There was probably a grain of truth to it—but Heimer suspected the explanation was simpler than that. For Allan Bjurwall, the trip was the highlight of the year, and he was still the company's biggest shareholder. He was a man with whom it was unwise to clash; even his daughter had to pick her battles carefully.

Heimer looked around the exclusive band of invitees. He made eye contact with Volker, who'd headed up the business in Germany for many years. They were the same age and both enjoyed discussing architecture. In many regards, he was unlike the rest of the AckWe honchos: more confident and less eager to impress the empress.

Heimer felt phony as he smiled at him. One morning two weeks earlier, Sissela had been in a bad mood and told him that sales were still falling in Germany.

"I'm getting sick of Volker's excuses," she had said.

Heimer felt sorry for the man. It wasn't Sissela's style to give people second chances. Once people stopped delivering, the trap door would open beneath them.

There was the ring of a spoon against a wineglass and Heimer turned his gaze toward Allan, who apparently wanted to say a few words. AckWe's chairman looked old—the man was almost eighty, after all.

"First and foremost, I'd like to offer my thanks for the splendid few days we've had together. Tomorrow, we all return to the daily grind—but before that there are still a few things left on the program. This afternoon, the board and management team are going to work together on a number of key strategic issues. For the wives, we've arranged an excursion to a nearby market."

There was polite applause around the table but at the same time Heimer saw a few of the guests exchange glances with one another. Had he actually said "the wives"? Had he forgotten that half the management team and several of the members of his own board were women? Not to mention the chief executive officer.

If Sissela was embarrassed, she didn't show it. She sat calmly beside Heimer and appeared to enjoy the Chablis he'd selected to go with the fish.

A younger version of Heimer would've been provoked and spent the rest of the day sulking. But he'd learned to accept that things were the way they were. He was the person he was and the same applied to Sissela and her father.

After Emelie, it had been all about surviving. Every evening when he closed his eyes, he still saw her before him—but he didn't talk to Sissela about it anymore. She didn't like it when he let thoughts of their daughter paralyze him. His wife was grieving too—he knew that—but in her own way.

In the beginning, she'd been patient with him. But after a couple of years, the urging to move on and find meaning in life had stopped feeling encouraging and started feeling mandatory. Eventually, he realized their marriage was in danger. At some point, the shame of divorce in the public eye would be easier to deal with than being married to him.

Heimer had done some soul-searching. He was in no position to start his life all over again by himself. For as long as he was married to Sissela, money was no issue—but in the event of a separation the source would quickly dry up. The family's lawyers had made sure of that when they'd had him sign a prenuptial agreement.

The solution had been to separate his inner life from the outer one, an advanced role-play in which he acted the part of the husband rising from depression for Sissela, while trying to deal with his emotions in the wake of losing Emelie alone. Over time, he had grown accustomed to it. There were days—or at least parts of days—where it no longer felt like he was playing a role. Times when there was genuine congruity between the emotions he displayed on the outside and the ones he felt on the inside.

Heimer lingered on, enjoying the view, as the other guests broke away. Majorca's coastline, with its steep cliffs and burnt red-brown earth, was truly dramatic. On the north side of the island, it was also surprisingly calm—at a safe distance from the parties and budget hotels in Magaluf.

Hugo Aglin, the director of finance, and the one he liked best out of Sissela's colleagues, kept him company by the rail surrounding the terrace.

"You know there's a golf course right nearby," he said. "If you don't want to go to the market with the wives, I mean."

Heimer smiled at him to show that he had recognized the allusion to Allan's faux pas.

"Thanks for the tip—but I'm happy to go, actually. I'm on the lookout for a special bottle of wine."

They returned their gazes to the open sea and silently took in the magnificent view. The afternoon breeze had picked up and it felt good on Heimer's sunburned face.

"Hugo, we're starting."

Sissela was standing by the open sliding door in her dark formal dress, a laptop under her arm.

"Of course, just coming," he said, nodding to Heimer before following his boss into the bowels of the hotel.

The bus ride along the winding road up to the mountain village had been a nightmare, but once they arrived Heimer's mood improved. The young lad on the market stand had grasped that Heimer was a connoisseur and that it would pay to give him some attention. He had called his father, who'd come to pick up Heimer and had driven him to the family's vineyard a few kilometers away. The man had opened the door to their wine cellar and gestured that he should browse. However, when Heimer asked him to get out his own favorite, he shook his head.

"Sorry, no sell," he had said in broken English.

Heimer insisted on at least looking at the bottle, so the man accompanied him into the innermost chamber of the cellar, where the wines were stored behind a barred black gate. He opened the heavy lock using a key on the ring in his pocket before handing over a bottle.

"Best wine at vineyard. Only six bottles left. For my daughter's wedding."

The man hesitated for a long time, but when he realized that the amount Heimer had offered for just one bottle would pay for the whole wedding, he gave in.

When Heimer got back to the hotel room, he got the wine to temperature and decanted it into a carafe. The wine was a blend of the local grapes, Mantonegro and Callet, and it smelled wonderful. It felt good knowing that he and his wife would share this very bottle. Bought today, for this particular moment.

When Sissela opened the door to the hotel suite fifteen minutes late, her face was the picture of irritation.

"How was the meeting?" he said.

"So-so," she muttered. "Allan doesn't understand why we should expect lower margins for a few years while we invest in the new e-commerce platform. He gets that physical stores cost money—but he doesn't seem to be able to understand that digital ones do too. He's stuck in a different age."

Heimer nodded, sensing that the meeting had gone somewhat worse than "so-so." Sissela only ever called her father by his first name when she was angry or an outsider was present.

"After his speech at lunch, I doubt you're the only one who thinks he's stuck in a different age," he said, in an attempt to lighten her mood.

The result was the exact opposite. Her eyes darkened and she turned her back to him to get his help with the zipper on her dress.

"Sometimes I just get so tired of him. Doesn't he know what it feels like for me to sit there as a woman and hear him being so out of touch?"

Yes, or for me as a man, Heimer thought to himself—but he was sensible enough to keep the comment to himself. He didn't want to make the atmosphere any worse.

Sissela explained that she needed a shower before dinner and vanished into the bathroom. When she emerged, she had put on one of the hotel bathrobes. Heimer had changed into a clean shirt and put out three wineglasses on the small round table between the rattan armchairs on the balcony.

"Let's sit outside," he said.

Sissela looked at him and then the clock on the wall above the sofa.

"We don't have time. I have to get dressed and do my makeup."

She went into the bedroom in their suite and he heard her opening the sliding doors of the wardrobe. Had she forgotten? Surely that wasn't possible.

"What do you mean, don't have time?"

"It's almost dinnertime and I'm not going to piss off that old fogey any more than he already is by being late."

"Do you know what date it is?" he said in a low voice.

"No, why?"

He waited and let her realize by herself why he had put out three wineglasses on the balcony. That was what they did each year on Emelie's birthday. One for Sissela, one for him, and one between them that they drank on behalf of their daughter.

"Surely it isn't?" she said.

He nodded, gazing at her gravely.

"Oh, forgive me, Heimer. Forgive me."

She sat down next to him on the edge of the bed. Part of him wanted to push her away and ask what kind of mother forgot her daughter's birthday. But the years of practice at separating his inner emotions from his outer appearance meant he was able to control himself. He needed this period of shared sorrow that their daughter was no longer with them. So it would have to be on Sissela's terms—better that than not at all.

"You've got too much to think about," he said. "Do you think we can sit outside just for a little while?"

She smiled and gently kissed him.

"Let's sit outside for as long as we like," she said, leading him toward the open balcony door.

25

John looked at his brother through the window into the interview room. Billy was sitting perfectly still on the uncomfortable chair with his hands resting on the table. The officers who had carried out the arrest overnight hadn't given him long to clean up. His holey jeans were dirty, and his t-shirt bore the washed-out logo of a lighter fluid brand.

The man sitting beside him was decidedly more neatly turned out. His shirt was carefully ironed and his tie impeccably knotted, despite it being half past seven in the morning. The nonexistent chin made his face look like a rodent's.

Then the door opened and Primer stepped into the interview room. He glanced at the window, even though he couldn't see his colleagues through the one-way glass. Ruben checked that the video was on and then turned to John.

"Why the hell haven't you spoken to Primer?"

"There hasn't been a chance to," he said. "You gave me until the end of the week."

Ruben snorted at him.

"I didn't know you were going to dig up Emelie Bjurwall's body, did I? As soon as this interview is over, you need to tell him. I'm serious."

"Of course."

"Really, I ought to throw you out of here, but it'd only lead to a lot of questions. And don't you dare say anything about me already knowing your true identity. One of us getting fired is enough."

"Calm down. I'm not going to get you mixed up in this."

John discerned the sour odor from his colleague's armpits. He presumably smelled just as bad himself. There was rarely time for showers and deodorant at critical points in investigations.

On the other side of the glass, Primer greeted Billy and the lawyer—then he sat down at the table. He had no notebook. It was a conscious strategy to make the conversation feel more informal.

"Well, Billy," he heard his boss say through the speakers.

He didn't get any further before a woman stumbled into the interview room. The guard on the door received an annoyed glance from Primer and a silent question about why he had let her in.

"She says she's the guy's legal counsel," he said apologetically.

"You already have a lawyer, though, don't you?" said Primer, turning to Billy.

"Mr. Nerman wishes to change counsel with immediate effect," the woman said firmly. "As of now, I'm his public defender." John studied Erina Kabashi through the glass. She had large almond-shaped eyes and golden skin. Her hair, once again tied back in a tight bun, was as glossy and black as the paint on a grand piano. He guessed she had family roots somewhere in the Balkans.

John turned his gaze to his brother and followed the drama. Two lawyers fighting for the right to defend him—now he needed to make his mind up. The rodent made it easy for him. He got up of his own accord and carefully put his notebook and pen back in his briefcase.

"Good luck," he said, as the guard opened the door.

Once he had disappeared, the woman took the seat next to Billy—and immediately the dynamic in the room shifted.

"I need to speak to my client, and hereby call for a one-hour break," she said.

Primer didn't even answer.

He simply got up, pushed his chair under the table, and left the room.

"How on earth did she know we had arrested him?"

Saliva sprayed from the boss's mouth as he spoke. The rage he'd managed to suppress on the other side of the glass was now being expressed with double intensity in the observation room.

"Billy Nerman hasn't contacted her—I know that much," he added. "He didn't have any specific request when he accepted the offer of a public defender and it's not in the media yet. So it can only have come from us."

He crashed his fist into the desk holding the control panel for the recording equipment. The coffee in Ruben's cup sloshed over the rim and he hurried to wipe it away with a napkin before an ugly ring stained the wood.

Primer paced back and forth in frustration.

"This godforsaken building is full of nothing but fucking blabbermouths," he said, pounding the desk again for good measure.

John waited a few seconds until the boss had gotten out the worst of his aggression.

"Is it really that bad? It's just a lawyer."

Primer sank into the black leather sofa by the wall.

"Erina Kabashi isn't just a lawyer. She's the devil incarnate. She'll cause us more grief than you can possibly imagine. You saw how that weakling reacted when she came in. He just handed over his client like that."

"It might say more about him than her," John said.

"Yes, that's possible—but I've had so many bad experiences in cases where that woman's been involved."

The boss leaned back on the sofa. He was breathing heavily after his outburst and needed time to calm his large body. After a period of silence, he looked happier—as if he'd had a good idea.

"You're going to lead the next interview," he said.

John met Primer's gaze and froze.

He realized the impossibility of the situation. He couldn't stay quiet any longer; the bandage had to be ripped off. Ruben was sitting next to him and if John didn't open his mouth now, his colleague would.

"That won't work. I'm afraid I can't interview him."

"Why not?" said Primer, getting up.

John turned toward Ruben.

"Could you give us some privacy?"

"Absolutely," his colleague replied, feigning an expression of confusion. Then he took his mug of coffee and left the room.

Primer still looked quizzical.

"Why can't you interview him?" he asked again.

John felt his body perspiring under his clothes. Without saying anything, he took off his jacket and hung it on one of the chairs. He crossed his arms in front of his chest and looked at his boss.

"I have a personal connection to him."

Primer looked surprised.

"A personal connection?"

"Yes."

"To Billy Nerman?"

"He's my half brother."

John didn't know what reaction he was expecting, but the laughter that burst out of Primer took him by surprise.

"You're messing with me."

"I'm afraid not. It's the truth."

His boss's smile died as the news sank in. He looked through the window into the interview room where Billy was still sitting with Erina Kabashi. It was as if it had only now occurred to him that John had the same color skin as the suspect.

"I don't understand. You mean you're siblings?"

"Yes, we have the same mother."

"But . . . why the hell didn't you say something before?"

John took a deep breath and told Primer about the letter that his mother had sent to him and the decision he'd made in his hospital bed in Baltimore. How he wanted to find out the truth about his brother and make sure the investigation was fair. That it was personal for him and something he had to do in order to move on with his life. Primer listened attentively without interrupting once. He just stood there, hands to his cheeks, as though he were being doused by a cold shower. His face grew redder and redder. Once he'd heard enough, he came up to John and held out his hand.

"Give me your badge and service weapon."

John took the piece of plastic out of his wallet and checked the safety on the pistol in his shoulder holster before handing it over.

"And what happens now?" he said, careful not to lower his gaze.

"You're on a leave of absence until further notice at your own request. What happens then, I don't know. You've committed gross negligence and this will have consequences."

"Of course, I understand. But I still hope this can be dealt with discreetly. If word gets out around the police station it'll leak to the media and my real identity will be exposed."

Primer snorted and shook his head.

"Well, you should've thought about that before you blundered in here and sabotaged the investigation. You put yourself in this mess. I'm not responsible for your witness protection status."

He was so angry that John realized it was meaningless to try to warn him of the risks of the story getting out. Primer was neither willing nor able to make any promises of secrecy. The decision would be made at a higher level and in consultation with Mona Ejdewik in Stockholm. Maybe even Brodwick would get involved. John could imagine his old boss's thirst for revenge. He would love to remind John that he had been opposed to the idea of Sweden from the very beginning.

John dismissed the picture of the lopsided smile from his mind and glanced into the interview room. Through the glass, he could see his brother's morose expression as he listened to Erina Kabashi. The lawyer seemed to be talking without interruption, and John wondered what was going through Billy's mind. Being forced once again to spend his nights in the police station cells was probably not what he had been hoping for when his big brother had finally come back to help him.

26

Heimer slowly jogged the final stretch back to the house at Tynäs. He had done the last kilometer in 3:34 and it had finished him off. His legs felt like lead and he wanted nothing more than to flop onto the sofa. But if he was going to cut any more seconds from his time, he had to take care of his body after a workout. Which is why he so slavishly followed the routine from *Runner's World*.

The magazine's guide was taped to the hall wall. Step one—slow jog. Step two—stretch. Step three—water and protein powder. Step four—hot shower. Step five—oil and massage. Step six—rest and mental visualization training for thirty minutes. He'd started doing it after the trip to Majorca and noticed that his body was recovering more quickly after a workout and that his muscles were more malleable the morning after.

He thought about Sissela. She was just as obsessed with the family firm as he was with running. Right now, she was presenting the new partnership with Nyla. The Finnish star designer had agreed—after much hesitation—to do an exclusive collection for AckWe, on the condition that the launch took place in Karlstad, the company's birthplace.

Sissela loved the idea and had talked of nothing else lately. Models and stylists had been flown in from New York, and together with editors from the world's leading fashion magazines they turned the town's hotel into a significantly more fashionable place than it usually was.

The lunchtime showing was taking place in an old warehouse that had once been AckWe's first factory. Heimer had been there the night before, at the general rehearsal. The show was fantastic. The contrast between Nyla's urban, scaled-back designs and the projected images of seamstresses from the first half of the twentieth century would definitely make an impression on a discerning audience.

He had considered being there today too but had decided against it. Heimer always felt slightly in the way when AckWe was beating its drum. He struggled to handle the double emotions of being fussed over because he was the queen's husband, and on the other hand feeling lost since he had no role to play.

He took an extra long stride to avoid a puddle and then looked toward the gate up ahead on the road. There was a car parked outside—as if it were waiting for someone to come home. The man leaning against the driver's side door was someone he hadn't seen in many years, but seeing that face still made his stomach cramp.

This could only mean bad news. Heimer had spent the last ten years developing a strategy to cope with daily life. Nevertheless, its structure was so fragile that all it would take was the slightest prod to bring his existence tumbling down.

The man had seen him and raised his hand in greeting. Heimer nodded in response and jogged over to him.

"Have you been waiting long?" he said, sounding as relaxed as he could.

"Don't worry, I only just got here," said Bernt Primer.

Heimer felt the warmth in his body from the run disappearing, to be replaced by the uncomfortable feeling of cold sweat lingering on the skin under his running clothes.

"I've been trying to get hold of your wife on the phone but didn't manage to get through," Primer added.

"She's busy with work," said Heimer. "What's it about?"

Primer fidgeted and seemed to struggle to get the words out.

"I'd prefer to speak to both of you together," he said eventually.

Heimer only needed a couple of seconds to understand what this was about. Why else would the policeman standing before him have gone to the trouble of coming all the way out here?

"Emelie . . ." he heard himself say. "You've found her."

"You know what, Heimer? I think we should go inside and . . ."

"Answer me. Have you found her?"

Primer lowered his shoulders and scanned the neighborhood with his eyes. After what felt like an eternity, he took a deep breath and opened his mouth.

"Yes, we've found her. She's dead. I'm so sorry."

Heimer had to fight to keep his balance. The black reinforced steel gate, the cars on the drive beyond it, the hornbeam hedge with its brown leaves running alongside the fence down toward the big band king's house—everything in his field of vision took on strange shapes. As if he was seeing the world through the peephole in a door.

"Where . . . Where did you find her?"

"She was buried in the woods alongside Hallerudsleden. I know this must be a shock to you. Shall we try to call Sissela again?"

The policeman got a phone out of his pocket, but Heimer waved dismissively at him.

"That's not necessary," he said. "I'll speak to her myself."

Primer appeared to hesitate.

"Shall we go inside anyway?" he insisted, nodding toward the house. "I think it would be best if we could get your wife to come here, so that we can all talk together."

Sissela, Heimer thought to himself. He wouldn't be able to play his role any longer. Wouldn't be able to pretend to be the grieving but strong husband who had moved on and found a life after losing his daughter. There was no life after Emelie—there never had been.

Primer put a hand on his shoulder and gestured that he should open the gate.

"No," Heimer said in a voice he didn't realize he possessed.

Then he began to run.

It was about ten kilometers to AckWe's old factory on the outskirts of Karlstad. The asphalt felt hard under his feet, but he ignored the pain in his joints from the rough surface. The rain had begun to fall without him noticing. His hair was suddenly wet and there was spray flying off the tires of passing cars.

Sissela had to know, he thought to himself as he increased his speed. The voice in his headphones said his pulse was 152 and that the last kilometer had taken 3:42 minutes. Heimer took them out, leaving the buds dangling around his neck. For each step he took, he got a little closer to his wife—he didn't need to know more than that.

He licked the drops of water from his lips and felt his lungs filling with air, bringing him oxygen. The images he was trying to ward off were still forcing their way into his head. His daughter, buried in the ground. Her beautiful face covered by the dirty soil. Worms slithering between locks of her long blonde hair.

He wondered what she looked like after ten years. She was presumably unrecognizable. Her body must be decomposed. Nevertheless, it wasn't as a rotting body that he thought of his daughter. In the pictures appearing in his mind's eye, Emelie's face was peaceful—as if she had just closed her eyes as life had left her. Shovelfuls of earth covering it, spade by spade, until there was nothing left to see.

He passed the bridge and looked down into the water below. The raindrops formed small circular ripples that kept colliding—turning into one large effervescent mixture. The railing wasn't high—Heimer guessed it was about a meter. It wouldn't be hard to climb up, lean out, and then feel the relief of free fall.

He increased the frequency of his stride. It had worked before: physical exertion as a way of subduing anxiety. What unpracticed runners thought was their max was in fact just half of the power it was possible to squeeze out of the human body.

When the red brick building appeared on his right, his heart was thudding so hard he thought his rib cage was going to burst. The red carpet was out, and the parking area was full of cars. Inside he could hear sharp, electronic music—but it was almost desolate outside. Heimer slowed down to avoid running straight into the security guards manning the entrance.

The oldest of the four broad-shouldered men approached him with a skeptical expression. He wasn't keen on leaving the shelter of a marquee outside the entrance which was keeping him out of the rain.

"Sorry, but you need an invitation to get in here," he said.

Heimer bent forward and rested his hands on his knees while catching his breath.

"Are you alright?" the bouncer added in a friendlier voice, when he saw how worn-out the man in front of him was.

Heimer nodded and then straightened up slowly.

"I need to go in and speak to my wife."

"Sorry, but like I said, I can only let in people with an invitation."

"You don't understand. My wife . . ."

Heimer paused to catch his breath again. The bouncer brushed his neck to stop raindrops from running inside his shirt collar.

"My wife," Heimer continued. "She's in there. She's Sissela Bjurwall."

"*The* Sissela Bjurwall?"

"Yes."

The bouncer looked doubtful, but Heimer must have been sufficiently credible to avoid being immediately taken for a madman.

"Wait here," he said, disappearing beneath the protective roof of the marquee.

He dialed a number on his phone and a moment later a young woman came out. Heimer recognized her. She was one of his wife's assistants and had been on the trip to Majorca. The bouncer waved at him to come closer.

"Come with me," the woman said, opening the door into the cacophony.

Heimer followed her. They walked through a foyer full of abandoned champagne flutes and plates of half-eaten lunch canapés.

"The show is almost over," she shouted in his ear, nodding at a new bouncer who opened the next door leading onto the old factory floor.

The woman put a tag reading *VIP* around his neck and pointed at an empty seat at the very front, by the stage. The audience was sitting on temporary raked seating on either side of the catwalk running through the center of the room, while the end was reserved for photographers. The music had been loud enough in the foyer, but in here it was deafening. The deep bass bounced between the red brick walls and made the steel structure he sat down on vibrate.

On the stage, young women were showing Nyla's collection for AckWe under bright lights. Camera flashes went off and the models assumed poses to show the clothes in their most flattering light.

Heimer saw the man next to him lean away. The woman on the other side did the same. He suddenly became aware of his running kit and the fact that he was dripping with rain and sweat. His mouth felt dry after running and he regretted not asking the assistant for a glass of water.

He looked up at the stage again. The models had changed into new outfits and were earning appreciative applause as they faced the audience. He tried to make eye contact with the woman at the head of the procession. Her face was covered in mud and her hair tangled in rotten leaves. The models following her looked the same. Their lips were bloodless and white, and their eyes lacked all signs of life.

He forced himself to keep watching.

Then he saw it—they all had Emelie's face.

Heimer turned to the man next to him. He didn't seem to be reacting to the grotesque parade before them—all he did was make a note in a small notebook.

The tunnel vision he had experienced earlier with Primer returned. His field of vision began to contract and Heimer was unable to take in enough air, no matter how much he breathed through his mouth.

The models processioned back out and a woman in black jeans and a strangely cut gray top came in. The adulation in the room increased. It was Nyla herself. Next to her was the company's CEO and public face—Sissela Bjurwall.

Heimer could feel the music hurting his ears and he put his hands over them to shut out the noise. The lack of oxygen was getting worse and he stood up in an attempt to start breathing again. Once he was up on his legs, he felt how wobbly they were. The man next to him looked at him with irritation when Heimer grabbed hold of his shoulder to stop himself from falling, but continued writing in his notebook. On the stage, Sissela took a couple of steps back and joined in the applause, to show that the adulation belonged to Nyla alone.

Heimer felt the nausea rising up through him and fell forward toward the small barrier separating the seating from the catwalk. He put out his hands to stop himself and promptly threw up. The yellow-green contents of his stomach sprayed across the shiny white stage floor, just a few inches from his wife's high heels.

27

Despite the rain pouring down, he stood outside the car to eat. The hamburger he bought from a street vendor in the town center was on the greasy side, and John didn't want to risk it on the leather seats of the Chrysler. Two hours had passed since the confrontation with Primer at the police station, and it was only now that he could feel the adrenaline beginning to subside. He hadn't slept in thirty-six hours and was drained of all energy after recent events.

In the course of just a morning, he'd gone from being the hero who found Emelie Bjurwall's remains to a liar being kicked off the investigation. He'd no longer get updates on the case, and that bothered him. But maybe there was a way to change that . . . It was at least worth a try.

His phone beeped and he read the message. The person on the other end had agreed to meet. He threw the rest of the burger into a trash receptacle and put the address into the GPS. It took only five minutes to reach his destination. He pulled over to the curb. The place across the street didn't look how he had expected. He checked the text message again to make sure he'd come to the right place. He compared it with the sign on the façade in front of him. Yes—it was correct.

He got out of the car, crossed the street, and opened the door to Rat Chance Thai Massage. The sign in the shopwindow comprised colored lights flashing out of time with the unobtrusive pan flute music coming out of the speakers on the reception counter.

The young Thai woman who greeted him was wearing a red kimono with beautiful embroidered butterflies on it. She smiled and bowed slightly toward him.

"I must have the wrong address," John said.

"Follow me, mister."

The woman spoke broken English. She held back a curtain made from colorful plastic beads that concealed an arched opening in the wall. On the other side was a corridor with rooms on both sides. She knocked on the door of one of them, and a voice inside asked them to come in. John saw a familiar face look up from the massage table.

"Sit down."

Erina Kabashi sounded just as commanding as she had when she had taken over as Billy's lawyer. John looked around for something to sit down on. Another much older Thai woman, who was busily kneading the lawyer's shoulders, looked up at him. She nodded toward a stool in the far corner. John fetched it and sat down at the head of the table.

"And now I'd like to know who you are," Erina added, groaning on the final syllable as the masseuse's powerful thumbs dug into muscles glistening with oil.

John hesitated. The number of people who knew that Fredrik Adamsson was just a front was already too high and he had no wish to include the lawyer in that party. On the other hand, it was important that he kept her on his side. Right now, she was the only way of maintaining any ongoing insight into the investigation against his brother.

"Don't worry about Gewalin—she doesn't speak a word of Swedish," said Erina. "I've often had confidential meetings here. Not all of my clients want to be seen hanging around outside my office."

John's quizzical look made her elaborate.

"I represented the family that runs the place in a civil case a couple of years ago and they ran out of cash. So in lieu of the final installment I accepted three massages every week. It was that or bankruptcy—and then I wouldn't have gotten a penny."

A new groan of pleasure-filled pain escaped the lawyer's lips.

"That's enough, Gewalin. Do my backside," she commanded in English.

The masseuse shifted the white towels on her back so that her shoulders were covered and the lower part of her body was bared. John tried to avoid looking at the lawyer's ass.

"You must realize that I'm wondering who you are," Erina continued. "First you write to me, anonymously, to tip me off that Billy Nerman has been arrested again and needs a lawyer. There's nothing unusual about that. I get tip-offs like that all the time. But then you write again and this time you want to meet—that makes me suspicious."

John was annoyed by his own awkwardness in the woman's presence and tried to take control of the conversation.

"Who I am doesn't matter," he said. "What does matter is what I have to say."

"Who a person is and what they say can't be separated," she replied, as quick as a flash. "I've been a lawyer long enough to know that. If you don't want to tell me I'm sure you have your reasons, but then I'm afraid I'll have to pass on the assignment."

Erina looked at the floor through the hole in the head end of the table, as if the conversation were already over. The Thai woman smoothed oil onto her rear and then began to knead her backside with brisk movements, up and down.

"Pass on the assignment," he repeated. "I don't believe that for a second. The media's going to be all over this case. Passing up all that attention isn't like you."

"It's only good PR if I win. And I usually do—do you know why?"

"Because you're a divinely good lawyer, I assume?"

"You might very well think that," said Erina, choosing to ignore the irony. "But no—it's because I work harder than everyone else. I anticipate what the prosecutor is going to do and I make sure I'm prepared. That's why it's not forensics and witnesses that keep me awake at night—it's the X factor. The unknown element that's been concealed from me and that I haven't had the chance to prepare for."

The lawyer lifted her face from the table so that she could turn her head toward him.

"That's why I have a nonnegotiable policy," she continued. "If I sense there's an X factor, I quit the assignment immediately. And you—my friend—smell like X factor from a mile away."

John held out his hands and did his best to look injured.

"I don't understand how I'm gumming up your chances of successfully defending Billy Nerman. All I've done is to tip you off about a job. Without me, he wouldn't even be your client."

"And that's exactly what's bothering me. How did you know he'd been arrested? And why do you want me to defend him? You haven't asked for a tip-off payment. Not yet, at any rate. It's obvious you're hiding something from me. So, either you tell me who you are or I'm out."

John searched for something to say but couldn't find the words. His attempt to apply the principle that a good offense was the best form of defense had failed, and now he had no idea what to do next.

"I think you should consider two things before you make up your mind," she said, fixing her gaze on him. "One: I have a zero tolerance policy toward lies. If you lie and I find out, then I'll quit. Two: our conversation is taking place within the scope of my defense of Billy Nerman. That means anything you say is protected by confidentiality and will never leave this room."

John looked at the woman on the massage table. Erina Kabashi meant business. Her conditions weren't the opening of a negotiation—they were absolute demands.

"I want her to leave the room," he said, nodding toward the masseuse. Gewalin seemed to understand John's gesture. She put a warm, double-folded towel over the lawyer's backside and then vanished noiselessly out the door.

"What I'm going to tell you is confidential. If it gets out, my life will be in danger. Do you understand?"

"Let me repeat what I just said: everything you say to me is protected by lawyer-client confidentiality. If I violate that, I'll never be able to work as a lawyer again."

John met the serious gaze. He had no choice but to trust her. If he wanted to keep the promise he had made to himself and his Swedish family, he had to make sure his brother got the best possible defense.

"Billy Nerman is my half brother," he said, pausing to let her process the information.

"Yes—it was either that or you're his lover," she said without even a hint of surprise in her voice. "And why is that a secret?"

"Can we leave it at the fact that I'm currently in witness protection? There's a threat against me that has nothing to do with the accusations against Billy."

Erina clicked her tongue against the roof of her mouth while she considered whether the answer was sufficient.

"Okay," she said. "But then I need to know who you're posing as. I assume you've been given a new identity?"

"Yes, Fredrik Adamsson."

The lawyer sat up rapidly, struggling to ensure all the towels continued to cover her body.

"The Fredrik Adamsson? The one who appears in the preliminary investigation I just read? The one who found the body?"

John nodded reluctantly.

"Wait, let's take this nice and slow so I can keep up. You're part of the cold cases team investigating the AckWe case—in which your own brother is the prime suspect?"

"Half brother," John corrected her.

"Okay, half brother. But that doesn't change anything. And you've managed to find out where Emelie Bjurwall was buried all by yourself?"

"I understand that it must seem odd," John said.

Erina sighed at the understatement.

"It's the most absurd thing I've ever heard. You give the prosecutor the final piece of the jigsaw to put Billy Nerman away for life while also leaking information to his defense. Seems kind of schizophrenic. Which side are you actually on?"

John crossed his arms and looked at her.

"That of the truth," he said.

"Oh no, not one of those," Erina groaned. "Turn around, please."

John did as he was told while she wrapped herself in a dark blue kimono and sat on the table with her legs dangling.

"I have absolutely no interest in the truth," she said. "For me, it's not about whether someone has done this or that—it's about whether the prosecutor can prove it. So if you want to help your brother, I suggest you think less about the truth and more about the evidence."

"I don't want to help my brother like that."

"No, I gathered that," she said. "If you had, you would've left that girl in the ground. So what is it you want?"

"For him to get a fair trial—and I don't think he'll get that if Bernt Primer leads the investigation. There needs to be a counterweight—that's your role."

The lawyer looked at him. She tried to hide it, but John still spotted the hint of an amused smile beneath the serious facial expression.

"So, you've found out that he doesn't care about the truth either."

John felt the flames of anger beginning to rise. Erina Kabashi might be good at what she did, but she completely lacked a moral compass. Like hell was he going to let her treat him like a schoolboy! If there was anyone who knew how rotten the world could be, it was him. But that didn't mean you had to throw all your principles overboard.

"Sorry if I provoked you," she said, sensing the atmosphere in the room.

John didn't reply. It felt good that Erina was now on the defensive. She could stay there a while longer.

"You had something you wanted to say to me—that was how this conversation began," she said. "Now you've told me who you are, I'm happy to listen."

John pulled the stool closer to the table but was careful to ensure the distance was still big enough that she wouldn't interpret it as a silent acceptance of the apology.

"It's about the DNA evidence against Billy. I want to know if he's said anything new about it in his conversations with you."

"No comment. To answer that would violate his confidentiality."

"Okay, I understand. But let me put it like this: how are you going to deal with the fact that your client's semen was found right next to Emelie Bjurwall's blood?"

"I don't know yet. But I can tell you that the strategy he's relied on until now won't work."

John thought about what Ruben Jonsson had said to him in the car outside the tattoo parlor. The DNA evidence was the prosecutor's strongest weapon and the defense would have to expend a lot of energy neutralizing it.

"So you'll ask him to tell an alternative narrative?"

"I'm not in the habit of asking my clients to lie."

"But you're not especially interested in the truth either," said John, regretting it right away. It wasn't in his interest to provoke her. "My brother has stuck to the same story over the years," he added. "Isn't that strange, given how easy it would have been for him to come up with a lie that explained why his semen was found there? Maybe there's a slim chance he's telling the truth."

"What do you mean?" the lawyer said.

"Well, what if it isn't his semen? It wouldn't the first time a lab had screwed up."

"Sounds far-fetched."

"But worth checking—if only to rule it out."

That was his best argument. The lawyer had nothing to lose by requesting a new test.

"I'll think about it," she said at last.

"Thanks. That's all I needed to hear," John said, heading for the door.

"Are you going back to the police station? Confidentiality or not, I have to say I think it's highly inappropriate for you to be involved in the investigation."

John turned around.

"Don't worry about it. Primer took my badge."

The lawyer looked surprised.

"So, he knows?"

"He knows about my relationship to Billy, yes."

Erina made the irritated clicking noise with her tongue against the roof of her mouth again. It seemed to be a tic of hers whenever she received and processed new information.

"Now I understand better," she said. "You want me to be your mole in the investigation now that you don't have eyes on the inside."

"I want you to represent my brother and nothing else."

"That's funny," she said, disregarding his interruption. "Here I was, thinking you'd give me information—and it turns out your plan is the reverse. I assume Primer is going to launch an internal investigation?"

"I don't actually know," John replied truthfully.

He took a few steps back into the room and sat down next to her on the massage table. Out in the corridor he could hear new customers being shown to their rooms.

"Does this change anything for you?" he said.

"How do you mean?"

"Well, are you going to continue defending Billy, now that you know I'm a police officer and that I've been tossed off the investigation?"

She looked at him in surprise.

"Of course. You're no longer an X factor."

28

Heimer looked at his wife's eyes. They were red from crying. When he told her that the police had found Emelie's remains, she'd fallen into his arms. It didn't matter that he had thrown up on the catwalk and was wearing sweaty running clothes. She still pressed herself against him.

They were sitting on two plastic chairs in a windowless room behind the stage. Outside they could hear the rattle of the roadies taking down the banked seating. The steel parts clanked against each other as they were carried onto the loading.

There was a cautious knock on the door.

"The press conference," Sissela said in a low voice. "Tell them they'll have to manage without me."

Heimer took his wife's face between his hands and kissed her gently on the forehead. Then he got up to open the door. He was worried the nausea would return when he changed position, but he noticed that he was steady when he stood up. In the corridor outside, the young assistant who had gotten him past the bouncers earlier was waiting.

"We need Sissela for a bit," she said, smiling at him.

Heimer smiled back.

"I'm afraid she needs some time to herself."

He was ashamed to admit it, but saying no to the assistant was almost intoxicating.

"But the press conference starts in ten minutes. Nyla's team is asking where she is."

"You'll just have to handle it. You should assume that she'll cancel all appointments in the short-term," he said, before closing the door without any further explanation.

He returned to Sissela and crouched in front of her.

"Do you feel up to leaving?"

Sissela didn't let go of Heimer's hand in the back seat of the taxi. She cried again, but differently this time: more calmly and with greater depth in her inhalations. He imagined that a frozen ball of grief inside his wife had finally been allowed to defrost. Perhaps she felt just like he did but hadn't dared admit it. Perhaps all the talk of moving on and not getting stuck in the past had just been a way of protecting herself from the pain. Perhaps thoughts of Emelie also came to her during the hour of the wolf.

He squeezed Sissela's hand extra hard as the taxi drove up to the entrance outside the forensic medicine center. Bernt Primer was standing on the steps waiting. Heimer had spoken to him on the phone and apologized for his behavior outside the house earlier. The policeman had reassured him that he understood but was still reluctant to show them the body. When Primer learned it was also what Sissela wanted, he gave in and promised to be there in person.

The first thing Heimer thought about when they entered the building was disinfectant. The place smelled and looked like a hospital, but the crucial difference was that the staff in the corridors weren't in a hurry. And why would they be? The patients were already dead.

Primer went up to a door and turned to face the visitors.

"She's been in the ground for ten years. You won't recognize your daughter in there."

"We understand," said Heimer.

Primer nodded and pressed a button on the wall, making the electronic door swing open. They followed him into a room with tiled walls and a linoleum floor. There was a man in a green coat standing by a stainless steel gurney—he raised a hand in greeting. What was on the gurney was covered with a white sheet.

"I just want you to know that we treat the deceased with the greatest of respect here," he said. "The goal is always to leave as few traces as possible on the body when we carry out our examinations."

Heimer thought the phrases sounded like lines that had been memorized. Like a flight attendant going through the safety procedures before takeoff.

"I'm ready when you are," said the pathologist, taking a step toward the body.

Heimer put his hand on Sissela's shoulder.

They were ready.

The man slowly pulled away the sheet. Heimer stared intensely at what was lying on the gurney in front of him. Their daughter had been transformed into a skeleton with naked bones exposed in many places. There was rotting tissue on top of the rib cage that still hadn't decomposed fully.

Heimer swallowed and forced himself to look at the head of the gurney. All that remained of Emelie's once-beautiful face was the cranium. On the right-hand side there was a clear contusion. Two cracks ran from an impact point—one slightly longer and wider than the other. It looked absurd and unreal, as if someone had played with the props for a production of *Hamlet* and had dropped the skull on the floor.

"The cause of death is almost impossible to determine this many years after the fact," the pathologist said. "It's not possible to identify any injuries to the soft tissue. On the other hand, she has been subjected to head trauma—as you can see. That may have been what killed her—either by itself or in combination with other injuries."

Sissela quickly looked away and hid her face in her hands.

"I think we're done here," said Primer.

The man nodded and covered the body again.

"Just one more thing," he said, handing over something that had been lying on the table behind him. It was a sealed plastic bag containing a metal object.

"We don't need this any longer."

Heimer took the bag and held it up to the light. Inside was Emelie's silver heart.

It had gotten dark by the time they got home to Tynäs. They were sitting on opposite sides of the glass table in the living room, waiting in silence for the kettle to boil. Heimer thought there was an understanding in the silence between them. They both probably needed some time to process the experience. The point was, they had done it together.

The kettle began to whistle and Heimer got up to make the chamomile tea that Sissela liked so much. He took the kettle off the heat and waited a few moments so that the temperature would fall a few degrees.

Once the drink was ready, he sat down in the Lamino armchair again. He usually didn't have much time for chamomile, but today it tasted good. Sissela's phone was next to her cup on the glass table. It was set to silent, but it would light up at regular intervals as the world tried to penetrate into their bubble. She turned it over so she didn't have to look at the screen and leaned back against the soft cushions on the sofa. Heimer got up and sat down next to her.

"Shut your eyes," he said.

"Heimer . . ." she protested quietly.

He hushed her and stroked his hand over her face to make her close her eyes. He took the plastic bag given to him by the pathologist out of his pocket. He opened the seal and took the silver necklace out of the bag, his hands trembling. The heart had been a gift from both of them to Emelie on the day she started middle school. Despite her changes in fashion taste, new haircuts and styles, their daughter had worn it every day.

Heimer fumbled as he tried to attach the chain around his wife's neck. But he finally managed to get the thin silver hook to slip into the eyelet. He carefully turned it so that the heart fell on her breast and the fastener was on her neck.

Sissela opened her eyes and smiled weakly at him. She took the heart in her hand and rubbed her thumb on the shiny surface.

"The bite marks are still there," she said.

Heimer smiled too, remembering Emelie with the heart in her mouth. They had nagged her that it wasn't good for her teeth, but she had kept on chewing on the necklace when she needed to concentrate that extra bit harder on her homework.

Sissela let go of the heart and Heimer saw a flash of concern cross her face.

"Don't take this the wrong way, Heimer. It's a beautiful necklace and I'd like to buy a good case to store it in. But I don't want to wear it every day. I can't do it."

Heimer tried to stay calm. He didn't want to show how disappointed he was. So that was how Sissela regarded the memory of Emelie: like a millstone around her neck that she couldn't bear to carry.

"I can see that you're upset," she said.

"Don't worry. You shouldn't wear anything you don't feel comfortable with."

She smiled at him again. It was forced this time.

"I'm worried about you," she said.

"What do you mean, worried?"

"That you won't cope. You remember what it was like in the early years. I don't want to go back there. For your sake and ours. Nothing has really changed. She's gone from our lives and is never coming back. The police finding her is just confirmation of what we already knew."

"So seeing the remains of our daughter on a gurney means nothing to you?"

"You know it does. It was as hard for me as it was for you."

Heimer felt the taste of the chamomile growing bitter in his mouth. The fact that anyone could drink this dishwater was beyond comprehension. He got up, took his cup, and poured it down the kitchen sink.

"Please, don't be like this. Come back so that we can talk about it."

His wife's voice from the sofa was harsh in his ears. She'd cried some tears on his shoulder and now it was done. He had been an idiot—imagining things between them might be different. Instead, he was back at that point in their relationship it seemed impossible to move past. He just had to accept it. He would sink in the depths without Sissela—he knew that—which meant he had to live within the boundaries she set for him. What was visible on the outside belonged to her, but what was on the inside was his own. She would never be able to take that from him.

He poured a glass of cold water and returned to the sofa.

"Sorry," he said mildly. "I didn't need to say that. I know we have to move on and make the best of our life together. It's what Emelie would have wanted. But you have to give me some time."

Sissela looked at him with new warmth.

"It's me who should be asking for forgiveness. We've just experienced something very disorientating and it wasn't my intention to make you feel like I was jumping down your throat. It's just that I don't want you to lose your way again."

Her lips felt soft when she kissed his cheek. He moved closer and asked her to lift up her hair.

"I'll help you take that off," he said.

Sissela leaned forward and let him release her from the burden of Emelie's silver heart.

29

When John woke up, he sat on the edge of the bed for several minutes, staring out the window. The night had been the same eternal flux in and out of sleep with only the noise of tractor-trailers on the adjacent highway to keep him company.

Almost a week had passed since he'd met Erina Kabashi at the Thai massage parlor. On several occasions, he'd been about to call or text her, but he stopped himself. If he pushed her for information about the investigation, there was a risk she'd lose patience with him.

There had been nothing from the police station either. Neither Primer nor any of his colleagues had contacted him. Of course, they were busy questioning Billy, but John guessed that was only half the explanation. The situation had begun to smell of scandal, which meant they needed to distance themselves from the person at the center of it.

Sooner or later, he'd hear from them. If the police authority decided to air its dirty laundry in public then an internal investigation awaited—followed by dismissal and maybe even corruption charges. The witness protection program would wash its hands of him, and John's identity would be exposed. He'd become an easy target for Ganiru's hired killers.

At the same time, there were powerful forces pulling in a different direction. John's relationship with the Bureau had already been frosty when he left Baltimore. But the fact remained that the conviction of Ganiru and his men was a feather in the FBI's cap. It wouldn't look good if the Bureau just sat by and watched as the life of their star witness was put in danger. How easy would it be to recruit new undercover agents after that?

In a tug of war like that he thought he knew who would win. It seemed likely that they'd keep the story quiet and John would be offered a discreet exit through the back door, but he couldn't be completely certain.

The frustration at being unable to influence the course of events seared through his entire body and he missed Trevor again. In situations like this, his friend was the only one he could share his thoughts with. After the first, brief email he'd sent from the pub at Bryggudden, it became easier to find the words. They'd written to each other several times since then.

He lay in bed with the laptop propped up on his bent legs and logged in to the encrypted email service to see whether Trevor had been in touch. There was a new message in the inbox with the subject line "Am I imagining things?"

Hello eager beaver!

Hope you're getting settled and that the ladies are all over you, you being such a cool dude and that (well sometimes).

John could almost hear his friend's rumbling laughter and realized that the corners of his mouth had involuntarily curved upward. Trevor's sense of humor was infectious even by email. But the subject line suggested that his friend was worried about something and it didn't take long to find out what.

Look . . . I think I'm losing it. Everything gives me the creeps. There's been a car on the street outside my house for a week. It's not there when I get home at night, but then it's back there every morning. Probably just my imagination . . . if it was them they wouldn't stay in the car would they? I'm sleeping badly even though I'm dog tired. Just imagine. ME—sleeping badly even though all I've done for fifty years is sleep! When I go to the bar I've started taking back streets. I've found this totally cool place, by the way. Wish you could try their Caipirinhas—they're the best I've ever had.

I think I need to think less.

Take care. T.

John sat up, the computer still open on his lap. Trevor was probably right—his friend was seeing things. It was only a few days since John had let fear get the better of him in the tattoo parlor.

He began to write about his own paranoia and what it had done to him. The sentences almost wrote themselves. He just wanted to keep writing—about the colleague who had uncovered his identity, the body he had found in the woods, and the suspicions against Billy.

John could picture his brother in the interview room. Sulky, his arms crossed, as if he didn't care about any of it. If the lawyer didn't manage to get him to change his account, the question of how his semen had ended up next to Emelie's blood would remain unanswered—and Billy would probably be convicted of murder, or in the best case manslaughter.

He wanted to tell Trevor all of that—but he didn't. It would be impossible to discuss the investigation without his friend figuring out where John was. And that would be a violation of their unspoken agreement never to reveal such information to each other.

Instead, he read what he'd written about the figments of his own imagination at Awesome Ink. He deleted a couple of words to ensure that his email didn't include any geographic markers and then hit send.

Forty-five minutes later when John stepped into the lobby, he was wearing one of the two wool jackets that he had ordered from a tailor on Mulberry Street in Little Italy. The day was unlikely to include any meetings or other events where his appearance mattered. But becoming careless with his clothes would be a step in the wrong direction. It was evidence of a lack of self-respect—and who knew where that might end? Maybe he would look in the mirror one day and realize he looked like his coworkers at the police station—mustard stains on his trousers and faded polo shirts.

Rain pattered onto the roof above the entrance and there was a cold draft when the automatic doors slid open to let out a loud conference delegation. The bus waiting for them outside had its engine running. Diesel fumes wafted into reception, mixing with aftershave and the smell of fresh bacon.

John headed to breakfast. He filled his plate with protein in all its forms and complemented this with freshly pressed juice and black coffee. The last guest had left a newspaper on the table. John opened it and froze when he saw the headline on the inside page.

MISSING ACKWE DAUGHTER'S BODY FOUND—30-YEAR-OLD MAN REARRESTED

It was hardly a surprise to see the story. There was a limit to how long Primer and the police could keep Billy's arrest off the front pages. It still felt unpleasant. He looked around before turning to the relevant page—as if it were a secret document he was going to read, rather than the country's biggest paper.

The story was dominated by a photo of Emelie Bjurwall's face. She looked serious—as if she knew the article was about her own death. In the text, it said the cold cases team was in the process of finally solving the crime. The girl's parents and loved ones would at last have closure, and the perpetrator—as the reporter unhesitatingly chose to describe his brother, despite the lack of a conviction—would face punishment.

The newspaper had refrained from publishing the name, but it wouldn't be hard for readers in Värmland to figure out who the police had arrested. Everyone in the area knew that Billy Nerman had been the prime suspect ten years ago and that it was the lack of a body that had prevented charges being laid.

The article said nothing about Fredrik Adamsson or how the police had found out where the girl was buried. However, Bernt Primer was quoted several times and emerged as the hero who had steered this challenging investigation into port. John was grateful for that and hoped he could stay out of the eyes of the media in the future too. He had a strained relationship with the front pages of the papers. Each and every day he was scared that one of them might proclaim the truth about his two identities: *Swedish FBI agent investigated own brother suspected of AckWe murder in Värmland.*

The only thing he could do to minimize the risk of such a story was to limit the number of people who knew his true identity. Each name that got added to that list increased the likelihood of gossip spreading at the police station and then on to the newsrooms.

John's breakfast was disturbed by the driver outside revving the engine. All the conference delegates had gotten on the bus. From the table, he watched it pull away with a shudder from the hotel entrance, making way for another, rather smaller vehicle. It was a yellow minibus with the words *Ring and Ride* on the side. Thankfully this driver was considerate enough to turn off the engine to stop fumes from drifting into the hotel.

John looked around at the guests murmuring in the breakfast room. Several of them had copies of the newspaper open. The story about Emelie Bjurwall was front-page news and would remain so for several days. Readers would think they knew more about the case than they really did. They would gape, then chew and swallow the story of Billy Nerman as a selfish rapist and murderer without caring about any doubts or nuances. In the world of the newspapers, reality was black and white—the printing presses didn't deal in shades of gray.

From the entrance he heard a new racket. He turned his head and looked toward the minibus. A woman in a wheelchair was shouting at the driver, who was apparently using the ramp in a way she didn't appreciate.

John shook his head and shoveled scrambled eggs onto his fork. What was wrong with people—why couldn't they talk instead of shout? He pushed away the plate and continued reading.

"So this is where you're hiding away, you damn coward!"

The voice from the far side of the room cut through the air and all the guests turned around. The woman in the wheelchair had come into the dining room and stopped by the welcome desk. Her face was partially concealed by strands of dark brown hair. Her right arm had slipped off her knee and was hanging loosely toward the floor.

The guests curiously tried to locate who the malice was directed at. John froze when he realized it was him she was talking to. The glances from the couple next to him told their own story. The situation couldn't be rescued. He was naked in the spotlight and he had to say something.

"John! I'm talking to you! Surely you can look your mother in the eyes?"

He got up so quickly his chair tipped over. On his way between the tables, he happened to knock into a little girl balancing a bowl of cereal in her hand. The sound of the bowl crashing to the floor echoed through the room.

He was angry now—really angry.

Once he reached his mother, he turned her wheelchair around and wheeled her into the lobby. Both elevators were on the third floor, so instead of calling them he wheeled her on down the corridor toward the spa.

"What the hell are you up to?" he hissed, speeding up.

"John, I—"

"Quiet!"

A cleaner wearing the hotel's collarless gray uniform approached them pushing a cart. The corridor was too narrow for the two vehicles to pass so John opened the first door he could and pushed the chair inside.

It was a small changing room with ribbed wooden benches and two showers. The smell of chlorine and essential oils was very strong on the warm, moist air. His mother was breathing heavily as John shut the door. He sat down on one of the benches and turned the chair around so he could look his mother in the eye.

"Have you completely lost your mind? I thought I was more than clear when I explained my situation to you. Didn't you understand what I was saying? Do you think there's one single person out there who didn't hear you?"

He fell silent.

Her face had gone an angry shade of red and her eyes were wide open, as if they were about to pop out of her head. The sound of the subsequent coughing fit bounced off the walls of the white-tiled room. The wild ride had been too much for her lungs—smoked to pieces as they were. It was painful to see her gasping for breath, large globs of thick mucus dripping out of her drooping mouth.

John reached for a tissue from a dispenser on the wall and passed it to her. He wondered what on earth they did in Swedish rest homes. His mother's hair was white with dandruff and very greasy—it couldn't have been washed for weeks. Her light gray tracksuit bottoms were stained all over the thighs, offering a map of recent meals. At the same time, he instinctively understood that the nurses caring for her were picking their battles.

"Shame on you," she croaked, as she threw the mucky tissue to the floor. "Billy is your damn brother."

"Yes, he's my brother. My half brother," John replied.

"Half or whole, what the hell does it matter? He's your little brother and you have no idea what the poor kid has gone through. But it's just as I thought—you don't give a shit about him, just like you've never given a shit about us."

She was back there again, John thought to himself. Little Billy—so small and fragile and in need of protection at any cost, regardless of his behavior or the trouble he caused.

"I do give a shit about him," he sighed.

"You do? You promised to help. You sat by my bedside, held my hand, and promised he wouldn't have to go through this again."

"No, Mom. I didn't promise that."

"Yes, you did!" she screamed.

There was a rattling in her windpipe and she had to straighten up to take in more oxygen.

"I promised to make sure the investigation was done properly. That Billy would be treated fairly. But if he did it, then I have no intention . . ."

"So, you're happy now?" she interrupted him.

"What do you mean?"

"Well, you must be happy now that you've managed to dig up that shameless upper-class whore and make your own brother a candidate for murder."

She exaggerated her emphasis on the final words and stared at him, her mouth open.

John paused.

"How do you know it was me who found her?"

His mother snorted, so that saliva dripped from her lower lip, making her dry chin shiny.

"Because Billy called me after you'd been there. He was just crying. He didn't understand anything. Even though he's not heard a word from you all these years, he's always looked up to you and your father. And now that you've finally come back here, the first thing you do is knock his legs out from under him."

John felt the sweat dripping down his back. It wouldn't be long until his shirt was soaked through. It was as if the walls were closing in by the second, and even he was struggling to breathe in the moist warmth.

"Please, Mom. Don't you see why things have ended up the way they have?"

"What are you talking about?"

"Can't you see why Billy is where he is? Why everything has gone to hell?"

"Because you came home and made him a suspect again," she said, with what was probably the closest she could get to a grimace with her paralyzed face.

"This has nothing to do with me. It's about Billy . . . and you."

"About me?"

John saw his mother's eyes narrow. Maybe he ought to stop talking, but he couldn't.

"You're doing it again . . . over and over. And now you want me to do the same thing."

"Do what?"

"You're protecting him."

"He's my son!"

"But he's also a grown man who has to take responsibility for his actions. That rape that Billy was mixed up in . . ."

"Rape?" his mother hissed.

"Yes, the rape he was reported for, not long before Emelie Bjurwall disappeared."

"That wasn't rape—that girl had . . ."

"That girl was sleeping," John interrupted her. "And Billy had sex with her without her consent. It was rape and you damn well know it. But instead of letting him take responsibility, you told him to lie to the police and say that the girl had been up for it. And then you got his buddies to give false testimony. Isn't that what happened?"

"It's sad to see," his mother continued.

Her voice was calmer now, but full of disgust.

"What?"

"That you're the exact likeness of your father. A family has to stick together but neither of you seems to get that. So, it's just as well that you leave. Do what he did—to hell with all of it, just leave us here."

"You seem to have completely forgotten that it was you who got pregnant by another man."

His mother stared at him, her eyes red-rimmed. But before she had time to say anything, the door to the pool opened and a man in a bathrobe, fresh from his swim, stepped into the changing room.

"Occupied," John snapped, putting his hand against the man's hairy chest and forcing him back to the pool.

When he turned around, his mother looked away.

"Take me out of here," she said. "We're done."

John took hold of the wheelchair and pushed it into the corridor and toward the lobby. He collided with a fire cabinet, making his mother's right foot slip off its footrest and drag along the floor. He left that for the Ring and Ride crew to deal with. He didn't plan to spend a minute longer than necessary with this woman who—through one of the universe's worst flukes—happened to be his mother.

He continued toward the sliding doors by the entrance and waited while the ramp from the minibus was folded down. She slowly turned her face toward him again. The worst of the rage seemed to have dissipated.

"Have you thought about what'll happen to Nicole?"

John pictured the girl on the turquoise bike. His mother's words had touched a sore spot. He hadn't given much thought to his niece since he had hit the body in the ground with his shovel.

John lay on his bed on the third floor. He had been there for almost an hour. He knew that his mother was a world-class manipulator. It was masterful, playing on his conscience by bringing up the risk of an eight-year-old growing up with her father in prison.

John reminded himself that even if he felt genuinely sorry for the girl, it didn't matter. Or rather: he couldn't let it matter. It was that kind of sentimentality that had put him in this position in the first place.

He'd thought he had a debt to settle. That he owed Billy and their mother his help. But it was all bullshit. He was twelve years old when his father dragged him to New York. It hadn't been his decision—he didn't have to take responsibility for it.

His mother had expressly asked him to leave and that was his intention. She, Primer, Brodwick, and all the others trying to control his life could go to hell. He was going to create his own witness protection program. Head to Germany using Fredrik Adamsson's passport and then buy a new identity. Maybe go on to France. Or Italy. Europe was wide open for anyone with money and time—and he had an excess of both.

He got up and threw the black suitcase onto the bed. Hanging behind the sliding doors of the wardrobe were his neatly ironed shirts in a row. Sorted by color. White on the left, blue in the middle, and then other colors on the right.

He pulled the first one from its hanger and threw it into the bag. Then he continued with the next one. It felt good—a suitable ending to a trip that had been a mistake from the start.

With just a couple of shirts to go, his phone beeped. Annoyed, he pulled it out of his jacket pocket and saw there was a text message from Erina Kabashi. It was short and informative like last time. "Massage 11:30."

He left the remaining clothes and sat down on the edge of the bed. According to the time on his phone, that was in twenty minutes. A scene from *The Godfather Part III* sprang to mind. For some unfathomable reason, Trevor liked that one best when they'd binged the trilogy in the Baltimore safe house. Michael Corleone trying to escape his past and complaining: "Just when I thought I was out . . . they pull me back in." John remembered the eyes. They were filled with a darkness that only a young Pacino could deliver.

He rose to his feet and kicked the wardrobe with his black leather shoe, making the sliding doors rattle on their rails. With a final glance at the half-packed suitcase, he left the room and hurried down to the parking garage.

"No massage today?"

Erina Kabashi was alone in the room at Rat Chance Thai Massage. She was wearing the same kimono as last time.

"Gewalin is coming after our meeting is finished," she said. "But first you and I need to talk, and I would prefer not to be lying down this time."

John sat on the massage table and waited for her to get to the point. She had asked to meet him and he didn't want to seem too keen.

The lawyer stood in front of him.

"I was skeptical—I'll freely admit that."

"Skeptical about what?" he asked.

"Your long shot. It might seem risk-free to take a new DNA sample from my client and demand that it's compared with the semen found near Emelie's blood. A match doesn't really change anything—he's already tied to the scene. But you're forgetting the psychological impact. The defense risks looking desperate."

He hadn't thought about it like that, but she was right. A trial was about so much more than hard facts and evidence. The psychological dimension was at least as important in determining the outcome.

"But after thinking it over, I decided it was still worth a chance," she said, before falling silent—as if she wanted to keep him on tenterhooks.

"And?" said John.

Erina grinned from ear to ear.

"A conclusive result. It's not Billy's semen. Never was and never will be."

John struggled to believe what he had just heard. Even though he was the one who had suggested a new DNA test, he hadn't expected this.

"So, he was telling the truth?" he managed to say.

"It seems that way," she said. "At any rate, the police have absolutely no proof that Billy was ever near the girl."

"So, what happens now?"

"I'm going back to the police station to sign some papers. Then he's free to go."

Erina poured two glasses of cucumber water and handed one to John.

"Thanks for the idea. If it hadn't been for you, I'd probably still be trying to persuade your brother to change his story to a hand job in the woods."

"I take it that wasn't easy?"

John thought she sounded slightly more hoarse than usual when she laughed. She'd presumably been using her voice nonstop since the results had come back from the lab.

"I've never met a more pigheaded person in my life."

He thought about the suitcase on his hotel bed. It would be easier to keep packing after this news. His job in Sweden was done. Billy would be able to get on with his life, without the cloud of suspicion hanging over him. Just like John would get on with his own. Far away from internal investigations and impossible family relationships.

Erina interrupted his train of thought.

"The question is how on earth the samples got so messed up in the first place."

"Technical error?"

She shook her head.

"No, technical errors mean no results at all. For safety's sake, the lab has to rerun the comparison between Billy's old DNA sample and the semen on the rock—and there's still a one hundred percent match."

"So, the DNA sample labeled with Billy's name ten years ago belongs to someone else."

"Yes, and not just any old person. Right?"

"No, it is likely to belong to the perp."

"Exactly," said Erina. "How likely is it that the mix-up happened by mistake?"

There was an uncomfortable silence. The lawyer pulled the kimono tighter around herself, as though the chill they both felt at her rhetorical question was a real blast of cold air. Erina sat down next to him on the massage bench.

"I think that the real perp panicked when he gave a sample," she went on. "He realized he was going to be found out and wrote Billy's name down on the sample instead of his own."

"What you're saying presupposes two things," said John. "One: the perpetrator must've lived in the area or had been asked to give a sample for some other reason. Two: he must've had access to the samples."

Erina said nothing. She didn't have to. John saw she'd reached the same conclusion he had: everything suggested that the perpetrator worked somewhere in law enforcement. In other words, he was a police officer, prosecutor, lawyer, or lab employee in Linköping.

"There's a third thing you ought to add to that list," she said.

"You're thinking of the choice of Billy as a scapegoat?"

Erina nodded. She had clearly done her research on his brother and read the report from the closed investigation into what happened at the party a year or so before the disappearance of Emelie Bjurwall.

"He was never charged with the rape of that girl," she said. "So, the information isn't public. But you can get hold of it if you have access to the police computer system."

"So, when the perp needed a name to write on his own sample, he searched old investigations for suitable candidates," John added.

"Yes, and Billy was the perfect match. He lived in an area on Hammarö that the investigators had already decided to take samples from. All the perpetrator had to do was get hold of both samples and swap the labels."

There was a knock on the door and Gewalin's face appeared in the crack.

"Time for your massage," she said in her soft, accented English.

Erina looked at John apologetically.

"Sorry, but I need a good massage before I head back to the police station. It's going to be a long day—not that I'm not looking forward to it."

30

"It sounds completely unlikely to me."

Once again, Heimer heard the sharp edge to his wife's voice. It was the way she spoke to employees at AckWe when they provided unconvincing excuses for their failures.

"I know it must sound strange to you."

Primer's voice sounded slight and seemed to lack authority. The police detective was troubled by the conversation and for a good reason. The investigators had had all the evidence they needed to get a murder conviction against Billy Nerman. Yet they'd screwed it up and had to let him go again. There was apparently no limit to these people's incompetence.

Sissela seemed to feel the same way. She continued to push Primer, who seemed to shrink inch by inch behind the desk in his office at the police station.

"What happened to the strong forensic evidence you told us about?" she said.

"It no longer holds up."

"What does that mean?"

"It means it no longer holds up."

Heimer did his best to contain his anger. But Primer's robotic manner was galling. It sounded as if the bastard was reading from an internal teleprompter.

"Yes, that much I gather," Sissela said. "But what happened to it?"

"I'm afraid I can't go into details about that for investigative reasons."

She fixed her gaze on him and lowered her voice.

"Are you seriously going to take that line? We're Emelie's parents and we're entitled to know what's happening."

Primer looked unhappy and shrank a little more in his office chair. He had slipped so far forward on the seat that he would soon fall off it.

"I don't want to seem unnecessarily formal, and as next-of-kin you have every right to be frustrated. But at the moment, I can't tell you any more than I already have."

"Then I'll have to speak to the commissioner of county police," she said.

"That's your prerogative. But I should tell you that he's the one who made the decision."

Sissela didn't seem to have been prepared for Primer's reply and for a moment she lost her thread. The policeman appeared to regain some of his authority for a moment. He adjusted his position on the chair and pulled it closer to the desk. Heimer looked at him and felt disgust. The man was as mediocre as the office he was sitting in, from the yucca plant in the corner to the IKEA storage units.

"I understand if you—" Primer continued.

"What is it you understand?" Heimer interrupted him. "What it feels like to have a bunch of amateurs investigating your daughter's murder?"

Sissela gave him a look that was unmistakable in meaning. She thought he'd crossed a line. Heimer didn't.

"You mess up the whole investigation, and then you won't even tell us what's happened. Fucking hell, it's a disgrace."

"Like I said, preliminary investigations are confidential. And I would appreciate it if you calmed down."

"You want me to calm down?"

Primer held out his arms to indicate there was nothing he could do. The decision to keep things under wraps wasn't his.

"I understand if you—" he began.

He didn't get any further before Heimer smashed the wall with his fist so hard that his knuckles sank into the plasterboard.

"If you say 'I understand' one more time, I'll smash up your whole damn office."

Sissela was implacable when, after a few brief apologies, she led him out of Primer's office. Heimer regretted his outburst even before the elevator had made it to the ground floor of the police station, and he knew it was the prelude to a long conversation.

One step forward, two steps back.

He had to learn to control his emotions. What was inside him belonged only to him. It couldn't influence how he acted out in the world.

31

Just like last time, John parked a few hundred meters from his childhood home so as not to draw unnecessary attention. He had spent the whole afternoon weighing whether to say goodbye to his brother or not.

He decided the risk was acceptable. The Chrysler was already packed and if he took a ferry down to the continent tonight, it wouldn't matter if someone connected it with a visit to Billy Nerman. He'd sell the car for cash in Germany and all traces of Fredrik Adamsson and John Adderley would vanish when he bought his new identity.

What had made him hesitate was more to do with the emotional aspects. John wasn't sure whether he wanted to see his brother one last time. The visit might unleash a lot of emotions that he had neither the time nor inclination to deal with. Better to let the story end here. That way, he could at least pretend that Billy was living his life happily, now that all suspicions against him had disappeared.

Nevertheless, he walked up the gravel road toward Nerman's Autos. It was dusk and John felt his father's sermons resounding in his ears. *"There's nothing more important than family, John. When all is said and done, that's all we have."* That was what he'd said at the kitchen table in their apartment on the Lower East Side, with the poorly concealed expectation that his son would give him a grandchild or two. It hadn't worked out like that. Instead, the old man's words had driven him back here—to his childhood home.

John was aware that his father didn't include either Billy or his mother in the concept of family. That branch of the family tree had been chopped off with an axe the moment they stepped on the plane to New York. But it was different for John. It didn't matter how many times he tried to erase his Swedish family from his consciousness. They would always be there, a pang of bad conscience. And leaving the country without saying goodbye was the coward's way out.

John stood outside the front door. He rang the doorbell but no one came to open it. The bell had been broken back when they were kids, and it seemed Billy hadn't gotten around out to fixing it. Maybe not many guests came to visit.

John knocked on the door a few times. Now there was some movement inside. He heard a chair being pushed back, scraping the floor—and then footsteps approaching. Billy's face lit up when he opened the door, and he gave John one of his bear hugs.

"I was just wondering if you were going to turn up. Come on in! We're celebrating. There's cake and everything."

He let go of John and showed him into the kitchen. John had to make an effort not to brush away the dirt he imagined his brother's hands had left on his jacket.

The kitchen looked just as John remembered it from childhood. The walls were still covered with that white wallpaper with thin blue stripes and a border of flowers. On the gateleg table that his father had won at an auction, there were party provisions: a cake, whiskey, a wine box, and a bottle of pear juice.

"Didn't I tell you to leave?"

His mother spoke harshly, huddled in her wheelchair at the far end of the table. She gave him a hostile look as she washed down her cake with a large mouthful of red wine. John ignored her and fixed his gaze on the girl sitting on the bench. Her ears were concealed by a pair of red headphones with a sticker on one ear. It had half peeled away and depicted a snowman in a cartoon winter landscape. She'd looked up from her tablet when he came in, but then became engrossed in her screen again.

"Nicole," his brother said loudly and clearly, to make sure she heard him through the noise of the game or movie.

The girl removed her headphones.

"Go up to your room. You can take your snack with you."

She balanced the plate of cake in one hand and glass of juice in the other as she walked through the kitchen and into the hall, the tablet tucked into the waist of her trousers. Billy waited until he heard her steps on the stairs and a door being shut upstairs before he said anything.

"Mom—I haven't told you yet."

"Told me what?" she hissed.

"I know you're angry with him, but it was John who got me out. He arranged for the lawyer and suggested a new DNA test. Without him, I'd still be locked up."

"It was because of him you ended up there," she muttered.

"Yeah, but for ten years everyone in town thought I killed that girl. Now everyone knows it was someone else—and it's all thanks to my brother."

"Is this true?" she said to John. "Were you responsible for the new test?"

John could hear that she was slowly thawing. It would probably take a while, given the permafrost that had characterized their encounter at the hotel.

"It was technically the lawyer who requested the DNA test," he said. "But it was my idea."

"Jesus—you're not as dumb as I thought," she said, taking a fresh gulp of her wine. This reminded Billy that his own glass was empty and that John didn't have a drink. He got up, rinsed a glass in the sink, and put it on the table.

"You like Jack Daniels, right?" he said, pouring at least three fingers for each of them.

John nodded and didn't have the heart to say that all he had drunk for years were Scottish single malts. It was a habit that had come with the money left by his father.

"You should have seen Primer's face when he had to let me go . . ."

Billy laughed and managed to breathe in the smell of the whiskey so heavily he began to cough.

"Oh wow," he said. "I must've been inside so long I can't handle hard liquor."

"You'll get used to it," John said, raising his glass.

Billy reached across the table and the brothers were united in a toast.

"There's one thing I did think of while I was stewing in my cell thinking about how much I wanted to beat the shit out of you," he said. "How did you know where to look for the girl? I assume you didn't just grab a shovel and take your chances?"

"A cell phone," John replied cryptically.

When both Billy and his mother looked at him blankly, he explained how his inquiries had led to him finding the body close to the old dump next to Hallerudsleden.

"Not many people go walking around there," Billy said.

John readied himself for an onslaught of questions about where the investigation would go and whether the police had any new suspects. But to his surprise there were none. Tonight, his brother seemed happy with his company and the warmth of the contents of his glass.

"Can you call Ring and Ride, Billy?"

John glanced at their mother. She looked pale. Her cheeks, which had been blooming red, seemed to have lost their color.

"Don't you feel well, Mom?" said Billy, who had also noticed the change.

"Nothing to worry about, I'm just a bit tired."

She smiled briefly, revealing a mouth in urgent need of dental work. Some of the teeth on her lower jaw were so worn down and discolored from cigarettes that they looked like small, dirty yellow stones sticking out of her gums.

Billy ordered the minibus. Then he went into the hall and shouted upstairs.

"Nicole, come down and say goodbye to Grandma."

John got up and went over to him.

"She can't find out who I am," he said in a low voice.

Billy smiled at him, happy that the brothers were once again sharing a secret.

"Don't worry. I'll just say you're an old friend from back in the day who's moved back."

He took a few steps up, stumbled, and had to grab the bannister to avoid falling over.

"Come down now," he bellowed upstairs.

A door opened and soon the girl appeared, sauntering along with her eyes on the tablet—headphones still attached to her ears like a protective membrane against the world. She had long since outgrown her t-shirt and her black trouser bottoms were covered in jam from the cake.

"Billy, I need to go to the bathroom before I leave. If I wet myself again they've said they'll stop taking me."

Their mother had rolled into the hall and was using her functioning arm to point between her legs. She had propped the wine box in between her thighs—she apparently intended to smuggle it into Gunnarskärsgården. Billy accompanied the intoxicated woman into the bathroom. John didn't envy his brother, who would have to lift her out of her wheelchair onto the toilet and then back again once she had emptied her bladder.

Nicole walked past him into the kitchen. She took a spoon from a drawer and shoveled what was left of the cake right off the plate into her mouth. John stifled the impulse to stop her. It wasn't his job.

When their mother returned to the kitchen after her visit to the bathroom, the girl took off her headphones and stood up. She went up to the wheelchair and leaned forward to hug her grandmother. John saw her shudder when her cheek touched the slack skin. The smell of her grandmother's body must have stung her nose.

"Grandma's sweetheart," said the woman, digging in a pocket with her good hand. She found a two hundred kronor note, which she handed to the girl.

"What do you say?" Billy encouraged from the doorway leading into the hall.

"Thank you," Nicole said quietly, returning to the table and her headphones.

Fifteen minutes later, the minibus pulled up outside. John moved instinctively away from the window into the living room to avoid being seen. It seemed to take Billy and the driver a while to get the wheelchair up the ramp and into the minibus. Eventually, John heard the rear doors close and the gravel crunch under the tires as it left.

He went back into the kitchen and saw the whiskey glasses had been filled again.

"You'll stay to watch the match, won't you?" said his brother, draining his in one go.

It was still the same sofa that he and Billy had sat on so many times in childhood. The screen, on the other hand, had grown in comparison with the square brown box that had provided their entertainment back then. The TV screen was at least fifty inches and was showing the American football field and all its white lines in the highest possible resolution—every blade of grass was visible.

"Jesus Christ! Not Latimer! Why are they bringing on that meathead?!" Billy shouted, spreading out his arms.

The New York Giants were losing against the San Francisco 49ers—and John decided he shouldn't delay his departure any longer. Given the speed with which the whiskey had gone down his brother's throat, very soon it wouldn't be possible to talk to him at all. But it didn't feel right to raise the subject. This was clearly Billy's idea of a reunion of brothers and he would probably be upset by John's plans to leave Karlstad tonight.

"How wide can he go?" Billy complained in response to a failed attempt at a field goal. "I don't know what's up with the Giants this year. It's like they don't want to win."

"Do you watch all the games?" said John.

Billy grinned proudly and pointed at a blue-and-white cap on top of the bookcase.

"Haven't missed one in years. I really went nuts for the Giants after you and Dad left."

John thought it was strange that his brother still referred to the man who had left him and never got in touch again as Dad. Billy hadn't asked one single question about the old man and presumably didn't even know he was dead.

On the field, the Giants had finally managed to secure the ball again and launched a decent drive with only twenty yards to go.

"She's not got much going for her nowadays," said Billy.

"Mom, you mean?" said John, wondering where the conversation was going.

"Yes, of course. You should have seen the lady in her prime. There were men left, right, and center falling all over her after you left. She was the belle of Värmland."

Billy explained that he had stopped sleeping in his own room and moved into their mother's double bed after the separation. One night he had woken because there was an unfamiliar naked man moving next to him. Billy had lain still and pulled the duvet over his ears in an attempt to shut out the bastard's groaning and his mother's hushing.

The morning after, their mother had left for work but the man had stayed in bed, snoring. Billy had been so scared he had crept out, locked the bedroom from outside, and gone to school. It had ended with the man kicking the door to pieces when he woke up and realized he was locked in an empty house. Their mother was angry and had stopped his pocket money until the carpenter was paid off.

Billy laughed and filled their glasses again with what remained in the bottle. He didn't seem to be looking for John's sympathy—he just considered the story to be a comic childhood incident.

While Billy had been in high school, their mother crashed badly and had been admitted to a psychiatric ward for a few months. After that she changed. She quit the hard liquor and stuck to wine. The men stopped turning up and at times she even painted.

"Do you know who your biological father is?" John asked.

"No, Mom's never wanted to say. But I guess he was one of Dad's friends. She always did like exotic guys."

Billy got up from the sofa so quickly that the whiskey splashed over the edge of his glass and began to run down the outside.

"Now we're talking!"

He turned up the volume on the TV, filling the living room with the racket from the Giants' home crowd. They had come to life, hoping the game might be turned around. At that moment, Nicole stuck her head around the door.

"Dad, I'm hungry."

"There's some fish fingers," he said. "Do you want to bring the plate in here and sit with us?"

The girl shook her head.

"It's too loud. I can hear it," she said, pointing at her headphones, which were at that moment hanging around her neck.

She had turned around to leave when Billy called out to her again.

"Haven't you forgotten something, Nicole?"

She went over to the sofa, took the two hundred kronor note from her pocket, and put it on the table in front of him.

"Sorry."

"It's okay, darling. I'm sorry it has to be like this. But living in this house costs money."

"I know, Dad."

The girl vanished into the kitchen and the money disappeared into Billy's jeans pocket. Then he turned his attention back to the TV and what little whiskey there was left in his glass. He licked the rim to avoid missing any drops that had spilled over.

John thought about the millions in his own bank account and how they'd ended up there. He wanted to help his brother financially, but it had to be done in a way that couldn't be traced back to him or wrongly interpreted. Billy was broke enough to take small change from his own daughter, but also proud enough to turn down charity from his brother.

"Do you think she's fat?" Billy said, his eyes fixed on the game.

John was surprised by the about-face.

"Nicole? No, definitely not. What do you mean?"

"She's a bit plump, but that's just how she is. I just don't want them to bully her for that too."

"Are they mean to her at school?"

"Hmm, well, I think she finds it tough sometimes. Hardly surprising, given who her dad is. But she doesn't want to talk about it and I'm not really the kind of guy to get involved either."

John felt sad and angry all at once. The false accusations that had ruined Billy's and their mother's lives were harming the next generation too. The misery he saw everywhere in this house all stemmed from one thing: an unknown perpetrator had picked his brother as a scapegoat in order to get away himself.

For Nicole, it wouldn't help that her father was no longer suspected of rape and murder. Her classmates had already heard how their parents talked. They had learned that Nicole Nerman was a lesser person. You weren't to go back to her house to play after school.

Billy tried to refill his glass and looked at the bottle in disappointment when all that came out were a few solitary amber drops. He went into the kitchen and returned with two bottles of Budweiser and a bottle opener.

"Did I miss anything?" he said, slurring his words.

"The 49ers fumbled."

Billy's face lit up. He turned the volume up a bit more before sitting down on the sofa. Or flopping onto it. The springs under the cushions creaked under the weight of his clumsy movements. His eyes were clouded and John could see that his brother was struggling to keep up with the game. The curses and celebratory cries no longer correlated with what was happening on the field.

John went to the bathroom for a piss and when he returned Billy had drifted off. He had his head resting on the arm of the sofa. He was covered with a brown duvet with feathers coming out of a hole in it. Nicole had come out of the kitchen and was sitting next to him, still staring at her tablet. She must have been the one who turned off the TV and put the duvet over him.

John remained standing in the doorway looking at her without her seeing him. The girl wasn't very old. It was really Billy who ought to be putting her to bed, not vice versa.

He cleared his throat loudly enough for her to hear it through her headphones. She jumped and looked up from her tablet.

"I thought you'd left," she said, taking her headphones off.

"Sorry if I scared you," he said. "I was just in the bathroom."

He sat down in the armchair next to the sofa and smiled at her.

"I think you should probably go to bed and sleep as well," he said.

Billy turned on the sofa and grunted a few times. Then his breathing became more regular again and the blanket rose and fell in time with his loud snores.

John touched his shoulder and shook him gently.

"Billy, you need to wake up."

The girl looked at the visitor and almost imperceptibly shook her head.

"He won't wake up now," she said.

There was a part of John who wanted to hug her. Put down the screen and whisper that another life was possible. Later on. When she got older and could make her own decisions. But it wasn't up to him to look after Nicole. The girl was fragile and he didn't know what her reaction would be.

"I have to go now," he said, and she nodded in return.

During the short walk to the car, he felt the anger return. Someone was responsible for this—and the fact that the bastard might be a police officer didn't improve matters. Was he really going to get in the car? Enter Berlin into the GPS and never look back?

He kicked a pebble across the gravel and heard it bounce into the shallow ditch, startling an animal in the darkness. Whatever decision he made would be the wrong one. If he just left, the image of Nicole on the brown cord sofa with her sleeping father next to her would haunt him for all eternity. They both had a right to find out who had done this to them. But if John stayed in Karlstad, his own life would have to take a back seat again—and that wasn't part of the plan.

In short: he needed time to think.

The cloying taste of the whiskey grew acrid in his mouth and he regretted letting Billy refill his glass. He was tired and frankly too drunk to drive the Chrysler. But that was exactly what he was going to do. Not south on the highway, though—back to the hotel instead. With a little luck, his old room would still be available.

32

Heimer really had no desire to eat at AckWe. But he would sometimes meet Sissela there at lunchtime, and after what had happened at the police station he didn't want to say no. The skin on his knuckles was still sore and hadn't healed completely after the assault on Primer's plasterboard wall.

He knew that his wife took pride in eating in the staff canteen together with everyone else at the corporate office. She loved to talk in the business press about how she always made sure at least once a week to take her tray and ask to sit at one of the tables. The routine presumably scared the living daylights out of the employees, who might at any given moment have the top boss appearing unannounced at their lunch table.

The canteen was on the ground floor of the headquarters that Allan Bjurwall had commissioned in the mid-seventies next to the old factory. Heimer struggled to find redeeming features in his father-in-law, but he had to admit that he'd dared to carve out his own path. All of the major architectural firms of the time had submitted proposals for the new office—but Allan had selected an unknown agency from Oslo. The Norwegians had designed a five-story building whose whole façade was covered in weathering steel—long before the rust-colored surface came into fashion. It was an inspired choice that created a design rapport between the brick-built factory and the new rusty-looking office.

Sissela walked ahead of him with her tray through the minimalist canteen, photos from AckWe fashion shoots adorning its walls. Eventually, she found a table with a view of the lawn by the parking area.

"Hope I didn't ruin your plans for today," she said, sniffing the chicken curry casserole appreciatively.

"Definitely not," said Heimer, thinking about the run he had been planning to do before lunch. Now he would have to digest the food and wouldn't be able to head out until two at the earliest. But it was worth it. Sissela was in a good mood, which was a rarity in recent times, when their conversations had mostly covered his lack of impulse control.

Heimer looked at the line of diners. A familiar face was paying the cashier before heading for his table. It was Hugo Aglin—the director of finance.

"Heimer, old boy. It's been a while," he said, standing by the table.

"Yes, I suppose I last saw you in Majorca."

"That must be right. The tan is all gone by now, sadly."

"You had time to sunbathe?" said Sissela. 'The program must not have been busy enough."

Hugo laughed and asked whether he could join them.

"Have a seat," Heimer said, pulling out one of the empty chairs.

They were still talking about the retreat when Sissela's phone rang. She got up and took the call over in the lounge area. After a minute or so, she returned with her hand over the microphone.

"I'm so sorry, but something has come up. You stay here, guys, and finish your lunch in peace."

Heimer received a kiss on the cheek before she vanished upstairs with the phone glued to her ear. He was actually relieved she'd left them. With Sissela at the table, conversation almost always shifted to the company. When she left, it was easier to talk about other, more stimulating subjects. Hugo was knowledgeable about both wine and architecture, but this time the finance director changed the topic to Emelie and the impending funeral. This wasn't especially strange. He and Hugo often discussed serious things at the dinners that were part of life at AckWe—without being particularly in each other's confidences.

"It must open up a lot of wounds to have to go through all this again," he said. "But don't let it ruin what you and Sissela have built. What's happened has happened and you can never do anything about that, can you? But the stuff that's ahead you can influence—and that's what you have to focus on."

Heimer's first thought was that this must've come from a self-help book Hugo once read. But then he realized where the line of argument was coming from. He recognized the reasoning. The encouragement to move on. To not get stuck in the past. To look forward, not back.

It was his wife's doing.

It was no coincidence that Hugo sat down at their table and that Sissela left shortly afterward. Her colleague was supposed to do what she had failed to do herself—get him under control.

He couldn't really blame her. After all, he'd smashed up a plasterboard wall at the police station. But still. It felt humiliating to be treated like a child being made to see reason. The fact that it was Hugo who'd been given this assignment made it even worse. He was the only one of Sissela's colleagues who seemed to respect Heimer on his own merits—not because he was married to the boss.

Heimer wanted to storm out of the canteen. But causing another scene—and in such a public place—wouldn't go down well with Sissela. So, he took a deep breath and made an effort to control his voice.

"I see she's asked you to talk to me," he said.

Hugo looked unhappy. He adjusted his black-rimmed glasses that had slipped down his nose slightly.

"Sorry, I'm not quite with you . . ."

Heimer continued staring at him. The director of finance fiddled with the cutlery. He was no poker player. If Heimer exploited the silence for his own ends, the truth would soon come tumbling out.

"She means no harm," Hugo said at last. "Sissela's worried about you . . ."

Heimer remained silent and looked at the man's mouth. A red tinge was spreading surprisingly quickly from his throat and cheeks up to his ears and brow. Hugo Aglin was blushing. The director of finance, who looked after billions of kronor, looked like a schoolboy caught cheating on a test.

"I was there when it happened, and I remember how you were in the years after. Sissela says you were sometimes still in bed when she got home from work. It hit her hard too. She doesn't want you to end up in the same place—nor do I, for that matter."

There was a sincerity in his voice. As if Hugo really did care about him and wasn't just acting as Sissela's errand boy.

"I lost my wife many years ago, as you know," he added. "It's not the same as what you've gone through, but eventually I got so sick of the anger and grief that I just decided to start living again. It wasn't easy but it worked."

Hugo dared to meet Heimer's gaze again.

"So don't let your life fall apart again. If not for Sissela's sake, then for your own and Emelie's."

Heimer nodded slowly. There was nothing he could do except play along. Hugo probably had the best intentions, but he would never understand.

"Thanks for sharing," Heimer said. "I really appreciate it. But you don't need to worry. I've grieved for my daughter and come out the other side. Nothing that's happening now changes that."

Hugo looked relieved and for a brief moment Heimer was afraid he'd get up and try to embrace him.

"If you want, Sissela never needs to know that you saw through our little arrangement," said Hugo. "I'm guessing you need some peace and quiet at home."

"Thanks, I appreciate that."

Hugo Aglin's phone buzzed.

"I need to take this," he said, looking slightly guilty for interrupting the moment.

Hugo left the table and hurried up the stairs toward the offices. On the way up he almost collided with someone coming in the opposite direction—a man whose face was so grim that Heimer didn't recognize it at first. Not until the man had made it almost all the way to the front door did Heimer see that it was Volker, head of the German office. Sissela must've wielded the axe and notified him that his services were no longer required.

The German stopped mid-stride and looked toward the tables in the canteen. Most people were staring down at their plates, reluctant to meet the gaze of someone with eyes that bleak. Then he caught sight of Heimer and seemed to hesitate about whether to continue into the parking area or to approach the man whose wife had just fired him. He opted for the latter. The sound of the soles on his leather shoes on the stone floor was amplified by his deliberately heavy paces. The man walked like a German general refusing to admit defeat.

Heimer wiped his mouth with a napkin and prepared for the worst. When Volker reached the table, he leaned on it with his hands and looked at him. He spoke quietly in Swedish with a German accent.

"That man you just had lunch with. Hugo Aglin. He's sleeping with your wife. And the whole damn company knows about it."

Then he turned on his heel and marched out of the rust-brown corporate headquarters.

33

John attached the visitor's badge to his jacket and sat down at one of the tables to wait. It was strange to be back at the police station and forced to sign the register. He vaguely recognized some of the faces of those using the staff entrance behind the information desk. Most were heading out and John knew why. It was lunchtime, and if there was anything that got police officers moving, it was the prospect of food.

There was something that felt fated about the fact that Primer had called him this morning. If John had followed through on his plan to leave the country last night, his work phone would've been in a ditch somewhere next to the E18 highway by now. And John would be on the autobahn, halfway to the German capital.

But it hadn't ended up like that. Instead, he was in reception at the police station going over his strategy ahead of the meeting he'd been summoned to.

If Primer wanted to initiate an internal investigation, John would play along and not protest any more than he had to. Then he'd have no choice but to leave the country as soon as possible and vanish on the continent.

But if things went the way he expected—that he would be asked to resign and discreetly leave the police force—then he'd take the risk of staying in Karlstad a little longer. His visit to Billy had moved him deeply. Regardless of whether he was on the police force or not, he intended to find out who murdered Emelie Bjurwall and ruined the lives of his brother and niece. He'd made up his mind by the time Primer had ended the call.

An initial step in reconciling himself with the thought of remaining in Karlstad had been to start looking for an apartment that morning. There were several listed for sublet on the website he checked. He created an email account in Fredrik Adamsson's name and sent around ten inquiries.

The first reply arrived just a few minutes later from a woman who had moved to Marseille. She was going to stay there indefinitely and wanted to rent out her one-bedroom apartment right away.

The advertisement hadn't included photos, and the rent was absurdly high. But after the incident with his mother at breakfast, he didn't want to stay on at the hotel. The woman offered to let him view the apartment immediately. There were no keys—she emailed him the address and a temporary code to unlock the door.

The building was in the Bryggudden neighborhood, just a stone's throw from the pub where he had written his first email to Trevor. The dark brick building was right by the water and soared into the sky as if it belonged in a bigger city. Värmland's Empire State Building, John had thought to himself as he took the elevator up to the twenty-first floor.

His jaw had dropped when he opened the door.

The apartment was no apartment.

It was one single room.

A large area of more than two-hundred-square meters with gigantic floor-to-ceiling windows with panoramic views in all four directions. As soon as he stepped across the threshold, he'd noticed the faint smell of turpentine. It was coming from one of the balled-up rags lying on the floor next to an easel with a half-finished oil painting on it. It was as if the artist had gotten bored mid-brush-stroke and taken the first flight to France.

A carelessly made-up double bed with bloodred sheets was positioned in the middle of the room under one of the skylights. The rest of the furniture could be counted on the fingers of one hand: a dark brown Chesterfield sofa, cracking at the seams, a kitchen table made from raw pine, and three old fruit crates to sit on.

John thought of his mother. As a child, he'd heard her dreaming of the day she would get her own studio. When she'd finally have time for painting and not have to be disturbed by her husband or her rowdy boys. She'd had sorrow in her voice when she spoke about it, as if she'd known that she would probably have drunk herself to death in that studio if she'd ever gotten the chance.

He had emailed the landlady to say he was interested. But he couldn't confirm he wanted the apartment for sure until later that day. Everything depended on what Primer did.

John looked at the time. There were still twelve minutes until the appointment. The door behind the reception desk opened and two men emerged from the staff area. Ulf Törner headed into the parking area without saying anything, but Ruben Jonsson came up to him for a chat.

"How's your brother?" he said, once he'd checked that no one could over-hear them.

John couldn't tell whether the question was meant seriously or whether he simply wanted to remind him that he'd uncovered the truth.

"I don't know, but I'm guessing better than he's been for a long time."

"I understand. And how about you?"

"I'm not really sure," said John. "It depends on what happens in this meeting with Primer."

"Oh, Jesus—are you meeting him now?" said Ruben, sitting down at the table.

"Yes. Have you heard what he's going to do?"

His colleague shook his head.

"He hasn't said anything about anything. It's been chaos here since your brother was released. We don't even know why Billy was ruled out as a suspect. Just that the forensic evidence no longer held up—whatever that means. Maybe you know?"

Now it was John's turn to shake his head.

"I'm completely out of the loop."

"And Erina Kabashi hasn't said anything?"

The question was posed innocently, almost in passing.

"Billy's lawyer? She doesn't even know who I am."

"No?" Ruben said thoughtfully. "I wouldn't be so sure of that if I were you. That woman is remarkably well-informed. I still don't know how she managed to turn up at the police station so soon after the arrest."

John knew better than to continue the conversation in the direction Ruben was heading. If he wanted to know something, he'd have to ask a direct question rather than drop hints.

"How's Ulf?" John said, changing the subject.

"Oh, you know, busy with everything except police work. He's still pissed off with you about the coffee mugs."

"Does he know?"

"That you chucked them in the trash? Absolutely—everyone in the building knows. The caretaker found them. You've got us split into two camps: a few who like the rebel, and the rest who think you're an all-around asshole."

John looked sternly at him.

"I meant whether he knows why I'm not at work."

"Like I said, Primer is keeping everyone in the dark and I've no reason to talk more than necessary. Ulf doesn't know why you were taken off the case—and it's bothering him almost as much as your protest against the kitchen chore schedule."

The conversation ended abruptly when the woman at the reception desk came up to them. She escorted John to a conference room on the management corridor on the second floor. "Just come in," called an unfamiliar voice after she knocked on the door.

John realized the rumbling baritone belonged to the commissioner of county police. The man looked like a bloated walrus standing next to Primer, whose usually imposing body shrank into insignificance. The third person in the room was somewhat trimmer and it was her presence that made John hopeful.

Mona Ejdewik.

The fact that his contact from the National Criminal Police unit was there meant that the issue of an internal investigation had gone beyond Värmland to higher powers—just as he'd expected.

The Walrus asked him to sit at the table and waited until the receptionist closed the door.

"First and foremost, I want to make it clear that what we say has to stay within these walls. Any problems with that?"

John shook his head. That was the thing he wanted—to keep the number of people who knew who he actually was to a minimum.

"In that case, I'd like to start with your incredibly poor judgment," he said. "You investigated a serious crime without informing your boss that the prime suspect was a close relative. It's against the law—and it's something that makes me damned angry."

The man paused to take a sip of mineral water from the glass on the table in front of him. His belly was straining against his white uniform shirt and small beads of sweat were visible on his forehead.

"I understand . . ." John began, but he stopped when the commissioner held up a hand.

"I'm not finished yet," he said sharply, wiping his face with his shirt sleeve. "You deserve to lose your job and face a corruption charge—that's my honest view and I want you to know it."

He let the words linger for long enough for them to be followed by a *but*. However, John had no intention of saying anything aloud. He'd already interrupted the Walrus once and had no intention of doing so a second time.

"But . . ." said the commissioner, taking another sip of mineral water.

John clenched his fist in his pocket. Maybe everything was going to be okay.

". . . there are arguments for taking another view. Mona Ejdewik has reminded us that there's a threat against you. Precisely what that consists of is only known to you and your protectors at the FBI. However, she's convinced me that we must try to keep your identity secret. If nothing else, the Americans would be furious if we sold you out—and we can't have that, can we?"

John threw a grateful look at Mona. Until now, she hadn't said anything during the meeting—but it seemed she'd been involved during the preparation. He guessed that Brodwick had put a lot of pressure on her bosses from across the Atlantic.

"The question remains of what we should do with you," the commissioner continued. "I can't sack you for gross misconduct without launching an internal investigation. And that would inevitably lead to charges, which would mean your identity would be disclosed. So as far as I'm concerned, it would be easiest if you resigned of your own accord. Are you willing to do so?"

"Yes, I am," John said without hesitation.

"Good, because you'll have to do that if you break the rules again."

John tried to take in what he had just heard. *Again*? Was it wishful thinking, or had he just been given a second chance? He looked at Mona but received no help in interpreting the situation. Her face was as expressionless as when he'd entered the room.

"We've decided to let you keep your job," said Primer, in an attempt to sound as if he'd been involved in the decision, when it was clear to everyone around the table that he hadn't been.

"I assume I should thank you at this point," he said.

The commissioner looked him in the eye.

"No, this is the point where you fall to the floor, kiss our boots, and promise never to cause us any trouble again. Understood?"

"Understood."

He couldn't help liking the Walrus. Underneath, he was refreshingly un-Swedish.

"What exactly do you want me to work on?" he said.

"You're going to work together with Mona to find out who killed Emelie Bjurwall."

John couldn't hide his surprise. This conversation kept getting stranger. He'd been expecting to lose his job—not to be put back on the investigation he'd originally been thrown off.

"I can see you wondering whether we've all lost our minds," said the commissioner. "I can understand that. When Mona first suggested it, I thought it was the stupidest thing I'd heard in my forty-year career—and that's putting it mildly."

John wanted to ask what had made him change his mind, but by now he'd grown accustomed to the commissioner's dramatic pauses. This man delivered more cliff-hangers than a series on HBO.

"None of us knows what you worked on in the States," he said. "But I'm guessing you were involved in investigations on a completely different level to what we do in this place. Those are skills we could use."

John looked at Primer and tried to determine what he thought about the turn the meeting had taken. It wasn't a wild guess to suspect he felt left out, in between his boss and the woman from Stockholm.

"Who else is going to work on the investigation?" John asked in an attempt to understand how the previous team fit into the picture.

"Initially, no one. It'll just be you two."

The commissioner pushed his chair back and got up. The parquet flooring creaked under his feet as he laboriously moved around the table to stand at the end.

"It's at this point the conversation becomes extra sensitive, and I need to remind you of its confidentiality. Information has emerged in this investigation that is extremely troubling to us institutionally," he said.

John realized they'd reached the point of the meeting where he had to use his acting talents. They couldn't find out that he already knew what happened to Billy's DNA samples. When the Walrus wrapped up his account, John did his best to look surprised.

"So you mean the perp is with the police?" he said.

"Not necessarily. But at the very least he must've had some insight into the investigation and access to the DNA samples. That's why we've brought Mona in to head up the investigation. She's an outsider, just like you, and we don't want to risk the esprit de corps mucking things up for us."

"The investigation will still be led by county CID, but with me on loan," Mona clarified, in the same formal voice she had used at their first meeting in the hotel.

The commissioner waddled back toward his chair, but on the way, he stopped behind Primer and put his big hands on his shoulders.

"Bernt will help arrange what you need to get started, won't you?"

"Absolutely," Primer said with forced enthusiasm.

Just a few days ago he'd been depicted in the newspapers as the man who had solved the AckWe case. Now he was downgraded to administrative assistant to his former subordinate and a bigwig from Stockholm—and a woman at that.

The Walrus sat down again and drank what remained of the mineral water from the bottle.

"You're lucky that I'm retiring next year and don't have a career to protect," he said, pointedly addressing John. "If I did, this meeting might've ended differently. But now all I care about is finding the rotten egg that killed Emelie Bjurwall and my big fat gut says you're our best chance."

After the meeting, Mona was waiting in the corridor. She pulled John into the nearest room with a closable door, which turned out to be a small space for confidential phone calls.

"What the hell happened?" she said.

The balanced facial expression she'd maintained during the meeting was replaced by bitter anger that made her eyebrows angle down toward her nose and the skin around her eyes wrinkle.

"I'm not sure I understand the question."

She pushed him down onto the one chair there was and stood in front of him with her arms crossed.

"When you go into witness protection and you're given a new identity, you have to cut all ties to your former life," she said with exaggerated slowness—as if she were giving a lecture in the first week at the police academy. "But you moved to the same town as your mother and brother, and—to cross the t and dot the i in idiot—you got a job investigating a crime for which your brother was the prime suspect. How can I guarantee your safety in those circumstances? You and the FBI must both have been out of your minds to approve Karlstad. So, my question again. What the hell happened?"

"I was the star witness against some really bad dudes," he said. "The Bureau owed me after the trial and this was where I wanted to go."

"But why take the risk of moving back here?"

"Because I had to."

The answer came out so quickly he was surprised. Mona sat on the floor and leaned against the wall. She'd touched a sore spot and she wanted to proceed in a more trusting tone. It would be hard if she were looking down at him.

"Why did you have to?" she said in a calmer voice.

John wasn't going to take the bait. Mona wasn't a friend. She was the person responsible for ensuring that witness protection was maintained in Sweden. He had no desire to discuss this with her, but he had to say something. She had, after all, just persuaded the Walrus to let him keep his job.

"I wanted to find out whether my brother was the murderer and rapist that everyone claimed he was. I owed that much to him and to myself."

"And you didn't think Primer's team would manage to do that without you?" said Mona.

John examined her face. The wrinkles around her eyes had changed in character. They were finer and her eyes were less hostile. She was listening attentively to what he said, open to his side of the story.

"No, that team was a joke. They weren't looking at the case with fresh eyes—they were just looking for evidence to tie Billy to the crime. They had absolutely no interest in alternative suspects." John decided to stay on the offensive. "Why did you ask the commissioner to keep me on? The Bureau would've been satisfied if you'd kept the story quiet and I'd resigned of my own accord."

Mona needed no time to answer.

"Self-interest," she said. "This lousy investigation has been dumped on me and I need help. County CID has been at it for ten years and has gotten nowhere. You found the body in less than a week, and in my book that's worth something."

John looked at her again. The woman was honest—he had to give her that.

"How are we going to do this?" he said.

She waved her hand dismissively.

"That'll have to wait. First we have to discuss your security. Your friends at the FBI are worried and they're breathing down our necks. You must really have gone the extra mile for them."

John smiled grimly.

"I don't think it's me they're worried about—it's themselves. If things go south for anyone in witness protection, it'll have consequences. It'll leave the Bureau's credibility in shreds."

"In the same way that it'll hurt the Swedish police if your identity gets out while you're still in the country," Mona said. "How many people know who you are?"

John tried to think quickly. Lying unnecessarily was stupid. At the same time, he might put himself and others in trouble if he was too honest. He'd promised Ruben he'd keep him out of it. Erina Kabashi was someone else he couldn't mention. It couldn't emerge that he had leaked information to the lawyer.

"Just the commissioner, Primer, and you," he replied.

Mona seemed satisfied that the list wasn't longer.

"And your mother and brother—you've not had any contact with them?"

"No, I decided it was too risky," he answered, unsure whether that lie was truly necessary.

Maybe Mona would've understood why he'd looked up his family. But it had happened while Billy was the prime suspect in the investigation, and it would create doubts about John's loyalties. He was probably right to keep quiet about that too.

"Good. I want you to avoid them in the future as well. Do you think they'd recognize you if they saw you in town?"

"I don't think so. I was only twelve when we left—and my brother was eight."

He heard the sound of a phone vibrating in Mona's handbag. John sent silent gratitude to whoever was calling as it interrupted the interrogation. She got up from the floor, got the phone out, and showed the screen to him.

"It's Primer. Maybe he's found us an office."

"I hope there's room for two chairs," he said. "It'll be a pain if we have to take turns sitting on the floor."

Mona's mouth twitched into something that might charitably be perceived as a smile.

34

Heimer was lying in bed listening to the jet of water hitting the tiles. Sissela had just gotten home and said she was going to take a quick shower before an evening meeting with the management team.

That meant he would be there—Hugo Aglin. The only proof Heimer had that Sissela was actually cheating on him with Hugo were the words that Volker had spat in his face in the AckWe staff canteen. Could he trust him? After all, he was a desperate man who had just been fired and had every reason to cause problems for Sissela.

Heimer hadn't sensed anything. During the long dry spells, it wouldn't be surprising if she'd sought out other men. Emelie had more than hinted at this to him—but he hadn't wanted to listen. He dismissed it as yet another of his daughter's provocations.

But Hugo.

No, he just couldn't believe it.

He tried to think back to all the times he'd seen them together. He had seen friendship and mutual respect between them—but nothing else. No hand resting too long on a shoulder, no hug indicating anything more than a colleague's appreciation. He didn't doubt that his wife was capable of hiding things from him. But the unforced manner Hugo had in his company would surely be impossible to sustain if he were screwing Sissela.

Heimer looked at the translucent glass walls of the bathroom. Was it for her colleague that she was shaving her legs and applying skin lotions that cost more than a month's wages for the employees in AckWe's Bangladeshi factories?

He got up from the bed and went into the kitchen. Sissela's phone was charging next to the coffee maker. He picked it up and entered the PIN: 1931—the year AckWe was founded. The display came to life and Heimer clicked on the message symbol. He scrolled until he found one from Hugo. It was serious and concise. "The F2 is in your inbox."

Heimer had heard his wife use AckWe-speak for long enough to know that F2 meant "forecast two"—the second evaluation of the year for how business was going compared with the original budget.

He scrolled on through the messages between Sissela and Hugo backward in time. There were hundreds of messages over the course of several years. He glanced through them quickly—Sissela might turn up at any moment and wonder what he was doing with her phone—but he found nothing to indicate that they were more than colleagues.

Heimer switched to email. He searched for Hugo's name via the search field at the top and pulled up a seemingly infinite list of hits. The emails were harder to glance through than the text messages. All he could see in the preview were the sender, date, and subject line. If he actually wanted to know what they had written to each other, he would have to click on them.

Heimer wondered what order to tackle them in—old or new emails first? He decided to start with the most recent and work backward. After all, Volker had said "sleeping with your wife"—the present tense.

He was struck by how dull Hugo's work seemed to be. Emails had subject lines like "cash flow analysis" and "currency hedge," but that didn't stop Heimer from opening every single one. Even if he had written something that gave away that they were in a relationship, he would hardly have titled the email "shag tonight?"

Heimer was about to close an email about AckWe's new auditors when he noticed that the email had been sent to two recipients. One was sissela.bjurwall@ackwe.com and the other was to sisbjuw452@gmail.com.

The Gmail address suggested his wife had a separate email account and that Hugo had mistakenly put it in the address field as well. He searched for Gmail among the phone's apps and found it. The familiar logo was hiding in a folder labeled *Practical* along with some weather apps and a step counter.

Heimer felt his fingertips moisten with sweat and the phone refused to obey his commands. He put it down on the countertop and wiped his hands on his trousers. All the time, he kept listening for Sissela. The sound of water from the bathroom was still audible.

He picked up the phone and clicked on the Gmail app and ended up going to the inbox without having to enter a password. His heart almost stopped when he saw all the emails. Hugo and his wife appeared to write to each other almost daily. Sometimes more than that.

The subject lines were reminiscent of the intense communication that Heimer imagined formed part of a healthy marriage. There were practical "I'll be a bit late" emails, confiding "There's something that worries me" emails, considerate "Thinking of you" emails and sometimes—but only sometimes—lustful "I want you NOW!" emails.

Heimer forced himself to open email after email. He didn't follow any particular order—he just clicked on the ones that would hurt the most to read. It wasn't the ones with sexual references, as he had first thought. Instead, it was a different kind of intimacy that turned the knife in his heart. Everyday things—he couldn't think of another way to put it. Over the course of many years, Sissela and Hugo had formed a secret life together and—like all couples—they had their own jargon. It had a sense of humor and warmth that contrasted sharply with the formal atmosphere in his own marriage.

Heimer realized that Sissela's true husband was Hugo.

He clicked on an email that was just a week old. It had been written the day after he and Sissela had been shown Emelie's remains.

Sorry that I disappeared from the Nyla show without speaking to you. But now you know what's happened I'm sure you understand.

Heimer and I went to the pathologist to see her. It was awful. There was almost nothing but bones left of my darling beloved Emelie. It does feel good to know that we can finally bury her. I need somewhere to go where I can be close to her when those moments hit me.

Heimer is acting strangely. I'm worried about him. He's clearly on the verge of becoming manic again.

He wanted me to wear Emelie's old necklace that's been in the ground with her. How macabre is that? If it had been something else then I guess I could have accommodated it, but the necklace was just too much. I tried to say it as gently as I could—but he didn't take it well. I could tell.

Hugo, I don't know how this is going to play out. But I have a bad gut feeling. I'm ashamed to say it, but if it means Heimer making my life hell again, then I almost wish she'd never been found.

Heimer felt his arm shaking and it was hard to hold the phone still enough to keep reading. He forced himself to open another email. Who cared if Sissela caught him now? He was fully entitled to read every single word these people had written to each other.

We went to the police today. The head of the investigation said they've let Billy Nerman go. I don't understand and the police refused to say what's happened. One day they had concrete forensic evidence against the guy and the next he's free and we're told there is no further suspicion. It's all very weird.

Heimer was an absolute disaster (obviously). He was really unpleasant and aggressive. He punched the wall, damaging it and making his knuckles bleed. The mere thought of the funeral turns my stomach. There will be TV cameras and God knows what he'll do.

Could you talk to him? I know he values your opinion.

PS. I'll try to call a "management team meeting" soon so that we can spend some time together. I need someone to hold me.

Heimer put the phone back down on the kitchen island. His pulse was as fast as it was after his most challenging runs, and the blood was throbbing through his temples.

He went to the window and stared across the dark water outside. He had no idea how long he stayed there. All sense of time dissolved. All he could perceive was his own breathing and the slow movement of the waves.

A hand on his shoulder made him turn around. Sissela was standing there in fresh clothes, car key in hand. Her makeup was painstakingly done but discreet. Her hair was still damp and had a faint smell of lavender.

"Everything okay?" she asked.

He tried to find a smile.

"Of course—I'm just tired."

"You have to look after yourself," she said, kissing his cheek.

He had to exercise all his self-discipline not to turn away from her. It was almost impressive how easily she was able to deceive him. There wasn't a trace of guilt in her voice or movements.

"It'll probably be a late night."

She wiped lipstick off his cheek with her thumb and then slipped her phone into her handbag. It was no longer plugged in. He wondered if she had noticed that—or maybe her thoughts had already turned to Hugo.

35

They had requested an office, but had been given an entire floor. Primer started the workday by issuing them each a pass and telling them about the police station basement. Not only did it house the garage, but it also had extensive office space—partially subterranean. County CID had previously been located there.

Two years ago damp had been found during an inspection of the building. The risk of mold meant the basement had to be emptied until the problem was addressed. Then they'd been told that the facilities in Karlstad were being looked at: they were talking about building a new, bigger police station. While waiting for that decision, the authorities had no desire to invest in the old building. As a result, the basement remained unused.

"But now we've found a use for it," Primer said, vanishing before John could ask any questions about the mold and whether it might be a health hazard.

"Look on the bright side," Mona said in the elevator on the way down. "It's not like anyone's going to disturb us."

She was in a good mood and took the basement allocation in stride. After the conversation the day before, the air between them had been cleared—for now at least. John had spent his first night in the new apartment at Bryggudden. He was looking forward to getting back to work. His suitcase had been unpacked and his shirts were back in the wardrobe.

The elevator stopped with a soft thud and they got out into something that looked like a gloomy dentist's waiting room. Two worn-out leather armchairs, a coffee table, and a plastic flower to add a pop of color. John picked up one of the magazines on the table. It was from 2016.

To the left were a couple of large doors with covered windows that prevented anyone from seeing in. John swiped his card and heard the lock release. He pushed down the door handle and stepped into what would be their new base.

Neither he nor Mona said anything for a long time. The open plan office that stretched out before them was big and divided into groups of four desks using partition walls. Some of them still had family photos tacked up next to faded newspaper clippings about old cases. There was a dark blue jacket still hanging on a chair by one of the desks closest to the doors. It was as if someone had blown a whistle and everyone had simply put everything down and headed for the door.

Mona went to the chair with the jacket on it and set it spinning. The fabric fluttered, raising a layer of dust from the desk.

"Where do you want to sit?" she said.

"Somewhere in the middle. As far away from the walls as possible."

"Good idea," she said, heading toward a group of four desks that were completely empty.

John searched for a light switch and before long he found an entire set of switches by the bathrooms. He pressed them all, and row by row the fluorescent lights on the ceiling came to life, casting their harsh radiance over the room.

Mona ran her hand over the cushion of the office chair before sitting down at one of the desks. John sat at the desk opposite. Then they went over together what had to be done.

Their theory of the case was that the murderer had inside knowledge of the investigation. When—for whatever reason—he had a DNA sample taken, he panicked and switched his own sample with Billy Nerman's. Mona found a whiteboard on wheels and rolled it over. Using the only pen that hadn't dried out, she drew a circle.

"These are all the men who gave samples during the investigation."

She paused, then drew another circle that partly intersected with the first one.

"And these are all the men who worked in law enforcement at the time: the police, the prosecutor's office, the law firm that defended Billy, and the national crime laboratory."

Then she colored in the area where the two circles overlapped.

"It's here—at this intersection—that we'll find our perp."

John looked around the abandoned office. Despite everything, he was glad they were in the police station basement. These kinds of meetings didn't need anyone listening in.

"Getting a list of everyone who gave a sample shouldn't be hard," he said, pointing at the first circle. "It must be in the investigation files."

"Good—you can take care of that," said Mona. "I'm going to get hold of the staff lists so that we have something to cross-check your list against."

John had no objections to the division of labor. He was glad to avoid the thankless task of ass-kissing and threatening stretched HR staff who wanted to avoid checking old databases.

He tried inserting an ethernet cable into the nearest socket and was happy to find that the connection still worked in the basement. It took just a few clicks to get into the police's internal system. He pulled up the AckWe case and began to review its contents list. It was very familiar to him by this stage. All the documents that had been created were assigned reference numbers, and using this list, he'd be able to find the one he needed. He scrolled slowly until he found what he was looking for.

"File 32078:657. DNA samples sent for analysis."

John typed the number into the search field and hit enter. An hourglass appeared while the search was being processed. The answer came quickly. "No file found."

John repeated the process, but this time he copied and pasted the document reference number from the contents list to avoid any typos. The same answer again: "No file found."

Mona must have noticed his confusion.

"Is something up?" she asked from across the desk.

"Maybe. Come and take a look at this."

She stood behind him so she could see the screen.

"According to the contents list, there should be a record of all the people who gave a DNA sample. But the file seems to be gone."

"Let me try," she said, taking his place at the keyboard.

John watched the document reference number being inserted into the search box for the third time, resulting in the same negative response.

"That's odd," she murmured, as she began to search the system.

John leaned forward and tried to keep up. He'd always liked hanging out with the nerds in the NYPD's technical department, and he considered himself more knowledgeable than most detectives when it came to IT. Nevertheless, Mona seemed to be sharper. Her fingers were flying across the keyboard and soon she accessed a system overview.

"You're searching the logs?" he said.

"Yes—every change made to the system is recorded and if someone deleted the file, we ought to be able to see who it was," she said, pointing at the screen.

Her finger left a mark. In New York, the detectives had called those marks BPs—Boss Prints. Pictures of suspects, CCTV footage, interview transcripts—the boss needed to point at all of it. But this was hardly the moment to get annoyed by something like that. If Mona could dig up something about this file then she could stick her ass against the screen for all he cared.

"Look," she said, making a new mark.

John leaned in and read the row she was pointing at.

11/21/2019. File 32078:657 deleted. User: parker3

He checked the date again. November 21.

The file had been deleted just a week ago—the day after Billy was released.

Primer balanced three paper cups filled with coffee in a triangle in his two hands.

"Jesus, they're hot," he said, blowing on his fingers after he had put them down on Mona's desk.

"Don't you have any real mugs?" Mona asked.

"Yes, but we seem to have lost a lot of mugs from the kitchen and when the cupboard's bare we use these delightful things."

John searched for a sarcastic undertone to what Primer had just said but didn't find one. The rumor about his revolt against the kitchen schedule hadn't yet reached the boss.

"What do you want to talk to me about?" Primer added.

Mona got right to the point and explained what had happened to the missing file and how suspicious the date of deletion was. Primer sank into one of the chairs and slowly shook his head. He looked tired and concerned.

"This isn't good," he said.

"According to the logs, the user who removed the file was 'parker3.' Do you know who has access to that account?" said Mona.

Primer ran a hand self-consciously through his hair.

"Quite a few people, I'm afraid."

"Quite a few? What do you mean?"

"Well . . . everyone in the building knows that keystrokes are logged in this place and sometimes you might want to read a file you have no reason to read. Just out of interest. So some genius in IT created that account and the details got around. 'Parker' as in nosy parker . . ."

Mona looked at him blankly. She couldn't believe what she'd just heard.

"So, it could be anyone?"

"Yes, unfortunately so. Those logins have been around for as long as I can remember," he said. John was almost beginning to feel sorry for the big man. First he'd been cut from the investigation and now he was being humiliated in the police station basement.

"Is there a parker1 and parker2?" Mona asked.

"To be honest, I don't know how many parker accounts there are. You'd have to check with the boys in IT."

It looked as if Mona had a number of profanities on the tip of her tongue, but she wisely chose to save them for another time. Primer might be useful to them and there was no point kicking a man when he was down.

"Is there a printed copy of the list of people who gave DNA samples anywhere in the building?" she said.

"It'd be in the archives if there was," he said.

Mona asked him to take her there and before John had time to even finish his coffee they were back. With them was a rubber-wheeled cart with six boxes of case files on it. All the documentation from the AckWe case.

John soon saw that the person leading the investigation ten years earlier had been very thorough. The papers were sorted in numerical order. Document 32078:657 ought to be in box three or possibly four.

As he approached the magic number, he felt his hands becoming clammy. The sheets of paper stuck to his fingertips, making it harder to get through the piles of paper. He stopped and leafed back a few pages to double-check that he hadn't mixed up his numbers. No—there was a gap in the series.

"The list is missing here too," he said, looking at his colleagues.

Both of them appeared to shrink by a few centimeters from the gravity of the news. If there had been any doubt, it was now erased. Someone had cleaned up after themselves and deliberately made any further investigation difficult.

"Let me guess," said Mona, unable to contain her sarcasm any longer. "There's no guard, CCTV, or sign-in sheet for the archives."

Primer squirmed.

"We've been talking about honing our procedures, but we never got round to it. We have to stretch the budget as it is. Well, you know what it's like," he said, attempting to solicit sympathy.

Mona's silence said it all.

Fucking country bumpkins.

John thought about a final opportunity to retrieve the list that he didn't want to share with either Primer or Mona: the flash drive he'd been sent in the hospital in Baltimore. It would probably be another dead end. His mother—or rather, the lawyer who helped her compile the investigation files—had omitted a lot of this kind of background information. Just to be sure, he would check that evening when he got back to the new apartment.

"Could the samples still be in some database?" he said.

Mona replied without looking at him.

"No, they're only kept if the people who provided them are subject to reasonable suspicion, and in this case, we're dealing with a mass collection of DNA."

"What about the lab?" said John. "Even if the results weren't kept, maybe they still have a list of those tested."

"I find that hard to imagine after this length of time. But it's obviously worth checking up on," said Mona, reaching for her phone.

A short phone call later, her suspicion was confirmed. The lab monkeys in Linköping couldn't help them.

"Somehow, we have to re-create the damn list," she said, turning to Primer. "How were people chosen to give samples?" she said.

John was impressed by the decisiveness of his new boss. He was the same. The best cure against setbacks at work was to try to find alternative ways of achieving the same goal. Plan A was something any cop with two brain cells could come up with. It was the ability to come up with and execute Plans B, C, and D that set the real police apart from the amateurs.

"Well," said Primer. "This wasn't exactly yesterday. But I assume we followed protocol and started with men in the victim's direct vicinity—family and friends."

"Did any of them have a job that would've granted them access to the DNA samples?" said Mona.

Primer shook his head.

"No, it was mostly people who were Emelie Bjurwall's own age. Most of them were students."

"Then we'll put them to one side. What next?"

"When we didn't get any matches, we started taking more samples. I seem to remember we used postal codes on Hammarö. We started with people closest to the crime scene and worked outward. There was a hell of a fuss about it."

"How so?"

"There were people who thought we were invading their privacy. The papers wrote about it and there was a big debate. Mass DNA collection wasn't that common back then and the lower age limit was pretty low."

"How low?" said Mona.

"I seem to remember that all men who were fifteen or older and registered at an address in the postal code area had to submit a sample."

"How many postal codes did you get through before you got a match to Billy Nerman?"

Bernt Primer tried to remember, but then shook his head.

"Three, maybe four. I can't remember precisely. We must've taken DNA from hundreds of people on Hammarö."

Mona saw she wouldn't get any more information out of him and let the man return upstairs. While she escorted him to the elevator, John searched online. Primer's remark about public debate relating to the DNA collection had caught his attention.

His search for "DNA + AckWe + criticism" brought up several hits. He clicked on an article from *Nya Wermlands-Tidningen* that had been published in September 2009 after Billy was arrested. A female professor was interviewed and compared the investigation in Karlstad with one in Linköping a few years earlier. On that occasion, mass DNA samples had been taken in connection to a double murder. She particularly emphasized the problematic issue that the police might be tempted to run DNA samples against biological evidence from other investigations, thereby securing evidence for less serious crimes by the back door.

John shook his head. Sometimes he felt as though he didn't understand anything in his old home country. Surely it didn't matter how criminals were uncovered—they were still criminals.

He was about to click away from the article when he read the sidebar under the headline. The newspaper had reported that more than eight hundred men ranging from fifteen to eighty-seven years old had provided DNA samples in the AckWe case before the perpetrator had been arrested. There was then a list of the three postal codes on Hammarö where samples had been taken.

He clenched his fist in a spontaneous gesture of victory. This information would make it easy to produce a usable dataset from the national population register.

John had just told Mona the good news when his phone rang. He didn't recognize the number but he still answered. The voice on the line sounded metallic; it reminded him of a robot in a bad movie.

"She's come back."

He realized immediately that it was Torsten Andreasson—the manager at the Björkbacken treatment center. He could picture the man pressing a hand against his throat to generate that unusual voice.

John put the phone on speaker so that Mona could listen in.

"Are you sure?" he said.

The manager's voice sounded even more artificial as it echoed out of the phone.

"I just drove past the cabin and saw a light was on in the window. It has to be Matilda. She's the only one who knows where the key is."

"Where are you right now?"

"A couple hundred meters from the cabin."

"Has she seen you?"

"I don't think so. I drove past and she can't see the car where I am now."

John thought for a moment.

"Go back to the treatment center," he said. "I'll drive to Charlottenberg right away and talk to her. I'll let you know when we're done."

"So, I should just pretend nothing out of the ordinary has happened?" said the metallic voice reluctantly.

"Yes, and under no circumstances should you visit Matilda. Do you understand?"

There was silence on the line.

"Yes, I understand," said the manager.

"Good," said John, ending the call.

He looked at Mona.

"Coming along?"

She waved her hand dismissively. "No, you go. I'll stay here and try to get hold of the staff list. I'd like to cross-check it against the population register before the end of the day."

John nodded and then headed to the elevator.

With a little luck, he and Mona would come up with the same name—by two different means.

36

Heimer usually woke up after his wife, and he was surprised to see the car still in the drive. He called out for her and at first he couldn't hear her reply through the closed double doors at the far end of the hall. Only when she raised her voice did he realize that she was working from home.

He wrapped his dressing gown more tightly around him and went to her study. Sissela was sitting at the big desk, just as meticulously dressed as if she were going to the office. Heimer didn't know how she did it. There were no signs of fatigue. No rings around her eyes, no tousles in her hair.

He heard her come home late the night before after the "management team meeting." She had crept into the bedroom and lain down on her side of the bed. Feigning sleep, he had turned toward her to see whether he could smell any trace of Hugo Aglin. But no matter how much Heimer had sniffed, he hadn't discerned any hint of aftershave or lingering note of bodily secretion. All he was able to make out was the soft rose scent in his wife's skin lotion.

Sissela was a professional when it came to infidelity—that much he grasped. She hadn't made him suspicious by showering when she got home. At the same time, she must have washed away the smell of her lover some other way. He remembered the scentless wet wipes she always had in her handbag. Maybe that was what she used them for.

He looked around the study—the only room in the house that Sissela had furnished. The sofas by the window had been imported from Italy. Had they fucked there some time when Heimer was away? Was Hugo Aglin's hairy ass on the white calfskin while Sissela rode him until he came inside her?

His wife continued to look at him. As if she were expecting him to say something, rather than merely stand there in the doorway like an idiot.

"Do you want coffee?" was all he managed to say.

Sissela said yes and asked him to put on a pot. She would join him in the kitchen in ten minutes.

He shut the door behind him and staved off the impulse to tear the doors open again and demand to inspect her computer. It was one of his new fantasies: making

Sissela take off all her clothes and read everything she had written to Hugo Aglin aloud while he videoed it all. The oldest emails on the phone had been from 2013, and given the contents of them it was clear the relationship had been going on for some time before then.

Emelie had named no names. But maybe she had been referring to Hugo Aglin when she taunted him for not being man enough to satisfy her mother in bed. In that case, Sissela and her colleague had been a secret couple even back when his daughter had been alive. That meant at least a decade of infidelity. Probably even longer.

Heimer didn't know exactly when Hugo's wife had died from cancer, but he remembered that they had had to get a babysitter for Emelie so they could attend the funeral. Was it once he had become a widower that it had all started? Sissela had been there to support him and suddenly she'd had his cock in her mouth? Was that how it happened?

Heimer would never know unless he put his wife's back against the wall, and he had no intention of doing that. Quite the opposite: this was a new challenge in the art of separating the inside from the outside. From now on, the wall between what he felt and what he showed would be so dense that nothing would be let through that he hadn't decided to let through.

He switched on the coffee maker and went to check the mailbox. He threw the newspapers right into the recycling. They weren't a good way for either him or Sissela to start the day. Billy Nerman had been a free man for several days, but the hungry reporters refused to stop gorging themselves on the case.

He didn't have time to start opening the letters before his wife sat down across him at the kitchen island. She poured milk into her coffee—Heimer never understood why she ruined the taste like that—and she watched him as he opened the first envelope. It was the bill for the gas credit card. He checked the summary, then tore it in half and put it next to his cup.

Sissela raised her eyebrows quizzically.

"Direct debit," he said.

She managed the big finances and he managed the small stuff. Sissela hadn't paid a bill for as long as he could remember. The next envelope in the pile was from the postal code lottery. Personalized direct marketing was a nuisance that the polite notice on the mailbox didn't prevent. Nevertheless, he opened it and saw a game show host fanning himself with a span of lottery tickets. *Neighbors' delirium in Bergeforsen* it said in large letters above the picture. One hundred fifty-two winners had shared sixty-five million kronor. Heimer did the math. That wasn't even half a million per person. He doubted whether anyone in Tynäs bothered to play the lottery.

He put the advertisement to one side and opened the third envelope, on which the address was handwritten in a mixture of upper- and lowercase lettering. The letter inside was written on white office paper with pre-punched holes. He unfolded it and began to read.

Sissela noticed his changed facial expression immediately. He could feel how pale his cheeks had gone.

"What's that?" she said, nodding at the letter.

"Some nutter trying to con us out of money," he said, folding the sheet up again so that it would fit in his dressing gown pocket.

"Let me see," she said, reaching out.

Heimer gave it to her. It wasn't worth fighting over. She unfolded it and read it aloud.

I know who killed your daughter. How much is that information worth to you? I'll be in touch.

Heimer saw how affected she was by it—but also how quickly she shook that discomfort off and replaced it with something else. Sissela was furious.

"Who sent this?" she hissed. "Is there no limit to how awful people are?!"

Heimer didn't reply. He couldn't think clearly. The letter had short-circuited every wire in his brain.

Did someone actually know?

Sissela couldn't wait for him to regain his capacity for speech. She answered her own question.

"Apparently not. But I'm not going to be swindled."

She picked up the envelope from the table and put the letter back inside it. Then she fetched her handbag.

"What are you going to do?" Heimer heard himself ask.

"Take it to the police. Sending this kind of thing has to be a criminal offense."

"Criminal offense?"

"Yes—it's just as you said. He's trying to con us. Or she. But I have difficulty believing a woman would do something like this."

Heimer felt the situation slipping away from him as Sissela started making decisions on her own.

"Wait a second," he said. "What if it's not a bluff? What if they really do know something?"

She looked at him blankly.

"I find that very hard to believe. But if they do then there's even more reason to hand it over to the police."

"Why?" he said. "It says *I'll be in touch*. If we go to the police and the sender finds out, they'll never tell us anything."

"You don't seriously believe that the person who wrote that crap actually knows anything about what happened to Emelie?"

"Probably not. But I can't be sure—and neither can you. I think we should wait and see what happens."

"Someone is trying to exploit our vulnerability, Heimer," Sissela said. "Someone has read in the papers that the suspect has been released and thinks we'll be willing to pay anything to find out what happened to our daughter."

Heimer said nothing, conscious that she had logic on her side.

"The only right thing to do is hand over the letter to the police," she continued. "I'm going to the office now anyway, so it's on my way."

Sissela got up and Heimer knew he had lost.

"Wait," he said. "You're right, of course. We shouldn't let ourselves get dragged into something like this. I'll make sure the police get the letter—save you the trouble. I suspect you've got more on your to-do list today than I have."

He tried to smile but felt as though the skin on his cheeks was straining unnaturally. Sissela handed over the envelope.

"Thanks, darling," she said, before disappearing down the stairs.

37

John had covered the one hundred kilometers between Karlstad and Charlottenberg in less than an hour. He picked up a scent again and this time there was nothing stopping him. No opposition. No divided loyalties about what he might find out. He knew that Billy had had nothing to do with events at Tynäs that night and it was liberating. Nevertheless, he could still feel his brother's presence in the investigation. Someone had tried to frame him and it was John's task to find the real perpetrator.

He left the main road and drove down the small country lane leading to the Björkbacken treatment center and the manager's small cabin. The woods began to draw closer. The trees beside the narrow road were dense and their long branches cast dark shadows over the car. Even though it was the middle of the day, the sky was almost black—as if the clouds were filled with a torrential downpour but they couldn't make up their minds whether to let it go or not.

When John thought about Matilda Jacoby, he saw the investigation piece in his mind's eye, with MAJA written in slanting capital letters above the roof of Hugo Aglin's house in Tynäs—the house where she had gone to a party together with Emelie Bjurwall and all the other young people Magnus had invited. Then she was gone without a trace. She'd vanished into the darkness—the only link to the outside world being Björkbacken's manager and the abandoned cabin in the woods.

John slowed down so that he didn't miss the unassuming building. There, after a sharp bend, it appeared just as he remembered. He turned right onto the gravel road and drove toward the gateposts that marked the edge of the yard.

He cut the engine and got out. The Chrysler wasn't the only vehicle in the drive. There was a black Land Rover parked by one of the fruit trees, its front wheels on the grass. It was covered in grime, but it was a new model that would've cost at least as much as John's car. In other words: hardly the vehicle one would expect for a junkie with no fixed abode.

"Damn," John murmured as he waded through the uncut grass toward the house, which stood around ten meters away.

He stepped onto the porch and noticed that the door he had forced on his last visit had been replaced with a new, paneled dark wood version. The sound of his clenched fist on the sturdy wood echoed among the trees.

"Matilda Jacoby," he called out. "I'm Fredrik Adamsson from the police. I'd like to talk to you."

He heard the scrape of a chair and steps approaching.

"About what?"

The voice was a woman's and it sounded muffled through the door.

"I've got a few questions about Emelie Bjurwall. From what I understand, you hung out with her for a while. It would be really helpful if you . . ."

The lock turned and John fell silent. He waited for her to open the door, but when nothing happened he pushed the handle down and peered through the crack. The woman had vanished and the hallway was empty.

He stepped across the threshold and noticed that everything else seemed unchanged. The lightbulb hanging from the ceiling swayed slowly in the draft and the rat droppings were still under the coatrack. The only difference was the temperature. On the last visit, the cabin had been damp and freezing cold—but now he encountered pleasant warmth. There was a smell of burning wood and the sound of crackling from an open fire in the kitchen.

He took a few steps into the hall. On one of the chairs at the kitchen table, there was a slender woman with her knees drawn up to her chin, staring out the window. Opposite her was Torsten Andreasson—just as he had expected.

"Are you Matilda Jacoby?" said John.

The woman didn't answer—she simply continued to stare at the garden. She was wearing a large woollen turtleneck that concealed half her face. Her black tights ended at her ankles and she wore a pair of gray socks on her feet. On the table in front of her was an open pack of tobacco, and next to that a smaller pack of cigarette papers.

"That's right," said Björkbacken's manager, nodding at him as if he wanted to create some kind of trust between them.

"Torsten, come outside with me."

The man seemed to hesitate at John's instruction and put his hand to his throat to activate the voice generator.

"Matilda, is it alright if I . . ."

"It's okay," she replied dully, without looking at him.

He leaned back on his chair, as if her answer hadn't convinced him.

"Now!" John ordered.

The manager jumped up and together they went outside into the over-grown garden.

"I think it might be a good idea if I sit in while you talk to her. You know she's not very well and . . ."

He went dead silent when John grabbed him by the collar and pushed him up against the shabby façade, so that one of the planks came loose and fell into the grass.

"What did I tell you?"

Torsten Andreasson waved his arms around, trying to free himself. The only sound that came from his voicebox was a low hissing.

"Didn't I make myself clear when I told you not to come here? I said you shouldn't contact Matilda before I had spoken to her."

The man tried once again to hiss something.

"Shut up! I'm sick of your excuses. If you don't get the hell out of here, I'll pull that damn thing right out of your throat. Do you understand?"

The manager's eyes were wide and sweat was running down his brow. He panted, whining loudly, but he finally managed to hold up his hands in a gesture of resignation. He walked unsteadily back to his car.

"I'm just worried about her," he said, before closing the door of his Land Rover.

John waited until the vehicle had disappeared behind the tall trees in the direction of the Björkbacken treatment center. Then he adjusted his tie and went back inside.

The woman was still sitting at the table in the same position as before. She had lit a cigarette and was blowing out smoke that lingered beneath the low wooden ceiling.

"Thanks," she said.

John got out his police badge and sat down at the table on the same chair Torsten Andreasson had just vacated.

"Thanks for what?" he said, holding the plastic ID card under her nose.

She glanced at it briefly without answering his question. There were big bags under her eyes. She didn't appear to have eaten or slept in a week. Her black hair was shaved on one side and mid-length on the other, and her cheeks were covered with small, inflamed pimples.

"So Emelie is dead then?" she said, taking another drag.

"Yes. But the body has only been found now."

"Where?"

"Someone buried her in the woods on Hammarö. A few kilometers from the house where you went to the party."

"So, you've arrested that perv again then? Wasn't it just the body you were missing last time?"

John saw that Matilda Jacoby did not keep up with the news. She seemed to have missed Billy's arrest and subsequent release in relation to the murder.

"It wasn't him," he said, without going into detail.

"No?" she said in surprise. "Who was it then?"

John looked gravely at her but said nothing. She laughed and he saw that she was missing one of her canines.

"You don't have a clue and you hope I'm going to help you, don't you? Is that why you've come all this way?"

The hand holding the cigarette trembled, while the other continuously sought out the pimples on her face. He knew there was an all-out war going on under her skin. This was what the junkies looked like on the night shift in New York City, their bodies screaming for more amphetamines.

"Are you going cold turkey?" he said, leaning back.

"Yeah—what the fuck did you think? That I was out in the woods just 'cause it's cozy?"

"How many hours?"

"Almost seventy-two. There's not much to do out here."

"I get it. Is there anything I can do for you?"

"You could leave me alone—like you're going to do that."

She sounded resigned but not directly hostile. If he was careful and kept up with the rapid mood swings caused by her withdrawal, he would probably get what she knew out of her.

"How well do you know Torsten Andreasson?"

Matilda grinned, as if the question amused her.

"Know him is a bit much. He just wants to help me and I exploit that."

"How does he help you?"

"He usually gives me cash. Cute, right?"

She took a bundle of money out of the waistband of her tights. John could see it was several thousand kronor.

"And I get to stay here for free," she said. "He spoils me—brings me breakfast, lunch, and dinner. Full fucking board."

"And what does he get in return?"

"Nothing. I've tried." She laughed again as she stubbed out her cigarette on the saucer. "I think it turns him on in some messed-up way."

"What does?"

"Spoiling me without getting anything in return. Torsten isn't stupid. It's not that he doesn't get that I'm using him."

"But you're not sleeping together?"

She shook her head.

"I don't mean turned on in the usual way. I've offered to suck him off countless times, but he doesn't want that. He gets something else out of it. It's like a game we play. I go cold turkey and promise to quit drugs, which he knows I never will. And he strokes my brow and tells me everything will be okay, which I know it won't. And we go on like that until I've squeezed enough money out of him or just can't put up with the guy any longer. Then I get on the bus back to Stockholm."

John put his arms on the table and clasped his hands. It was time to get to the point.

"When did you find out Emelie was missing?"

She licked a cigarette paper and began to roll a new one.

"A few days after that party."

"And what did you do then?"

"I was on the underground in Stockholm. I saw a picture of her in the newspaper on the seat next to me."

"And why didn't you get in touch?"

"Why would I? I didn't have a fucking clue where she had gone and I don't like talking to cops if I don't have to."

"You were never contacted by the police?"

"No. I didn't exactly move in the same circles as her other friends, so I guess I wouldn't have been easy to find. I always slept in different places—wherever there was a couch to borrow."

John let a few seconds elapse.

"There are witnesses who say Emelie left the party to meet someone. Is that your recollection too?"

"Yes."

"Okay. Do you know who she was going to meet?"

"No."

"You have no idea?"

"No."

"Come on, Matilda. You and Emelie arrived at the party together and several witnesses say you were the last person she spoke to before she disappeared. You must know why she . . ."

"She was going to get some more flake."

John fell silent and tried to digest this. She was hardly referring to the chocolate bars he and his brother stuffed their faces with when they were kids.

"Cocaine?" he said.

"Yes. She had been emailing some dude earlier in the day and they had agreed to meet. He was going to come to us and bring the stuff. I'd brought some from Stockholm, but we'd used that up the night before."

"I understand," said John, remembering the empty bag that Emelie's parents had found in her desk drawer. "But you never found out who this person was?"

"No. She called him something or other—but I can't remember what."

John took a deep breath in the hope that it would at least pull some oxygen into his lungs in addition to cigarette smoke.

"It's important, Matilda. We haven't been able to identify this person and you're the only one who can help us."

"Is he the one who killed her?"

"We don't know. But we really need to talk to him."

Matilda's short, sharp nails left red marks on her cheeks as she continued to scratch away.

"If I could remember, I'd tell you. But it was a long time ago. It's not so easy to remember."

"I understand. But Emelie called him something?"

"Yeah—like, a nickname."

"Like what?"

"Jesus. I said I can't remember."

John saw a wave of comedown wash over her and resolved to use only his kindest voice.

"Why didn't you go with her?" he said. "I mean—you wanted coke too."

"She wanted to go by herself."

"Okay—how did she seem?"

"What?"

"Well, was she worried about meeting this person? Scared? Nervous?"

Matilda sighed and rolled her eyes.

"No."

John brushed his hand over his mouth and massaged his cheeks. It was hard work getting a junkie going cold turkey to remember things that happened a decade ago.

"Do you remember anything else that happened at the party? Anything that stood out—anything at all?"

Matilda thought. "I remember the dad of the guy throwing the party coming home and being absolutely fucking furious."

"Magnus's father? Hugo Aglin?"

"I don't have a fucking clue what his name was."

"What was he angry about?"

"That we were having a party, I guess. He probably hadn't expected the house to be full of messed-up kids. He raised hell for a while, but I think he finally just went to bed, because we kept partying."

"And you don't know why Emelie wanted to go to the meet-up alone?"

"No, I don't know!"

Matilda got up and went over to the hearth. She crouched in front of it and added a couple of logs to the fire. She sat down, staring into the flames.

"If I'd gone with her maybe she'd be alive now."

John saw her turn her face away, and he heard quiet sobbing. The reaction surprised him. He went to the fireplace, grasped the slender shoulders, and helped her back to the table. She weighed almost nothing—as if she were made from Styrofoam.

Matilda wiped her tears on the sleeve of her sweater and began to roll yet another cigarette. Her hands were trembling more than before. John asked if she needed help, but she shook her head.

"Won't you tell me about Emelie?" he said. "Was it at the treatment center that you first met?"

"Yes."

"And what was it like? Were you happy there?"

"Oh, we were deliriously happy. To be honest, we just wanted to get out of there, but I guess it was okay. If it hadn't been for them, I would've left right away."

"Them?"

"Emelie and that other girl—Kirsten. The whole place was stuffed with spoiled upper-class bitches, but those two were different. Especially Emelie. Her parents were more loaded than anyone else's—but she didn't talk about it. Actually, she bad-mouthed them. Said it was their fault she ended up there and stuff."

"Why was it their fault?"

"I don't know. She thought they'd deserted her. Families were allowed to visit on Sundays, but Emelie's parents never came. She'd banned them from coming, she said. Her dad would call, but she hardly ever wanted to talk to him. I remember Robocop tried to get her to go easier on them, but she was a tough cookie."

"Robocop?" John asked, guessing who she was referring to.

"Torsten. It was Emelie who started calling him that. He sounds like a robot," Matilda laughed, dragging more smoke into her lungs. "She liked nicknames, Emelie did. When we were on our own, she used to call me Maja. She thought it suited me better."

Silence followed and John waited a while before continuing.

"A few days after you were discharged from Björkbacken, you went to a place in Karlstad and got tattoos on your forearms. Why?"

Matilda put the cigarette down and her eyes filled with tears again. It was as if the question had touched on something that she long ago buried at the bottom of a mound of tragic memories.

"It was Emelie's idea," she said.

"So, it was her idea to tattoo a bucket list onto each of your arms?"

He stopped talking when he saw Matilda's reaction to what he had said.

"It wasn't a bucket list."

Now it was John's turn to be surprised. The witness statements from Magnus Aglin and Emelie's parents correlated. According to them, Emelie had said the tattoo was a list of things she wanted to do before she died.

"If it wasn't a bucket list, then what was it?" he said.

Matilda took a drag on her cigarette.

"It was an extra life."

"Extra life?"

"Yeah."

"Tell me a bit more," he said, leaning over the table.

"There was fuck-all to do in the evenings in that place, so we were always up in the attic playing video games. You know, those things from the stone age—Zelda, Super Mario and the rest."

John nodded. He remembered the old 8-bit games and the gray Nintendo console that you put cartridges into. He and Billy had been given a used one for Christmas.

"And what was the connection between the games and the tattoos?"

"Emelie used to say that it was unfair that it was only in Super Mario that you got an extra life. People like us needed it, she said. We had all attempted suicide before we got to Björkbacken. So we made a pact. Three extra lives—just like Mario."

Matilda scratched a loose flake of skin off a pimple on her cheek, making it bleed. John saw no reason why she would make up the story about the tattoo. All things considered, it was no surprise that Emelie had lied to those around her. Her parents would've gone through the roof if they'd found out that she was keeping a list of her suicide attempts on her arm.

"So you all tattooed a tick into the first square because you had all already used up one life?" he said.

"Exactly. It was like a promise to each other. If you ended up so depressed that you wanted to end it all, you had to tattoo a tick into one of the boxes. Only after all the lives were used up would it be okay to, like, jump in front of a train."

John thought back to the photo that had been posted on Emelie Bjurwall's Facebook page and the pictures from Kirsten Winckler's autopsy. Both girls had used up all their extra lives. The only difference was that Emelie's last tick wasn't tattooed—it had been carved right into her skin.

He tried to get a handle on the sequence of events. The first tick had been there right from the beginning, while the third had been added by Emelie herself—or the perpetrator—on the evening she disappeared. But the second tick—where had it come from? He asked Matilda, who for once didn't have to think before answering.

"She added it in Stockholm the year after she was at Björkbacken. It was when she started at that dorky university and had the worst-ever makeover."

"Makeover?"

"Yeah, you know, like on TV. At Björkbacken, she wore black jeans and edgy t-shirts. But when we got out . . . All she wore was expensive designer stuff. She looked like some crappy model and she said she was going to study. It was like she wanted to change herself and her life completely."

Matilda stubbed out the cigarette but immediately began to gather the tobacco to roll the next one.

"And then?" said John.

"Studying was harder than she expected. She had to fight for every damn credit and during the autumn term I didn't ever see her. I thought she didn't want anything to do with me anymore. That I didn't fit into her new life. But she got in touch around Christmas."

"And how was she?"

"Really down."

"Why?"

"Because she'd screwed up almost every single test. I got the feeling she had really tried, but that it had all gone to shit anyway. Her dyslexia meant she struggled to keep up."

"Emelie struggled to read and write?"

"Yeah, she blamed it all on her poor genes. Apparently her old man has the same problem."

Matilda laughed and rolled a new cigarette. She licked the paper with her tongue and reached for the lighter.

"Did her parents know how badly school was going?" said John.

"Christ, no. They thought their little princess was a model student. She lied right to their faces."

"I see. And did you hang out during the spring term?"

"She came around a lot to the apartment where I was staying, and on the weekends she always slept over."

"And it was then that she tattooed in the second tick?"

Matilda nodded slowly, brushing her hair away from her pale face.

"It all went downhill pretty fast. She stopped going to classes and didn't bother with most of her exams. We partied pretty hard."

"Did that include drugs as well?" John asked.

"Yeah, of course. I had a friend who could always get us good stuff. He would give it to you for free if you blew him or one of his buddies in the bathroom—we didn't mind that. They were alright, at least most of them were."

"Didn't Emelie have money to pay with?"

"Yeah, obviously. And sometimes she coughed up—but usually she didn't."

"So, you mean she preferred to prostitute herself instead of paying for drugs?"

"She wasn't fucking prostituting herself. We hung out with the guys, they fixed us up with some stuff, and sometimes we had sex with them. I think she liked it. It was as if she . . ."

Matilda felt silent, seeming to disappear into her own thoughts.

"As if she . . . what?" John prompted.

"As if she wanted to get dirty, or something. These were totally different guys from the kind she usually hung out with. Not exactly mommy's boys flashing daddy's credit card around. You have to understand the pressure that chick was under. She was going to take over the whole company one day. Everyone at that college kissed her ass and she pretended she was Little Miss Perfect. But my friends didn't have a fucking clue who she was. She usually told them she worked in an AckWe store and complained about how bad the pay was. Typical Emelie sense of humor."

Matilda shook her head and looked out the window.

"There was something about that transformation into a career girl that didn't fit. She had always hated everything her mother stood for, and now all of a sudden she was trying to be exactly like her. It was so fucked up—I never really got her."

John noticed Matilda hesitating, as if the memory of Emelie had made her remember a story she might not want to tell. He sat in silence and hoped she would keep talking.

"You know, sometimes we'd be in some bar drinking and suddenly she'd point out some disgusting bastard and ask what she'd get if she made out with him."

"People she knew?"

"No, no. Always strangers. Then she'd go up to them and do it. And when she came back she'd just laugh and go back to drinking, as if nothing had happened. I thought it was cool back then, but I've thought about it since and it was actually really weird—I don't understand why she did it."

John could feel the picture of Emelie Bjurwall changing into something much darker and more destructive. She seemed to have been in a much worse state for far longer than anyone around her had been aware or had been willing to acknowledge.

"Was there anything in particular that made her get the second tattoo?" he asked.

"It was in the spring—just before Easter. She hadn't been in touch for a week and wasn't picking up my calls. Eventually, I went round to her place in Östermalm. She lived there in an apartment her parents had bought for her and . . ."

John saw the woman in front of him struggling to get the words out.

"And what, Matilda?" he said. "What happened?"

"She was lying on the bathroom floor when I got there. Everything stank of vomit and booze. I got her up and put her on the sofa. She was so miserable, she just cried and cried. After a while, she told me she totally fucked up a test the day before. She had tried to study but couldn't. Afterward, she'd got drunk and decided to go to the party where her classmates were celebrating that night. She'd apparently lost it after some bitch talked shit about her behind her back. The cunt asked if Emelie had even managed to spell her own name right on the test."

John could feel the cigarette smoke irritating his airways, and he really needed a break to get some fresh air. But he didn't want to interrupt Matilda. He had the feeling she hadn't talked about her friend even once in the last ten years.

"She just wanted to die," she said. "I kept trying to cheer her up the best I could. I said we'd promised not to give up until all our extra lives were used up. I don't remember how I convinced her, but that evening we took the underground to see a guy I knew who had tattoo equipment."

"And he did Emelie's second tick?"

"Yes," Matilda replied, laughing. "While we were there, Emelie's mother called. And what do you think Emelie did? She answered and told her the test had gone brilliantly."

John struggled to respond to the laughter and managed to force a smile.

"Would you say that Emelie was addicted to drugs?"

"No, she wasn't. She sometimes went for a long time without taking anything. She even said no sometimes when I'd gotten hold of some—the ungrateful cow."

Matilda laughed again and put her hand to her mouth—the deep, mucous cough sounded as though it came from a patient in the late stages of lung cancer.

"Do you know anything about the third tick?" John asked.

"No."

"But you know about the photo that was posted on Facebook the same night she disappeared?"

"Yeah, it was in the papers after."

"Did anything happen that night that could've affected her so much that she carved the final tick into her arm?"

Matilda looked at him. "Are you sure it was Emelie who did it? She was killed. Maybe the murderer did it."

"Maybe. We don't know how she got it. But assuming she carved it herself . . . Was there any reason for her to?"

"She'd been found out," said Matilda, pointing her cigarette at him—as if she had just remembered something she hadn't thought about earlier. "Like, on the morning of the party."

"Found out?"

"Yeah. Her parents discovered her studies had gone down the toilet."

"And how did Emelie take it?"

"Said she didn't care, but I could see she was in crazy agony."

"Enough to use up her last extra life?"

"I don't know. Maybe. It seemed important to her mom that she went to this college," said Matilda, spreading out her arms.

John imagined the pressure Emelie Bjurwall must have been under. Not daring to tell her parents about her failure at business school said it all. The heiress couldn't show any cracks in the façade.

After trying to persuade Matilda Jacoby to share more memories of the evening, he saw she had nothing else to tell. He took her phone number and handed over his card.

"If you remember anything else—anything you think might be important—you have to call me."

Matilda nodded and looked out of the window.

"How long are you staying this time?" he asked, getting up.

"Mister Hyde," she said suddenly.

"Sorry, what?"

"The nickname. The person she was meeting that evening."

"Mister Hyde?" John repeated.

"Yeah."

"Like in the book?"

She looked at him blankly.

"I don't know anything about any fucking book—that's just what she called him."

"Are you sure?"

"As sure as a junkie can be. But I stopped trusting myself a long time ago. You know, your head goes funny when you've been at it for as long as I have."

John put his hand on her shoulder and thanked her. He headed for the door but stopped when he heard her get up from her chair.

"Two thousand kronor and I'll let you do whatever you want to me."

He turned around and saw her pull the thick sweater over her head and let it drop to the floor. Her bare torso looked anorexic and her thin arms were covered in scars and track marks. The silicone was the only thing not affected by the malnutrition, making her breasts look oddly out of proportion.

He was disgusted. Not by her, but by the men who paid to have sex with her.

"Fuck it," she said apathetically, bending down for her sweater.

"Wait a second," he said, going up to her.

He took hold of her left forearm and turned it to the light. Under the fading scars he could see three squares tattooed onto her skin in black ink. Each one contained a tick.

She looked at him and laughed.

"I ran out of extra lives long ago."

38

Sissela surprised him by returning just after lunch. She only had a few phone calls scheduled for the afternoon and she might as well take them from home, she told him as she headed for her study.

Heimer wondered whether a guilty conscience brought his wife home this early. Nevertheless, he didn't like it. During the daytime, the house was his domain and it felt as though she was invading his personal space. He would never rush unannounced into her office.

It didn't matter that she was in the study with the door shut. The atmosphere changed somehow and he couldn't get anything done. The wine bottles he bought in an online auction the week before were still on the kitchen counter waiting to be carried down to the wine cellar and sorted.

Then he heard her voice in the hall. At first, he thought she was talking to him but then he realized she was in the middle of a phone call. The steps got closer.

"Just a second."

She turned the corner, put the phone down on the kitchen island, and gestured for him to come closer. "The police," she mouthed, pointing at the phone. Out loud, she said: "You're on speaker."

"Thanks—that's great. Are you there too, Heimer?" said a voice from the phone.

Heimer didn't recognize the voice. Someone other than Primer was speaking. The man had a subtle but easily identifiable accent. He sounded like an American.

"Of course, with whom am I speaking?"

"My name is Fredrik Adamsson and I work at County CID in Karlstad. I'm working on the investigation into Emelie's death. I need to ask you and your wife a question, if that's alright."

Heimer looked at Sissela, who shrugged her shoulders. She didn't seem to know what this was about either.

"I thought Bernt Primer was leading the investigation," he said cautiously.

"There's been a changing of the guard," the detective replied in a neutral tone.

Heimer waited for it to continue, but when it didn't, and Sissela didn't object, he said: "Of course—we want to help the police as much as possible."

The man who had introduced himself as Fredrik Adamsson said something, but the sound was cut off for a moment before returning.

"Sorry, we didn't catch that last bit," said Sissela.

"I'm in the car—the connection may be patchy," the detective apologized. "So, this might be a strange question, but I wondered whether you know someone called Mister Hyde?"

Sissela looked at Heimer with her eyebrows raised. She was as surprised as he was.

"Hyde? As in Doctor Jekyll and Mister Hyde?" Heimer asked.

"Yes, I assume so."

"Why are you asking?" said Sissela.

"The name has come up in the investigation," said the detective. "Your daughter was supposedly in touch with someone called that. But you never heard her use the name?"

"No, I don't think so," said Sissela. "I mean, the kids had nicknames for each other. Magnus Aglin was called Mange and Emelie was sometimes called Emmy—even if I didn't like it. But Mister Hyde—that sounds more like a joke."

"Who said that Emelie knew someone by that name?" Heimer interjected.

"One of the girls who was at the party the night she went missing. But I agree it sounds a bit weird and she may be misremembering."

"Well, we've never heard of any Mister Hyde except for the fictional one," said Heimer, exchanging a glance with Sissela.

She rolled her eyes as if to say that if this was the best the police could come up with then it wasn't a promising start to the new investigation.

"What do you think about the letter that was sent to us, then?" she said, changing the subject. "I've got to say, it was upsetting."

The voice on the other end of the line took its time to reply. The sound of tires on asphalt and the faint hum of the engine were transmitted through the phone and into the Bjurwalls' kitchen. Heimer realized the detective was confused. He couldn't possibly know what Sissela was talking about. The letter was hidden in an atlas in the bookcase.

"My husband handed it in this morning," she continued. "Haven't you read it?"

"I think there's been a misunderstanding," the detective eventually said. "I just spoke to my colleague on the case, who's been at the station all day, and she didn't mention a letter."

Sissela looked at Heimer in irritation. He considered shrugging his shoulders and feigning surprise but knew it wouldn't work. She was aware of his views about the letter but only now realized he'd lied to her.

"I think we got our wires crossed here at home," she said without divulging any of her frustration to the detective.

Sissela described the letter that arrived that morning and what it said. She got all the relevant follow-up questions: was the envelope postmarked? Who was it addressed to? Was it handwritten or printed from a computer? Did they have any idea who might have sent it? And so on.

Once the detective was satisfied with the answers, he asked them not to touch the letter again. He would ask someone to pick it up right away and make sure it was sent for forensic analysis.

"You're unbelievable," said Sissela, after the call ended. "We agreed you'd hand it over to the police—and then you didn't."

"Listen to me—"

"No, you're going to listen to me. How could you lie to me?"

It was a question he would've liked to fire back at her. Sissela's phone was still lying on the kitchen island between them. He had to muster every ounce of willpower not to pull up the emails to Hugo Aglin and shove them in her face. Instead, he tried to revel in his own self-control. Mastering himself in this kind of situation was a tough challenge and he had pulled it off.

"Sorry," he said. "I don't know what got into me. I just thought we might wait a little. This person might really know something—and I didn't want to scare him or her off by getting the police involved."

Sissela looked at him seriously, almost sadly. He had disappointed her, she explained. Heimer had heard her use that word many times—both when they had fought and when she had been on the phone to employees who'd fallen short in some way. Heimer was convinced it was a highly conscious choice of words. If she simply became angry, the emotional reaction in the other party wouldn't be as strong. Anger was short-lived by nature. People got angry and then it passed. But disappointments weren't like that. They lived on in the body and created long-term feelings of useful guilt.

Heimer slowly walked to the bookcase and took down the atlas. Inside the cover showing Europe's borders before the fall of the Soviet Union was the envelope. He was about to hand it to her when she blocked his arm.

"Didn't you hear what he said? We're not supposed to touch it," she said.

He nodded. Then he shut the atlas and pushed it across the kitchen island to her.

"I'll wait here until the police arrive," she said, placing both her hands on the cover of the atlas, as if preventing him from hiding the letter again.

39

John had decided to give Rederiet another chance. The pub was in a good location—on the ground floor of the building next door to his at Bryggudden.

Mona had accepted right away when he'd suggested they should discuss the investigation over dinner. After a day spent in the musty basement, she needed a change of scenery. The menu featured Spanish tapas dishes. They decided to let the waiter pick his own favorites and serve them alongside a Pinot Noir from the very decent wine list.

The décor was rustic, with dark wooden tables and subdued lighting from chandeliers. Large floor-to-ceiling windows looked out onto the harbor promenade and the water. In order to talk undisturbed, Mona and John had picked a spot toward the back, near the kitchen.

"Read it aloud," Mona said, taking a sip of wine.

The novel is set in nineteenth-century England and is about the charming, conscientious Doctor Henry Jekyll.

Doctor Jekyll's friends are surprised when this respectable doctor begins to socialize with a strange, ugly little man guilty of knocking a child down in the street. Not only are they friends, but Jekyll has also left all his possessions to the strange Mister Edward Hyde in his will.

It transpires that Mister Hyde is in fact Doctor Jekyll when he consumes an elixir of his own making, which appears to release his most primitive and brutal side.

Doctor Jekyll becomes addicted to doing what he wants in the form of another. The temptations of transformation are too great and he cannot stop using the elixir. This story is about mankind's inherent capacity for both good and evil.

John looked up from the screen and noticed that Mona was looking for the waiter. Apparently, she needed to replenish her reserves after a workout in the hotel gym she managed to squeeze into her schedule. Her hair was still damp and her cheeks were rosy.

"The inspiration for it is apparently some Scottish cabinetmaker from the eighteenth century who did carpentry by day and robbed banks by night," he said.

"Wilhelm Brodie," said Mona.

John raised his eyebrows.

"Almost. William Brodie."

"I read it when I was little. I was more fascinated by the story behind it than the book itself."

John couldn't help being impressed. How could she remember such an insignificant detail from childhood? He wished he had the same ability to preserve memories. His early years in Sweden before the move to New York were mostly fragments of events that were impossible to piece together into a timeline.

"But why did Emelie use a name from an old book?" Mona continued.

"Right. Maybe she thought it was somehow appropriate?"

"You mean the person that Emelie was going to meet had similarities to this character? A respectable citizen by day and a primitive animal by night?"

"Something like that."

She swirled her wine in her glass.

"I assume that a police officer or lawyer would fit the bill."

"Yes—or a therapist," said John.

She looked at him searchingly.

"You don't like the manager at Björkbacken much, do you?"

"He may have gotten close to Emelie during her time there. He treats depressed girls as Doctor Jekyll and sells drugs to them as Doctor Hyde."

"You're forgetting one important thing, surely?" Mona objected.

"I know, I know," he said. "Torsten Andreasson didn't give a DNA sample and is unlikely to have known anything about the investigation. But there's something not quite right about that man. Why was it so important that he spoke to Matilda Jacoby before I got there? He disobeyed my direct instructions."

"Maybe he wanted to protect the poor weak girl from the big, bad police detective. Does it have to be anything more than that?"

The food arrived and Mona filled her plate. John had never seen a woman eat with such fervor. He would have to up his pace if he was going to get his fair share of the goodies on the table.

"There's one thing bothering me," she said, her mouth full of chèvre and walnuts. "Why did Emelie go to the meeting with Mister Hyde alone? Matilda Jacoby was more used to buying cocaine and offered to go with her."

"If it was cocaine she was buying."

Mona looked at him in surprise.

"You think it might have been about something else? That she lied to Matilda?"

"I don't know. It's a thought. In any case, it would explain why she didn't want company."

"A secret relationship?"

"Maybe," he said. "Look at it like this. Emelie leaves the party and has consensual sex with Mister Hyde down by the water. Then she declares her love for him. But when he doesn't reciprocate she gets upset and threatens to reveal their relationship. For some reason, Mister Hyde is terrified of this. Maybe he's married—who knows? It all ends with him panicking and killing her."

Mona stuck her fork into the goat cheese.

"And the tick carved into her arm?" she said.

"It wasn't about failing at school—it was about unrequited love. Maybe she carved it herself in front of Mister Hyde. To show him that life wasn't worth living without him. Then she posted the photo on Facebook as a melodramatic gesture. Step one in exposing their affair."

Mona shook her head almost imperceptibly. John didn't know whether she was aware she was doing it or not. But he understood her skepticism. Now that he had tested his hypothesis, he could see how flimsy it was.

"I don't know," said Mona. "It doesn't tally with the Emelie that Matilda Jacoby told you about. It all sounds a bit . . ."

"Teenager-y?" John said.

This time Mona nodded.

"Yes, something like that. Emelie seems to have been a confused but tough girl and she wouldn't have sacrificed an extra life for a married man who had dumped her."

Mona got her notebook out of her coat and he saw she wanted to change the subject. He had nothing against it. When they'd spoken on the phone earlier, she had promised to tell him about the results of her research efforts.

"I've found some interesting names in our cross-section," she said.

John remembered the circles she had drawn on the board and their overlap. She had apparently already had time to cross-check data from the population register against old records.

"How many?" he said.

Mona leafed through her notebook.

"I got seven hits," she said, showing him a page of handwritten names.

John read them quickly but didn't recognize a single one.

"Who are they?"

"Two are lawyers with the prosecutor's office. Then there's a local forensics specialist who might have handled or had access to the DNA samples. The rest are police."

"Are they all still working?"

"I don't know. But that doesn't really matter. Even if the perpetrator has retired or changed jobs, he could still have made his way into the police station somehow and deleted the list of DNA samples."

John looked at the list of names again.

"So these men all lived in one of the three postal codes that got checked and they all submitted DNA samples ten years ago?"

"Yes, and I've put my guys in Stockholm on the job of tracking them down and making sure they give another sample."

"Your colleagues at National Crime?"

"Yes."

He didn't have to ask why. The commissioner of county police had been quite clear. Every measure to minimize the risk of a leak had to be taken. There were good reasons for them working in the basement of the police station.

"And on what basis will your guys be taking new samples? These seven will wonder what's going on."

"I told them to be creative," said Mona. "They know what's at stake—none of the men can be allowed to find out why they're giving a sample."

John nodded.

"And once they're done, we'll run them against the semen from the rock and then we should—"

"Yes," she interrupted. "Then we'll have found Mister Hyde."

The waiter cleared away their plates but left the wineglasses.

"Did you make it to Tynäs?" said John.

Mona pushed her chair away from the table and stretched out her legs.

"Of course. I went as soon as you called and I got to meet Sissela Bjurwall herself. What a place they have—completely unbelievable."

"Did she give you the letter?"

"Yes, and it's gone off for analysis. But I took photos and made copies."

She reached for her bag and pulled out a plastic folder containing a sheet of paper with a close-up photo of a brown envelope. It was postmarked in Karlstad and the address was handwritten.

HeiMer BJurWalL
TynÄsvägEn
663 42 HaMmaRö

John examined the sprawling letters. It was clear that the anonymous sender wanted to conceal their handwriting by using upper- and lowercase letters at random.

Mona handed him another plastic folder with another photo of the letter itself. It hadn't been written by hand—it had been written on a computer and printed on white office paper.

"We'll get a report from Forensics tomorrow," she said. "The Bjurwalls think it's someone trying to con them out of their money."

I know who killed your daughter. How much is that information worth to you? I'll be in touch.

John read the short message several times. He was inclined to agree with the Bjurwalls. To him, it looked like attempted fraud. Someone had read about the case in the papers and wanted to exploit the situation.

"Is it even worth following up on this?" he said.

"Probably not. But let's assume for a moment that the letter writer is actually telling the truth—that he knows who killed Emelie. Why hasn't he gone to the police?"

"That's obvious. The writer wants money—everyone knows the Bjurwall family is rolling in it. Maybe they're a criminal and don't want anything to do with the police."

"But why wait ten years?" she said.

"The investigation has been reopened. They're short on cash now and have just had the idea."

John watched Mona pour her second glass of wine. He was still halfway through his first.

"The fact that the letter is addressed to Heimer Bjurwall is interesting," she said. "If someone is just after cash, surely it would have been sent to the wife? She's the celebrity and the one with the money."

"Unless it's someone who knows the family and knows that the husband is the better mark. Maybe he was closer to the daughter."

"Who might that be?"

"Someone familiar with the family and its relationships, and in need of dough." Mona looked at him.

"That sounds like Matilda Jacoby."

John thought about it and realized she was right. If Matilda was desperate enough to try to sell sex to him, she was probably capable of something like this too.

"So you think she tricked me—that she actually knew who Emelie Bjurwall left the party to meet?" he said.

She shrugged her shoulders.

"Don't blame yourself too much. Some people lie so much and so well that anyone will believe them."

It irritated John that Mona perceived him as so egotistical that he'd consider it a personal failing if he had been tricked. And it bothered him even more that she was right.

"It was just a thought," she said. "We'll wait for the analysis. If it doesn't give us anything, maybe the letter writer will get in touch again. Regardless, we have to prioritize the new DNA samples."

John looked at the page of seven names again. Mona was right. There was no reason to spend a lot of time and energy on a possible witness when they would soon be able to identify the perpetrator using DNA. He leaned back and allowed himself to savor the Pinot Noir.

"I've got something for you," said Mona, pulling out a package wrapped in brown paper with a red ribbon around it. "Something I've got the idea you might need."

Her phone buzzed and she turned it upside down so that the screen was facing the table. John tore the paper off and took out a white coffee mug. It was equipped with two handles—one on either side—like a child's sippy cup. He laughed when he saw what it said on the side.

Bad Cop.

"Is that what you think I am—an evil bastard?"

"Turn it round," said Mona, standing up beside the table.

On the other side, it said *Good Cop* in the same italicized typeface.

"A mug for all occasions," she said with a smile. "And now you won't have to burn yourself on coffee in paper cups."

John smiled as she headed off for the ladies'. Now he realized why the mug had two handles. It was so he could choose which kind of police officer to be.

He liked this woman. He thought of her as more of a partner than a boss, which reflected well on her. She was clearheaded and to the point—and she didn't waste time on trivialities. And—as it turned out—she had a sense of humor.

John was grateful that the missing list of DNA samples hadn't been on the flash drive that his mother had sent him in Baltimore. He had checked just before they met in the pub. It meant he didn't have to explain to Mona where he found it. He was sure it would've resulted in a different atmosphere. After all, he had answered a direct question about whether he had been in contact with his mother or Billy in the negative.

Rederiet filled up with more patrons and there was a cheery hubbub from the tables. He was about to order coffee when Mona's phone vibrated again. She was still in the ladies' and he couldn't resist the temptation to turn over her phone. He recognized the name of the app that the notification had come from and the red-and-white logo in the corner: *TINDER—Martin sent you a new message.*

John had thought dating sites were an American invention, but apparently they had them in Europe too. He'd had colleagues in New York who sang the praises of Tinder, saying it was the easiest way to find a lay if you couldn't be bothered to go to a bar. But he would never have thought it was for sixty-year-old women. Maybe things were different in Sweden. He wasn't that surprised that Mona was using the service. She was probably just as focused on the goal when it came to sex as she was with everything else.

It occurred to him that he hadn't been with a woman in nine months and even then it had been while on duty. An up-and-coming drug dealer who didn't take an interest in women would be seen through sooner or later. Or accused of being a faggot, which was almost as dodgy in those circles.

The phone's display went black just as Mona reappeared and he quickly put it back on the table. She paid her half of the bill at the bar and then came over to him.

"I need to go," she said, picking up her phone. "See you in the basement in the morning. Eight o'clock."

"Sounds good," John replied, raising his glass to her. "Thanks for the gift."

"It was nothing. Hand it over."

"What?"

"Give me the mug and I'll bring it to work," Mona said. "I don't for a second trust you to do it."

He laughed and handed it to her. She put it in her bag and vanished into the darkness, the collar of her coat turned up against the rain.

40

Heimer thought it was a taxi that he had let in through the gates to pick up Sissela. But when he looked out the window he saw the director of finance standing there waving at him.

"Is he here already?" said Sissela, sounding stressed. She seemed to be searching for something.

"Is Hugo going to Paris with you?"

Heimer made an effort to sound unconcerned. It always hurt the most when he wasn't given any time to protect himself. He only needed seconds to assume his mask—he maintained it most of the time—but surprises like this were still hard to handle.

"I need my bean counter with me," she said. "We're going to check out some new opportunities."

There was no trace of hesitation or guilt in her voice. A beginner would've oversold it. Provided lengthy justification of why it was so vital for Hugo to come along on this trip. Perhaps even lied about something that could be double-checked. But not Sissela. The lies came as naturally to her as rain did on Midsummer's Eve.

We're going to check out some new opportunities.

A claim so vague it was impossible to poke any holes in it.

Eventually, she found her scarf, pushed it into her hand luggage, and kissed his cheek. Then she disappeared out to the whoremonger and his silvery penis substitute of a Mercedes for a few days of romance in the capital city of love.

Heimer filled a large glass with water and drank as much as he could in one long gulp. He poured what was left at the bottom over his head. Small streams made their way through his hair and opted to trickle down his face or run down inside his shirt collar. He closed his eyes and fumbled after the dish towel double-folded over the oven door handle. The coarse fabric smelled a little funny when he rubbed it against his skin, but at least he was dry.

After a hundred push-ups and a cup of coffee he was back to himself. It was just after eleven o'clock in the morning, which meant the postman ought to have come. He put on a pair of old clogs in the hall. Then he opened the door and went down the drive toward the mailbox. It had been custom-ordered from Italy and was installed in an enclosed niche in the wall. He put the key in the lock, turned it, and opened the door to retrieve the contents of the metal box. There it was, on top of a boat accessories catalog that he had forgotten he had requested.

A new letter.

He held it up to the daylight to get a better look. The sender was the same as last time—there was no doubt about it. The address had been written in a mixture of upper- and lowercase letters using the same black ink pen.

Heimer left the catalog and locked the mailbox again. He looked around, as if expecting the sender to be lying in wait somewhere in the bushes, spying on him. It was a creepy, unpleasant sensation—but also completely irrational. The envelope was postmarked Karlstad, just like last time. The person who wrote it would hardly be here.

He hurried back inside and found himself locking the front door behind him. This was out of the ordinary. The front door was usually left unlocked when he was at home in the daytime. He went upstairs taking quick steps and put the letter on the kitchen island. Then he paused—he took a few steps back and looked at the envelope.

The sender hadn't waited a week or a month to get in touch.

He or she had waited a day.

Heimer noticed his right hand shaking as he inserted his index finger under the flap and began to open the envelope. Part of him wanted to know what the letter said, while another part wanted to throw it in the trash and pretend it had never arrived. The sheet inside was folded in half like last time and he had to flatten the paper with his hand to make it lie flat on the surface. Then he read it.

Select the Lobby chatroom at chatta.se. Log on at 7:30 P.M. on Friday. Call yourself Froggy and search for Nadja6543.

Heimer tried to comprehend the meaning of those few sentences. Apparently he had to visit a chatroom and talk to the letter writer. He had never done that before. The word "chatroom" alone made him feel like he was a hundred years old. He took a deep breath in an attempt to reduce his heart rate but his heart continued beating even more wildly inside his ribs. It bothered him that he'd have to wait three days before he heard from the letter writer again.

Three days and the same number of nights.

During which he wouldn't be able to sleep.

Nor eat.

He wouldn't be able to think about anyone except Nadja6543 and what the person hiding behind the name had to tell him.

41

John leaned back in his chair with the sketch pad on his lap and his feet on the desk. The last few days had consisted largely of waiting, so this morning he decided to bring both the investigation piece and the pencil case with him to the musty basement.

Mona's colleagues in Stockholm needed more time than expected to locate the seven potential perpetrators and take new DNA samples. But eventually everyone had been tracked down, with one exception—a former detective inspector who now lived in Frankfurt. Originally, they thought they'd ask the Germans for help. Germany's Federal Police had turned out to be unreasonably bureaucratic. After spending a frustrating hour on the phone, Mona gave up and booked herself a plane ticket.

That was barely twenty-four hours ago and she had only been in touch once—to say that the man in Frankfurt had given a sample and that the sample was being shipped by air courier to the lab in Linköping. Soon the wait would be over and they'd know whose DNA was a match to the semen.

John put the pencil between his teeth and reviewed the latest adjustments to the investigation piece. The question mark signifying the person that Emelie Bjurwall had agreed to meet the evening she went missing had been reshaped into a two-sided face. One half was friendly and inviting, the other was dangerous and aggressive. Doctor Jekyll and Mister Hyde—different sides of the same person, just like in the novel.

He closed the sketch pad and put it in the desk drawer along with the pencils. Mona would be back soon and he didn't want her to see the piece. It had been bad enough being called "Picasso" in New York.

Outside the small windows it had stopped raining. A faint shaft of sunlight was seeping down through the dreariness and penetrating into the police station basement. John considered whether to go to the gym on the first floor and spend an hour on the treadmill. His gym bag was on the floor by his desk and he knew the exercise would make him less restless.

He thought about Trevor and the time in the safe house where they had hidden while waiting for the trial to begin. Each time John had tried to take him out for a run, his colleague had shaken his head.

"I've run enough this year," he had said, referring to their escape from the container at the port.

Trevor had been certain that all those hours, days, and months in police gyms had been nothing but preparation for those few minutes when he had saved John's life. Now that he'd passed the final test, he could quit working out, his conscience clear.

"That's how it is for all us top athletes—we know when it's time to quit," he had chuckled.

John smiled at the memory and pulled his chair closer to the desk before logging on to the encrypted email service. He hadn't checked it for a few days and he cheered up when he saw there was a new message. Trevor's email had arrived early that morning. To begin with, the tone was as lighthearted as before and he didn't mention any paranoia or mysterious cars watching him. But when John reached the last few lines he got an unpleasant surprise.

My stomach has been causing me some trouble. It started around the time I got here. It's hurt since then. I thought it was the food here and that my belly couldn't deal with it, or a stomach ulcer or something like that. I've been doing nothing but popping pills lately. On Saturday it became unbearable. I went to the hospital and stayed there overnight. They did an X-ray and found three tumors in my large intestine. Bingo! Waiting for more tests to come back, but I guess it'll be surgery. It'll be fine—they seem pretty damn good at their jobs here. Just sick of hospitals. Our stay was enough and then some.

Just wanted to tell someone.

Take care. T.

John read the final sentences one more time. Cancer. The whole thing was a broadside. Not Trevor. Not now. Not after everything he had gone through.

John pounded the desk with his fist so hard that two files fell to the floor. Slowly, and suddenly feeling weak, he bent down to pick them up. It had to be okay, he thought to himself. Trevor had mentioned surgery. There was probably some way of getting rid of the shit in his stomach. There had to be. His friend couldn't die. It would make him lonelier than he could imagine.

When Mona showed up in the basement an hour later, John had just about managed to collect his thoughts after the bad news. She had come straight from the airport with her wheelie case.

"The DNA analysis is done," she said, hanging her coat on the chair. "I got the reports by email, but I wanted to wait until we were together to check them."

She opened the computer and connected to the network. They'd been waiting for this for days. The man who buried Emelie Bjurwall's body and blamed Billy would be given a face. She pulled up the report from Linköping on full screen. John stood behind her and read over her shoulder. He had made it halfway through the first paragraph when Mona threw her arms up in despair.

"What the hell is this?!" she shouted, jumping out of her chair so abruptly that John took a step back.

"What?" he said.

"No matches. This can't be fucking possible!"

But it was. John leaned forward and double-checked the screen. None of the seven samples that had been analyzed was a match with the semen on the rock.

Mona called the forensic specialist responsible to check how the testing had been done. Only after he explained that all the samples had been analyzed three times and that none of the DNA profiles was even similar to that of the semen did she calm down and apologize for her angry tone of voice.

"We must have missed someone," she said. "Someone who didn't live in the area but was sampled anyway."

"And are we sure that the population register was exhaustive?" John asked, hoping she wouldn't take it as criticism.

"Yes, I think we can assume so. This is the state we're talking about—not corner shops paying wages under the counter."

Mona went up to the whiteboard with the two overlapping circles and turned to him.

"What was the name of the old lead investigator?"

John didn't need to check any documents to answer that question. He had reviewed the investigation enough times to remember the name of the now-retired detective chief inspector. If there was anyone who knew who had given samples of their DNA and why they had been picked, it would be him.

"Why the hell did you let Billy Nerman go?"

John looked around Anton Lundberg's apartment. The décor was more welcoming than that of the place he was staying, he thought to himself. However, it was no surprise that the conversation had started the way it had. Police who left unsolved cases behind rarely liked it when new investigators questioned established truths.

"The forensic evidence against him no longer holds up," he said, sticking to what the papers had said.

"You mean it wasn't Nerman's semen on the rock?"

"Yes, that's what I meant."

Lundberg fell back into his chair and grinned superciliously.

"Bullshit," he snorted. "There must be another reason."

"It's not bullshit," said John. "It's fact."

He had started to grow weary of this bitter old man with the big birthmark on his forehead.

"There's one thing you should know," Lundberg added, jabbing his index finger in the air. "I spent two whole weeks trying to crack that bastard—and I'd bet my grandchild's life it was him."

His eyes were burning with contempt. This was what his brother had encountered from day one in the investigation. The forensic evidence and how well Billy fit into the role of perpetrator had blinded the investigators. They hadn't been interested in hearing anything from him except a confession.

"I've got a few questions for you," he said in an attempt to move on. "Is that alright?"

Lundberg shrugged his shoulders as if he didn't care. John didn't allow himself to be provoked, simply steering the conversation on to the new topic.

"How did you decide who to take DNA samples from?"

"Doesn't it say in the investigation?"

"I'm asking you."

"As I recall, all men living in the area around the crime scene had to provide their DNA. We used postal code areas."

"Anyone else?"

"Yes, close family and several of her male acquaintances. Including ones who didn't live on the island."

John sighed silently. So far, the retired detective chief inspector had offered no new information.

"Can you try to remember what you did before you got the DNA match? What was the investigation focused on?" he said coaxingly.

"Hmm, well," said Lundberg, at any rate looking as if he was trying to think. "We talked to the parents, obviously. Tried to establish a picture of the girl. We worked on the timeline. I remember we questioned several of the kids who were at that party the night Emelie disappeared."

"Okay, anything else?"

Lundberg shut his eyes and put his hand over his birthmark, as if digging deep into his memory.

"We watched videos."

"Videos?"

"Yes," he said, opening his eyes again. "Hours of CCTV footage from a gas station. It's gone now, but it was on the road out to Tynäs. We hoped that the perpetrator had stopped to fill up or buy something. We took the registrations of all the cars that stopped there in the hours before and after the disappearance. Then we found the owners. If they were men and hadn't already given their DNA, we took samples from them too. But it didn't turn up anything."

John felt his hope reignited and extinguished all within the same conversation. If Lundberg was right, there were other people who had given DNA samples. But finding out who they were would require the CCTV footage. Given the thorough cleanup job the perpetrator had done, the likelihood of it still being in the archives was pretty much zero.

"What format were the videos in?" John asked.

"DVDs. I remember that because I made copies of them. We were working long hours at the time and I thought it would be useful to watch them at home in the evening too. That way at least I could drink some coffee with the wife during my breaks."

"You don't still have the videos, do you?"

Lundberg looked at him suspiciously.

"Does it matter? The originals are in the archives with all the other stuff. All you have to do is get them from there."

"It's been a bit of a mess lately," said John. "Some material went missing in a move."

"The archive has moved?"

"No, but some older materials have been archived differently to how they were before. Lack of space."

John might as well have been telling him about Santa Claus and the tooth fairy. He had lost his touch since his days as a field agent when the lies had come naturally to him. Lundberg got up and disappeared out of the room. When he returned he had two DVD cases that he handed over to John.

"You're lying, obviously. I just need to point that out, so you don't go away thinking this old man is completely past it. But if the videos are of any use then I won't stand in your way."

Police work according to the assembly line principle—that was how they structured their afternoon in the basement. They used a big old-school TV they'd wheeled in from one of the abandoned conference rooms. Mona handled the remote, pausing the videos at the right moments, when people's faces were visible as they filled up with fuel. John ran the license plates against the motor vehicles register and found the names of the men who lived at the addresses. Then Mona would step in and compare them with the personnel lists from the law enforcement agencies. Once they had gotten into the swing of it, the procedure took barely a minute for each car. Henry Ford would have been proud.

On the computer John looked at the spreadsheet filled with rows of license numbers and names. After two hours of staring at screens and searching databases, his eyes needed a break.

"I'll get coffee," he said, getting up.

"Thanks, you do that. I'm going to try not to think about how many cars we've got left to check," said Mona.

John took the elevator up to the first floor, where the kitchen was. It was the afternoon, but there were still a few hours left of the working day. The atmosphere was sleepy and most of the office doors were shut. He could see the blueish light of the computer screens and the silhouettes of detectives sitting in front of them through the thin blinds covering the windows onto the corridor.

When he reached the small kitchen, he opened the cupboard door over the counter to get out the mug Mona had given him as a gift. It wouldn't budge.

Glue.

Jesus Christ.

Someone had glued his mug to the cupboard. This silent war was getting out of control and John was beginning to have serious regrets about starting it. He now realized that his protest against the kitchen schedule had been seen as so much more than that. It was an attack on the Swedes' perceptions of solidarity and fairness. No one was above taking part in the kitchen chores. John expected even the damn prime minister was probably giving the tables "an extra wipe" in the government break room right now.

He sighed, filled two paper cups with coffee, and took them back to the basement.

"Where's the beautiful mug I gave you?"

John put the cups on the table. He blew on his hands, which were stinging after the ride in the elevator.

"You don't want to know."

She shrugged and turned the TV back on. A new car was arriving at the gas station, but it didn't even make it to the pump before she paused the video.

"Actually, I do want to know," she said with an amused smile.

John sighed and told her the whole story. Mona didn't even try to control herself. She threw her head back, howling with laughter—if they hadn't been in the basement everyone in the building would have heard it.

"And this was your plan for maintaining a low profile?"

John didn't answer—he just looked at her, annoyed.

She laughed even more and put a hand on his shoulder.

"I'll deal with the problem for you—I promise."

"How?"

"Just trust me, okay?"

She pressed play. The cars continued to flicker by. The same tedious procedure repeated over and over: park at the pump, get out of the car, insert credit card, fill up, and then pull away. The only variation came from those customers who chose to pay at the counter and had brought some unnecessary purchase out with them.

As the evening got later, the cars became less regular. John checked the time counter in the bottom corner of the screen. When Mona paused for an Opel Estate it was 10:46 p.m.—about an hour until Emelie Bjurwall would leave the party to meet Mister Hyde.

An old man got out of the car with difficulty and approached the pump.

"Hundred kronor says he pays cash," said John.

"Two hundred kronor says he buys some ciggies," Mona countered.

In silence, they watched the man stumble into the shop and emerge with an ice cream.

"He's got the cigarettes in his pocket," she said, hitting fast-forward.

The time counter moved on. John saw it turn eleven and watched the manager close up. He took the windshield washing fluid and garden toys that had been outside into the shop before locking the door. Then he vanished out of view on a bicycle.

There couldn't be many cars left to check up on now, and so far they'd scored no wins. John stared at the screen. If it hadn't been for the time counter moving on, he would have thought Mona had paused again. Absolutely nothing was happening—just time passing at a deserted gas station ten years ago. An episode in history that was so trivial and meaningless that it barely deserved to be kept on file for posterity.

Then the camera captured a Subaru pulling up to the forward pump. The driver seemed busy with something in the car and stayed at the wheel. Maybe he wanted to wrap up a phone call or finish listening to a song. John checked the time. It was 11:42.

"Is he just going to stay inside?" Mona sighed.

At that moment, the door opened and the driver went up to the card terminal. He was wearing a cap, which together with the angle of the camera made it impossible to see his face. He put a card in the terminal and chose his pump. Then he unhooked the hose and began to fill up. While gasoline flowed into the car he unintentionally turned toward the camera. In that movement, he also pushed the cap up, making his face visible.

Mona paused.

She seemed as mesmerized by the screen as John was.

Could it really be?

The man on the screen was ten years younger and considerably less heavy than the person they had gotten to know at the police station.

The years had not been kind to Bernt Primer.

The hit in the motor vehicles registration database confirmed what they already knew. The owner of the black Subaru Impreza in August 2009 had been Bernt Gunnar Primer, resident at Löwenborgs väg in Karlstad, where he still lived.

If it hadn't been so far to the coffee maker, John would've fetched a refill. Or even better, put a nip of whiskey in his paper cup. The irony was not lost on him. The man who had thrown him off the AckWe case due to his relationship with Billy was a potential suspect. Rules about conflict of interest apparently didn't apply when you were investigating yourself.

"What the hell do we do now?" John asked, as much to himself as to Mona.

"What we would do if it were any other police officer in this video," she said, pointing at the TV where Primer's frozen face was still staring at them. "Talk to him nicely. Ask what he was doing on the island at that time of night and ask for a DNA sample."

"And the commissioner?"

"Not a word to him until we've run Primer's sample against the semen."

John liked what he was hearing. Mona was no politician—she was a cop just like him. There was no reason to pull the top dog in until they had more to go on.

"Why didn't Lundberg say anything?" said Mona. "He must surely have remembered that one of his own officers was in the footage from the gas station. Especially given the time. Primer filled up half an hour before Emelie Bjurwall left the party and went missing."

"Yes, but I didn't tell him we were looking for one of our own. And back then Primer was just one of many who gave DNA samples as a matter of course. Nothing back then suggested a police officer was mixed up in this."

She nodded and seemed to accept his reasoning. What was more, a decade had passed. If anyone had asked him questions about investigations he had been involved in or even led in New York City years ago, he probably wouldn't be able to remember a thing.

"We'll talk to him down here, right? Out of sight, away from his colleagues on the corridor," said John.

"Yes, but we don't want him to suspect anything. If he has time to prepare we might miss his spontaneous reaction."

"So, we need a pretext?"

"Something innocent. Preferably administrative."

John watched Mona's cogs turning.

"What about money?" she said.

"Money?"

"Yes, a budgetary issue. I'll call him and ask him to come down to discuss a request from Stockholm for county CID to cover part of my expenses. He'll buy that. If I stay somewhere for a long time, the boss usually wants to try to send the bill to someone else."

"Won't he be suspicious if I'm here in that case?"

"Not if you stay in the background. We need two of us keeping an eye on him."

John listened as she called Primer. He took the bait and promised to come right away. The cops in Stockholm wouldn't get the better of him.

"As the old jungle saying goes," she said with satisfaction when she had hung up, "if you want the boss's attention, tell him something costs money."

"Jungle saying?" said John in confusion.

She looked at him.

"Sometimes I forget you've not been in Sweden long."

Just a few minutes later, Primer thundered into the big office, ready to fight for every last krona of his budget.

"We'll have to sit down and sort this out," he said, looking at Mona.

"Absolutely. There was just one other thing I wanted to check with you first, if that's alright?"

"Of course," he said, crossing his arms across his large stomach.

John didn't know whether the distancing gesture was part of his financial negotiation or whether Primer already sensed something was wrong. It fell to him to observe the former lead investigator. To search for the shifts in his facial expression and hesitations in his voice. It wouldn't be easy—especially not when the man they were about to confront knew every trick in the book.

"It's about the DNA samples," said Mona. "We've managed to re-create the lists and make a file with the names of everyone who gave a sample during the last investigation—and we've run these against the personnel lists from the law enforcement agencies."

"Oh?" he said, cautiously.

"But we've not found any hits."

"No?"

John listened for undertones but found none. Primer sounded genuinely surprised.

"No, and that's very strange. Everything suggested the perpetrator gave a DNA sample and then swapped their own sample for Billy Nerman's. For them to have been able to do that, they would have needed knowledge of the investigation and access to the DNA samples. Yet we've turned up nothing. Do you have any ideas?"

Only now did Primer sit down on the chair Mona had pulled over for him.

"I don't know what to say. It sounds strange."

"Our conclusion is that we must have missed some of the people who gave samples ten years ago. That's why John and I decided to visit Anton Lundberg."

Primer perked up and looked at John.

"Lundberg—it's been a while. How was he?"

If he was acting, it was impressive. There was no tremor in Primer's voice and no signs of nervousness.

"He seemed well."

John paused for a long time before moving onto the more sensitive issue.

"Lundberg said there was a gas station near Tynäs back then."

"Yes, that's right, but it didn't break even. People out there were always complaining about bad service and they tended to go elsewhere."

"There was CCTV on the forecourt and according to Lundberg you took DNA samples from everyone who filled up there in the hours before and after the disappearance."

John met his gaze. This was a crucial moment. If Primer was innocent and had simply forgotten the video, he would confirm Lundberg's account and say that he had given a sample.

The talkative Värmlander fell silent and seemed to be thinking.

"Yes, that's right. We reviewed the footage and followed up on the male drivers to get samples. I'd forgotten about that."

John gave him space to keep going, but when the silence became uncomfortable he knew Primer wasn't going to say anything else. There were only two reasons why that might be. Either the man had a very selective memory that allowed him to remember the CCTV footage but not that he had featured in it. Or—and this seemed more probable—he was coolly reckoning that the footage would never be retrieved.

John glanced at Mona who nodded discreetly at him. She wanted him to bring in the heavy artillery.

"We checked the archived investigation files for the CCTV footage," he said, thinking about the boxes in the archives that he had gone through after his visit to

Anton Lundberg just to be sure. "According to the contents list there should be two DVDs, but just like the list of DNA samples, they're missing."

"Stolen?" said Primer with a frown.

"Yes, it would seem so."

"So, you think the perpetrator took the DVDs because he's one of the people who filled up at the gas station?"

"It's a theory at least, but it'll be hard to get anywhere with it if the videos are missing," said Mona.

"Yes, of course," said Primer.

John thought he saw a flash of relief in his expression, but it might have just been his imagination.

"But this time we got lucky," he said. "Really lucky, actually."

Primer looked interested.

"Oh, how so?"

"Lundberg made copies of the DVDs to watch at home. He's kept them all these years and he let me have them. Mona and I have been watching them all afternoon."

Primer's expression didn't change. His insides were presumably a chaotic mess of stress and tactical considerations of what he should and shouldn't say, but none of this showed on his face.

"We thought we'd play you a clip," said John, turning on the TV.

He reached for the remote and a moment later they watched a Subaru Impreza pull onto the forecourt. The former lead investigator followed what was happening on the screen attentively, but said nothing about the car being his. John played the video all the way up to the moment when the man at the pump pushed his cap up and turned toward the camera. Then Primer began to laugh.

"Fuck me, I'd forgotten about that. Dementia is apparently well and truly on the way."

"So that's you in the video?" said Mona.

"Yes, of course it's me. A bit less ballast, but definitely me."

More laughter. Not nervous, booming. The way Primer sounded when he was amused.

"Did you give a DNA sample?" she said.

"Of course. Lundberg made no exceptions. I had to give a sample like everyone else."

"And what were you doing out on Hammarö just before midnight?"

"Checking on my boat. There had been some shenanigans in the harbor that summer. Some trifles and other valuables had gone missing."

"Did you meet anyone?"

"No, it was late at night and there are no guest berths out there."

John listened attentively. His body language was still relaxed, but Primer had started making mistakes. His account of the evening was emerging too rapidly and it was too detailed. From not even remembering the visit to the gas station, he had suddenly remembered why he had been on the island that late and that the harbor had been deserted.

"I hope you've no objection to us taking a new DNA sample," said Mona, sounding at once friendly and formal.

"Of course not. Now?"

She nodded at John, who unscrewed the lid from a plastic tube, pulled out the swab and waited for Primer to open his mouth. He leaned forward and ran the swab against the tissue on the inside of Primer's cheek a couple of times. Then he put the swab back in the tube and screwed the lid back on.

"There we are then," said Mona neutrally.

"And the expenses that Stockholm wanted us to cover—what are we going to do about those?"

John's amazement at Primer's brazen manner did not cease. If the sample matched the semen on the rock then he had just handed over the crucial evidence. Such an outward display of cool composure at the very moment the roof was caving in was something few people could've pulled off.

"I'll talk to Stockholm and see whether we can resolve it internally. If there's a problem, I'll get back in touch," said Mona.

It was a bad lie that Primer saw straight through.

"Well, that's fine," he said with a smile as he got up. He uttered a dutiful *good luck* and then they were alone again in the basement.

"So, what are we supposed to make of that?" said John.

"It's strange," said Mona. "The harder I pushed, the nicer he got. Not exactly the response you usually get from suspects."

"He didn't react at all when I played the video," John said. "It's almost superhuman."

"Assuming he's not in fact innocent."

John raised his eyebrows.

"Do you think that?"

"I don't think anything. I'm trying to be professional. As you may recall, this investigation has already hit a wall once thanks to police with tunnel vision."

John was about to object and point out that it was different this time when he realized that it wasn't. Everything had pointed to Billy then—just like it was pointing to Primer now.

"Okay, you have a point," he conceded. "So what do we do?"

Mona stood up.

"I'll make sure this gets analyzed as soon as possible," she said, taking the plastic tube from John's desk. "And you keep an eye on our suspect. I want to know what he does next."

"Bernt Primer has gone home."

John twitched and turned on his heel in the management corridor on the second floor. The woman speaking to John was the same one who had escorted him to the meeting with the Walrus. She seemed to divide her time between the reception desk and administrative tasks for management.

"When?"

"Just now. Said he felt off."

John peered through the blinds again. The desk chair was pushed under the table and he couldn't see a jacket or bag in the room.

"Not to worry—it'll keep until tomorrow," he said, hurrying back to the stairs. There was a big window with a view of the parking lot. He cast his gaze over the expanse of asphalt and managed to spot Primer squeezing his large body into a blue Nissan SUV.

John wouldn't make it downstairs in time to follow him. It would also be a bad idea to do it in the Chrysler. It drew too much attention. Instead, he took the elevator to the garage in the basement. They issued him a civilian surveillance car with an automatic transmission—a white Volkswagen Passat.

He took a chance on Primer having headed straight home and entered Löwenborgs väg into the GPS. The mapping software instructed him to take the E18 highway west and then exit just before the big shopping center he could never remember the name of, even though he had been there countless times as a child.

As he got close to the address, John slowed down. He saw identical red brick houses in neat rows with well-tended hedges bordering small front lawns.

Primer's house was on the left-hand side of the road. The blue Nissan was on the drive and John stopped at a safe distance.

John got his phone out of his jacket pocket and called Mona, who picked up after one ring.

"Where are you?"

"Outside Primer's house," he said, explaining that the former lead investigator had feigned illness and gone home for the day.

"Interesting. Considering how calm he was, I would've thought he'd keep working."

"Maybe it's starting to dawn on him what's going to happen."

"Let's not get ahead of ourselves," said Mona. "But it's a good idea to keep an eye on him. What time shall I relieve you?"

John smiled to himself. Clearly she wasn't unaccustomed to working at uncomfortable hours of the day.

"No need," he said.

42

For the first time in years, Heimer had blisters from his shoes. He sat on the sofa with the laptop next to him and twisted his leg into an uncomfortable position so that he could examine the bubble of skin on his heel. It was red and hurt when he pressed it. The combination of new shoes and the manic running of the last few days had been painful. But pushing his body to the limit was the only way to silence the anxiety gnawing away inside him.

He leaned back against the sofa, rubbed his eyes, and tried to relax. All he had thought about in the last few days was the anonymous letter. Heimer had visited the site the evening before to familiarize himself with the setup. There hadn't been many chatters online. But now, when he opened the laptop and logged on, the situation was different. There was a Friday night vibe and the chatrooms were filled with people who preferred socializing on their screens to meeting up in real life.

Heimer wished the letter writer had given him another nickname. Froggy divulged nothing about gender, and it made him more popular than he would've liked. After just a few minutes, his screen was filled with messages from screen names like HotGuy and his mates. They wanted to know whether he was a girl and whether he wanted to get to know them a little better. When he ignored them they raised their voices.

Come on. Pics please.

Don't be such a cunt.

Heimer wanted to reply to the chatters and tell them he was a man of almost sixty who was NOT going to send any pics. But that would only trigger a fresh avalanche of messages. He was already busy enough keeping track of the stream of visitors logging in and out of the Lobby of the chatroom.

The clock in the top right corner of the screen moved forward. It was 7:26—just four minutes left until the appointed time.

Is it your time of the month or what?

The messages kept coming, but there were gradually fewer of them. The boys—many of them no doubt men his own age—had presumably found someone else to harass.

He thought about Sissela and how angry she got when he hadn't given the first letter to the police. This time she wouldn't find out, given that she was occupied with her director of finance. The thought of the two of them naked in a Paris hotel room made him sick.

He glanced at the time. Still no Nadja6543.

Had the letter writer gotten cold feet and called it all off? Doubtful. The sort of person who started something like this probably had sufficient nerve to see it through. He found himself thinking of the person as a woman, even though it could just as easily be a man.

Then it arrived—the message he'd been waiting for. Nadja must have entered the chatroom without him noticing. He or she was as taciturn online as they were in their letters. *Switch to Salon* was their instruction.

Heimer felt overcome by nerves. The thing he had visualized so many times over the last few days was now happening. He read the message again and tried to find the Salon. The mouse was harder to move when his fingers were slick with sweat, but he eventually managed to open the virtual door to the new chatroom.

The letter writer was waiting for him inside.

Are you alone?

Yes, Heimer replied.

Good. Listen carefully.

Heimer nodded at the computer and then remembered that Nadja couldn't see him.

I'm listening, he wrote, instead. He found himself holding his breath.

It was as if the letter writer were reaching through the screen with their hands and squeezing his throat. Nadja had all the power and he had none.

The text appeared so quickly that it had to have been written in advance and then pasted into the chatroom.

In ten days' time, have 300,000 kronor ready in a bag. Drop it off in locker 109 at the train station in Karlstad at exactly 2:00 P.M. Lock the locker, take the key with you, and get on the bus to Säffle leaving at 2:12.

Heimer scribbled the information into a notebook. His hands were shaking so much that he struggled to write. Despite the absurdity of the situation, he wasn't surprised. He had spent several days and nights thinking—and he had been expecting something like this.

He put down the pen and returned to the keyboard.

Can I trust you? he wrote.

The answer came quickly.

Yes.

Heimer brushed his hair from his forehead. It wasn't reassuring. The answer was so brief and automatic. Just *yes*—nothing else. However, he knew that more words wouldn't have made him feel any better. He had asked a question and Nadja had answered. He'd have to be satisfied with that.

How do you know? he wrote.

This time the answer took some time. The letter writer needed time to think. The emptiness of the Salon seemed to echo. It was just the two of them in there. Heimer stared intensely at the screen, as if it were possible to see through it and make out the contours of the person on the other side.

Eventually, his vision began to flicker and he had to close his eyes for a bit until it calmed down. When he opened them he still hadn't received an answer. He hesitated for a moment and then wrote:

Who are you?

The answer came quickly.

Nadja6543 has left the room.

43

In order to avoid starting the engine—and giving away their position on a stakeout—some of the unmarked police cars in New York City were equipped with portable electric heaters that could be plugged into the cigarette lighter. They were like gold dust during the winter months when officers working surveillance at night were freezing their asses off. The Swedes didn't feel the cold the same way. John had searched both under the seats and in the trunk without finding a heater. Either the Scandinavian cops were hardened to it, or they hadn't come up with the idea yet. He guessed the latter.

His thin suit trousers felt cold against his thighs and his toes had begun to go numb in his Loake shoes. He'd already dismissed the idea of driving away from the residential neighborhood to warm up the car a bit. Primer could still be awake and might get suspicious if there was activity out on the quiet street in the middle of the night.

John lowered the side window a crack to clear the foggy windshield and checked the time.

11:45 P.M.

Thus far, the surveillance had been undramatic. Primer had spent most of the afternoon and evening at the kitchen table with his laptop, and then he had gone to bed. The house was dark and the whole neighborhood seemed to be asleep.

John turned on the radio—for the umpteenth time during the stakeout—and twiddled the tuner for a while before turning it back off.

He didn't feel like himself.

How many hours, days, weeks had he spent like this? Keeping an eye on people under police protection or watching suspected criminals had been part of his daily work as a detective in New York City and he never had any issues with it. Quite the opposite—he liked it.

But now it was different. After everything that had happened in Baltimore, situations like this made his skin crawl—times when he was alone with just himself and no distractions to divert his thoughts. He found himself putting his hand to his stomach, as if looking for Trevor's tumors in his own body. The friends' fates were so closely entwined that it wouldn't have surprised him if he too had cancer.

He took a deep breath and reclined the seat back a notch. Then he saw lights in the rearview mirror and sat up again. On the other side of the sparse clump of trees, there was a taxi that had just stopped. John turned toward the house. If Primer had called a cab and he jumped into it, he'd have a head start. He was relieved when he saw the door of the taxi open and a woman get out. It hadn't been ordered for a pickup—it was doing a drop-off.

The woman took a shortcut through the trees and then walked along the dark path past the bus shelters and toward John. He saw her weaving between puddles glittering like small lakes on the asphalt. In the meantime, he noticed that the taxi hadn't left—it was still there with its engine running. He sank farther down into his seat while waiting for her to pass. When no one appeared, he looked around and out the back window. The woman was no longer in sight. She must live in one of the first houses and had presumably vanished into the front yard.

A gentle tap on the driver's side window made him jump.

"You're not drifting off, are you?" said a familiar voice through the crack in the window.

"No. How the fuck would I in this cold?" said John.

Mona walked around the car and got in. She handed him a brown paper bag.

"Only McDonald's was open, I'm afraid. But I guess like all Americans you like fast food . . ."

"Stereotype or fact?"

"Both, I suspect."

Mona looked at him searchingly.

"You look tired. Go home and get some sleep—I'll take over. I asked the taxi to wait."

John looked in the rearview mirror and saw the black car was still there, ready to take him home to the apartment at Bryggudden and his warm bed. But what would he do there? Lie, sleepless, staring at the night sky through the skylight? He was barely fifty meters from the man who made Billy's life hell. Leaving now would feel like betrayal.

"Don't worry," he said, retrieving a hot cup of coffee from the paper bag.

Mona ran her hand through her wet hair and then opened her bag.

"You left this in the basement," she said, handing over John's rolled-up overcoat.

"Thanks."

She used her phone flashlight to signal to the taxi, which slowly departed into the darkness.

"Which one is his?" she said, nodding at the row of identical houses.

"On the left, with the blue SUV outside. He hasn't left all evening."

"No visits?"

"No."

John took a sip of coffee and felt its warmth spread through his chest. He could smell from Mona's breath that she had drunk wine and he stifled the impulse to ask where she'd been. It was none of his business and he didn't really care. When it came to life outside of work, she had an aura of integrity around her. During the short time they had worked together he'd found out nothing about her private life—apart from the fling with Tinder Martin, and he got that through spying.

He dug into the bag and found chicken nuggets, fries, and dipping sauces, before opting for a hamburger. However, after he'd pulled off the wrapper and taken a few bites, he put it back. Even though he hadn't eaten since lunch—apart from the bar of chocolate someone had left in the glove compartment—he wasn't hungry. Smelling the fast food was all it had taken to kill his appetite.

"I've checked him out," said Mona, pulling her notebook from her pocket.

She angled it toward the windshield so that the streetlight would illuminate the text.

"Primer has been registered at this address since 1989. He's never been married and doesn't appear to have any children. He trained as a police officer in Stockholm and did a six-month assignment in Helsingborg. After that he came back to Karlstad and spent three years working as a beat cop before taking his detective inspector exams at the end of the nineties."

She paused and flashed one of her barely perceptible smiles at John.

"You'll like this."

"What?"

"From the autumn of 2001 he worked in narcotics—and he was there for almost a decade."

"Jesus—that's how he got the cocaine and sold it to Emelie."

"It's a theory, at least," said Mona. "But he must have done a pretty tidy job. There are no reports about missing evidence."

"Mister Hyde," said John, looking at the dark house. "If Emelie knew Primer was a police detective and also dealing drugs, she might very well have called him out on it."

"Yes, and it wouldn't surprise me if he let her pay with sex."

"What a bastard," he said, thinking about how well the scenario correlated with what Matilda Jacoby had told him about Emelie's destructive behavior.

Mona looked at her notebook again.

"Apparently he was on temporary assignment in Anton Lundberg's department in the summer of 2009 when Emelie went missing. Anyway, Primer went back to narcotics once the AckWe investigation was closed and stayed on for another year or so before ending up with Lundberg again."

John pulled out his phone and started searching through his contacts. Eventually, he found the name he was looking for.

"What are you doing?" said Mona.

"I'm calling Matilda Jacoby. If it was Primer that Emelie went to meet, she may be able to confirm it."

She pulled the phone away from him and ended the call before it started ringing.

"We're not going to call anyone until we can tie him to the scene."

"But Matilda might have kept quiet precisely because he was with the police."

"Matilda Jacoby is a junkie," said Mona. "If we give her sensitive information, she won't hesitate for a second to sell it to the media as soon as her comedown gets too tough and she needs cash. We need to talk to her—but not until we hear back from the lab in Linköping."

She handed the phone back to John and kept her gaze on him to emphasize the seriousness of what she'd just said.

John was woken by Mona tapping his thigh. He pulled his coat off his face and glanced at the clock on the dashboard. It said 2:31 A.M. What felt like a quick nap had been almost two hours of sleep. He shifted his seat upright and stretched his aching body as best he could in the cramped space.

"He's up and moving about," said Mona, pointing through the windshield.

John rubbed his eyes and turned his gaze to Primer's house. A light was on in the downstairs hall.

"He came downstairs a little while ago and disappeared into the room with the small square window."

"That's the bathroom. He's probably just having a piss," said John.

"Maybe. But I'm not so sure."

"No?"

"No, it looked like he was carrying something."

John looked at Mona.

"Carrying what?" he asked.

"I don't know."

John felt the last of the sleepiness leave his body. They sat in silence for a long time, trying to see what was happening inside the house. The light was switched off and a dark figure emerged into the kitchen. The fluorescent tube above the sink flashed and an angry white hue illuminated the room.

"He's dressed," said John.

Mona nodded tensely.

They watched Primer open the fridge door and get out a carton, which he drank from. John guessed it was milk or juice. Then he returned to the hall, turned left, and disappeared once again from sight.

"What's he doing?" Mona whispered to herself.

It had begun to drizzle and John closed the side window to stop water from getting inside the car. A moment later, Primer returned to the kitchen—he was now wearing a coat—and turned off the light.

Mona fell back into her seat.

"Jesus! He really is leaving," she said.

Then the front door opened and Primer emerged onto the front step carrying two suitcases.

At the same time, the rain grew in intensity. Water streamed down the windshield and it became harder to see what was happening by the house. John didn't dare turn on the wipers in case Primer noticed.

"Do we arrest him?"

He could see Mona thinking as she stared out into the wet darkness.

"No," she said finally.

"Why not? If he heads off in his car there's a high risk of something going wrong. It's two against one here and we have the element of surprise on our side."

"We can't arrest a senior detective until we're absolutely sure," she interrupted. "It'll be a damn mess if we happen to be wrong."

"We're not wrong. He got up in the middle of the night and put two suitcases in the trunk of his car. Surely that says it all?"

Primer shut the trunk, turned on the engine, and reversed into the street. The headlights swept across the unmarked police car while John and Mona crouched down in the front seats. When they looked up again they saw two taillights leaving the neighborhood.

"Follow him," she said.

John waited until Primer had vanished from sight before pressing the ignition button. He drove slowly with his headlights off along the narrow streets, before eventually reaching the main road. He put his foot down, and didn't ease up until he was at a safe distance from Primer and could hang back.

"Oslo or Stockholm?" said Mona, plugging her charger into the car's USB port.

John put on his seatbelt to silence the beeping safety warning and focused on the red lights ahead. They got their answer at the first exit. Primer turned left and headed onto the E18 going north—toward the Swedish capital.

Mona scrolled through her contacts and made a call.

"Hello—this is Ejdewik at National Crime. I need to check whether a certain individual has a booking with any airline today, and if so, where he's going."

She waited on the line.

"His name is Bernt Primer—and he's probably traveling from Arlanda," she added, and read out his social security number from her notebook.

She waited again while the person searched the database. Meanwhile, Primer was stuck behind a truck and the distance between them was shrinking rapidly. The illumination from the many lights on the back of the truck shone into the blue SUV. The figure ahead was still as a statue at the wheel. John eased his foot off the accelerator.

"Okay, great," said Mona after a long pause. "Gate number?"

She offered concise thanks, ended the call, and turned to John.

"He's booked on a flight leaving Arlanda at 7:10."

"Destination?"

"Bangkok. Connecting in Vienna," she said. "What a damn fool."

Thailand, John thought to himself. Primer had mentioned the country—his holidays there and his plans to buy a house once he retired.

"We don't need to wait for the lab results," he said. "We've got enough to stop him."

"I know," said Mona. "But I don't want to get more people mixed up in this than is necessary. I'd prefer to do this with my team in Stockholm. We'll arrest him when he parks his car at the airport."

While she woke up her personnel at National Crime and dispatched them to Arlanda, John tried to keep pace with Primer. The blue Nissan SUV had overtaken the truck and was about two hundred meters ahead of him. Initially there weren't many cars, but once they had passed Örebro, the morning traffic began to pick up, forcing their suspect to slow down.

Mona connected her phone to the built-in Bluetooth system so that the next time it rang it was on speaker through the car's audio system.

"Morning, Einarsson," she said. "Are you in position?"

"Absolutely. We're at Arlanda and fresh as a daisy," said a thick voice. It seemed to belong to a man of advanced years who sounded anything other than fresh. "Bergting and I just had some coffee. Where are you?"

"On the E18 at Enköping."

"You've made good time."

"We should be with you in about forty-five minutes. Is it just the two of you?"

"Vladimir is here too. I've just sent him to the Radisson Blu hotel. He's waiting in a car there and will pick up your tail when you pass."

"Good," said Mona. "I want to arrest him as soon as he arrives. Nice and calm."

"Understood. Do we know where he's going to park?"

"Probably in one of the long-term areas."

"Do you want me and Bergting there too?"

"No, you go to the gate. Plan B is to arrest him there if anything gets screwed up."

"Sounds good. What about comms?"

"I'll dial us in to a group call when we're approaching."

"Great. Speak to you then."

Mona hung up and called her colleague waiting at the hotel. Vladimir said he had a good view of Route 273—the road that Primer would most likely choose. Mona gave him the information he needed and then leaned back in her seat and shut her eyes.

John said nothing, letting her recharge her batteries for a while. As they got closer to Stockholm, Primer drove more slowly. The traffic was heavier, making it easier to follow Primer. John only had two cars between him and the target. After a while, the Nissan SUV's right turn signal began—surprisingly—to flash.

"He's turning off," said John, and Mona looked up.

She pulled up the map on her phone and zoomed to get an idea of where Primer was going. Then she made a group call to her colleagues.

"The suspect turned off at Bålsta and is probably going to make his way to Arlanda on Route 263, going through Sigtuna and Märsta. It shouldn't change anything for you, should it, Vladimir?"

"Nope—he still needs to cross the E4 and join route 273 to get to the airport. So my position should be okay."

"Good. I couldn't remember exactly where the hotel was, but we'll just stick to the plan."

"Do we think he's armed?" asked the third police officer, who hadn't spoken much before. From what John understood, that was Bergting and he was inside the airport at the gate with Einarsson.

"He may have his service weapon with him," Mona replied. "But he'll probably leave it in the car."

Once Primer was on the smaller roads, he sped up again. John had to speed up, but he also had to make sure he didn't get too close. There were no other cars to hide behind out here and it was a straight road. They rushed through several small villages and after twenty minutes of challenging driving Mona spoke again.

"We're getting close. He's on Route 273 and about to drive under the E4. What car are you in, Vladimir?"

"A black V70. Registration Kilo, Echo, Papa—three, nine, two."

"Roger," she said, pointing out of the window.

John glimpsed the blue-and-white Radisson sign above the treetops up on the hill. On the left, he could see the light from the runways. The speakers crackled and Vladimir's voice spoke again.

"I can see him. A blue Nissan SUV . . . and I can see you . . . and I'm on your six."

"Roger," Mona said again.

John could see the Volvo a few cars behind them in the rearview mirror. Primer slowed down, turned left at an exit, and continued toward the airport. He passed several long-term parking lots without stopping.

"I'm guessing the parking garage," Mona said, nodding at the round building close to the Departures area.

Primer slowed down and signaled right.

"Suspect is turning right," said Mona. "He's not going to the garage. We're heading for a smaller parking lot. If he goes there we'll swoop in."

Her voice had taken on a new sharpness and she was leaning forward in her seat. John eased his foot off the accelerator.

"He's passing that one too," she said, checking the map on her phone. "And he's turning onto Driftvägen instead."

"There aren't any parking areas there—not so far as I know," said Vladimir on the speakers. "Has he spotted us or what?"

It wasn't out of the question, John thought to himself. Primer might be turning onto a small, quiet road as a test to see what the cars behind him did.

"Drop back, Vladimir—and stand by," Mona said.

The Volvo carried on straight ahead while John continued to follow the Nissan SUV.

"There aren't any other turnoffs," she said in confusion. "Where's he going?"

John slowed right down and drifted along the dimly lit road while waiting for Primer to make his next move.

"The suspect is pulling up at a guard's hut," said Mona, before reading aloud from the black-and-white sign on the fence. "Staff parking—how the hell does he have access to that?"

John accelerated to get closer and saw Primer stick his arm out of the window. He held a card to the reader and the barrier lifted.

"He's driving in," Mona said.

The barrier closed behind Primer and they were forced to watch his taillights vanish into the underground parking garage beneath the terminal building.

"Einarsson here."

The gruff voice filled the car.

"I've asked around and staff parking is under Terminal Five. There are two ways in. Elevator or stairs. The problem is they come out in different places."

"I want you to watch both exits," said Mona.

"Then we have to split up and leave the gate."

John saw her stop to think.

"It's okay. Vladimir can take the gate instead. Hurry."

Three voices rapidly acknowledged that they had understood their orders. John drove up to the guard's hut. When Mona saw it was unmanned, she pounded the dashboard.

"Damn it—we can't get any farther," she said, opening the car door. "I want to be there when they arrest him," she called out. "You stay here in case he decides to leave again. Call me and I'll add you to the call with the others."

As she ran toward the terminal building, John put his headset on and joined the group call.

One by one, the breathless voices reported that they had taken up their positions, but that so far they hadn't seen Primer. Hopefully, he was still in the parking garage. The alternative—that he was on the move around the terminal unobserved—wasn't one John even wanted to contemplate. He could feel what had initially been irritation growing into pure, red rage. If he'd been in charge they would have arrested Primer that morning at the house, avoiding this circus.

He muted the microphone on his cell so that no one could hear him. Then he reversed about fifty meters from the barrier and stopped. He put the car in drive and floored the accelerator.

The red-and-white barrier gave way more easily than he expected. He looked in the rearview mirror and saw pieces of hard plastic and metal on the road behind him, while a dazzling yellow light on the guard's hut began to flash.

He entered the underground garage, slowing down to avoid scraping the side-view mirrors as the concrete walls closed in. A few seconds later, he reached the half-full parking area. Cars were sparsely spaced out between the pillars and the level of lighting was low. He glanced around looking for the blue SUV and spotted it two rows over.

If Primer had been quick, he may have had time to park and get into the terminal with his suitcases before Mona's colleagues managed to take up their positions by the two exits. The distance from the car to the elevator and to the stairs was about the same, so it was hard to guess which way Primer went.

John parked the Passat in an empty space behind a minibus. Then he turned off the engine, unmuted his phone, and got out.

"I think we've missed him," he said into his headset. "I'm in the garage and can see his car. He probably made it up into the terminal before we got into position."

"You're in the garage?"

Mona's voice sounded surprised.

"Yes."

"How did you get in?"

"I found a way," John replied as he slowly approached Primer's Nissan.

"How?"

"Hang on."

He suddenly fell silent and stepped behind a concrete pillar. When he stuck his head out again, he saw that the movement in the car wasn't something he imagined. Primer was still in the driver's seat.

"The suspect's still in the garage," he whispered.

"Can you see him?" said Mona.

"Yes."

"Has he seen you?"

"I don't think so."

"What's he doing?"

"Just sitting there at the wheel. It looks like he's waiting for something."

There was a sound from Primer's corner of the garage. John stuck his head out again and saw that the driver's door was open. The shirt tucked into his jeans was taut across his stomach as he got out of the car.

"What was that noise?" said Mona, who had clearly heard the sound on the phone.

"He just got out of the car," said John.

"Then we'll get him as soon as he gets up here. Let us know which way he comes—stairs or elevator."

"Will do."

John checked that his service weapon was where it should be in his shoulder holster without losing sight of the target. He saw Primer get the suitcases out of the trunk, pull on his jacket, and start walking.

"He's taking the elevator," John reported.

"We're ready for him."

When the lift doors had closed behind Primer, John hurried up to the SUV and peered through the window. He was just wondering to himself whether Primer's service weapon might be in the glove compartment when someone shouted in his ear.

"Shit!"

"What's going on, Bergting?" Mona called out.

There was a scraping sound in his earpiece, as if someone was running again.

"I think he spotted me and realized I was police. He went back into the elevator and pressed the Down button. I couldn't get there in time. Too many damn people everywhere!"

"Okay, did you catch that, John? He's coming back down to the garage."

John heard Mona's voice, but it sounded different. It took a second before he realized that there wasn't something wrong with the phone, it was him. He could feel what was about to happen. Contorted sounds and a pulsing pain at the back of his neck. The dizziness came out of nowhere and forced him to slump against a pillar.

It couldn't be happening. He was having one his attacks in the middle of an operation—and in a situation where everything depended on him. John tried to reason with himself through the tangle of thoughts. The man in the elevator was most certainly unarmed. This morning, he'd felt no qualms about arresting him outside his house and there was no reason to feel differently now. Primer was an obese cop in his late middle age, while John was a well-trained FBI agent who had the advantage of being armed. This was just stupid. He would never be able to look Mona in the eye again if he went to pieces now.

"Can you hear me? Are you there?"

Mona's voice bounced around inside his head. The more she talked, the louder it got. He could no longer make out the individual words. All he heard was a buzzing feedback loop that was going to blow his brain to bits if it didn't stop.

He pulled the headset off. His body wasn't listening to him. His feet and legs were going numb and soon he wouldn't be able to move. John looked over at the elevator.

His vision was blurry, but he could see the illuminated arrow showing that Primer was on the way down. To him.

He pulled the pistol from his shoulder holster in a final attempt to take command of the situation. He realized too late that it was adding fuel to the fire of frying synapses in his brain. The sight of the weapon in his hand accelerated the inevitable, bringing memories of the container in Baltimore to the surface.

The pain in his neck exploded. Somewhere, far away, he heard the chime from the elevator. He turned toward the sound and at the same moment the weapon slipped out of his hand. He saw the doors open and then saw Primer come running toward his car. John tried to make his legs take a few steps forward, but he couldn't. It was as if he were frozen to the pillar in the darkness.

Primer unlocked his car remotely, threw the bags onto the back seat and got behind the wheel. John desperately tried to shout something at him, but his mouth wouldn't work. The only sound he could get past his lips was a faint groan as his knees gave way and he fell to the floor.

"What the hell is going on down there?"

The voices in his headset dangling on his chest were drowned out by the sound of the engine as Primer turned on the ignition and reversed out of his spot. The last thing John noticed before the headlights obliterated his vision was Mona emerging from the stairs with her weapon raised.

Then he lost consciousness.

"What happened?" Mona asked, while overtaking several cars at once.

John was in the passenger seat of the Passat with his forehead leaning against the cold window. Pine forests rushed by outside. He looked down at his right hand, which was resting heavily against his thigh, and carefully tried to flex his fingers. Ten minutes ago they hadn't even been able to hold his service weapon, but the messages from his brain seemed to be getting through again.

"I have migraine attacks sometimes," he said, clenching his fist experimentally.

Mona glanced at him doubtfully.

"Migraine?"

"Yes. I've had this shit since I was little."

The police radio crackled.

"He's come off the E4 and is heading east on Route 77 toward Husby-Långhundra," said a male voice.

Mona put the microphone to her mouth and pressed the button.

"Roger."

When Primer had escaped from the garage, Mona had been forced to contact the Stockholm Police. Roadblocks were in the process of being deployed at key strategic locations north of Stockholm. What should have been a calm arrest had turned into a full-out police operation guaranteed to draw attention. Mona accelerated to 160 kmh but still sounded composed when she spoke.

"I'd appreciate it if you'd stop lying to me and tell me what this is really about."

"It's not about anything other than that," John mumbled.

"No?"

"No."

He ran his hand over his face and felt that his cheeks were wet. He didn't remember crying. His eyes stung and there was snot in his nose. He was ashamed of what had happened in the garage. He'd regained consciousness when she had pulled him from the concrete floor and then tried to escape her grasp, convinced that she was Ganiru, about to drag him into the sunlight to shoot him.

"I've no idea what you've been through and I don't need to know. But you've just screamed at me not to kill you and then had a tear-filled panic attack in front of half the National Crime team. I'm not sure a headache pill is the solution."

"It won't happen again," said John, beginning to feel sick.

He turned around to see whether the McDonald's bag was still in the back seat. He wanted to vomit. He wanted to throw up the self-contempt and be rid of it forever.

"How can you be sure?" said Mona.

John heard himself mumble something inaudible in reply. Then he sat in silence hoping she'd stop asking questions. At that moment, a voice on the police radio reported that Primer had just passed Husby-Långhundra and was still on Route 77 toward Rimbo and Finsta. Three roadblocks had been deployed and all junctions onto the E18 highway were blocked.

"Where's he going?" John asked, in an attempt to change the subject.

"Nowhere, probably. Just away from us."

"Have we got anyone in the air?"

"A chopper's taking off from Arlanda shortly. The pilots were asleep," said Mona, pulling off the highway.

She drove through a red light to make it onto Route 77 and avoid getting stuck behind two buses. There was a loud honking as one of the drivers hit their horn.

Dawn was breaking, but there wasn't much traffic on the small road. The yellow streetlights in the small villages were still on and people inside the houses were getting ready for another day at work.

"I didn't leave my apartment for five months after an armed raid went to shit," said Mona, out of nowhere.

"Okay," John said hesitantly, unsure where the conversation was going.

"One young lad died. I thought it was my fault and I took on all the guilt. It made no difference that Internal Affairs decided I'd followed the rulebook, I knew that boy would have made it if I'd acted differently."

The police radio demanded their attention once again. A new report stated that Primer had turned off at Norrtälje and was heading along Route 76 toward Hallstavik and Östhammar. The roadblocks on the E18 could be removed and shifted to other positions. There was talk of a pincer movement to cut off the suspect's escape routes. The helicopter had also joined the hunt and the pilots reported visual contact with the target.

Mona glanced at John again while passing. A farmer was taking up a large part of the road in his tractor and refusing to budge.

"You need to take control of your thoughts," she said.

"There's nothing wrong with my thoughts," John replied.

"No, of course—you're an FBI agent. I forgot. You just take an aspirin and get on with it."

He closed his eyes to shut out the sarcasm. It was irritating when someone didn't hold back as they touched his most sensitive nerves.

"When do they hit?" said Mona.

"What?"

"The attacks. What triggers them?"

John thought about it without showing her that he was. He was fully aware that the pain in his neck came at moments of pressure, when his thoughts returned to the mock execution at the port in Baltimore. The moment when he'd been certain his life was over.

"Five months after that boy died, I was back at work," Mona said. "Just the idea of holding a weapon again made me anxious, so I requested desk duty. I did that for almost a year before deciding to take control of my own head."

She hesitated for a moment, as if searching for the right words.

"I can't explain where the strength came from, but one day I realized that I couldn't undo that raid. I would always hate myself for the fact that the boy died, and that was okay. I could live with that. The next day I spoke to my boss. A week later I was back in my old job and did my first operation without having a panic attack."

John squeezed the leather upholstery of the passenger seat with one hand. He knew where she wanted to go with this story. But was it even true? He doubted it. She was probably just trying to get him to open up to her. He had used the same method to get close to some of the guys in Ganiru's gang. Shared stories about childhoods with absent fathers, when in reality his own had been more present than he sometimes would have liked.

"I'm really sorry I fucked up. It was rotten luck to have a migraine hit today."

Mona took a hand off the wheel and held it up in an apologetic gesture.

"Like I said, I don't know anything about your baggage. But I know one thing: you are in charge of deciding how to deal with it. What's done is done and there's nothing you can do to change that. You can only do it differently next time. And you have the power. It's there. You just haven't found it yet."

John felt a new bout of nausea and put the window down a crack. He managed to hold it down until Mona hit the brakes hard and stopped at a crossroads. He couldn't wait any longer. He opened the doors, stumbled to the ditch, and threw up what little there was in his stomach.

"Anything new on the radio?" he said, shortly after getting back into the car.

Mona looked at him sympathetically. He sincerely hoped the psychoanalysis session was over so that they could concentrate on catching Primer.

"It's okay. I just needed to get it out," he said, trying to convince both himself and Mona that it was true.

A patrol car with its blue lights flashing and siren blaring passed them at high speed. Mona switched her attention to it and accelerated.

"Primer has turned off and is heading toward Älmsta. He'll get caught in our roadblock in just a few minutes," she said.

They continued following the patrol car. Tall pines flew by on either side of the Passat. John held firmly on to the handle above the side window to avoid slipping out of his seat on the turns. Then the landscape opened up before them. The forest gave way to meadows and open fields. A few hundred meters farther ahead on the other side of one of the fields he saw what they were heading for.

It looked like a spaceship had landed in the middle of the rural idyll. Three patrol cars, their blue lights flashing, and two more unmarked cars were positioned in a circle around something that had to be Primer's Nissan.

"We've got him," the radio crackled.

They quickly looked at each other before Mona pressed the button.

"Roger that. We're almost there."

They reached the roadblock, but just as Mona was getting out of the car, her phone rang.

"I've got to take this," she said, stepping to one side.

John hesitated for a few seconds, but then he opened the door and stepped onto the asphalt. He walked slowly toward Primer's car, where three uniformed police officers were standing with their weapons drawn. An obese man in a white shirt and with hunched posture struggled out of the driver's seat.

"It's him," said Mona, who had appeared at John's side. "Linköping is done with the analysis. It was Primer's semen on the rock."

PART 4
2019

44

John came out of the front door of the apartment complex that recalled the Empire State building and squinted up at the sky, which was clear blue for the first time in ages. He pulled his sunglasses out of his coat pocket and polished them with his sleeve. They hadn't been used since he was in Baltimore.

It was twenty-four hours after the operation in Stockholm. Primer had been taken to the prison in Karlstad, where he was in custody, awaiting questioning. When Mona had dropped John off outside the apartment, she told him to rest. She told him he needed to recover before they got back to Primer.

The mandatory leave was connected to the migraine attack—or whatever he was supposed to call it—in the underground garage. But he didn't intend to dwell on it. Mona could stick with her idea of what happened. The most important thing was to pull himself together and focus on at the questioning ahead.

Since the Chrysler was still parked at the police station, he took a taxi. On the way, he scrolled through the news to see if there was anything about the arrest. It seemed Mona's efforts to keep a lid on it had worked. Despite the helicopter and roadblocks, no reporter made the connection to the AckWe case.

When he got out of the taxi, it was already quarter past eleven in the morning and he hurried inside. As he entered the station, he almost bumped into Ulf Törner, walking through reception with a bundle of papers under his arm. The fine weather appeared to have had no positive impact on the man, who glowered resentfully and walked on without greeting him. Ruben was standing behind the information desk holding open the staff entrance. He saw it all and was laughing loudly.

"What's up with him?" John asked.

"What do you think?" Ruben grinned and took a big bite from the doughnut in his hand. "I guess Yanks are good for something after all. Damn good idea if you ask me."

He laughed again as he wiped chocolate from his mouth.

"What are you talking about?"

"The kitchen, obviously," he said, letting John into the inner sanctum of the building. "You coming up or going down to the den of mold?"

John felt his curiosity growing. Primer could sweat a little longer.

"Up," he said, heading for the kitchen with Ruben in his wake.

The formerly soulless coffee room had been transformed into something that was akin to a cozy café. A short-haired young man, wearing a well-ironed shirt and black trousers, was moving among the tables with a practiced air. The worn-out tables were covered with linen tablecloths and adorned with cut flowers in white vases. In the middle of the room was an old-fashioned tea cart. On it was a large basket of doughnuts and Danish pastries, as well as a silver platter of fresh fruit.

John's first thought was that he had missed Ulf's birthday and that his colleague was pissed off about it. But then he saw what it said on the back of the young man's shirt.

Fredrik Adamsson's Kitchen Week—in partnership with Manpower.

This was Mona's promise to solve the kitchen chore issue. The battle of the kitchen schedule was over and with her help, John had triumphed.

"I was about to go and take a dump—do you think he'll wipe my backside too?" Ruben whispered.

John couldn't help grinning.

"I'll ask," he said.

His colleague departed for the men's room laughing, and John headed for the elevator. Mona was waiting for him in the basement. She waved at him to follow her into one of the rooms on the narrow corridor that ran around the edge of the office. The room was no more than ten square meters and furnished with two chairs and a desk with three ancient computer screens squeezed onto it.

Two of the monitors were off, and the third was showing a black-and-white image of a bleak room with a single chair in front of a rectangular table. John looked at the tangle of cables trailing from the screens down to a similarly antiquated control panel where there was a bulb faintly glowing yellow.

It's old stuff, but it should work," said Mona.

John wished he was back in the more modern spaces a few floors up in the building, where the interviews with Billy took place. But that wasn't an option. The rumor about Primer would spread through the building like wildfire.

"Are you sure?" he said.

"Yes, we tested them earlier."

She looked at him.

"How are you feeling?"

"Just fine."

"Did you get some sleep?"

"Yes."

"Good," she said, breathing in as if she was about to continue. Instead, she slowly exhaled through her lips. John was grateful. He wasn't up for a lot of questions about his mental health.

"Ruben Jonsson will be acting chief and will take over Primer's duties until further notice," she said, changing tack to something less loaded.

"Okay," said John, smiling slightly. "I just ran into Ruben. He seemed to appreciate my week on the kitchen schedule."

"Good. I hope your lovely mug gets left alone in the future," she said with a smile.

The sound of a door opening made them both direct their attention at the monitor. For a moment, John thought the prison guard had brought in the wrong person for questioning. The poor resolution of the screen and the big t-shirt flapping around his body made Primer look both older and fatter than he actually was. His panting breaths rattled through the speakers and Mona adjusted the volume down.

John leaned toward the screen and saw Primer clumsily squeezing in between the table and chair, both of which screwed into the floor. A second later, he quickly turned his head to look up toward the camera, as if he knew someone was watching him. His face was as blank as when he was arrested.

"Let's do this," said Mona, pressing the control panel a few times before heading for the door.

The yellow light went red to show it was recording and the counter in the bottom corner of the screen began to run.

"Do you want anything before we get started? Water? Coffee?" Mona asked, once she and John had sat down at the table in the interview room.

Primer said nothing. He merely shook his head slowly without raising his gaze from the table. The skin around his reddened eyes was swollen and his cheeks were shiny. It was apparent he had been crying.

Mona pulled a few tissues from her bag and placed them in front of Primer, who immediately put them to his face.

"Jesus Christ," he said, once he had blown his nose and crumpled the tissue into a ball. "This is unfortunate. Tragic from start to finish."

"What do you mean by that?" Mona asked, exchanging a quick glance with John.

Primer was noticeably affected and it took a few seconds for him to reply.

"Everything . . . all the circumstances that led to this mess. I should've said something a long time ago, but I couldn't. Call it cowardice, fear, ego, or whatever you want. But . . . I couldn't do it."

His voice was thick and halting, as if the feelings of guilt were growing in his throat and on the verge of suffocating him. His eyes filled with tears and he reached for a new tissue.

"Are you ready to talk about what happened?" said Mona, once he pulled himself together again. "I assume you know why you're here?"

"Because I'm a gigantic idiot," he mumbled.

Mona ignored the comment.

"Forensics ran the sample you provided the day before yesterday," she said. "Your DNA matches the semen found next to Emelie Bjurwall's blood on the rocks out at Tynäs."

John studied each shift in Primer's teary, red face. He was still struggling to look them in the eye. He sat in silence, squirming on the uncomfortable chair.

"Let's take it from the beginning," Mona said eventually. "I'd like you to tell me about your relationship with Emelie Bjurwall. How did you first come into contact?"

Primer once again attempted to look at them and this time he managed to make eye contact with them.

"I became acquainted with her father."

"Heimer Bjurwall?"

"Yes, exactly. We met through the boating club and went out fishing together a few times."

"Did Emelie come with?"

"No, it was just Heimer and me. But that was a long time ago, when Emelie was still little."

Primer spoke slowly and the words stumbled out, as if he had to process each sentence.

"She was one of the kids you saw running around down by the jetties when families were heading out onto the lake. It was only many years later that we were introduced."

"When was that?"

"When she was nineteen or twenty. I was working in narcotics here in Karlstad back then, and I would give talks about drugs and addiction at different schools and treatment centers around Värmland. I used to go up to Charlottenberg."

"To Björkbacken?" John interjected.

"Yes. We had a fairly close partnership with the therapists there and I usually went four or five times a year."

"And that's where you came into contact with Emelie?" said Mona.

"Yes, that's where I met her. She came up to me after one of my visits and asked if I recognized her. I didn't. But when she said who she was, I could tell it was her.

She'd grown up so much. We chatted briefly on a couple of occasions, but then I tried to avoid her."

"Avoid?" Mona repeated. "Why?"

"I don't know. I got the feeling that she was . . . flirting with me."

"And that wasn't something you reciprocated?"

"No." Primer fell silent. "Not then and there," he added, clearing his throat.

He looked ashamed and John noticed that his breathing had become heavier. His neck had turned flaming red and beads of sweat were forming on his brow.

"Once she got out of Björkbacken, she looked me up again," he said reluctantly. "Obviously, I should have said no, but she wouldn't give up. Eventually . . . well, I couldn't hold out anymore."

"And it was at this point you started your relationship?" said Mona.

"That's right. Somehow, I felt for her. Things at home with her parents were messy. I just felt sorry for her."

John felt his irritation rising. Primer's way of painting himself as a victim and laying the responsibility on a young girl was galling him.

Couldn't hold out anymore.

I felt sorry for her.

It was the worst bullshit he'd heard in ages. The asshole had likely taken every chance he got to sleep with her.

"It was a sexual relationship?" Mona asked, her mind on the same track.

Primer wiped away the sweat running down his fleshy face.

"Yes," he admitted.

"Okay, and how long did your relationship with Emelie last? Did you see each other right up until she disappeared?"

"Do you know what, Mona? It doesn't feel good talking about this. I know it's important and everything, but it's really hard."

She glanced at John again and then switched into a different, softer tone of voice.

"Yes, I know it must be. You should take all the time you need. And if you want a short break then just let us know."

Primer nodded slowly and sat in silence for a long time. Mona asked John to get a glass of water, and when he returned the agonized man looked more composed.

"We saw each other on and off for a few months," he said, once he had drained the white plastic cup. "Then in the autumn she moved to Stockholm and started school."

"But you stayed in touch?" said Mona.

"She got in touch when she came back to Karlstad for the holidays."

"Did you see each other then?"

"Yes, but it wasn't sustainable. I was going to end it several times . . . but I never did."

"Why not?"

"I don't know. I just never seemed to get around to it."

Mona opened the folder on the table. She picked out several of the photographs from the promontory at Tynäs and put them on the table in front of Primer.

"You've probably seen these photos a thousand times."

He laughed bitterly.

"At least."

"Did you have sexual intercourse with Emelie Bjurwall on August 14, 2009—the night she went missing?"

Mona nodded toward the photographs. Despite the fact that all three of them knew there was only one answer to the question, Primer seemed to be reluctant to tell them.

"Yes, I did," he said eventually, looking down at his hands. "That was a big fucking mistake."

John glanced at Mona. Her face was still grim, but he could discern a certain satisfaction behind the determination. The interview was taking the direction they had hoped. Now they needed to encourage Primer to keep talking and give a timeline.

"Why did you meet there in particular?" she said.

"Emelie had sent me an email earlier—she said she was going to a party nearby and wanted to see me out there at midnight."

"An email?"

Mona looked thoughtful and John realized why. The girl's computer had been seized early on in the investigation and reviewed thoroughly on several occasions. Forensics had even recovered deleted emails, but they hadn't found anything that moved the preliminary investigation forward.

"I got her to create a Gmail account," Primer said, noticing her frown. "It was anonymous and that's how we kept in touch. I wanted the relationship to be as discreet as possible."

"I understand," said Mona. "So she wrote that she wanted to meet you out on the promontory at Tynäs in the middle of the night?"

"Yes."

"And you went there?"

"I got there just before midnight, after filling up at the gas station. But she was late. At first I thought she might have forgotten. I waited for a while and eventually . . . well, she turned up and we went to the rocks and sat down."

"What time was that?"

"I don't know. I might have waited twenty minutes or so."

"And was it at this time that your semen ended up on the rock?"

Primer sighed in resignation and ran his hand over his face.

"Yes, I suppose it was."

"Could you tell us what happened out there after Emelie arrived?" said Mona after a brief silence.

"I don't know if there's much to tell."

There was suddenly a distance in his voice, John noticed. They were approaching a minefield.

"I'd still like you to tell us what happened," she said. "Was there any particular reason Emelie wanted to see you there and then, so late at night?"

"Yes, I guess there was," he said, crossing his arms over his chest.

"And what was it?"

"She wanted to have sex."

"Okay," said Mona. "And what happened?"

He snorted and glowered at her, as if what she just said was the stupidest thing he'd ever heard.

"She sucked me off, if you want to put it plainly."

In a flash, Primer's embarrassed demeanor vanished, replaced by a chilly shrug of the shoulders. John recognized the behavior. He'd seen similar transformations when interrogating suspects back in New York, pushing them to put their actions into words. Nonchalance was a defense—a way of distancing themselves from the crime and making their feelings of guilt more bearable.

"I'm sorry, Bernt, but I need to ask these questions and you know that. So Emelie performed oral sex on you, but you didn't have penetrative intercourse. Is that how I should take it?"

Primer said nothing but nodded.

"Is that how I should take it," Mona repeated, pointing at the microphone.

"Yes, that's how you should take it. We didn't have penetrative sex."

"And what did you do next?"

"We talked for a bit. I said I wanted to end it."

"You wanted to end the relationship?"

"Yes."

"And how did she react to that?"

"She was upset. Angry. Mostly upset I think. She claimed it was a shock. But it couldn't have been. We talked a lot about how impossible our relationship was."

"And this conversation was after you'd had sex?"

"Yes."

"And then what happened?" said Mona.

"She cried and started shouting at me. We weren't getting anywhere and in the end we decided to talk again the next day. Then I went back to the car and left."

John felt a shiver run through his body. Maybe this wasn't a straight line to a confession after all. But he couldn't show his frustration or disappointment—that would give off the wrong signals. Instead, he concentrated on Primer. Gone was the shifting, uncertain gaze.

The eyes that met his were decisive now.

"So Emelie was alive when you left her?" said Mona.

John could hear her making an effort to sound neutral.

"Yes."

"And you didn't hear from her again?"

"No."

Primer picked up the empty plastic cup and sucked up the final drops of water. John looked at Mona. Her face looked relaxed, almost amused. As if she wanted to show Primer that his bullshit was entertaining, but that she didn't believe a word of what he had said.

"Where did you go once you had parted ways?"

"Home," Primer said curtly.

"Why didn't you say you had been with her? I think you must've been the last person to see her alive—apart from the perpetrator, that is," she added in a tone that couldn't be interpreted as anything other than ironic.

"It was impossible. No one would've believed me. You don't know what the mood was like in Karlstad back then. Emelie wasn't just anyone. There was pressure from every fucking direction and those of us working on the case were getting more and more frustrated when we weren't making any progress. All we had to go on was the semen. If I had said it was mine, then it would have been over."

"So, the fact that Emelie was murdered the same night and in the same place where you'd had sex with her is just an unlucky coincidence?" said John, making no great effort to conceal his sarcasm.

"Yes, you might say that."

John clenched his fist under the table. Primer's obvious approach of playing innocent was infuriating. His thoughts kept returning to Billy and the hell that his brother had been forced to go through because of this man.

"You must have panicked when you appeared in that CCTV footage from the gas station and realized that you would have to provide a DNA sample. Was that when you came up with the idea of swapping the labels to cast suspicion on Billy Nerman?" he said.

"No, I didn't do anything like that."

John waited to see whether there was anything else to come. But when Primer sat there quietly with his arms crossed, Mona took over again.

"But if you didn't switch the labels, how could your sample get mixed up with Billy Nerman's?"

"I don't know."

"So, you don't have a theory about what might have happened?" said Mona, who no longer had it in her to maintain her amused expression. Now she mostly sounded tired and irritated.

"No, I've thought about that all these years. I gave a sample and assumed it would be pinned on me. But when Billy Nerman was arrested instead, I was very surprised. The only explanation I can think of is that there was some kind of bungle with the samples."

"What kind of bungle do you mean?" said John.

"Well, they got mixed up. There were hundreds of samples that were collected. From what I remember, most of us were working twenty-four seven and were completely exhausted. It's not impossible that someone made a mistake."

"I assume you don't have an explanation for why the list of everyone who gave a sample was deleted from the investigation files either?"

"No."

"Yet another occasion when your guardian angel stepped in?"

"Yes, it would seem so."

John leaned back in the chair and clasped his hands behind his neck.

"You must hear how stupid this sounds. Why would anyone delete files from the investigation if it wasn't to save their own skin?"

"I'm afraid I don't have an answer," said Primer.

"It's clear as day that it was you."

"I'm sorry, but I don't know anything about the list of samples."

Primer sounded like a robot repeating preprogrammed answers. John sighed and shook his head. Mona put her elbows on the desk. She leaned forward so that her face was just a few inches from Primer's.

"Supposing it was all as you say," she said. "You got dragged into this by an unfortunate coincidence and you don't have anything to do with Emelie Bjurwall's death. So how come you tried to run?"

"I panicked," he said. "This is a small town. Even if I told the truth, everyone would think I was lying. I booked a ticket to Thailand and I was going to dump the car in the staff parking garage. I got a pass card as part of an investigation years ago."

"But you didn't have any problem with Billy Nerman being accused when he was innocent?"

John regretted it the moment he said it. He saw Mona react from the corner of his eye. She had warned against him letting the ties to his brother get in the way of the investigation.

"You heard what I said," Primer replied. "I'm completely aware that I didn't do the right thing ten years ago. And it's unfortunate that your brother had a tough time. But things went the way they did, and you can't turn back time."

John felt Mona's hand on his arm. He had to calm down, otherwise he risked being sent out of the room.

"So, to summarize," she said. "You're saying that Emelie Bjurwall performed oral sex on you at Tynäs on the night she was murdered, but that she was alive when you left her."

"That's correct."

"And you don't know who swapped your DNA sample for Billy Nerman's. Or how the list of DNA samples and the DVDs from the gas station disappeared from the investigation files."

"No, not a clue."

Mona closed her notebook and stared at him for a long time.

"I'm going to be honest with you, Bernt. There are slightly too many coincidences for your story to seem credible. I know it must be hard, but wouldn't it be easier for everyone if you just confessed to what you've done—here and now? You had sex with Emelie Bjurwall and somehow it went wrong and you killed her."

Primer shook his head.

"No, it wasn't like that."

"You must see that the evidence against you is very strong. Maybe there are mitigating circumstances we're not aware of. I think you'd feel better for telling us."

"There's nothing else to tell," he said. "When I left Tynäs, Emelie was alive."

Mona put her pen down. John thought she was going to suggest a short break, but instead she merely stared at Primer. The sweat had soaked through her white blouse and left damp patches at her armpits. The room was stifling and the whirr of the ventilation system in the metal ducting on the ceiling was neither adding nor removing air.

John straightened up in his chair.

"Can I ask something?" he said, reaching for the folder on the table.

He took out the picture that had been posted on Emelie's Facebook page—the one they now knew was anything but a bucket list.

"When you left her at the rocks, did her arm look like this or was the final square still empty?"

He held the picture up in front of Primer, who merely glanced at the photo.

"I don't know," he said.

"So you don't remember whether the final tick—the one that wasn't tattooed but was carved into the skin—was on Emelie Bjurwall's arm when you left?"

"No."

"Do you think she could have done it to herself?"

Primer looked at the picture again and this time he stared at it.

"Given how she felt, I imagine she might have, yes."

"Did you consider her to be self-destructive?"

"Yes, I think most people who use drugs are."

Mona took the photo from John and put it back in the folder.

"According to witnesses, Emelie claimed she was leaving the party to obtain drugs—specifically cocaine," she said. "Why do you think she said that, if she was going to meet you?"

Primer immediately looked worried and John took note.

"I don't know."

"What do you think? Why would she have said that?"

"The only thing I can think of is that she wanted to keep her friends in the dark. Or she met someone else before she came to see me. Maybe that's why she was late."

"So it wasn't you who gave her the drugs?" said Mona.

Primer looked shocked and then laughed.

"Me? No, absolutely not. Why would I do that? I wanted to keep her off that stuff."

Mona balanced a pair of reading glasses on her nose and took a sheet out of the folder.

"You worked in narcotics at the time and you were . . ."

"Hang on just a second, Mona," Primer interrupted her, holding up his hand. "I know what you're doing, but you can drop it. It's ridiculous to try that line."

"As an officer in narcotics, you had access to . . ."

"Aren't you listening to me?!" Primer bellowed, pounding the table with his fist. "I didn't give or sell drugs to Emelie or anyone else. Full stop."

Mona closed the folder and took her glasses off.

"I think we'll take a short break and continue in . . ." She looked at her wristwatch. ". . . let's say twenty minutes?"

John nodded curtly and they got up from the table.

"He's lying," John said as he tried to wander around the limited floor area. "He's going to fight us with every last ounce of strength."

Mona hadn't said a word since they left the interview room and once again went into the adjacent room. She was leaning forward in the chair in front of the monitors, drinking from her water bottle as if she were in the dugout during an ice hockey match.

"Yes, it seems that way," she said, between swigs.

John could see that she was grappling with the same disappointment that he was.

"Obviously he was the one who swapped the DNA samples and got rid of the list," he hissed. "And the story about Emelie—I don't buy it."

"You don't think he had a relationship with her?"

John shook his head.

"The sense of Emelie you get from the witness statements is that she was a girl who could have anyone she wanted. The idea that she'd fall for a man twenty-five years her senior who isn't much of a looker doesn't seem at all plausible."

"So, you think she performed oral sex on Primer not because she was in love with him but because she was self-destructive?"

"Yes, maybe. And for some reason they started to fight, and she fell and cracked her head on the rocks."

Mona watched him pace.

"How about you sit down and breathe deeply for a minute? I'm as frustrated as you are, but we'll get there. We've just begun. We'll break him down."

John reluctantly sat down.

"How can you be so certain? We need a confession and he knows it. Primer won't give up—not at first."

"He won't be able to hold out forever. Now we know his attitude to the accusations, and we've got enough to hold him, on remand. We'll crack him with time."

John still didn't feel convinced. He looked at the black-and-white monitor, his gaze lingering on the man hunched over a cup of coffee while munching on a cheese sandwich.

It struck him that Primer had what Billy had always lacked.

An explanation for why the semen had been on the rock.

45

Heimer looked around. The office in the basement of the police station was full of desks but devoid of people. He thought about one of those popular zombie series that he'd tried to watch on TV. It felt as if this place had been hit by the apocalypse and he was about to encounter a horde of shambling, bloodthirsty creatures. He glanced at Sissela. She was reading emails on her phone and didn't seem to have noticed the surroundings.

"We've got issues with damp—that's why there's no one down here," the female detective who fetched them from reception said, when they got out of the elevator and she saw Heimer's reaction.

They'd met once before when she picked up that confounded letter from the house in Tynäs. Her name was Mona Ejdewik and she was the new lead detective who had taken over after Primer. Heimer tried to guess her age. The woman was definitely older than he had first thought. Her hands gave her away too—that was something she had in common with Sissela. Fit bodies, but slack and wrinkly sections of skin on the back of the hand.

She got a tray with the mandatory coffee cups and put it down on the desk in front of them. Heimer saw Sissela look up from her phone to check that there was milk. And there was. Small packets of milk were set out in a bowl along with sugar in eco-friendly paper packaging.

Heimer saw that something important was happening. The whole situation oozed importance. The fact that they were here in the basement of the police station rather than on the sofa at home. The way the woman carefully pushed the cups toward them and the patience with which she waited for Sissela to put her phone in her handbag. And then, of course, there was the language. The formal tone that people relied upon when important things had to be said. Like an anchor on the TV news reporting a tragic accident—two tones lower on the scale than usual.

"Thank you for coming in so quickly. I want to update you on the latest events in the investigation," she said.

"We appreciate that," said Sissela. "Over the years it's been a bit hit-and-miss when it comes to information from the police."

It bothered Heimer that in every new encounter with a person, Sissela would try to induce guilt in the other party to gain the upper hand. However, the new lead investigator wasn't drawn into making apologies, merely continuing with her formal tone.

"I'm about to share confidential information with you and must request that you don't discuss what's said here today with anyone else. Do you understand?"

"Yes," Heimer said quickly, before his wife had time to ask any follow-up questions.

"Well then—it's my duty to inform you that this morning, the prosecutor took an individual into custody, and there's reasonable suspicion that they murdered your daughter."

The room was silent. Heimer felt his heart pounding. Sissela had just picked up a packet of milk but now she put it back in the bowl.

"Who is it?" she asked, in a voice that he thought sounded steadier than she probably felt.

"Before I tell you, it's important that you understand the full picture. Sooner or later, the press is going to learn who's been arrested, and I think once that happens it would be wise for you to go away or at least be unreachable."

Sissela looked at her with that look that Heimer knew gave AckWe employees stomachaches.

"I appreciate the thought, Mona. That was your name, wasn't it?"

A new show of power. His wife never forgot the name of anyone she met.

"Yes—last name Ejdewik."

"My husband and I are quite capable of dealing with any reporters who may not honor the boundaries of our private life. But right now, all I want to know is who did this to Emelie."

Heimer put his hand on Sissela's shoulder to show that he agreed with every word she said. This was a conversation between two women used to getting their way and the best thing he could do was keep quiet and show loyalty to his wife.

Mona leaned back in her chair before continuing.

"The person who has been arrested is Bernt Primer."

Heimer let go of his wife's shoulder. Who exactly was this woman? Was she even a police officer or just some crazy person who somehow got into the building? Bernt Primer had been to their house many times over the years. He'd posed for newspaper photos and talked about how important it was to solve the case. Primer in custody? This was irony beyond belief.

"Surely not *the* Bernt Primer?" said Sissela.

"Yes, I'm afraid so," said Mona.

"But he was in charge of the investigation until recently, wasn't he?"

Her voice was fainter now. Not even Sissela Bjurwall could be unaffected by what she had just heard. Mona nodded gravely and held her arms out in a gesture of resignation, as if she wanted to apologize on behalf of the entire force.

"Are you sure?" said Sissela.

"We've got strong forensic evidence."

Sissela shook her head. Heimer knew what his wife was thinking. The police had said that before. But this time she didn't opt for confrontation. Perhaps she was too dumbstruck by the news to apply pressure to the new lead investigator. But if Sissela wasn't up to asking the necessary questions then he'd have to do it himself.

"What does that forensic evidence consist of?" he said, clearing his throat.

He had been quiet for so long that his voice felt raspy when he spoke.

"DNA. Bernt Primer's DNA matches the semen found near Emelie's blood."

"Now I'm confused," said Heimer. "You said that about Billy Nerman too."

"Our hypothesis is that Bernt Primer swapped his own DNA sample with Billy Nerman's in an attempt to frame him. We've rerun the samples and confirmed that it's Primer's semen on the rocks."

"So, he was there?"

"Yes, he was there—we're certain of that."

The dizziness was sudden; the room began to spin. The lights slid down the walls, creating an unpleasant halo effect. Heimer grabbed hold of the desk to stop himself from falling out of his chair. He moved his hand far too quickly for it to be perceived as a natural movement. His wife saw it—the detective too.

"Would you like some water?" asked Mona.

He shook his head.

"No thanks, I'm fine. What does he say, then?" he pushed on.

"We've not started to formally question him."

"When will you do that?"

"Later today. We're still preparing."

"I need to see him."

Mona looked at him in astonishment. Sissela also looked surprised, but slightly annoyed too—even if she tried to conceal it. Heimer hadn't meant to say the last thing—it had just spilled out.

"I'm afraid that's not possible," said Mona. "But obviously I'll provide updates on any developments."

Heimer wanted to scream. Putting three hundred thousand kronor in a locker at the station seemed instantly meaningless. He needed to speak to Primer. Now! It was moments like this that he needed to exercise self-control and avoid being overcome by his emotions.

Sissela warned him with a quick glance not to continue down that well-trodden path. He still remembered putting his fist through the plasterboard wall in Primer's office and the conversation afterward. He didn't want to end up there again. If he was ever going to stand a chance of meeting that bastard face-to-face, he needed to appear as calm as possible.

"I think I will take that glass of water after all," he said.

46

John turned up his collar and ran home from the parking lot through the rain that was lashing Bryggudden. As usual in the evenings, he stopped at Rederiet and asked the kitchen to fix some takeout for him to bring back to the apartment.

"Busy at work?" said the manager, who had begun to recognize his new regular.

John nodded, but was too exhausted to respond to the man's smile. He ordered peanuts and a beer while he waited for his food. He hung his wet coat over the back of his chair and rubbed his head irritably with a napkin.

The latest session in the police station basement had been fruitless. Primer was sticking to his story that the whole thing was an unfortunate coincidence and that he had had nothing to do with Emelie Bjurwall's death. Over the course of seven long interviews, they had listened him to describe the events on the night of the murder without being able to poke any holes in his account. Not once had he deviated from the timeline or changed any details. He'd had ten years to perfect his fictitious account and John guessed that he could probably reel it off in his sleep.

For each fruitless hour that passed, John had found it harder to remain patient. On a few occasions, he'd asked Mona to excuse him from the table and he instead followed the interview via the monitors from the adjacent room. He stood in front of the black-and-white screen and fantasized about being alone with Primer. Just the two of them, without any cameras on. John knew how to give someone a kicking without leaving even a trace on their body. Imagining it in detail was an effective way of channeling his frustration.

Mona had done better in keeping her spirits up—at least during the initial days—but that afternoon even she began to look discouraged. Especially once the news about Primer had leaked to the media. It took longer than they had expected, but now the circus was up and running and the reporters weren't holding back. They were writing reams about the chief of police being held on remand for the crime he had previously been investigating.

Trust in the police was at rock bottom. The commissioner of county police had waited as long as possible before calling a press conference and when he finally did, he sent Mona out instead. The Walrus said just a few words before he deftly referred all questions pertaining to the case to the executive lead investigator from Stockholm.

John stayed in the musty basement and watched the live broadcast from the press conference on his phone, a kebab in his hand. Again, he was impressed by his colleague, Mona. It wasn't the first time the woman had been grilled by journalists—that much was clear. She gave detailed answers that inspired confidence, while keeping a close eye on which details could be revealed. After thirty-five minutes she left the police station conference room and went straight back to questioning Primer in the basement.

John paid for his food at Rederiet, feeling frustrated as usual by the Swedish alcohol laws which prevented him from buying a few beers to take back to the apartment. He wolfed down the tapas dishes while half-reclining in bed. The sky above him was pitch-black and the raindrops on the skylight glistened like crystals. He followed the trails of running water until his vision became blurry and his eyelids closed.

After a brief snooze, he shuddered and came to—wide-awake. A thought had weaseled its way into his sleep. It made him glance toward the kitchen table, where the laptop was folded shut among the brushes and turpentine bottles.

John swung his feet down onto the floor and walked to the table. He opened the laptop and logged on to the encrypted email service. It had been almost a week since he got the bad news about Trevor's tumors. He'd written a short reply the day after and since then he hadn't dared look at his inbox. But now he couldn't wait any longer. The results from the new tests surely had to be ready by now.

John keenly felt the absence of beer to moisten his dry mouth as the server verified his password. He swallowed and then saw the screen light up. A red *1* flashed above the inbox. Trevor had sent the email early the morning before. He moved his finger to the trackpad to click on it but was interrupted by his phone vibrating in his pocket. He took it out and looked at the screen.

It was a text message from Erina Kabashi.

I'm outside. Can you let me in?

John read the message again and then jumped when he heard the door buzzer. How the hell did she know where he lived? No one except Mona knew his address and he knew she would never reveal it to anyone.

He closed the computer with the email remaining unread and went out onto the terrace. John squinted in the wet darkness. It was impossible to make out any visitor. The building was twenty-five stories high and the entrance was obscured by protruding balconies.

Immediately, images of Ganiru's sinister executioners appeared in his mind's eye. They must have threatened the lawyer and forced her to find the rat so they could make him pay for what he had done—once and for all. It was far-fetched—he knew that—but it still made the back of his head throb.

The buzzer went off again and he headed for the door. He picked up the handset without saying anything.

"Hello?" said a voice he recognized.

"Who is it?" he said anyway.

"It's Erina Kabashi. Can I come in?"

John remained silent as he deliberated.

"Let me in and I'll explain. I'm soaked through."

He hesitated briefly before pressing the button to open the main door. Then he put on the white shirt that was still wet from running through the rain earlier and peered through the peephole. The digital numbers above the elevator told him it was moving and was currently on the seventh floor. He went out onto the landing. The familiar numbness began to spread through his feet and up his shins. He supported himself on the wall and took a few deep breaths.

When Erina stepped out of the elevator, she was wearing a strappy black pantsuit with a belt accentuating her waist. Her gray leather boots were soaked and the coat hanging over her arm was dripping water onto the floor. In her other hand she was holding a bottle of red wine.

"You only get to try the wine if you hang this up to dry," she said with a smile, proffering the coat to him.

For a split second, his brain's paranoid alarm systems kicked into action and John imagined there was a weapon concealed beneath the wet fabric.

"Are you alright? You've gone pale . . ."

He managed to take the coat from her, but he was still leaning against the wall. Her hand was empty.

"Nothing to worry about—just a bit tired," he managed to say. "How did you know where I live?"

"Can we go inside?" she said.

"No, not until you tell me how you got my address."

The words came out more harshly than he intended and he hurried to add a quick smile.

"I saw you," she said unconcernedly, shaking her wet hair.

Her voice was low, almost hoarse, as if the rain had given her a cold.

"Saw me?"

"Yes. I live two blocks over and sometimes eat at Rederiet. I saw you come out of there with a bag the day before yesterday and then go in through this door. Then I saw the light go on in the top-floor apartment."

Erina sounded credible and the beginnings of a panic attack in John's body subsided. The pain in the back of his head faded and he regained most of his balance.

"Okay . . . ?" she said, waving the wine bottle in a gesture toward the door of the apartment.

John nodded and risked taking his hand off the wall. He moved aside so that she could go in.

"Amazing," she said once she was inside and saw the huge space. "Do you paint?"

"I used to do it a lot back in the day—but it's been a while. I didn't actually know it was a studio when I rented the place."

Erina ran her fingertips over the half-finished canvases. She seemed to be impressed by both the art and the size of the apartment. John hung the wet coat on a hanger and then accepted the wine she was holding out.

"Are we celebrating?" he asked, reading the label.

"Yes. Your brother clearing his name."

"Half brother."

"Yes, of course. I also want to thank you for giving me the chance to defend him."

"You didn't have to buy such good wine just for that."

"Given how much attention I got for freeing the notorious Billy Nerman, I reckon it's a pretty poor fee."

John headed for the kitchen. He didn't know much about his landlady, but she seemed to like her drinks given that there were plenty of wineglasses in the otherwise empty cupboard. He pushed the laptop aside and put two glasses on the table.

"What are you afraid of?" said Erina, once she was seated on one of the wooden crates and John had opened the bottle.

"What do you mean?"

"You seemed pretty jittery when I arrived."

John avoided the question and filled their glasses.

"Skål!" he said.

They clinked glasses and the sound bounced off the walls. It sounded as though someone had dropped a coin in an empty palace ballroom.

"So, are you going to answer the question?" she said.

John sipped the wine. Erina already knew too much about him. If the plan was to find out more, he wasn't going to let her succeed.

"Is that why you're here? To . . ."

"No," she interrupted him quickly. "It's not."

"Okay, so what do you want?"

"I'd like to keep that to myself for a little longer."

She sipped her wine but didn't drop her gaze. Was she actually flirting with him?

"So, Bernt Primer . . . ?" Erina said. "That was unexpected. How's the questioning going?"

John laughed.

"You really have zero scruples. Would you like me to hand over the full investigation report right now?"

"Yes, would you please?" she said, smiling at his ironic suggestion. "He doesn't have representation, does he?"

"No, he doesn't want any. I can see you're interested."

"Definitely, but unfortunately I can't represent a new client in the same case," she said. "By the way, has he confessed?"

"I can't discuss that."

"Of course he has."

"Again—no comment," John repeated, and he saw a spark ignite in Erina's eyes.

"Can I guess?" she said, leaning over the table. "He's admitted he fucked her, but nothing else. He has an explanation for the semen, but not the murder."

John steeled himself to avoid reacting.

"Is that what you think?" he said, in a tone that attempted to highlight the fact that she was just trying it out.

"Yes, and it's one hundred percent the right strategy. You'll try to prove Emelie didn't consent. Which I assume he claims. In that case he has an explanation for why the semen ended up on the rock and purely theoretically that version is just as possible as yours."

"Even if he's telling barefaced lies?"

"What is it about you and your obsession with the truth? I've told you it doesn't matter from a legal perspective. If he gets himself a decent lawyer, he'll go free."

The frustration that had been tormenting John over the last few days began to creep back into his body again. It was disheartening to have his own gut instinct confirmed. At the same time, it was refreshing to hear someone talking about the probabilities in layman's terms.

"So you don't give a shit about whether he did it or not?"

Erina sighed.

"We've had this discussion before, and you know my views. The idea that he would have fucked her and then left doesn't seem very likely. I doubt that she even had consensual sex with him."

John sat in silence and let her train of thought go the same way his own had already done on many occasions.

"Do you know how they got in touch with each other?"

John held up his hand to stop her.

"Sorry, I'll keep my mouth shut," she said, raising the glass to her lips.

The raindrops on her bare shoulders and upper arms still hadn't dried and her skin glittered under the kitchen lights.

"How's your brother?" she asked.

"I don't know."

"Haven't you spoken to him since he got out?"

"Yes, I saw him. He seemed relieved."

"He should be grateful to you."

"Yes, and I'm sure he is in his own way."

"In his own way?"

"We're very different, Billy and me. I guess that's what happens when you grow up in different worlds."

John topped up their glasses even though Erina had barely tasted hers. The wine was full-bodied and made his tongue tingle.

"It must be a shock for the girl's parents," she said after a period of silence.

"Mr. and Mrs. AckWe," he said. "Yes, it's not easy for them."

"Have you spoken to them?"

"No, not personally. But they were informed as soon as we arrested Primer. The dad was furious, apparently. He wanted to see him."

"What? See Primer?"

"Yes," said John, shaking his head. "But we'd probably have to scrub the blood off the walls afterward."

"It's a good idea."

"What?"

"To let the dad see Primer."

John waited for a laugh or at least a smile to cross Erina's lips.

"You're joking, right?"

"No, I'm not."

John laughed and put his hands behind his neck.

"You're out of your mind."

"You should exploit the opportunity to get Primer off-balance. Who knows?—maybe he'll start talking."

"And you don't see any risks in an encounter like that?"

"There's risk in everything. But you've hit a dead end—that much is obvious. And as long as he doesn't confess, you're in a corner."

"Yes, you've said that. But there's . . ."

"Primer has been living with this crap for ten years," she interrupted. "He's had time to distance himself. If he's forced to look the girl's dad in the eye it'll become real for him again. I once had a client who had stabbed his own half sister and was vehemently denying everything. I spent days with him trying to get him to confess. Even though it was the only chance he had of getting a reduced sentence, he refused. Four months later when he saw their mother come into court, he grabbed my arm and said he'd done it. He needed to see her. You get it? He needed to see the pain he had caused."

John shook his head slowly.

"We can't use her father like that."

"Use? What are you talking about? He wants it."

John fell silent and looked at her. There was something about her frank, almost arrogant attitude that was seductive. She knew how beautiful she was and didn't hesitate to use it in both her personal and professional lives.

"Sorry, I can't sit on this fucking fruit crate any longer," she said, getting up. "Why don't you get some real chairs?"

"Well, you've got free massages whenever you want."

John had expected a response to the taunt, but instead she tucked her hair to one side and headed toward the bed. She stopped by the crumpled sheets and glanced at him.

"Haven't you figured out yet why I'm here?"

John smiled and drained his glass before getting up to walk over to her.

"No, I haven't actually."

When he reached her, she surprised him by taking a step back. When Erina pressed her buttocks against his crotch and took hold of his neck with both hands, a thrill ran through him.

"Do you see now?" she whispered, putting her lips to his throat.

She turned around and kissed him. Her tongue was bitter from the wine and her lips hot. He immediately felt himself getting hard but he also knew what a terrible idea this was. If he needed sex, it would be better to head to the pub and pick up a stranger rather than sleep with the sharpest lawyer in town—who happened to know his real identity.

"You need to leave," he said.

Erina shook her head slowly and undid her shoulder straps. Her top fell down to her waist.

"I know you want me. You'll regret it if I leave. You know it."

John stopped resisting and decided that if he was going to do this then he might as well enjoy every moment.

Erina was dressed and standing by the bed, looking at him.

"I need to be in court in a couple of hours," she said.

John turned to look at the clock on the bedside table. The sex had been explosive for them both and before they'd had time to decide whether she was spending the night they had fallen asleep.

He got out of bed and pulled on his trousers. Then he went with Erina into the corridor and called the elevator. They stood slightly apart and listened to the whining sound as the elevator began to ascend.

"Hmm. I was thinking about something," he said tentatively.

Erina turned to him.

"What?"

"I was just wondering whether there are any legal obstacles to letting Emelie's father see Primer?"

She laughed and shook her head.

"Not if you guarantee the safety of both of them," she said, getting into the elevator.

Then she pressed the green button for the ground floor and the doors slid shut.

Once John was back in the apartment, he became aware of how grubby he felt. He went into the bathroom, urinated silently in the toilet bowl, and then got in the shower. The water was cold, but he still decided to move the dial another half-turn toward the blue end of the scale. The cold was his punishment for being unable to resist sleeping with Erina Kabashi.

He tried to tell himself that she had just wanted sex, and that he had simply been a suitable candidate for the job. Erina was unlike the women he'd been with in the past. They had all been so predictable and had never challenged him. But the lawyer was different. She knew what she wanted and was happy being the smartest person in the room. But this was hardly the right time to embark on a relationship. His own safety mattered more. Sooner or later they might fall out—he knew that—and then all bets would be off.

He turned off the water, wrapped a towel around his waist and picked up his toothbrush. As he looked in the bathroom mirror at his own reflection, the anxiety returned like a punch to the gut. The experience with Erina had been so intense he had managed to forget about the email from Trevor.

He dropped the toothbrush in the sink and went back into the still-dark apartment. He went to the laptop and opened it.

The email service had kicked him off due to inactivity. He logged in again and began to read the email. After getting through the first paragraph, he couldn't keep going. The message was simple, but still hard to take in.

Inoperable.

It's all over.

John's eyes filled with tears and a cold hand grasped his heart. It was the worst possible news.

He went to the kitchen and drank two glasses of water. Then he forced himself to return to the laptop and keep reading. Trevor told him what the doctor had said. The tumors had spread and were so bad that surgery would be highly risky. The best course was to give him the least painful, most worthwhile life possible until the unavoidable end. The doctor hadn't wanted to speculate about when that might be. But he had finally managed to squeeze a prognosis out of him. Eight to twelve months. He had no longer than that.

John pushed the laptop away so hard that the computer almost fell onto the floor.

Was this really happening?

It couldn't be happening.

The final sentences in the email were the ones that hit him hardest. Trevor asked whether they could meet one last time. He wanted to visit John before he *put on his wooden jacket*, as he put it. He still felt tolerably well between his hospital visits. If Trevor's trip to see John took place during one of these gaps, they'd be able to spend some time together almost like normal.

John felt his eyes fill with tears again.

It was him—a colleague—that Trevor planned to say farewell to. Not the wife he still loved or the child he wasn't allowed to see.

John thought it was the saddest damn thing he'd ever read.

47

Heimer had just gotten home from one of his increasingly punishing runs when he heard his phone vibrating on the hall table. The taste of blood in his mouth and his muscles throbbing with pain, he had answered without checking who was calling.

He recognized her voice right away. It had a particular clarity and precision that he appreciated but which also intimidated him. He was grateful that he could blame his breathlessness on the workout he had just finished. Mona Ejdewik didn't need to know that he probably would have sounded the same if she'd called while he was on the sofa.

The detective opened with "How are you?"

Heimer thought it sounded a little strained, as if she were obliged to say something pleasant before getting down to business.

"Fine given the circumstances, thanks."

That was what he was expected to say. In reality, that was as far from the truth as it could be. Not knowing what Primer was saying during questioning by the police was driving him insane. Over the last few days, he had been running farther, more frequently, and faster than ever before, while Sissela had her own method for distracting herself: working and screwing Hugo Aglin. There'd been several more late nights at the office. Heimer didn't have the energy to care about whether she was lying to him. All he could think about was Bernt Primer.

He grasped the phone tightly and tried to prepare himself for what was to come. His heart had been pounding in his rib cage as if he had taken the final, lactic-acid-filled steps up a long climb.

"I wanted to ask you whether you were willing to assist us with something," the detective had continued.

The question took him by surprise and he was slow to reply.

"Oh? With what?"

Mona Ejdewik explained that they had reached a dead end in questioning, so she was ready to try unconventional methods. When Heimer asked what that meant, he was told she was considering letting him visit Primer in lockup, hoping that it would provoke the man into confessing.

Heimer was surprised and also pleased but tried not to sound too enthusiastic.

"Let me give it some thought . . . I mean, if you feel it would help the investigation . . ." he said, trailing off into a meaningful silence.

"We don't know how Primer will react, and I definitely don't want to pressure you into doing something you don't want to do. But we need to break the deadlock, and I think this might work."

Shortly after, he gave up his feigned reluctance and accepted her suggestion. They agreed that he would come to the police station the next day and that Mona would meet him by the entrance.

Then Heimer ended the call and went into the bathroom, relieved. He tossed his sweaty clothes in the laundry hamper, shaved, and got into the shower.

Emelie, he thought to himself.

With his eyes shut and the water rushing over his face, he was able to feel his daughter's presence for just a brief moment.

Afterward, he massaged oil into his muscular legs and lay down on the bed naked. He could allow himself thirty minutes of rest, he decided. The remainder of the day would be spent preparing for the visit to the police station. He would only have one chance, so nothing could go wrong.

"How do you think you'll feel when you see him?"

Heimer caught Mona Ejdewik's gaze. She was sitting on the other side of the desk in the zombie basement of the police station. He pretended to think and then gave her the answer he had so carefully crafted the evening before.

"I don't think I can really know until I'm sitting face-to-face with him. I'd be lying if I told you anything else. For me it's about justice for Emelie. I need to know what actually happened—I need closure."

"And if you succeed and he actually starts talking about what he did to your daughter, what happens then?"

"I don't know. But I promise to try to think about Emelie and what's best for the investigation."

The detective was trying to get him to relax while simultaneously evaluating his mental state. The questions about how he felt were discreet and deftly smuggled into the conversation. If she saw even a tiny crack in his façade, she would call it all off.

Heimer made an effort to be the person she wanted him to be. He couldn't seem unaffected—that would seem psychologically aberrant. At the same time, he couldn't be too emotional—that might make him seem unbalanced or a downright liability.

"Will I be alone with him?" he asked.

Mona cleared her throat and he thought he glimpsed a flash of concern cross her face.

"As I said, this is an unusual situation. But my feeling is that you'll meet alone, with a guard outside and cameras recording everything. How does that sound to you?"

Absolutely perfect was how it sounded. But he couldn't show that.

"How quickly can the guard get into the room?" he said.

"A few seconds. But if you feel uncomfortable, he can be inside the room instead. It's up to you."

Heimer pretended to think about it.

"Let's do it your way. I feel okay with that."

He caught himself touching the outside of his jacket with his hand. He looked at Mona to see whether she had reacted to his body language, but the movement seemed to have escaped her.

"What do you want me to ask him about?"

"Our problem is that he admits he had oral sex with Emelie but denies everything else. He says it was consensual and that she was alive when he left the scene."

She paused to see his reaction to what she had said. Heimer felt disgusted and there was no reason to conceal that.

"I want you to try to ask open questions," Mona continued. "Ask him to tell you about what happened that night. Say that you have a right to know. After all, you are her father. If you want to take a break, then that's totally fine. Just call for the guard and you'll be let out. And above all, stay calm—otherwise we'll have to come in and break it off. We'll see and hear everything you say."

Heimer nodded. He understood.

"Do you have any questions before we get started?"

"No, I feel ready. Well, as ready as I'll ever be for something like this," he said, to soften the absolute certainty.

She made a call and shortly after the door to the office opened and a prison guard entered. The detective introduced the men to each other before the three of them headed for the interview room. When they were almost there, Mona stopped. After a quick "good luck," she disappeared into the adjacent room to check that the audio and video were working as they should.

Heimer nodded to show that he was ready. But the guard cracked his knuckles and adjusted the baton on his belt.

"Please spread your legs and hold your arms out."

The casual tone in which the man spoke the words contrasted sharply with the panic that had erupted inside Heimer. He couldn't permit a pat down.

Autopilot kicked in—or his survival instincts did.

"I need to go to the men's room before I meet him," he said.

The man shrugged his shoulders.

"Of course. It's just over there," he said, pointing.

Heimer felt the man's gaze following him and he made an effort not to walk faster than normal. As soon as he locked the door he sank onto the toilet seat and allowed the panic to take hold of his body. His legs trembled and his breathing was heavy.

After a while, the worst had passed. He had to be quick. There was a limit to how long he could stay in there without drawing attention.

He searched the room for suitable hiding places. There weren't many to choose from. It was either the toilet tank or the paper towel dispenser. He chose the latter. He carefully pried the lid off and put it on the sink. He stood on tiptoe and saw that the dispenser was half full. Then he took the stiletto switchblade from the inside pocket of his jacket and put it on top of the paper towels. It worked. The stack of paper supported the weight of the knife and there was plenty there in the event that anyone visited the bathroom.

He put the lid back on the dispenser and looked in the mirror. His face looked tense, but it was supposed to. His eyes were more indicative of his state. There was something there that was harder to conceal. A kind of intense energy bordering on obsession. He was glad that Sissela couldn't see him like this. She would have seen right away that something was wrong.

He opened the door and went back into the corridor, where his chaperone was leaning against the wall fiddling impatiently with his keys. Unprompted, Heimer held out his hands and stood with his legs wide apart. The guard searched him and then showed him into the empty interview room.

"She wants you to sit there," the guard said, pointing at the chair bolted to the floor with its back toward the door. "For the camera."

Heimer turned his head and saw a discreet camera setup on the wall, aimed at the seat opposite his own.

"Okay," he said.

"I'll go and fetch Primer," the guard said.

Heimer nodded while trying to find something to fix his gaze on. Given the absence of windows, it had to be the camera on the wall behind him. He turned around and looked into the lens. That was his only contact with the outside world—a black hole registering every flicker of expression on his face. He had to look resolute.

48

John looked into Heimer Bjurwall's eyes through the monitor in the observation room where he was keeping Mona company. The face on the screen reminded him of how the young men in the NYPD's SWAT team usually looked just before a raid. Emelie's father was certainly no twenty-five-year-old bodybuilder in a bulletproof vest, but there was something there that connected the two—determination, which streamed through the lens of the camera and into the room next door.

For a moment, John doubted the whole operation. Maybe it would hurt the investigation more than it helped. But it was too late now. He had suggested Erina's idea to Mona and she gave her approval.

"They're on their way now."

Mona repeated what the guard who had fetched Primer had just told her via her headset. John nodded and looked at the screen again. Heimer Bjurwall had turned his back to the camera and clasped his hands on the table.

There was a buzzing in John's pocket. His phone was on silent so Mona didn't notice anything. He discreetly rejected the call. It rang again after just a few seconds. This time he got the phone out to see who was calling. It was coming through the switchboard. Curiosity got the better of him and he accepted the call.

"Hello?"

"John, buddy!"

He pushed the phone tightly against his ear so that Mona wouldn't hear. The voice on the line had used his real name. It took a second for him to place it.

Billy.

His brother was calling.

He considered whether to go outside and take the call, but with Primer en route to the interview room that was out of the question. Mona would wonder what call could be so important that he would disappear at this moment.

"I'm busy right now," he said in a formal voice.

"You need to come by. There's something I've got to tell you."

Billy's voice was slurred. He clearly had been drinking, but the gravity of his tone penetrated the inebriation. This wasn't just any old drunk talk. His brother really did have something he wanted to say.

Mona looked at John in irritation and indicated he should end the call.

"I can't talk," he said, ending the call.

He sighed as believably as he could.

"I thought the switchboard had been told to refer all reporters to the press office."

Mona's gaze lingered on him for so long that for a few seconds he thought she had heard the voice and realized that it belonged to his brother. John hadn't forgotten their conversation when he had told Mona he hadn't been in contact with either Billy or his mother.

"They're very creative when it comes to getting past switchboard operators," she said finally, turning back to the screen.

John tried to relax. He could see Mona checking that the equipment was recording as it should be. It was the umpteenth time, but it was obvious she was nervous about what was to come.

He switched off his phone to make sure his brother didn't disturb him again. It was definitely not okay for Billy to call him at work. John could only hope that he hadn't said anything to the operator that might reveal his true identity.

He moved his chair closer to the monitor and looked intensely at Heimer Bjurwall's neck and back. His hands were resting clasped on the table, just as they had been when he had last checked.

"They're going in now," said Mona, who had been updated via the headset.

A moment later, they watched on the screen as Primer was led into the room by the prison guard, who then excused himself and closed the door. John wished they had two cameras in there so that they could also watch Heimer Bjurwall's face. But given the setup, they'd have to make do with Primer's.

It seemed to take a moment before the former lead investigator managed to grasp who the man sitting at the table was. But when he did, the reaction was all the stronger. John thought it was usually a bit far-fetched to talk about eyes being wide-open, but that was exactly what happened. Panic spread across Primer's face, giving it an almost contorted appearance.

Neither of the men had yet uttered a word to each other. Mona leaned forward and adjusted the volume. A faint snuffle was audible from the speakers and John saw tears running down Primer's cheeks. This was different from the human robot with preprogrammed replies that he and Mona had encountered during questioning over the past few days. Simply by being there, Heimer had managed to get past Primer's defenses. It was a big step forward. Now they needed to make him talk too.

Primer collapsed onto the chair and buried his head in his hands. The snuffling soon turned into sobbing and his large body shook on the screen before them.

"Guard!"

Heimer Bjurwall had called out. Once again, John cursed the fact that they didn't have a camera on him. It would've made it easier to follow the dynamic in the interview room.

"What's he up to?" said Mona.

"Maybe he couldn't handle seeing him," said John, as Emelie's father was led out of the room.

Mona pressed her headset against her ear to listen to what the guard had to say.

"Apparently he felt unwell and needed to go to the men's room," she said.

From the speakers, they could hear Primer's sobbing becoming even louder. John looked at the screen and saw that the man was almost slipping off his chair and onto the floor. Mona turned the volume down.

"The sensible thing would be to stop," she said, but she didn't look as though she wanted to do that.

"No, we have to keep going," he said. "It might be our only chance."

Mona looked thoughtful.

"What's up with Heimer Bjurwall?" she said into the microphone.

It took a while before she got an answer. The guard was apparently heading for the men's room.

"He's on the way back now," the voice in Mona's earpiece said.

"Good, make sure he gets back in there."

It didn't take long for the door to open again and for Heimer Bjurwall to return to his seat in the interview room. Primer couldn't look him in the eye. He turned his face away and continued crying. Heimer, on the other hand, seemed calm and collected. When he spoke, his voice was matter-of-fact.

"It's time for you to tell me what you did to my daughter."

It wasn't a question—it was an order. It came from someone with power and was issued to someone who was powerless. John was fascinated to see how Primer shrank on the screen in front of him. Was this really the same man who had spent a week casually lying to them?

"Forgive me," he sobbed, using his sleeve to wipe away snot.

"I'm not interested in your apologies," said Heimer.

He leaned forward across the table to drive home that he was serious.

"I'll tell you—I promise," Primer stammered. "I met her by chance when I was out one night, years ago. We knew each other—I'd given talks at Björkbacken when she was there. I worked in narcotics back then and I was in the pubs around town a lot." He stopped to catch his breath and wiped the palm of his hand down his moist face. It was as if each and every sentence was a struggle.

"It was obvious right away that she'd taken something," he continued. "I asked her to empty her pockets and she eventually took out two bags of cocaine. I explained that I couldn't let that go and that I'd have to take her to the station. She was distraught and she begged and pleaded for me to keep my mouth shut. And eventually I . . ."

"Eventually you what?" said Heimer.

Primer hesitated for a long time before filling his lungs with air.

"Eventually, I gave in. I said I'd look the other way about the coke possession if she . . . made me come."

Once he had said that, the sobbing returned and he turned his head away from Heimer Bjurwall and the camera.

"Oh, Jesus, I'm so ashamed," he said. "But I couldn't help it—there must be something wrong with my head."

John and Mona looked at each other. This was a breakthrough—maybe everything would come tumbling out of Bernt Primer after all.

"So you had sex with her?" said Heimer.

John didn't understand how the girl's father could stay calm. It was as if the confession related to a random young woman rather than his own daughter.

"Yes. She gave me a blow job. But I didn't make her. Afterward, she laughed and even said she liked it."

Primer suddenly stopped talking, as if he had reacted to a change in Heimer Bjurwall's facial expression. John got up. It was instinct that told him he should be ready to step in and assist the guard outside the interview room if necessary. Mona also stood up and put a hand on his shoulder. He noticed that she was holding her breath as they followed the drama on screen.

"Come on, Heimer—just stay calm and keep asking questions," she muttered.

They could see Emelie's father fumbling with his hands at his own chest.

"He can't be having a heart attack right now, can he?" said John.

But after a while, the hands returned to the table and Heimer seemed to be composed enough to continue what must have been the worst conversation of his life.

"What happened then?" he said.

Primer collapsed back against the chair and looked dejected.

"I told her that if she was ever in town in the future and wanted to party, it would be better if she got in touch with me. I could get her some good stuff. There's so much crap out on the streets—you never know what's in it."

"Did she do that? Did she get in touch with you again?"

"I remember she contacted me a couple of times during the spring. Around Easter, I think. It must have been during the holidays when she came back to Karlstad from college."

"And?"

"Well, what was I supposed to say? She wanted cocaine and I helped her with that, I'm afraid. Of course, I regret it now. But I wasn't thinking. I hadn't . . ."

"How did she pay?" Heimer interrupted.

Primer lowered his head again and avoided the gaze of the man across the table from him.

"She always paid the same way."

"With sex?"

"Yes. But I never slept with her. It was only her who . . . helped me."

Primer had stopped crying and was speaking more clearly in a voice that didn't seem to belong to him. The words came more quickly and readily.

"The night she disappeared, she emailed me in the afternoon that day. She was going to some party and wanted me to bring her some stuff to Tynäs at midnight."

Heimer Bjurwall said nothing, and in the absence of a camera, John tried to imagine his face. He wanted to draw it tonight when he got back to the apartment. Fixed and determined with those tense neck muscles and the darkness in his eyes.

"Emelie was late," Primer continued. "But eventually she turned up. And we . . . well . . ."

He crumbled again. His face contorted silently for a moment before a new wave of sobbing overcame him. It was less controlled than before and was followed by a cry reminiscent of a wounded animal.

"I know I'm disgusting, but I didn't kill her," he sobbed.

John tried to make eye contact with Mona, but it was as if she were hypnotized by what was unfolding on the screen in front of them. The fact that Primer denied the murder didn't worry him. Serious violent crimes with sexual elements resulted in strong feelings of guilt and shame in the perpetrator. That was why confessions usually came in stages, with the most taboo acts the last to be acknowledged.

John could see how Heimer Bjurwall appeared once again to be touching his chest with one hand. Maybe he really was having heart palpitations.

"Was it you?"

Heimer leaned forward and when he spoke to the man opposite him it was little more than a whisper.

"I know how it looks," Primer snuffled. "I swapped the DNA samples to frame Billy Nerman and I deleted the files from the investigation. I panicked and I didn't want to get mixed up in it. But Heimer, I promise you . . . I didn't kill her."

John looked at Mona again. Primer was crashing and the confessions just kept coming. But the question was how long they dared let the conversation continue. Heimer looked like he was teetering on the edge. The pressure inside the murdered girl's father might become too much.

"We need to stop!" he said to Mona.

She shook her head, her gaze still glued to the screen.

Heimer Bjurwall's breathing was so rapid and heavy that the speakers were rattling. His face was just a few inches from Primer's and he was fumbling at his chest with one hand.

"Jesus Christ, Mona . . ." said John, but got no further before Heimer Bjurwall suddenly leaned back in his chair.

"Guard!" Heimer cried out. "We're done here."

Heimer Bjurwall had been noticeably tired when Mona had escorted him to reception. He wanted to go straight home after the meeting, which was no surprise. The conversation in the confined room must have been draining.

However, John and Mona felt energized. They'd gambled everything on this gambit—and won. Granted, Primer hadn't told them about the murder itself yet, but they had made good progress toward a full confession. The new information that had emerged would allow them to push him further in future questioning.

Mona was eager to report their progress to the prosecutor and asked whether John wanted to join her. He declined. Billy's slurred voice was still ringing in his ears. He needed to talk to his brother before the idiot caused any more trouble.

In the car on the way to his childhood home outside Skoghall, John let his thoughts wander. They took diversions, jumping back and forth between different subjects: the breakthrough in the investigation, Erina next to him in bed, and his unruly brother—he wasn't quite sure what to do with *him*. Once he was almost at the bridge to Hammarö, the tornado in his head calmed down and his thoughts settled on what hurt the most.

Trevor.

He thought about his friend's question in the email. Whether he could visit him. John wished he could answer "yes, come," but was it really that simple? They had been careful never to reveal where in the world they were. Bypassing all that and letting a cancer-ridden Trevor get on the next plane to Sweden was hardly in keeping with the witness protection program handbook.

All ties had to be cut—that was what Brodwick had told them over and over. John shook his head. It was easy for him to say—he didn't have to deny a dying man his final wish. Trevor hadn't been following any instructions when he had saved John's life in Baltimore. He had improvised and followed his gut instinct. If John said no to the visit, he'd need a better reason than it being against the rules—and he wasn't sure he had one.

John parked in the same place as on his last visit to his brother and strolled the final stretch to Nerman's Autos. Billy was on the steps to the house with a cup of coffee. Someone—presumably Nicole—had wedged a collection of wooden ice cream sticks into a crack on the second step.

"Well, how about that. The supercop is on the move."

His brother was in his usual attire: oily jeans and an equally filthy t-shirt. He smelled of booze, but seemed to have sobered up enough to stop slurring his speech.

"You seemed pretty damn busy when I called earlier."

John was immediately perturbed by the attitude. The fact that he had come to hear what Billy had to say was apparently not enough. He had to grovel too.

"I didn't mean to be rude," he said. "But you can't call me at work. It's . . ."

"Relax, bro," Billy interjected. "I didn't use your real name. I asked the operator for Fredrik Adamsson."

"And you got put through just like that?"

John put his foot on the lowest step and leaned over him.

"Well, not quite. I told them I had important information about the murder of Emelie Bjurwall. And fuck me, somehow it wasn't a problem after that."

Billy chuckled at his own resourcefulness, as John sat down next to him on the step.

"Watch out for the ice cream sticks! Nicole is keeping count of how many she eats. There's some girl at school who called her fat again, so we've established a new rule—no more than five per week."

John shifted slightly to the right to avoid mistakenly treading on the collection of sticks. He wasn't in the mood to discuss his niece's weight.

"Listen to me, Billy," he said, hoping that he was managing to conceal most of his irritation. "I'm going to get a separate phone that only you can call."

"I don't even have your number," Billy muttered.

"I'll give it to you. But you can't contact me any other way. Can you promise me that?"

"Hell, I'm sorry. Okay? I just wanted to talk to my brother who's been gone for more than twenty years."

"Do you promise?" said John, using his final reserves of self-discipline.

Billy nodded reluctantly.

"Sure, whatever you say."

"Thanks," said John, taking a deep breath of autumn air.

The smell of sulfur from the mill was fainter today, but it still lingered in the air like part of the scenery. He didn't want to hassle Billy. His brother was damaged goods and he needed to cut him some slack.

"What did you need talk to me about?" he said.

"What?"

"When you called. You said there was something you needed to tell me."

"Oh, that. It's about Nicole. She needs help at school with her math. The teacher says she's not keeping up in class and I was going to ask whether you could help. I guess I'm as thick as she is."

Billy laughed, as if he had said something funny. John thought it sounded somewhat forced and it didn't line up with the serious tone on the phone earlier.

"Was it really just that? You sounded pretty worked up."

"Just that?" his brother repeated. "It's obvious you don't have kids. If Nicole is going to make it in this life, she needs to do alright at school—you must get that?"

Billy wasn't making it easy. If his brother was aspiring to be Dad of the Year, surely he needed to stay sober until at least lunchtime.

"Of course, I get it," he said. "But I'm not sure it's a good idea. She'll start to wonder who I am."

"You're right," Billy said quickly. "It was just an idea."

John looked at the yard dotted with bumps and potholes. Most of them were filled with water from the rain that morning. He spotted a cigarette butt a few meters away. It was dry, which suggested it had ended up there sometime that morning, after the rain had stopped. Billy didn't smoke, but there was someone else who did.

"Have you seen Mom lately?" he said, wishing he could switch off his cop brain once in a while.

"I was over there last week," said Billy. "It was the usual moaning about the food and the staff."

The cigarette didn't have to belong to their chain-smoking mother, but it still seemed likely that his brother was lying for some reason. Part of John wanted to challenge him. Retrieve the butt from the yard; check whether it was her brand. But he stopped himself. He didn't want to put any more strain on their relationship than he already had done. What was more, the feeling of injustice was always there. The fact that he'd managed to clear Billy in the AckWe case wasn't enough to repay the debt he felt he owed his brother.

The front door opened and John turned around. Nicole was standing there with her red headphones around her neck and clutching a laptop.

"What are you doing with my computer?" said Billy.

"The tablet died, so I want to play on it."

Her voice sounded raspy, as if she had a cold.

"No, you can't. It's my computer."

"Please, Dad."

"Nicole!" he said sharply. "Don't touch my stuff, and don't make trouble when we've got visitors. Dad's friend is here again."

John waved at her and the girl nodded in return. Billy got up and tore the laptop from his daughter's hands.

"You've got to learn to listen," he said, disappearing inside.

Nicole sat down on the step and began to fiddle with one of the ice cream sticks. It came loose from the crack in the concrete and she threw it toward an oil drum collecting rainwater beneath one of the downpipes. A gust of wind caught the light piece of wood and made it bounce against the rusty metal before dropping to the ground.

"Shouldn't you be at school?"

"Teacher training day."

Nicole stared at the ground ahead of her and John did the same. His gaze settled on the cigarette butt on the gravel again. He decided to take a chance.

"Did you have fun when your grandma was here?" he said.

She shook her head.

"Not really. She and Dad spent the whole time fighting."

John felt awful for exploiting his niece, but at the same time he wanted to know what was going on. Why was his brother lying about something as trivial as their mother coming to visit? And why wouldn't he tell him the real reason for the call earlier?

"That's too bad. Has she been gone long?" he continued.

"Nope."

"Do you know why they were fighting?"

She shook her head.

"Dad told me to go to my room and play with my headphones on. That's why my tablet died."

When Billy returned, she took the opportunity to sneak back into the house. His brother drained the last of the coffee from the mug he had left on the step.

"I'd put on a fresh pot for you," he said, waving the mug. "But it'll have to be another time. Some guy from Sunne is on the way over with his wrecked Impala."

He just seemed to want John to leave him and his daughter alone as soon as possible.

49

Heimer hadn't been able to sleep after the visit to the police station. Somewhere, deep down, he was relieved to look into Primer's eyes and be convinced that it wasn't him. At the same time, it was possible he was mistaken. In the witching hour, with the duvet tangled around his legs and Sissela snoring on the pillow next to his, he questioned the moment when he decided to believe Primer. Did he really trust the former detective, or was it about fear of actually using that knife? Did his courage betray him, and did he choose to see that failure as something else?

He tried to replay what had happened in the interview room several times during the night. Primer's face looked different each time. His memory couldn't be relied upon. Eventually, he managed to get to sleep by accepting that all he could do was trust his instinct.

In the morning when Sissela had gone to work, he began to work through it with precise logic.

If it wasn't Primer then it had to be someone else.

The only question was who.

Heimer checked the time and realized he had better get started. Sourcing three hundred thousand kronor in cash in just five hours wasn't all that easy—not even when your last name was Bjurwall.

He got into the shower. He hadn't thought he would need to leave any money in the locker at the station. But after his visit to the police station, the game plan had changed, and he now saw no option but to follow through with the letter writer.

Half an hour later, he reversed out of the drive while calling the bank. He introduced himself and was immediately put through to the private banking department. He told them a lie about an opportunity that had come up to buy a vintage Mercat, saying that the seller was insisting on payment in cash. The woman on the line didn't ask any further questions but promised that the money would be ready for pickup the next day.

"That won't work," he said. "I need it in an hour."

The woman said that might be tricky, but that she would do her best. He thanked her and said he hoped she would find a solution, adding that it would be a pity if he had to call other banks to get their help with a simple thing like this.

He ended the call and counted the seconds silently. This time it was a male voice, reeling off a title that Heimer didn't catch, but which was undoubtedly more important and better paid than the woman's. Of course the money would be ready for collection from the Karlstad branch right away.

A little while later when Heimer arrived at the bank and was handed the bundle of cash, the bank employee bowed so low he almost struck his head on the desk in front of him.

The next stop was the Clas Ohlson store near the railway station, which was where Heimer parked the car. Inside the shop, he grabbed a toolbox, a power drill/screwdriver combo, some workman's clothes, and a backpack. The purchase of the webcam took longer. He wanted to be sure it was of a good enough quality and that it could be connected to the internet.

He changed in the shopping center bathrooms. The carpenter's trousers felt uncomfortable and looked far too new when he examined himself in the mirror. He slid his middle finger along the edging on the tiled floor and spread the grime on the coarse material. The result was surprisingly good. With a few tools in his pockets, he would pass for a workman.

He dumped his own clothes in the trunk of his car and walked to the train station. The building on the other side of Hamngatan was a classic: red bricks, arc-shaped window frames, and a fancy clock tower. He ran up the steps and passed through the automatic doors.

Inside, he saw a beggar on the right-hand side, holding a paper cup from Pressbyrån, and on one of the benches there was a gaggle of schoolgirls giggling over a cell phone. The lockers were farther in and he wondered from what position number 109 would be most visible. He settled on one of the walls beside the information boards. The higher up the camera was positioned, the better the angle would be, and he began to regret not bringing a ladder.

Was it workmanlike to stand on the bench?

He thought back to when they had built the house in Tynäs and reassured himself that he could get away with any behavior he liked. The builders had pissed in the flowerbeds and stubbed out their cigarettes on the custom windowsills.

Heimer took out the mounting for the camera and stood on the worn-out wooden bench. Using a pencil, he marked the holes using the metal plate as a template and then drilled four holes in the wall. Then he inserted the anchors and attached the plate using the screws that had come with it.

He jumped down to the floor and looked around. The schoolgirls and the beggar seemed uninterested in what the workman was doing over by the wall. He got the webcam out of its box and checked that the battery was charged. Then he stood on the bench again, hooked it on to the mounting, and pressed the on switch. The technology worked. Using an app on his phone, he could watch a livestream from the camera. The image was better than he had dared to hope for, and after making a few adjustments, the lens provided exactly the view of the locker that he needed.

He returned the tools to his backpack and attempted to discreetly brush the brick dust off his feet. Once he was satisfied, he left the station and glanced at the clock in the tower.

The time was 11:54 A.M.

In two hours' time, he would return with the three hundred thousand in the backpack.

Heimer wondered whether the beggar sitting on the floor by the entrance recognized him in his normal clothes. It didn't seem like it. The man tilted his head back and shook the paper cup. Judging by how few coins were jangling inside, it hadn't been the most lucrative of days.

Heimer looked toward the wall where he mounted the camera. Everything appeared to be in order, which was confirmed by checking the phone in his jacket pocket. The livestream was still running and he had checked the picture quality just a few minutes earlier.

With a determined stride, he walked up to locker 109. He opened the door and stuffed the backpack containing the cash inside. There was plenty of space for it. He pulled a coin from his trouser pocket and put it in the narrow coin slot. Then he shut the door and locked it. He put the key in his other trouser pocket. The letter writer hadn't asked him to leave it there, so he assumed he or she intended to gain access to the locker by other means. Perhaps the lock would be broken. Or maybe there was a spare key.

Heimer left the railway station and began to walk toward the bus station. When he got there, the number 800 bus to Säffle was already there. He bought a ticket from the vending machine in the waiting room and got on. The driver nodded at him and he sat down on a seat almost at the back of the deserted bus.

After a while he heard the hiss of the doors closing and soon the driver pulled away. Heimer waited until the bus made it to the first red light before getting out his phone. He opened the app and watched the livestream from the railway station. It showed a peaceful scene with just a few people sitting on the benches waiting for their trains.

It didn't matter if the letter writer already had time to empty the locker. The system saved all video content for twenty-four hours. But Heimer didn't think that was the case. It was more likely they would wait until he had left on the bus.

On the walk from the station, he'd tried to see whether anyone was following him, but he hadn't identified any suitable candidates. Still, it didn't really matter. When the locker was emptied, he would know who was behind Nadja6543.

The bus turned onto the highway and the driver accelerated. The connection remained constant without any disruption. The footage was crystal clear and he had no difficulty seeing which brand of soft drink a snuggling couple on the bench closest to the lockers was sharing.

Heimer had to look up from the screen for a while to avoid getting travel sick. When he looked down at the mobile again, he saw the beggar get up. Maybe he was going to give up for the day or switch to a location where there were more passersby. He slowly ambled forward—not to the doors, but in the opposite direction.

Toward the lockers.

Heimer could never have anticipated what happened next. The beggar stopped in front of locker 109 and inserted a key into the lock. He turned it, opened the door, and removed the backpack. In one swift movement, he slung it over his shoulder and headed for the exit. As he passed the webcam, he stopped and waved at the lens before vanishing out of sight through the automatic doors.

The bus didn't stop until Grums. The smell of the paper mill was the same here as in Skoghall. It stank of cheap housing and people grilling ham steak and drinking boxed wine on their patios.

Heimer was the only person to get off at the stop and he had to wait for a bus going the other way to take him back to civilization. He sat down on the bench in the bus shelter and replayed the video on his phone. When the beggar looked into the camera, he hit pause. He could hardly be looking at the letter writer—surely it was a courier? A hungry member of the Roma community that God-knew-who had given a few hundred in return for collecting the backpack and delivering it to them? It probably wouldn't be hard to track down this person. After all, there weren't that many Roma in Karlstad. On the bus back to town, Heimer searched online and found an article in

Värmlands Folkblad about a camp behind the gym next to the I2-forest. Once he was back in town, and had collected the car from the lot, he drove there.

He strolled into the area behind the fitness center, noting that the heavy rain had made the trails muddy. His Italian calfskin shoes were made for walking from pizzeria to pizzeria along cobbled streets—not expeditions into the forests of Värmland. Mud splattered up the tongues of his shoes and he regretted not changing into the work boots from his carpenter's outfit.

The closer to the camp he got, the more trash there was lying around the forest. He saw an abandoned grill setup for cooking and some frying pans under a tree, together with several Lidl grocery bags. Animals had torn the plastic to shreds.

After taking a sharp right-hand turn, the first tents appeared in a cluster of trees a little farther on. There were children playing football outside and some of the women were cooking over an improvised fireplace built with loose bricks. The men appeared to be occupied with repairing one of the tents that had collapsed.

Heimer stopped on the path. No one had seen him yet, and part of him just wanted to turn on the heel of his Italian calfskin shoes and head back to the car. But leaving wasn't an option. He was here to find the beggar.

He carried on toward the men, who were trying to fix a broken tentpole using duct tape and wire.

"Hello," he said tentatively.

They didn't answer. They just looked at him with fear in their eyes. Heimer realized they thought he'd come from the city government and was there to chase them away.

"I'm looking for someone who might live here," he continued, still speaking English.

They didn't answer, but they seemed to relax a little. The eldest of them stepped forward and looked him over from head to toe. He was a thin wiry man with eyes well recessed into their sockets and a comb-over.

"Do you have a name?" he said.

He had a rough voice and his English was surprisingly good.

"No, just a photo on my phone."

He held up the phone and the man glanced at it.

"Why do you want to find him?" he asked.

Heimer decided to stick to the truth—or as much as he thought necessary.

"There's something I want to ask him. It's a private matter."

The man still looked skeptical, but he held out his hand. Heimer gave him his phone and let him study the photo from the webcam. He then showed it to the other men and an intense discussion erupted among the group.

"Do you recognize him?" Heimer asked after a while. His voice sounded more tentative than he had hoped and he saw the dynamic was changing. When they had thought he was from the authorities, they were afraid. Now that it dawned on them that he needed their help, the situation was different. He wished he understood what they were saying. Was he prejudiced, or was one of the men looking at Heimer's wristwatch a lot? It was worth more than the whole camp could raise in years from panhandling. He was crazy not to have taken it off and left it in the glove compartment of the car.

"His name is Danut, and he lived here last spring," said the older man. "But he moved. It's mostly families here, and he lived alone."

A football rolled up to Heimer. One of the children had kicked it the wrong way and came rushing after it, hotly pursued by one of his friends. When they saw the visitor both of them stopped, unsure how they were expected to behave. Heimer stopped the ball, flicked it up with the outside of his foot, and volleyed it toward the boys. When he turned back to the men, he had at least regained some of his authority.

"Do you know where he is now?" he said.

The oldest man translated and another heated discussion followed. Heimer hoped it wasn't about whether they should rob him and sell his watch.

"It seems that he stays in town. He doesn't stay here, anyway," said the man.

"Where in town?"

The man shrugged his shoulders.

"Our kind aren't popular, so I guess he moves around a lot. Check lumberyards and underground parking garages. Anywhere you can find a roof to put over your head."

Heimer thanked them and wondered whether to give the men money. But there was something humiliating about offering them payment without them having asked. At any rate, that was what he told himself. Perhaps he was just afraid of what he thought might happen if he got his wallet out.

Dusk had fallen, accompanied by a heavy drizzle. Heimer had left his coat on the back seat of the car. He turned up the collar on his jacket to protect himself from the raindrops. He was starting to lose hope. He had spent the last few hours trying to think like a homeless man and visited all the places in town where he would have chosen to sleep. He met society's castaways. Mostly Roma, but also Swedish alcoholics and the mentally ill who didn't want or weren't able to seek out the shelter offered by the government and the church. But no one knew anyone by the name of Danut. Most people didn't even want to look at the photo on his phone—if, that was, they even understood what he was saying.

When the rain intensified, he decided to give up and go home. The car was parked next to the Wermland Opera. He sat there with the engine running, waiting for the heater to remove the fog from the windshield. Then he drove out onto the empty street, around the block, and onto the bridge across the Klarälven River. Halfway across, he turned his head and traced the winding river through the town. He counted three crossings just in his field of vision and if he looked the other way he would probably see a few more.

Then it hit him.

Bridges.

They were such an obvious part of the urban landscape that he barely noticed them. Maybe Danut had beat a retreat to one of the bridge abutments in the town to seek shelter from the elements. It was at least worth exploring.

Heimer turned left as soon as he reached the other side. He stopped by the curb and stepped out into the rain to see whether there was any trace of nighttime guests under the bridge he had just crossed. There were the usual graffiti and empty beer cans, but nothing to indicate anyone lived there.

He jumped back into the car and drove alongside the river to the next bridge. It was impossible to see under the bridge from the car, so once again he had to get out in the rain. He parked on Bjurbäcksgatan in front of the big houses and made his way on foot through the park toward the bridge.

Even as he was approaching it, his pulse quickened. The site—if you could call it that when describing outdoor sleeping spots—was ideal, with greenery nearby and plenty of space between the concrete foundations and the water. When he peered into the shadows under the bridge, he saw several sheets of cardboard stacked on top of one another to form a mattress. There were also traces of a fire on the ground.

Someone had made the bridge underpass their home—that much was obvious. The question was who. Heimer had learned that there were more homeless in Karlstad than he had thought and there was nothing to suggest that Danut lived here. But it was clearly a spot to return to later.

On the way back to the car, he saw a man walking through the park toward the water. He was pulling a wheeled shopping cart, the sort old women used. His clothes were tattered, and he was limping heavily with his left leg.

Heimer kept moving to intercept the man. When they were around twenty meters apart, the man bent down into a trash bin to check it for deposit bottles. He put his finds in the bag and stumbled laboriously on.

The man was now so close that Heimer could see his face. It was the beggar from the station.

For a moment, Heimer thought the man would turn around and try to run away, but instead he took a couple of steps closer and looked at him in astonishment.

"It's you," he said in heavily accented English.

Heimer nodded.

"Do you live over there?" he heard himself ask.

"Yes, under bridge. Good place. Quiet."

It had stopped raining and Heimer pointed at a bench next to the path.

"Can we sit down?"

Heimer brushed the water off the bench with the sleeve of his coat. He sat down and a moment later the man sat down next to him.

"You took something at the train station today."

"I don't have now," the man replied quickly.

"What happened to the backpack then?"

The man hesitated again. He looked like he was thinking about how to make the best of the situation.

"I give it to someone."

"Why?" Heimer asked, even though he knew the answer.

"I get money. All I do is collect package and hand on. Nothing else."

"Did you look inside the bag?"

"No, not allowed. If I look, I not get money."

Heimer took a deep breath before asking the only question he needed to know the answer to.

"Who did you give the bag to?"

The man got up from the bench. He pulled a half-smoked cigarette out of his jacket pocket and lit it.

"Is important for you," he said, exhaling smoke. "I see you put up camera. You don't do that if not important."

"Yes, that's right. It's important to me. Can you describe the person?"

The man met Heimer's gaze. He even dared to flash a gap-toothed grin at him.

"I have photo."

"A photo?" said Heimer in surprise.

"Yes," said the man. "I think someone maybe ask. So I take photo on phone, secret photo."

Heimer couldn't contain his excitement. This was better than he had dared to hope.

"Can I see the photo?" he said as neutrally as he could.

The beggar shook his head.

"Costs five hundred kronor," he said.

Heimer dutifully protested, suggesting three hundred so that the man wouldn't realize how much the picture was actually worth to him. The man stood his ground. His price was the only price. Heimer got out his wallet and handed over a five hundred kronor note. The man looked at it for a long time before pocketing it. Then he bent down and pulled a bundle from the inside compartment of the cart. It was a towel, which he unfolded to reveal a phone with a cracked screen. He entered the PIN and appeared to spend a while scrolling through photos.

"Look," he said.

Heimer took the phone and contemplated the screen. The photo had been taken in profile, but the face was still clear enough that Heimer recognized it at once.

50

For the second day in a row, John parked the car near his childhood home. He realized that he ought to vary where he parked to avoid drawing attention, but it was late, and it would be hard to find somewhere new in the dark.

As he headed for the house, he summarized the day before for himself. Mona had been in high spirits. There'd been nothing but pats on the back from the prosecutor and the Walrus following the breakthrough in the case. Primer had been deeply disturbed by the encounter with Emelie's father and hadn't slept a wink all night.

The doctor they'd called in had more or less ordered them to postpone more questioning for at least twenty-four hours. The break gave John the time he needed to buy two prepaid phones. Giving one of them to his brother would be the surest way of avoiding any more risky calls to the police switchboard.

Billy really had a unique capacity for causing trouble for himself and others. It had always been like that and nothing seemed to have changed in the years the brothers had been separated.

When John entered the yard, he heard the characteristic sound of a hammer striking sheet metal emanating from the workshop. He remembered what Billy had said about the Impala that had crashed. John had thought it was a lie to get rid of him, but maybe there really was a car that needed repairing.

He was about to knock on the garage door when he realized that his brother would be wearing ear protectors, so he went on into the workshop.

Billy was bending over the hood of one of the cars. When he looked up, a wide grin appeared on his face. He put his hammer down and removed his ear protectors.

"There are some real idiots out there," he said. "A beautiful set of wheels like this and the moron runs into a lamppost. And he must have been going fast too."

Billy pointed at the car's buckled bumper and John went to examine the damage. The metal was in a truly bad state.

"Surely you can't just bash that back out?" he said.

"We'll see," said Billy with a blasé look. "A new one ain't cheap, so it's definitely worth a try."

His brother was definitely more relaxed this time—he wasn't at all on his guard as he had been during the last visit. There was a sudden thud from behind them and John turned around. Nicole had jumped down from a pile of tires. She waved at him as she went over to the fridge that was humming away. As usual, the red headphones were on her head and connected to the tablet.

"She likes hanging out here when I work in the evenings," Billy explained.

The girl bent down and grabbed a cold Coca-Cola. She removed the cap using the edge of the work bench and put the bottle to her lips.

"No more of those tonight, Nicole. You've had enough."

She looked up at him and nodded curtly before being reabsorbed by her screen.

"Did you want anything, by the way?" said Billy.

"No thanks, I'm good," said John. "I can't stay. Just wanted to give you this."

He handed over a box with one of the phones in it. His brother took it and weighed it in his hands.

"There's a prepaid SIM in it and I've saved my number to it. If you want to get hold of me then call it. And for the love of God, don't contact anyone else using this phone."

John could hear how condescending he sounded, and he thought his brother would be resentful. But instead, Billy took the phone out of the box, examined it for a while, and then put it in one of the many open drawers under the work bench.

"You don't have a bathroom out here that I can use, do you?" said John, looking around.

"He's dead, isn't he?"

Billy's answer puzzled him. He looked at his brother. His eyes were oddly shiny and he looked as though he were miles away from the workshop.

"Dead?" said John. "Who?"

"Dad. He's dead, right?"

Billy turned his faraway gaze toward him. John realized it was as he had suspected—his mother had said nothing.

"Yes, he's dead. He died four years ago."

Billy didn't react to the answer. He picked up his hammer and put his ear protectors back on.

"Maybe it's for the best," he said. "If you need the shitter you'll have to go inside. The door's open—you know where to go."

John left the workshop, followed by the sound of the hammer once again striking the bumper. His brother's relationship with the man he insisted on referring to as his father was incomprehensible.

The door to the house was unlocked just as Billy had said and John used the bathroom, which had been adapted for disabled use. He was about to leave the house again when he glanced into the kitchen.

The light over the kitchen table was on, emitting a soft, pleasant glow. The two plates on the counter had obvious traces of ketchup and macaroni. Next to them were a few empty beer bottles and a half-finished glass of milk.

On the top shelf in the niche next to the pantry there was something that caught the attention of the investigator in John—the laptop that Billy had torn out of his daughter's hands on the previous visit.

He listened for the sound of hammering from the workshop. His brother was still working on the bumper. John quickly considered the ethics of the situation. Billy had transparently lied to him about their mother's visit, so it was perfectly reasonable for him to check out the laptop and see whether there was any plausible explanation why.

He took it down, opened it, and touched the trackpad. The screen lit up and the wallpaper—a field of lavender—appeared, along with a password prompt. John tried to remember how old the girl was. Then he typed in nicole2011 and pressed enter.

It didn't work.

He fiddled for a while with the year and upper- and lowercase letters—and eventually he found the right combination. The flowers disappeared and it was open sesame.

He began by reviewing the browser history. Billy's interests were decidedly limited. His brother appeared to almost solely visit online retailers selling vintage cars or sites about American football. John tried to access the email account, but that needed a new password. He tried a few options, but once Outlook stopped letting him try again he gave up.

The sound of the hammer striking the buckled rear of the Impala was still just as frenetic. He clicked on the Microsoft Word icon and waited for it to open. He went to the menu and selected *Open Recent*. A sub-menu showed two options: *letter.docx* and *letter-1.docx*.

John was curious. Billy didn't seem the type to write letters, but maybe there were more sides to his brother than he had shown to date. He opened the first document and stared at the screen, stunned.

The words were not new to him.

I know who killed your daughter. How much is that information worth to you? I'll be in touch.

John hurried across the yard. The banging inside the workshop had stopped. If Billy stuck his head out, John wouldn't be able to stop himself from shouting at him.

He would tell him what an idiot he was, trying to con Emelie Bjurwall's father. But a confrontation would be stupid and only make matters worse.

The leather seats in the Chrysler were cold when he got behind the wheel and headed out onto the road. John unbuttoned his coat and looked up Mona's details on his phone. It irritated him to call her—he knew how pissed she would be. At the same time, he couldn't keep the information from her.

Mona answered on the first ring, pounding music in the background.

"I'm in the middle of a spin class. Can it wait?" she panted.

"Afraid not. You'll have to get off the bike."

John waited while she made her way somewhere quieter. Then he told her about the visit to Billy and the letter on the computer's hard drive.

"So, you've been lying to me," she said. "I asked whether you'd been in contact with your half brother and you said no."

"Come on, Mona. It couldn't be helped. Sooner or later I was going to have to see him. No one saw me, I promise."

"That doesn't matter. For me, this changes everything."

John stopped at a pedestrian crossing and stared absently at the elderly couple crossing the road. He understood and respected Mona's position. Once a liar, always a liar—and that meant the trust required between colleagues in this line of work was gone.

"I'm sorry," he said abruptly.

The silence between them was painful. There were occasional slamming sounds in the background. John suspected that Mona was in the changing room and that it was locker doors that he could hear.

"We need to meet. Where are you?" she said eventually.

"On the way home," he said.

Mona's face was still flushed red and glistening with sweat when they met outside the main door to his apartment building. Apparently she had skipped the showers to get here as quickly as possible. Once they were inside, John put a glass of water on the kitchen table for her while she took in his new abode.

He could tell it raised questions in her mind. How on earth could a police detective with a secret identity afford to live somewhere this expensive? At least he had a good answer to that one. The fact that he had visited his brother behind her back, and why, would be harder to explain.

Mona sat on one of the wooden crates and downed the water in one go.

"Surely you realize that I can't continue to be your point of contact for your witness protection? When we're done with this investigation, I'll speak to my boss at National in Stockholm and ask him to appoint someone else. Until then, I'll just have to trust that you're not lying to me."

"You can," he said, knowing that to her ears, his words carried as much weight as Primer's did during questioning.

Mona asked for more water and he got her a refill. Mona liked him, he knew that—because he felt the same about her. Maybe that was why she was more disappointed than angry.

"Did you take photos of the letters?" she said, when her glass was empty again.

John handed her his phone. She seemed to be ready to move on and focus on the investigation.

"We know the first one," she said. "The wording and typography is identical to the one sent to Heimer Bjurwall."

She ran her index finger across the screen to bring up the next photo-—the one showing the second, hitherto unknown letter. Mona read aloud:

"Select the Lobby chatroom at chatta.se. Log on at 7:30 P.M. on Friday. Call yourself Froggy and search for Nadja6543."

"Do you think he sent this one too?" said John.

Mona brushed the hair from her forehead. The sweat had dried on her body and she shivered.

"Wouldn't the Bjurwalls have been in touch if he had?"

"You'd think so, but . . ." he said, his voice trailing off.

"But what?"

"There was something about Sissela Bjurwall's voice," he said. "When she asked about the first letter and found out that her husband hadn't handed it over to us. I think she sounded surprised. Almost angry. I didn't give it any more thought at the time, but maybe I should have."

"You think he wanted to keep the letter a secret?"

"Maybe. It's possible that the Bjurwalls had different views on the matter, isn't it?"

"True. In that case I suppose we need to pay them another visit." Mona went back to the photo of the first letter and read it again.

"Do you really think your brother knows something about the murder?" she said.

"I don't think so."

"No, because if he did, then surely he would have said something to the police. He was almost charged with the crime twice."

"So, it's just as we suspected all along—it's a con," said John.

Mona looked at him.

"You tell me—he's your brother."

John remembered the money his mother had given to Nicole, which his brother had then taken away from her.

"He's hard up at any rate—so that much makes sense," he said. "And Billy is definitely no saint, even if he didn't kill Emelie Bjurwall."

"Did you check when the letters were created?"

John shook his head. He cursed himself for not checking that detail. Adrenaline had been coursing through him when he had realized exactly what he'd found on the laptop.

"Okay, we know when the first letter arrived at least," said Mona. "And if Billy sent the second one, it should have arrived soon after, right?"

"Yes, it must've been written before it came out that Primer had been arrested. Afterward, every person in the country who could read would have known who killed Emelie Bjurwall—it wouldn't have been possible to con the dad out of any money."

"We need to find out whether or not they made contact in this chatroom," she said.

Mona got up, as if she were about to leave the apartment.

"I'll pay Billy a visit early tomorrow morning."

"Do you want me to speak to Heimer Bjurwall?"

"No, you're not going to talk to anyone," she said sharply. "You need to stay out of this. Billy is part of the investigation again, and he's still your brother."

Half brother, John thought to himself, but he kept quiet.

He knew there was no point protesting.

51

Heimer looked at the time. He knew that it was crazy to take the rain personally, but right now that was how it felt. As if all the forces of the universe were working against him. The water was lashing the windshield and the wipers were working at full capacity.

He saw the sign on the right. *Nerman's Autos – 24/7 towing – garage – service.* He slowly passed the entrance and parked out of sight by a gravel pit a few hundred meters away. After checking that the car couldn't be seen from the road, he began to walk toward the garage. The hood of his jacket, which he had pulled up, wasn't enough to keep the rain off his face. Drops found their way through the small opening he needed in order to navigate in the darkness.

Billy Nerman appearing on the homeless man's phone had been a complete surprise. It didn't add up with the man depicted in the media, the outsider who repaired American cars. Sending the letter showed a level of resourcefulness he hadn't known Billy Nerman possessed. But what did he really know about other people? Presumably, no one thought that he—Sissela Bjurwall's obedient lapdog—could think for himself either.

He made his way to the yard, where he saw that there was a light on in one of the windows of the house. He knew that Billy had a daughter; she couldn't get mixed up in this. If she was awake, he would need to wait until she went to sleep.

Heimer crept up close to the house, where he was harder to spot. He leaned toward the window and caught a glimpse of the kitchen. Billy was sitting at the table with a bowl of cereal or something in front of him.

He quickly withdrew his head and continued to the back of the house. All the windows there were dark. The daughter was presumably in one of the upstairs rooms, asleep.

Heimer turned his face to the sky, closed his eyes, and let the rain fall onto his eyelids. He stood like that for a few seconds before putting his hand to his face and wiping away the raindrops.

He quietly crept around the end of the house and back to the front of the building. He crouched under the kitchen window and continued to the front step. There was a snapping sound under his feet as he broke several wooden sticks wedged into a crack in the concrete.

He stopped and listened. The snapping sound was deceptive. It had sounded like a bomb blast to his ears, but the likelihood of anyone inside having heard it was bordering on zero. Especially on a night like this, with the rain pattering against the roof and windows.

He slowly tried the door. It was unlocked. After a gentle nudge and a low creak from the wooden frame, it opened.

He was in.

52

It had been a long time since he had checked the clock on his phone so often. Mona had forbidden him from being there when she met Billy but promised to call as soon as she was finished. John knew she planned to visit Billy at around seven in the morning because his brother would still be at home. As if he wouldn't be, he thought to himself. The only places that Billy seemed to move between were his house and the workshop. A stretch of less than one hundred meters.

He pressed the home button on the phone to light up the screen again.

9:15 A.M.

More than two hours had elapsed and he still hadn't heard a peep out of Mona.

John looked at the painting in front of him. It was the first time since he had moved into the apartment that he brought himself to put one of the blank canvases onto an easel. It had been more than a decade since he had painted using oils and he was either rusty or it just didn't work when his thoughts were somewhere else entirely. The view from the apartment didn't come to life on the canvas. The sky became one-dimensional. The movements of the water were too heavy-handed and lacked the soft fluidity of real waves.

John's interest in painting had lain dormant after his separation from his mother and the move to New York. A committed art teacher in high school had discovered his talents and tried to encourage him to apply to art school. But John had never even considered it. His dad would never let him choose such an uncertain future and being a police officer appealed to John more.

He put down his brushes and went to the bathroom to wash the paint from his hands. Why hadn't Mona been in touch? Did his brother actually know something about Emelie Bjurwall's disappearance after all? He imagined the visit to Billy having precipitated a breakthrough in the investigation. Maybe Primer was confessing to everything at the police station right now, while John was off the case due to his relationship with the source.

He dried his hands on the towel, went back into the studio, and called Mona's phone again—but just like before, he got her voicemail. It would be pointless to leave another message.

He thought about Billy's aggression. The night he'd told him that Emelie's body had been found in the woods, his brother had raised a wrench against him. He would never know how close Billy had been to using the heavy tool as a weapon. But there was no doubt that he lacked boundaries. John had noticed that side to his brother even when they were children. It had always been Billy who'd been responsible for the most serious pranks. He was the one who had dished out—and received—the most beatings on the school playground.

John was restless with vague fears. If Mona pushed too hard, there was a risk it might backfire. John couldn't rule out the possibility that Billy might wield that wrench against Mona.

He looked at his phone again.

9:31 A.M.

It was too much. He couldn't just sit here on his ass while Mona was in the home of a potentially aggressive individual. John took the elevator to the ground floor and was soon heading for Skoghall in the Chrysler.

On the way, he felt the disappointment growing. Regardless of what Billy knew or didn't know about what had happened to Emelie Bjurwall, it was a low-water mark to try to blackmail her parents for money. They had lost their only child and they deserved to be left in peace. Billy had his own daughter. Surely he understood what the loss of a child must be like?

John drove so fast that he almost missed the turn for Nerman's Autos. This time, he was going to park outside the workshop. If any nosy neighbors wondered who the car belonged to, there was a reasonable explanation. Fredrik Adamsson was there on official police business.

He stopped when he saw the patrol car in the yard next to Mona's black rental. Something was wrong with this picture. She would never bring uniformed officers to this kind of sensitive conversation.

John parked and switched off the engine. He opened the driver's door just as Mona came out of the workshop. Her appearance reinforced his conviction that something was wrong. She didn't seem annoyed to see him there. Instead she walked slowly across the yard to meet him. Her steps were heavy, as if crossing the gravel expanse was challenging.

John jumped out of the car and began to run toward the workshop. Mona took two steps to the side to try to stop him, but he slipped out of her grasp and continued to the open garage door.

The first things he saw inside the workshop were two uniformed police officers. One of them was pointing a camera at the ceiling. John followed its angle and saw the lifeless body hanging from a rope suspended from one of the steel beams.

Billy was wearing the same clothes he had had on last John saw him, but his face was discolored. The rope ended in a noose that had cut deeply into his skin as a result of the weight of the hanging body. Blue stripes had spread out from his throat and into his gray cheeks. A few meters away was the rickety chair that his brother had presumably stood on while attaching the rope around his neck, before kicking it away.

John felt overcome by nausea. He leaned forward and put his hands on his knees to avoid falling over.

"You okay?" said the police officer not taking photographs.

John recognized him. He had been eating snacks in the kitchen during Fredrik Adamsson's week on the kitchen schedule. The round, apple-cheeked face seemed friendly and considerate. But John wasn't fooled that easily. If there was one thing that uniformed officers liked gossiping about, it was detectives who couldn't handle the pressure.

He reminded himself that the police officer didn't know that the dead man hanging from the ceiling was his brother. It was important it stayed that way. John couldn't behave in any way that would raise questions.

"Two cups of coffee for breakfast and a run after that. Not the best combination, sorry," he said breathlessly.

The police officer patted him on the shoulder.

"No need to apologize to me. But if you hurl in here, Forensics will be pissed."

"Are they on the way?" said John, straightening up.

Shop talk was good. It helped him to distance himself from his emotions.

"Yes, they should've been here ages ago. But apparently they've got a lot going on today."

"You're not touching anything, I hope?"

John turned around when he heard Mona's assertive voice. She had come into the workshop and was looking at them with a serious expression. She understood the situation just as well as he did. No kid gloves, no sympathy. Nothing could be allowed to give away John's relationship to the corpse hanging from the ceiling.

"Of course not," said apple cheeks.

He didn't seem to appreciate being patronized by a woman, and one from Stockholm at that.

John avoided looking at Billy's lifeless face. He was afraid his own mask might crack.

The officer with the camera lowered it and muttered something about Forensics doing the rest. He crouched and began to stow the equipment in the black bag on the floor. Suddenly, his hands stopped moving. He was facing the door and could clearly see something the others hadn't spotted.

John turned his head.

There was Nicole.

She was wearing dark blue pajamas with white stars and her bare feet were inside a pair of rain boots. Her face was turned up and she was staring at the ceiling. The image being burned into her retinas was one she would never be able to erase. She would carry it with her for the rest of her life.

Then came the scream. The high-pitched, piercing cry of an eight-year-old. John saw her look around and spot him, the only face she recognized among the strangers in the workshop. The girl rushed to him and clamped herself to his leg, like the survivor of a shipwreck clinging to the final piece of driftwood.

Mona carefully tore the girl away from him. Even though it felt wrong, John helped to pry away the small fingers from his trousers so that Mona could pick her up. Nicole must have been asleep in the house and not been woken by the knocking on the door earlier that morning. The fact that no one had thought to look for her was an unforgivable mistake.

"I'll drive her to the children's shrink," said Mona once she had put the girl in the back seat of her rental car.

John nodded. It was the right decision. Nicole needed professional help—people who knew how to handle that kind of trauma.

John needed to get away and process his thoughts. With the workshop filled with people in white masks, he was unnecessary at this point. Fredrik Adamsson could leave without anyone asking questions.

He got into the Chrysler and with a heavy heart he drove away from his childhood home. When he reached the road, he stopped and considered where to go. He decided to head for the old scout hut where he and Billy had played as children. It was nearby. Before long he was sitting on one of the wooden benches by the fireplace. The cabin had been repainted—it was now a brownish shade rather than the traditional Swedish red. But otherwise it looked just the same. The swings were in the same place and kids were still building dens in the grove of trees by the old outhouse.

Thinking about Billy physically hurt. John could barely breathe, though the air down here by the lake was fresh and rich in oxygen. He wallowed in guilt like a pig in mud, until he stank of self-contempt. It didn't matter that he had absolved Billy for the murder of Emelie Bjurwall. It was too late. Something inside his brother must have broken over all those years—something that not even being cleared could heal. His mother had said he had tried to end things once before.

All the same, the timing didn't make sense. His brother had finally gotten his life in order and had been looking forward to an existence in which the locals no longer thought he was guilty. Why put a noose around his neck now? It didn't feel right.

John thought about the letters. He couldn't see it as anything other than an attempt to con money out of Heimer Bjurwall. Maybe that was the motive for suicide? Maybe his brother had had bigger financial problems than he'd let on and had been in a pit of debt that was unbearable. John cursed himself for not simply ignoring Billy's ego and giving him a meaningful amount of money. If he had, Nicole might still have had a father.

It seemed a good idea to speak to Heimer Bjurwall. If he had paid for the information that Billy claimed to have, there was a possibility they had met. Maybe Emelie's father knew something that might explain why Billy had taken his own life.

John got up and stretched. He had been sitting in the same position for too long and needed to get both his circulation and his thoughts moving.

He went down to the water's edge and decided to reboot his reasoning from a new starting point. What if Billy really had known something about the murder—what would that mean? He tried to follow this train of thought, but he didn't get past the first obstacle. If his brother had known that Bernt Primer had murdered Emelie Bjurwall, why hadn't he said so when he was otherwise risking prison? It just didn't add up.

John tried again to break away from his habitual thought patterns. Something occurred to him. If Billy had only realized who the murderer was *after* being cleared the second time, that changed everything. It meant there was a logic to sending the letters to Heimer Bjurwall that John hadn't previously seen. At that time, Primer hadn't been under suspicion. Instead of going straight to the police—who would most probably have dismissed the accusation if it came from Billy Nerman—his brother had tried to kill two birds with one stone. By selling the information to Heimer Bjurwall, Billy would have earned some cash and made sure Primer didn't get away with it. Emelie's father was a powerful man thanks to his last name. He, of all people, would surely be able to get the police to launch an investigation into one of their own.

John began to walk along the path toward the observation point on the knoll beside the scout hut. The path climbed steeply and John had to stop for a moment to catch his breath. He wished he had his investigation piece and some pencils with him, but for now he would have to keep on reasoning in his head.

He continued to climb and soon he reached the observation point. The old bench was still there. He had kissed a girl for the very first time here. Susanne, that was her name. He remembered it because Billy had teased him all summer when she had left him for a boy on the ice hockey team.

It was a beautiful view, stretching away to the open horizon. As a child, he had gazed across the lake and imagined it was the sea; he had told himself that there was something much more exciting than the town of Lidköping on the other side. He bent down to find a stone to throw. A younger version of himself would have tried over and over to reach the water—it didn't look far from up here—never getting more than halfway. He was searching for a suitable projectile when he noticed several cigarette butts lying by one of the bench legs, which were embedded in concrete in the ground.

He started and had to sit down again.

His mother.

Some scouts sneaking ciggies had reminded him of the visit to his childhood home two days ago. The butt lying in the yard and Nicole having given away that she had just been there. His brother had always been a real mama's boy and it didn't look as though anything had changed while John had been in the States.

It could very well be their mother who had made Billy write the letters to the Bjurwalls. Her fingerprints were all over this, making the scenario much more credible. Unlike Billy, she had both the drive and the brains to do something like this.

He remembered Billy's phone call to the police station and the sound of desperation in his voice. Presumably, his brother had wanted to tell him what he and his mother were up to. But John had been too busy to listen, and that time she had gotten there in time to stop him. Maybe that was the fight that Nicole had heard when she was sent to her room.

John needed to go to Gunnarskärsgården to talk to his mother. The nursing home was only a few minutes' drive away.

John recognized the woman in the corridor as soon as he came through the doors of Gunnarskärsgården. It was Ruben Jonsson's wife—the one who had told her husband everything and revealed his identity.

"Come with me into the office so that we can talk," she said gravely, opening the door to the small space just inside the main doors.

John sat down on a visitor's chair and she rolled her own chair forward so that they were closer to each other.

"I'm very sorry," she said, tilting her head slightly in the way health-care personnel usually did when they had bad news to impart.

"So, the police have been to tell her about Billy?"

"Yes, about an hour ago. She didn't take it very well. It was after that we had to call the ambulance."

John looked at her suspiciously. Ambulance? What was the woman saying?

"Sorry, you've lost me."

"Your mother is in the hospital," she said. "Heart issues."

John was shaken. There seemed to be no limit to how much shit this day was going to throw at him.

"How is she?" he managed to say.

"I don't know. You'll have to check with the hospital."

Fifteen minutes later, John parked illegally outside the emergency room, leaving the left-hand wheels of the Chrysler on the pavement. Thoughts were whirling around in his head as he attempted to find a member of staff. He hoped his mother was still conscious and also felt a little ashamed for feeling like that. Was he there because he needed to know more about the letters to Heimer Bjurwall? Or because he was concerned about his mother? He put the question out of his mind and stopped a nurse walking down the corridor with a cart.

"I need to speak to a woman who was recently admitted here from Gunnarskärs-gården," he said, flashing his police badge.

"Ask someone over there," she said, pointing at a counter at the end of the corridor.

He followed her instruction and repeated his question to a gray-haired woman. She answered right away without consulting her computer. Old school, John thought to himself. A relic of the days when people actually had to keep things in their heads.

"She's in the cardiac cath lab. Balloon angioplasty. She came in with chest pain."

"Is it serious?" he asked.

"Yes, I'd say so. But she got treatment quickly, so the prognosis is good."

John thought about his mother surrounded by doctors and nurses. In his mind, he could hear the beeping sound from the equipment monitoring her vital signs, while the staff did its best to keep her alive.

"Can I ask what it's about?"

The gray-haired woman's voice was gruff, but friendly.

"Police business; I'm afraid I can't tell you any more than that. But please ask her to call this number as soon as she can."

He wrote down his number on a piece of paper on the counter and gave it to the woman, who pocketed it.

"It's important," he added.

She nodded and looked at him gravely.

"I'll pass on the message—I promise."

John thanked her and hurried back to the car outside. As soon as he shut the door, he began to cry without understanding where the tears running down his cheeks came from. They originated from a strange mixture of emotions he actually felt and others that he supposed he ought to feel. His mother was fighting for her life inside the hospital and his brother had chosen to end his—all within the course of twenty-four hours. It was chaotic and overwhelming.

At the same time, he couldn't help partly feeling like an outside observer. As if it were someone else's mother and brother this had happened to. They'd been absent from his life for so long. Maybe it was symptomatic of this feeling that his tears stopped the moment Mona called. It was as if they came out of a tap that he could turn on and off as he pleased.

"How are you?" she said.

John closed his eyes and once again saw his brother's discolored face hanging from the workshop ceiling. The image was projected in widescreen onto the inside of his eyelids and was unpleasantly detailed.

"I don't really know—I suppose not that great."

"Where are you?"

"In a car outside the hospital."

"The hospital?" she repeated in surprise.

John explained that his mother was a patient. That he suspected she had been the driving force behind the letters to Heimer Bjurwall, but that she had taken Billy's death so badly that it triggered heart issues. He went over his idea that his brother had figured out that Primer was the murderer after his own release, and that together with his mother they had sold the information to Heimer Bjurwall. The plan was to put Primer away while cashing in.

Mona listened and interrupted him just twice: first, to offer her sympathies that his mother was in the hospital, and second, to tell him about the bag found hidden in Billy's workshop. It contained almost three hundred thousand kronor in cash.

"Oh, Jesus—then they must have met," said John.

"It seems so."

"Have you spoken to Heimer Bjurwall?"

"No," said Mona, sounding slightly annoyed. "When would I have had time to do that?"

John heard a faint beep, indicating that Mona had an incoming call.

"It's autopsy calling. Stay there and I'll patch you in."

John waited and soon they were joined by another voice.

"I've just started the autopsy of the guy who hanged himself outside Skoghall. Billy Nerman," said the man without wasting time on introductions. "You'll get a full report tomorrow, but there's one thing you'll want to know right away."

"Okay, we're listening," said Mona.

"It's no suicide. Someone helped him."

John heard the sound of a motorcycle accelerating loudly in the background from one of the phones—presumably Mona's. The rumble faded away and was replaced by footsteps and her phone brushing against her ear as she moved somewhere quieter.

He closed his eyes and let the new information sink in. Then frustration washed over him. He slammed his head hard against the headrest and cursed himself for not taking his own intuition more seriously.

Someone had helped him.

Of course they had.

Billy hadn't want to take his own life. Not now that he had finally found salvation from all the misery he had gone through.

"Are you sure?" Mona said.

"Yes. He was already dead when he was put in the noose. Apart from the injuries from the rope, there were clear marks from two thumbs on his throat that had applied pressure to the softest parts."

"So, he was strangled?"

"There's no doubt about it. But, as I said, you'll have a full report tomorrow afternoon."

Mona thanked him and the pathologist left the call. John pictured the man putting on a new pair of latex gloves and returning to the sterile room where his brother was lying on a gurney under fluorescent lighting. As of now, Billy's body was evidence in a murder investigation.

"We need to meet up and talk," said Mona.

John leaned against the back of the Chrysler and listened as Mona tried to put her thoughts on Billy's murder into some kind of order. They had agreed to meet at a gas station near the hospital. She'd confined the conversation strictly to the investigation.

John appreciated that. Thinking about his brother as a murder victim—just one of many—helped him to distance himself.

"The money they found was in a backpack hidden in the trunk of one of the cars in the workshop. Neatly wrapped bundles of cash. They almost certainly came from Heimer Bjurwall."

John looked at the elevated black Buick in front of him which his brother had spoken of so warmly. It was typical that he would hide the cash there.

"He's the one who killed Billy. I'm fucking sure of it," he said.

"Who? Heimer Bjurwall?" said Mona.

John nodded and continued.

"Billy might've been bluffing after all. He had no clue who killed Emelie and when her father realized that he was being conned, he flipped."

"And strangled him?"

"Maybe. It's a reason for Heimer to lose it."

Mona looked at him doubtfully.

"Because he was conned out of three hundred grand? I visited the Bjurwalls—that's what their trash cans cost. It's hardly enough to be a motive for killing Billy."

"You're simplifying it," he said. "If Billy claimed to know who murdered his daughter and then couldn't deliver the goods, that lie is far worse than losing the money. Billy exploiting the family's grief would've made Heimer Bjurwall furious."

"It still sounds flimsy to me."

"Maybe. But we still need to talk to him as soon as possible. If he met Billy when handing over the money, Billy might have said something that could explain why he was murdered shortly afterward," he said.

Mona shifted closer as a truck turned into the gas station and the long trailer passed by her.

"What if we turn it around?" she said. "If Billy actually knew something about Emelie's murder, there's a motive right there. Maybe he saw Primer do it. Or at least he saw him together with Emelie out at Tynäs."

John shook his head.

"It doesn't make sense. If Billy actually knew something about the murder, he must have gotten that information after he'd been cleared. Why else would he have kept quiet all these years?"

"I know, I know," said Mona. "And what's more, Primer is locked up in solitary twenty-four hours a day."

"Exactly. He has motive, but no opportunity."

"Maybe he's working with someone on the outside who helped him to silence Billy."

"Seems far-fetched," John said. "Primer is a dirty old man who used his police badge and access to drugs to pressure a young woman into having sex. He doesn't have a criminal network around him—hard to imagine him ordering a murder."

John waited as yet another truck thundered onto the forecourt to fill up, putting a stop to further discussion.

"I still need the go-ahead from the county commissioner to initiate a more thorough investigation of the crime scene in the workshop," Mona said once the semi-truck had come to a halt and switched off its engine by the pumps. "And I need to make sure that he understands that Billy's death isn't to be investigated as an isolated incident—it's part of my live investigation."

John noticed her choice of words. *My live investigation.* That was what she said—as if he were no longer part of it.

"Regardless, you have to leave the investigation," Mona added, as if she had read his thoughts. "Your connection to Billy is a problem."

He had been expecting that remark. It was almost surprising that it hadn't come up sooner. This wasn't the first time that his relationship to Billy had caused problems for the police.

"I understand," he said, debating whether to tell her about the phone he'd given to his brother. Mona would be incandescent the second he said it, but he couldn't let the detectives go up a blind alley.

"There's something I need you to know in relation to the crime scene," he said.

"What?"

Mona's voice immediately switched on to the offensive.

John cleared his throat.

"You'll find a burner phone with a prepaid SIM in Billy's house. There's only one number in the contacts."

"Let me guess," she said, without hiding her irritation. "Jesus Christ, John. Forensics has probably already found it and made the connection. Now this whole brother-investigating-his-brother story is going to blow up in our faces."

John looked at the floor. Mona had reacted just as expected. Dead brother or not, the kid gloves were definitely off.

"Take it easy," he said. "The number is for another prepaid phone. There's no chance it can be traced to me. I'm just telling you so that you don't waste time on it."

"And I suppose it'll be my job to explain why we're not going to look into our best lead?"

Mona had raised her voice despite the sensitive nature of the conversation. She lowered her voice when two young men unhooking a trailer turned around to look at her.

"I'm sorry about what happened to your brother. I really am," she said. "As for the investigation, I guess I've only got myself to blame—it was a big mistake bringing you back in."

Now it was John's turn to be irritated.

"Without me, you'd still have no body and Primer would never have been arrested. You know that as well as I do, so quit with the bullshit."

Mona took a step toward him. She didn't seem to care now that the guys by the trailer were staring at them.

"That's true. But we would also have avoided a load of hassle. If it gets out that you were involved in the investigation into your own brother, the press won't stop writing about it until heads roll. The bigger the headlines, the bigger the sacrifice required."

"So, you care more about saving your own career than bringing the perp to justice?"

Mona's eyes darkened, but he had no intention of staying to hear her defense. She had already shown where her loyalties were and that was enough for him. The Chrysler's tires squealed as he left her alone at the gas station.

John switched lanes, ignoring the protests of other drivers as he made his way to Hammarö. Billy had been a victim the whole way through this tragic story. The police had done nothing but harass him for ten years. Demanding—now that he was dead—that John sit back and let the same team keep working the case was just absurd.

He turned left onto Tynäsvägen and accelerated, making the two-ton Chrysler leap forward. As soon as Mona had confirmation from the Walrus that she was in charge of the Billy Nerman murder inquiry, she would be off to visit Heimer Bjurwall.

But it would probably take some time, and John intended to use that head start and get there first. He couldn't drop the thought of Heimer and Billy having met and their encounter somehow going wrong when Emelie's father learned he'd been tricked.

Mona hadn't been exaggerating the details about the AckWe house. The place was truly magnificent with views over the water. He drove up to the gate, pressed the buzzer, and found himself expecting an English butler on the other end. But there was no stiff upper lip—just Heimer Bjurwall answering in his prim Värmland accent.

John explained who he—or rather, Fredrik Adamsson—was. Soon he heard a whirring in the electric lock and the large gates slid open. He parked on the drive next to a couple of expensive Italian sports cars and was invited inside.

The interior was just as understated and elegant as John had imagined. At the same time, there was a strong feeling of desolation—emphasized by Heimer Bjurwall being at home alone. There was something sad about having so little life in so many square meters.

"Sorry I've come here without calling ahead," John said after the man had shown him upstairs to the kitchen.

"Don't worry about it. You're just lucky I was home. I'm usually out in the middle of the day."

"No, of course. I understand."

"What was this about? I'm afraid I can't talk for long."

Bullshit, John thought to himself. You *want* to talk.

"I'll get right to it," he said. "We need to discuss the letters you received."

"Letters?"

"Yes, letters. You did receive two, didn't you?"

Heimer Bjurwall looked as though he was biding his time—as if he couldn't quite decide whether or not to tell the truth. But then he raised his hands in a disarming gesture.

"Yes, a second letter did arrive. I'm sorry I didn't say anything. But I wanted to keep it to myself. Not even my wife knows."

"What did it say?" said John.

"That I should visit an online chatroom at a certain time. I would receive further instructions there."

"Instructions about what?"

"I didn't know at the time. I assumed it was about money. The information about what happened to Emelie wasn't going to be free. That was why I didn't tell you about the letter. I didn't want to scare the sender off."

"You never considered that it might just be a bluff?"

Heimer looked at him, annoyed.

"Yes, the whole time. Sissela was convinced someone was trying to scam us and that's why I kept her in the dark. But I was prepared to take a chance for Emelie."

"So what happened? Did you make contact with anyone in the chatroom?"

"Yes, I did," said Heimer.

He was speaking more quickly now, as if his initial resistance had been broken down and he was willing to talk.

"I was told to put three hundred thousand kronor in a locker at the railway station. If I did that, I'd be sent the information."

"So, you never met the letter writer?"

"No."

John sharpened his tone.

"That's a bit odd. Giving that much money to a stranger."

"You might think it's idiotic, but I went into this with my eyes open."

John let a few seconds elapse, as if to show that he still wasn't convinced.

"Okay, let's move on," he said. "What information were you supposed to receive?"

"Evidence that would hold up in a trial."

"Evidence against Bernt Primer?"

Heimer shrugged his shoulders.

"I assume so. The letter arrived before he was arrested. I should have handed it over to you as soon as I got it. It sounds so stupid, talking about it now. But it felt like my last chance to really do something for Emelie."

"I understand. But you never received any evidence?"

The man across the table laughed. The laughter sounded bitter and resigned.

"Sissela was obviously right," he said. "It was just someone trying to con us. I paid three hundred thousand for nothing."

"And you still don't know who wrote the letters?"

"I have no idea," Heimer sighed. "And I don't actually care."

John met Heimer Bjurwall's sorrowful gaze while trying to evaluate his credibility. He had stopped trying to play the bigwig with a packed schedule. The stiff posture and detached voice had been replaced by something softer and more vulnerable. John was forced to admit that he was struggling to picture Emelie's father in the dirty workshop with his hands around Billy's throat.

"Can I get you some coffee?" Heimer said.

Before John had time to decline, the man got up and went over to the coffee maker. It was an expensive model with copper tubes visible inside the transparent shell that funneled the coffee into the pot.

"Are you getting anywhere with Primer?" he said, raising his voice to be heard over the built-in coffee grinder.

"We're making progress," said John. "Your visit was a great help—a real breakthrough."

Heimer looked pleased, lapping up the praise like a schoolboy.

"Has he confessed yet?"

"I'm afraid I can't tell you what he's said under questioning. Confidentiality, you know."

John's phone vibrated.

"Sorry, but I have to take this."

"You can talk in the library," said Heimer, ushering him down the hall to a large pair of double doors.

John went into the room and closed the doors behind him. He didn't recognize the number, but it began with 054—the Karlstad area code.

"Fredrik Adamsson," he said.

"Oh, John—it's all gone wrong."

He recognized his mother's voice right away. She was crying and whimpering uncontrollably, which made it hard to understand what she was saying.

"Mom," he said, glancing over his shoulder. It was a word he wasn't supposed to use and he was glad he had closed the double doors.

"How are you? How was the surgery?"

"It went fine—my heart is okay. But you have to listen to me. It's my fault Billy's dead. No one can convince me he did that to himself."

John pressed the phone closer to his ear.

"What do you mean?" he said.

She emitted a low groan and he realized she was in pain.

"Do you remember when you were at Billy's and we ate cake?"

"Of course."

"That was when I realized."

"Realized what?"

"You said where you'd found the girl. That she'd been buried near the old dump along Hallerudsleden."

John remembered. His mother had gone from being in a good mood to being distracted and wanting to go home.

"I saw him coming out of the woods that night when I was driving home from the mill. I thought it was odd for a guy like him to be out running at that time of night. With a flashlight and everything. But then I read about what had happened and it wasn't so strange any longer. He'd probably been out looking for the girl—that was what I thought."

"Wait, who are you talking about?"

His mother didn't reply. It was as if she were in a trance and talking to herself.

"But when you told me where the girl had been found, I realized I'd gotten it all wrong. It wasn't at all the way I thought it was. He wasn't looking for her—do you see? He was burying her."

John slowly began to understand. He should've thought of it sooner. His mother had worked nights at the mill—Billy said as much during the first police interview. The road to and from her place of work went right past the scene. She was the one who had seen Emelie Bjurwall's murderer—not Billy.

He raised his voice in an attempt to stop his mother's stream of words.

"Who? Who did you see?"

It seemed to have worked. The voice at the other end of the line finally went silent. A few heavy breaths were audible before his mother spoke again.

"Heimer Bjurwall, of course. Who else would it be?"

John gasped for breath. The atmosphere in the library was immediately stifling. He hadn't thought about the fact that the room had no windows. The walls were covered in bookcases from floor to ceiling and no natural light could make its way in. The only way out was through the heavy double doors made from a dark hardwood.

He had been a fool not to see the obvious. He and Mona had only considered Heimer as a potential murderer of Billy. That he might also be responsible for his own daughter's death never occurred to them, even though it was right there in front of them. He remembered what the first letter his brother sent had said:

I know who killed your daughter. How much is that information worth to you? I'll be in touch.

Weirdly, he and Mona had somehow gone astray and interpreted the message as an attempt to sell information. The truth was much simpler. The letter was an attempt at blackmail. A witness who wanted payment for their silence. That was why Heimer Bjurwall hadn't wanted to show it to the police.

"Hello? John? Are you still there?"

He heard his mother's distant voice on the phone.

"Yes, I'm here."

"The thing with the letters was my idea. Billy thought I should tell you—just tell it how it was. But who would've believed me? The word of a drunken old woman against his—a Bjurwall. But the money was for Billy—don't ever think anything else. Every last penny. It was the right thing to do. For the crap he put up with for all these years, with people shouting murderer and rapist at him all around town."

She groaned on the final syllable. She needed a higher dosage of painkillers.

"We were so careful, John," she continued. "Heimer Bjurwall was never going to find out who was blackmailing him. But I should've realized that a guy like him would never drop it. Someone with that much to lose is dangerous."

John heard a cautious knock and a second later one of the doors into the library opened. Heimer Bjurwall entered, carrying a tray with a white cup, a small jug of milk, and a bowl of raw sugar cubes on it.

"Your coffee's ready," he said in a whisper, so as not to disturb the conversation.

John looked at him and felt the first twinge of pain at the back of his head. A second later, it exploded and he saw flashes before his eyes. Instinctively, he let go of the phone, which bounced off the cushion of the sofa on which he was sitting, and onto the gray-hued rug. Everything happened almost noiselessly. The fibers in the thick carpet absorbed the impact.

"Sorry, did I startle you?"

"No problem," John managed to say, as he felt his feet go numb.

He tried to wriggle his toes inside his shoes, but nothing happened. If he gave in, the numbness would spread rapidly, to the point where his body stopped working altogether. He tried to remind himself that this was not a neurological issue. The doctors in Baltimore had examined him from head to toe. It was all in his head.

Heimer Bjurwall picked up the phone from the rug and looked at it.

"You've gone a funny color," he said.

"Just a migraine attack. They come and go, unfortunately."

John held out his hand to take the phone, but his host made no effort to return it.

"I understand—migraines are the worst," he said. "Any news about the investigation?"

John listened for changes to his voice, but it was just as friendly as before. Had Heimer Bjurwall sensed something? Maybe he had been listening to the call from outside the doors. John tried to remember what he'd said on the phone. Granted, it was mostly his mother doing the talking—but at one point he had interrupted her, raised his voice, and asked who she had seen.

"I'm afraid I can't discuss it."

The pain in the back of his head came in waves; it forced him to close his eyes. The numbness reached his arms and he was no longer sure he could stand up even if he tried.

Heimer looked at the phone in his hand. Then he put it on the bookcase behind him. That settled it for John. Emelie's father understood. If not everything, at least enough to realize he was cornered.

His holster was straining across his chest, but pulling out his service weapon in this state without knowing whether he could control it would be dangerous. At the same time, he had to do something. The back of his head throbbed with such intensity that it almost blotted out his hearing. His legs refused to move for fear of discovering that they were already paralyzed.

He concentrated on trying to read Heimer Bjurwall's face. Emelie's father was no Ganiru. While Heimer had already killed—not just once but twice—he still came from another world. John was an FBI agent, trained for situations just like this. If only he had just a tenth of his usual capacity, this would be settled in no time.

John waited for the next wave of pain to abate. Then he forced his right arm to obey him. He slipped it inside his jacket, grabbed hold of his pistol, and pulled it from its holster.

53

Heimer looked at the weapon being aimed at him from the sofa. He felt surprisingly calm. His heart might have been pounding in his chest, and his brain was probably doling out masses of chemicals to sharpen his senses, but something had happened when he had killed Billy Nerman. He'd stood there with his hands around his throat in that disgusting kitchen that smelled of cooked food, pushing his fingers into the cartilage until Billy stopped breathing. Then he had dragged the heavy body into the workshop and after much effort managed to get it into the noose hanging from the ceiling.

The anguish he had expected to feel in the car on the way home had failed to materialize. Instead, he felt relieved. Somewhere down inside, he knew that Emelie understood what he had done. He loved her so deeply, and no one—least of all a moronic car mechanic—was going to ruin their love.

The story Billy Nerman had threatened to divulge was about a father who had killed his daughter and then buried her. It was essentially true. But all the assumptions that would follow would be lies. Heimer would be portrayed as a monster lacking all human feeling, when in fact he was the one who loved Emelie the most. A life in prison with that story written on the walls would be unbearable, which was why he had decided to do something about it.

The staged suicide was the proof that he'd finally learned to control his anger. He hadn't acted on impulse and gone straight to Billy Nerman's when the homeless man had shown him the photo on his phone. Instead, he thought it through carefully and made a plan.

The car mechanic couldn't be allowed to hold this over him. He'd burn through the money and then ask for more. Or even worse, get drunk and run off at the mouth. Heimer had distilled the rage and let the adrenaline flow at the crucial moment. In the future, if anyone implied that he was Sissela Bjurwall's insignificant appendage, he would think about the moment when the life had gone out of Billy Nerman's eyes. They had gone white and swiveled in their sockets.

Heimer continued to look at the weapon being aimed at him. When he'd heard the buzzer and the voice with the American accent on the intercom, he thought it was all over. Only after quite a bit of conversation did he realize that the solitary man wasn't there to arrest him. But then the detective's phone rang and he disappeared into the library. Heimer stood outside and heard enough to know that the floodgates were open after all. Someone had given him away.

He shifted his gaze from the muzzle of the pistol to the dark face, waiting for the man to say something. But no words came. Instead, he staggered when he got up from the sofa and had to support himself on a bookcase. His breathing was rapid and shallow. His eyes were glassy and focused on one point across the room. Perhaps on the spot where the phone was.

Heimer thought he recognized the symptoms. The man appeared to be having some form of panic attack. The trembling in his legs only got worse and before long his muscles couldn't hold out anymore. He collapsed on the floor and landed shoulder-first on the thick carpet. The weapon fell out of his hand and slid across the floor.

Heimer considered what to do. He had the chance to escape now. But the detective would soon come to and immediately contact the police. It wouldn't be long before he was arrested.

He contemplated the humiliation ahead of him. Sissela and the Bjurwall family casting him to the wolves and depicting him as mentally ill. Then the gauntlet of the media, the trial, and finally the long prison sentence. He wouldn't survive it.

It might be better to end it all. Perhaps the pistol had ended up at his feet for precisely that reason. At the same time, Heimer knew that suicide wasn't an option. The thought had flashed through his mind so many times and he had never gotten further than Googling various methods.

The man on the floor appeared to be regaining control of his body. He'd spotted the weapon on the floor and was laboriously reaching out for it. Heimer reacted instinctively. Using his foot, he kicked the gun away from the outstretched arm and then picked it up himself a few meters away.

He hefted it in his hand, feeling the weight of the metal. It was the first time he had held a firearm since his military service. He looked for the safety and saw that the catch had already been released. It was just luck that it hadn't gone off.

"Give me the weapon," said the detective from his position on the floor.

His voice was weak and lacked authority. It was an entreaty, not an order.

Heimer shook his head. Instead, he took a step closer, raised the weapon, and aimed at the man's shaven head. He was surprised to feel an almost euphoric sense of power. For once, he was in charge.

"Who were you talking to on the phone?" he said.

John managed to lift his upper body using his forearms before turning around so that he was sitting on the floor with his back leaning against the sofa. Heimer brought the weapon closer to his face.

"I asked who you were talking to."

Still no answer. Heimer was unsure whether it was because the man didn't want to say anything or because he was physically incapable of speaking. Regardless, it was infuriating. He couldn't very well kill him until he found out who had been on the other end of that call.

Who? Who did you see?

That was what the detective said when Heimer was listening through the door. He had silenced Billy Nerman—and unless the bastard was calling from the mortuary, there had to be another witness.

Heimer remembered the headlights from the car that had appeared out of nowhere on the narrow road. He had just put the shovel in the trunk and closed it. But before he'd had time to hide in the woods, he was blinded by the lights and had to screw his eyes shut. The person or persons who passed by had presumably seen his face while he was too shocked to notice what make of car it was or the license number.

"Why?" said the man on the floor, suddenly. "She was your daughter."

The words came out in fits and starts, and he ran his tongue over his lips in the most unappealing way—as if he needed to moisten them to speak.

"It was an accident," Heimer hissed. "That goes without saying. Everyone knows I loved Emelie."

The detective cleared his throat several times to check whether his voice would work.

"If it was an accident, I'm sure people will understand," he said.

Heimer realized that the man was just trying to ingratiate himself and buy time. But it still felt good to hear him say it. At least someone was trying to understand.

Heimer had come close to telling Sissela several times over the years, on the occasions when he'd felt a connection between the two of them—when he thought that she might understand and see her own role in what had happened. But the ice had always seemed too thin for him to take the first step. Deep down, he knew that it would give way under his weight—he would crash through it alone into the cold water and she wouldn't reach out to him with her hand.

His thoughts returned once again to that night ten years ago. After Björkbacken, Emelie had promised to quit the drugs. Despite that, he had found the empty bag in the desk drawer in her bedroom. He could see his daughter's defiant face that morning when Sissela had interrogated her about her poor exam results. It was the last breakfast they ate together, and it had ended in chaos. Emelie had leapt out of her chair, run away, and never come back. Heimer remembered that he had wanted to search for her later that evening, but Sissela had stopped him. Eventually, his wife fell asleep and he went out anyway.

He had walked toward the Tynäs promontory and noticed that Hugo Aglin's house was full of young people partying. From the hedge by the road, he had looked for Emelie but hadn't seen her either through the large windows or on the terrace. After a while, he continued toward the promontory and that was where he found her.

She had been sitting on a rock, staring out across the water. When she heard him coming, she turned around. He saw right away that she was under the influence. Her eyes were glassy and her pupils bigger than usual.

"What are you doing, Emelie? Why are you so determined to ruin your life with this junk?"

She had given her usual response, that he was pathetic and had no right to have opinions on her life. He had been about to make her empty her pockets when he saw her bloodied arm and the smashed beer bottle on the slab of rock beside her.

"What have you done to yourself?" he'd said.

She showed him the tick carved into the final tattooed box on her forearm. The wound was fresh and still bleeding.

"Isn't my bucket list beautiful?"

"What the hell is wrong with you? Why have you cut yourself?"

"That's none of your fucking business, Daddy!" she said, reaching for the smashed bottle neck.

She let it rest in her hand, as if considering whether to use it on her own body again.

Heimer leaned forward and tore the bottle from her grasp. It hadn't been the first time she had provoked him, and he'd usually been able to take it. But she was different that night. Coarser and more brutal. As if she enjoyed hurting him.

She'd said he was so fucking worthless he couldn't even satisfy his wife in bed. That she knew her mother was screwing someone else and that she could understand why. That he was so weak it was disgusting, and that the worst thing was she had inherited it from him. It was his wretched sperm that had made her dyslexic and so dumb she couldn't even pass the easiest exams. She wanted to be more like her mother, but every time she tried, something went wrong and it was all his fault. His horrible genes that couldn't be washed away, no matter how much she scrubbed.

It had all been too much to hear from his own daughter. More than he could bear. Anger boiled over and he'd pushed her. For a split second he had been surprised by the wound on Emelie's neck. Then he had looked down at his hands and saw he was still holding the broken bottle.

He'd looked back at his daughter again and saw how she was losing her balance. He remembered her smiling before she fell backward. As if she'd finally gotten him where she wanted him. Uncontrolled rage.

The distance to the next rock hadn't been more than a couple of meters, but it had been far enough for her to crack her head. He would never forget the sound of her head striking the rock. The way she ended up on her back with the dark red pool under her blonde hair just growing and growing.

At first, Heimer had meant to call an ambulance, but then he realized it was too late. Emelie was already dead—there was nothing he or anyone else could have done. And what would he have said? That she had fallen? That it was an accident? That lie would have been seen through as soon as they had found the wound on her neck.

He couldn't bear the thought of being remembered as the man who had killed his own daughter. So instead of calling someone, he carried her to a thicket and hid her there while he went home to get the car.

Once he was back at the promontory, he put her in the trunk and washed the blood off the rocks as best he could. Once he finished, he drove around aimlessly for more than an hour. He threw the shards of glass into the water from a bridge, but it was harder to part with Emelie. He knew he had to get rid of the body—but it had also felt so final, so irreversible.

Eventually, he'd settled on a forest clearing along Hallerudsleden. It was an area not many people passed through. Everything had gone according to plan until the moment when that damn car had blinded him on the verge as it passed by.

It was odd, he thought to himself, that so many crucial moments in life happened by chance. If that car had come by a minute later, he never would've been discovered and he wouldn't have had to kill Billy Nerman or the detective he was now aiming a pistol at.

"You won't get away with it—surely you realize that?"

The man on the floor forced out the words. Heimer looked at him contemptuously. He could get away with anything. All he had to do was take control of the situation and dare to act.

It had been different in the early days after he had buried Emelie. He had imagined that both the police and Sissela could see right through him. Not a day passed by without him thinking he'd be found out.

But then the semen had been found on the rock next to Emelie's blood.

The multitude of twists in the investigation had been confusing to him. First there had been the surprising arrest of Billy Nerman. In the many years that followed, Heimer had learned to play the role of the grieving father with a carefully suppressed level of aggression toward the young man who had killed his daughter. Then had come the discovery of the body and Primer's involvement in the whole affair. Heimer was still unable to think about that fat pig without feeling sick.

Initially, Heimer had imagined that it was the former lead detective who had seen him on the rocks with Emelie and later sent the blackmail letters.

But then he met Primer in custody. The plan had been to slash at Primer's throat as many times as he could before the police intervened. He would prefer to be convicted as the father who took revenge on his daughter's murderer, rather than being uncovered as the true perpetrator. But at the last moment he stopped himself. He looked into Primer's eyes and realized he knew nothing.

Heimer was pleased with the way he had eventually figured out that it was Billy Nerman behind the blackmail and eliminated that threat once and for all. At any rate, he had thought he'd done that, until just a little while ago. But now he knew there was another person out there somewhere who knew his secret.

He raised the weapon again so that the muzzle grazed the detective's temple.

"For the last time: who called you?"

No reply this time either. Just two wide-open eyes and sweat running down the coward's brow. Heimer stopped to think and saw there might be an easier way to find out what he wanted to know. He turned around to the bookcase and picked up the man's phone. Then he bent down and put the immobilized man's thumb to the fingerprint scanner. It worked. The screen lit up and Heimer navigated to the list of recent calls. At the top was a 054 number that he pressed.

It rang five times before he heard a voice answer.

"Ward thirty-four; this is Linda."

The voice was prim, but slightly strained. The person on the other end seemed stressed.

"Sorry, who have I reached?" said Heimer.

"Ward thirty-four. At the hospital. This is the patient phone."

"Someone there called me about ten minutes ago. Do you know who it was?"

The woman was immediately on her guard.

"I don't think I can disclose that information. We have patient confidentiality rules."

"But I'm worried a relative might be sick," he tried.

"I understand, but it's against regulations. I'm sure they'll call you again."

"Please, I'm begging you. If someone called me, then clearly they want me to know that he or she is in the hospital. That's hardly breaching their confidentiality."

He noticed that the woman's tone softened.

"It might have been Gunvor Nerman," she said after a brief pause. "I thought I saw her by the phone when I passed earlier."

Heimer thanked her and ended the call. The first name meant nothing to him, but the last name was enough to clear things up. Nerman. It had to be Billy's mother or sister—if he had one. He would have to find out later. First he needed to deal with the detective slumped in front of him on the library floor. The hard part wouldn't be shooting him. Moving the body would be much more difficult.

Billy Nerman had been heavy, testing his limits, and Nerman hadn't weighed anything close to as much as this fit-looking man. But he was sure he would manage. Maybe he could use the rug to drag him.

Heimer gripped the weapon with both hands. There would be a strong recoil and he didn't want to miss. He squeezed the trigger carefully with his right index finger and felt it move.

He would usually have reacted to the sound of the front door closing and footsteps coming up the stairs. But at that moment he was so engrossed that he couldn't hear anything except his own breathing.

"Heimer, are you home?"

Sissela had to shout twice before the sound of her voice penetrated his barrier of concentration. He lowered the weapon and turned around at the very moment that his wife stepped into the library.

54

John looked at the woman in the doorway. Sissela Bjurwall was wearing a cream-colored dress with embroidered details on the shoulders and across the bust. Every last strand of her blonde hair was in the right place. In her hand she was holding a leather bag big enough to carry a laptop.

Heimer lowered the weapon and turned his head toward his wife.

"You're back already?"

His voice sounded oddly shrill. Sissela didn't answer. John saw her trying to take in what must have looked like an absurd nightmare—her husband aiming a pistol at another man. She slowly put her bag on the floor.

"Heimer, what's going on here?"

"You aren't supposed to be back yet," he replied. "You're flying back tomorrow."

"We finished early and changed the flights. Who's he?" she said, pointing at John slumped on the floor.

John perceived a forced composure in her—as if she were attempting to master the situation without quite succeeding. He wanted to say something, but he was completely paralyzed. When Heimer had put his finger on the trigger, his body had expected to die and in a fight-or-flight reflex it had emptied his bladder and bowels. He was sitting there like a statue in his own excrement, piss dripping down his thighs.

"Did he break in?" Sissela said.

John tried once again to say something. Sissela's unexpected appearance was a lifeline that he intended to grasp as firmly as possible.

"I'm a police detective," he managed to say.

His voice was low, but sufficiently clear to catch her attention.

"What did you say?"

"I'm a police detective," John repeated more loudly.

This time she heard what he said. Sissela Bjurwall looked confused. Her gaze flickered from the pistol in her husband's hand to the man claiming to be a police detective and back again.

"I can't understand why you always have to change everything. If you said you were coming back tomorrow, why couldn't you come back then?"

Heimer sounded annoyed—as if upset by someone forgetting to take out the trash.

"Is he really with the police?" she said.

"Sissela—this is what we're going to do. You call a taxi and go to a hotel. Then you can come back tomorrow just as you planned."

"A taxi?"

"Yes—you're in no state to drive right now. In the meantime, I'll deal with this."

"What are you going to deal with?"

"Everything—I'll deal with everything. No one needs to know anything. Primer will be put away and then everything will go back to how it was before."

John looked at Sissela and saw her slowly begin to understand. Her facial expression, which had been composed until now, dissolved into something unrecognizable. She began to wail like an animal, pressing her hands to her stomach. John couldn't keep looking at her. It seemed too private a moment.

"It was you . . ." she stammered. "It was you who killed Emelie."

Heimer didn't react to what was happening to his wife. He simply continued to repeat his mantra.

"All you need to do is come back at the time we agreed you would."

Sissela supported herself against the wall with one hand. The other one was still clasped to her stomach. Her body shook as she began to cry.

"We'll never get Emelie back," Heimer continued, calmly. "What matters is what we do now."

"But I don't understand. Why did you kill her?" she sobbed.

"You know that I loved Emelie. It was an accident. The less you know, the easier it will be to forget about it."

"What do you mean? How am I supposed to forget about it?"

"You have to if we're going to stick together. Think about everything we have. Life will turn into a living hell—not just for me, but for you too. You'll be the wife of the guy who killed his own child. And what for, Sissela? Think about it. What good will it do?"

Sissela looked at her husband. In spite of her tears, John saw frightened but intelligent eyes.

"Give me the gun, Heimer," she said. "This isn't you—I know that. You're not yourself."

She held out her hand, but Heimer simply shook his head.

"You need to stop telling me what to do. If this is going to work, you need to show me some respect—do you understand?"

"But Heimer . . ."

"Don't interrupt me! I know what I'm doing. I've got this. Do you know what you need to do?"

"Please, just give me the gun."

She held out her hand again and this time he struck it aside.

"Do you know what you need to do?" he repeated.

Sissela reeled backward and raised her arms to protect her face.

"Call a taxi," she sobbed.

"Good. And then what?"

"Go to a hotel and come back tomorrow."

Heimer smiled at her.

"Good," he said in a softer voice. "Darling, none of this was ever supposed to come out. All you have to do is forget about everything. And I'll forget about you and Hugo."

John saw how the last remark made her wince. He guessed there was an affair that Sissela thought her husband didn't know about. Heimer caressed her cheek with his free hand.

"I read what you wrote," he said. "Every single word in hundreds of emails. Everything that you chose to share with him instead of me. But I'm strong enough that I can put that behind me, if you can do the same for me."

Sissela ran her middle finger beneath her eye. The tears had stopped but her hand shook as she wiped away the makeup that had run.

"You're right," she said, squeezing his hand. "There's no other way."

She retrieved her phone from the bag on the floor and went out through the double doors. Heimer closed them behind her and turned back to John. His eyes were disconcertingly expressionless as he once again raised the weapon. Instinctively, John moved his hand to the painful spot on the back of his head. At that moment he heard Mona's voice. What was it she had said after the blackout in the parking garage at Arlanda airport? That he needed to take control of his own thoughts. That he could do it differently next time—he just had to find the strength.

For the first time since Heimer had raised the weapon, John managed to insert a small wedge between himself and his emotions. Panic was still coursing through his body, but his rational superego had come to life, whispering to him not to worry about all the other stuff. It was just a rush of impulses bouncing through his nervous system—it didn't have anything to do with him. He wasn't just the sum of his emotions and it was up to him to choose whether to be controlled by them or not.

Slowly, he felt the throbbing pain dissipate and the paralysis begin to lift. He tried moving the toes on his right foot. They worked. He tried his left foot with the same positive result. He was fairly certain that if he got up now, his legs would carry him.

He heard the dull sound of Sissela Bjurwall's high heels going down the stairs. His lifeline had come unstuck and he was floating helplessly in the black waters toward almost certain death. But instead of being paralyzed, his brain was working intensely to find a solution. There was still time. Heimer wouldn't do anything until the taxi had arrived and taken his wife away.

"Police are on the way. My backup will be here any minute," John said, thinking of Mona again.

Heimer didn't answer, but showed with his expression that he didn't believe him.

"You think I'm lying," John added. "But it doesn't really matter. What counts is that my phone is here. It'll be easy to trace."

Heimer continued to stare at him blankly, as if immune to John's logical arguments.

"Forensics is going over Billy Nerman's workshop. It wouldn't surprise me if they find something tying you to the scene. One strand of hair is all it takes for a DNA match."

Still no response. He couldn't get through. Heimer Bjurwall had gone into lockdown and John was frozen with mortal fear. He closed his eyes to seek solace. The image that appeared behind his eyelids took him by surprise. It wasn't Billy. Nor his mother. Or father.

It was Nicole.

He saw her on the corduroy sofa with her red headphones on and her face illuminated by the blue light of her tablet. There was no one else on the sofa—she was alone.

John opened his eyes again. Mona had said the strength was somewhere within him, that all he had to do was find it. Now, all of a sudden, it was there. The rational part of his brain took control and commanded his pulsing head to be silent. He tensed the muscles in his arms and legs. They were responding better each time he tried them.

He knew that both he and Heimer were listening for signs from downstairs indicating that his wife was ready to leave the house. They stared at each other in tense silence. Seconds became minutes, which gave John essential recovery time. Eventually, there was the faint sound of the front door closing. Sissela was apparently going outside to get in her taxi. Heimer turned around and the opportunity presented itself.

John braced himself against the floor and then hurled himself toward the other man. This was his last chance to escape with his life. Using his left elbow, he tried to knock the gun out of Heimer Bjurwall's hand. But at the same moment, the tall man twisted to one side, so that John's blow struck his shoulder blade instead. He lost his balance and fell to the floor but didn't drop the weapon.

John could feel shooting pains in his arms and legs following his exertion. It was a good sign—it meant that his nerve endings were working and he had managed to get his muscles to move in coordination, even if it hadn't been quick enough.

Once panic was no longer paralyzing his brain, his training kicked in: the countless hours spent at the FBI Training Academy at Quantico as he and his colleagues drilled a variety of scenarios and how to deal with them. When the enemy was armed and you had no weapon, there was one clear instruction: get to safety and summon reinforcements. Heroes only existed in movies—that was what the instructor had said. In reality, they ended up on the floor covered by a white sheet.

John tore open the double doors. He rushed down the hall and into the kitchen. He crashed into a man completely dressed in black. His face was covered in a helmet with a visor. The only things visible were his eyes—young and hyped up with adrenaline. Behind the broad shoulders John saw more men, all clad in black and heavily armed.

"Take it easy, he's one of us."

John had never thought he would be so pleased to hear Mona Ejdewik's voice.

"Where's Heimer?" Mona cried out.

John pointed down the hallway he had just emerged from.

"In there. Second room on the right. The one with the double doors."

"Is he armed?"

One of the black-clad police officers in the middle of the bunch had posed the question. He was probably heading up the task force.

"He's got my service weapon," John replied, moving to one side to let the men continue forward.

He realized what must have happened and why the taxi had taken so long. Sissela Bjurwall hadn't called a taxi—she'd called the police. Despite the shock of learning that her husband had killed Emelie, she'd managed to keep a cool head. She had played along with his delusions so convincingly that both John and Heimer had been fooled.

Mona came up to him.

"Are you okay?"

John nodded. There was a lot they would need to discuss, but this was hardly the right moment. He hoped that deep down she would understand why he had done what he had.

The leader of the task force reappeared in the kitchen.

"He's not there."

"What do you mean, not there?" said John. "He must be."

The large man didn't reply—instead he issued orders to his team, who initiated a search of the house. John heard crackling from radios as voice after voice reported that their rooms were empty.

He went to the large window with its view of Lake Vänern and saw the large outdoor terrace at ground floor level below them. On one of the benches there was a tall figure curled up. He had drawn his legs up into a fetal position and was lying absolutely still. Somehow, Heimer Bjurwall had gotten out of the library before the task force had struck. Then he must have jumped out of a window in one of the adjacent rooms.

John called out to the task force leader.

"He's down there, on the bench."

The sound of assault rifles against Kevlar vests and police boots making their way down the stairs to the front door filled the house for a few brief seconds. Then there was absolute silence. Mona joined him at the window.

The man on the bench looked lonely. Heimer Bjurwall pulled his knees even closer to his stomach as his body began to shake. Maybe he was crying—it was impossible to tell from this distance.

When the first members of the task force appeared from around the corner, John looked away. He knew what was about to happen and had no desire to watch.

55

Heimer was thinking about the wines in the cellar. He had sorted them by grape type and vintage. The ones that were ready to drink were on the left and the ones that needed to mature were on the right. He hated the thought of Sissela down there among the bottles. She would never keep them in order. It wouldn't be long before Cabernet Sauvignons were muddled up with Pinot Noirs. She would probably uncork the new bottles of Barolo while they were far too young and wouldn't decant them properly. If only he'd had more time, he would've run into the cellar and poured out every single bottle. It would have been a more worthy fate for his collection than being taken over by a know-nothing with no palate to speak of.

There was one case he would have saved. Six bottles of 1988 Margaux—from the same year Emelie came into the world. He found them on a trip to London and had immediately thought of her birthday. The wine was so expensive he'd blushed when he had been told the price. But he hadn't hesitated. There was something special about those moments, once every year. He felt so close to both Sissela and Emelie at those times. It was almost as if they forgave him.

He wondered whether his wife would visit him in prison. Heimer didn't think so—not even on his birthday. But maybe he'd be able to arrange to have the wine—just one glass, once a year. He needed it to remember, so that Emelie wouldn't fade and slip away from him.

He pulled his knees closer to his chest and put his hand tightly around the necklace. He had worn the silver heart with the bite marks hidden beneath his shirt since the night Sissela had refused to wear it. Slowly, he ran his fingertips over the metal to feel the traces of Emelie's teeth. The proof that she had been alive and had once been his daughter.

He didn't want to cry—yet he still did. A deep sob that made his body shake and the planks of the bench sag.

Then he felt two strong arms pull him onto the terrace. He got splinters in his cheek from the dry wooden boards. The teak needed sanding and oiling, but of course no one had bothered to make sure it got done.

He had to deal with everything.

Absolutely everything.

EPILOGUE

THREE MONTHS LATER

John took a step back and looked at the canvas on the easel. Something about the eyes wasn't quite right. They were sad; that was spot-on. But there was also a sense of dejection—an adult form of resignation that didn't fit with the girl. The last time he saw Nicole a month or so ago, she had been more talkative. She asked about her father and what would happen now that he was gone. These were not the questions of someone who had given up—rather, they were the expression of a desire to start living again. The child psychologist, whom he had spoken to afterward, had agreed. Nicole was really making progress.

Social services had placed her in a foster home. She had been there for two weeks now, but John still hadn't been to visit. He had to take care not to seem too closely involved. Officially, Nicole was just a girl he had taken a liking to as part of his job.

In reality, she was so much more. She was the strength that Mona had talked about. It was for her sake that he had tried to stay alive when Heimer Bjurwall had been pointing his weapon at him.

He closed his eyes and tried to picture Nicole in front of him. Then he made a new attempt at the eyes. After half an hour he was satisfied and he sent grateful thoughts to his landlady who had left her oils behind in the apartment.

John washed his brushes in turpentine and cleaned the paint off his hands. He sat down on one of the crates at the kitchen table and opened his laptop. The clock on the screen told him it was a quarter to eleven in the evening. Trevor's flight was scheduled to have landed at Arlanda an hour ago. If he hadn't spent too long in the baggage hall or customs, he would be at his airport hotel by now.

John logged on to the encrypted email service and saw that his inbox was empty. Anxiety gnawed at his stomach. Maybe it had been a bad idea to agree to his friend's final wish to visit him. He remembered how back in the hospital in Baltimore, Trevor had always insisted he was fine—even on the days when the pain was at its worst. There was a risk he had overestimated his health and collapsed on the flight.

John shut the laptop and reflected on the deadline he'd set for his stay in Karlstad. Three months to find out the truth about his brother. But he hadn't counted on the consequences of every successful investigation. Christmas and New Year's had passed by and he was having to work overtime. The preparation of the cases against Bernt Primer and Heimer Bjurwall were moving at breakneck speed and John had to be available to the prosecutor.

The same applied to Mona, who was traveling back and forth between Stockholm and Karlstad. His relationship with her was rocky. She was keeping a professional distance from him and there was no chance of further dinners at Rederiet.

A couple of days after the operation at Tynäs, they had been at the police station discussing what had happened. John explained why he'd gone to Heimer Bjurwall's home in direct contravention of her orders. Billy's death made everything personal and he hadn't been able to step away from the investigation.

Mona had admitted that on an emotional level she could understand what he had done. Nevertheless, she considered it completely irresponsible and she was grateful they wouldn't have to work together after the trials were over.

John had not yet been assigned a new witness protection liaison in Stockholm, but he assumed it was just a matter of time. It didn't really matter who it was. With his mother back at Gunnarskärsgården and Nicole in a foster home, he would be able to leave the country with his conscience clear.

His time in Karlstad had been a mere footnote—a necessary diversion before he went on with his original plans. He would cut all ties to the Bureau and create his own private witness protection program somewhere in Europe. First stop, Berlin: that was where he was going as soon as the trials were over.

John opened his laptop again and refreshed the inbox. There was still no sign of life from Arlanda. He went back through the old emails and reread the early messages from Trevor. Most of what he had written resonated with John. The loneliness. The difficulty in coming to grips with a new country. The paranoia and fear of being discovered.

Then he made some coffee and drank it while standing at the window. The harbor below was illuminated by floodlights as a boat unloaded its cargo. In the light, he saw the first snowflakes falling, forming a white blanket on the ground. He rinsed his mug and sat back down at the laptop.

Finally.

Trevor had sent an email. He opened it immediately.

Landed and checked in at the hotel. Time to sleep. Catching the train to Karlstad tomorrow. See you at 6pm as agreed. I've lost a few pounds, but I assume there's no need for me to look sharp. Have a good one, T.

John exhaled. Everything was fine and tomorrow he would see his friend again. He went to the fridge and discovered there was still a little of the Sancerre left in the bottle that Erina had brought the last time she'd been around. The two had been spending time together—both in and out of bed—on a regular basis. He poured the wine into a glass and sat back down at the laptop to answer.

He had just started writing when the final line of Trevor's email caught his eye.

Have a good one, T.

There was something about it that bothered him. Something he couldn't put his finger on. Trevor usually ended his emails with that choice of words—surely there was nothing strange about it?

He clicked back to the old emails again. Now he saw the discrepancy. It was subtle, but still as clear as day. In six of his first ten emails, Trevor had ended with: *Have a good one! T.*

An exclamation point before the T—not a comma, which was what he had just received.

John pushed the wineglass aside. He had only had two sips and he didn't want any more until he got to the bottom of his suspicions.

He continued to read the conversation in chronological order and flinched when he realized in which email the comma had appeared for the first time. It was the one about Trevor's stomach problems.

John took a deep breath and deleted the email he had just started writing. Instead he wrote:

Glad to hear it. I'm sure I'll recognize you. Hope you still eat fish. There's a great place in town that I've made a reservation at.

Then he hit send and waited.

The answer arrived just a few of minutes later.

Sounds great. See you soon.

John closed the laptop. He stared at the flecks of paint that had ended up on the lid during the recent period of intense painting. They fused together in front of his eyes. Trevor had never liked fish. He was a steak-and-burgers guy who had protested loudly on the few occasions that the FBI agents had brought anything from the sea to their safe house.

John got up and went back to the window. The snowfall had intensified and he could see a thin layer forming on the quayside below. Instinctively, he put his hand to his neck and felt for the pain in the back of his head.

But it wasn't there.

It seemed to have vanished for good in Heimer Bjurwall's library.

Instead, anger pulsed through his body. He thought about Trevor and what must have happened to him. He was presumably dead. Tortured and executed. The paranoia hadn't just been in his head. Ganiru's henchmen must have found him and obtained the email login. They'd used it to get John's location and made arrangements to see him. He hadn't been emailing his friend—he had been emailing Nigerian hitmen.

John looked at the time. It couldn't end like this. He had to find a way to escape—for his own sake and Trevor's.

He had just a few hours to figure out how.

ACKNOWLEDGMENTS

The authors wish to thank:
Our first editor, Erika Degard, at Norstedts. Her keen-eyed perspective made *The Bucket List* a better book. Our agent, Judith Toth, at Nordin Agency, who has taken John Adderley out into the wide world. She is an unstoppable force of nature. We're so grateful to have you on our side of the negotiating table. Our editor at The Overlook Press, Tracy Carns, and the Overlook/ABRAMS team, as well as translator Ian Giles, for their great work in bringing this book to English-speaking readers. Ralf Lyxell and Karin Jansson, who provided their invaluable knowledge of Karlstad and its surroundings. If there are any details that remain inaccurate, the fault is entirely our own. Gustaf Carlsson, who gave us insight into the world of forensics and taught us how incredibly difficult it is to get away with murder. Family, friends, and acquaintances who have read all or parts of the manuscript at different stages of the writing process. Your critical oversight and words of encouragement have been a great help.

Mohlin would particularly like to thank:
My wife, Anna, and my daughters, Märta and Ellen, for being there for me in sickness and in health, in writer's block and writer's flow.

Nyström, the best partner a writer could ask for. He always has one hand on the keyboard and the other on my shoulder for support.

Nyström would particularly like to thank:
My children, Smilla and Nicolas. Simply by existing you give meaning to everything.

Mohlin, for his ability to never give up. For the fact that (as long as he receives regular meals) he is always ready to go the whole mile. Thank you for being by my side in both headwinds and tailwinds.

AUTHORS' NOTE

Thank you for making it all the way to the end. We hope this book has kept you entertained for a while. If you happen to come from in or around Karlstad, or you're just particularly interested in the world of John Adderley, we'd like to tell you a few things.

The places mentioned in the books do often exist in the real world—although not always. We've taken liberties in terms of both exteriors and interiors. For example, the police station in Karlstad is on Infanterigatan, but to our knowledge it has no moldy basement.

A genuine newspaper mogul and a bona fide music star really do live in Tynäs. However, we've never encountered the Bjurwall family in that exclusive neighborhood.

The tower at Bryggudden where John Adderley lives also exists, but we doubt that the penthouse apartment consists of just one room.

In other words, the settings in *The Bucket List* are a mixture of truths, half-truths, and total make-believe.

Finally, we want to beg forgiveness from everyone who lives on Hammarö. We know it's been many years since the mill at Skoghall has smelled. But we couldn't resist using sulphur to set the scene for the events in this book. In our world, drama sometimes has to take priority over facts, and for that we apologize.

Peter Mohlin and Peter Nyström